PRAISE FOR *ONCE THERE WAS ME*

'Bobby Sachdeva's book *Once There Was Me* is at once raw and sincere. Filled with painful memories of a tumultuous past, this is a narrative that is deeply personal but one that the world must read – especially today when differences can be deadly' – PARO ANAND, author of *No Guns at My Son's Funeral*

'A riveting and interesting tale of one man's search for his identity, and his roots. It closely follows a real-life journey, exploring the clash between modernity and religious beliefs.' – KISHWAR DESAI, Chairperson, The Arts and Cultural Heritage Trust for setting up The Partition Museum, Amritsar and author of *Jallianwallah Bagh 1919: The Real Story*

'A deeply personal account on a sprawling canvas of history in which desires and conflicts intersect with borders and pogroms. An unsettling story of dispossession and displacement in a world where the earth keeps moving under the feet. Pointedly topical for the times we live in' – ANIRUDH KALA, author of *The Unsafe Asylum: Stories of Partition & Madness*

'A compassionate novel about lives distorted by the tragedies of Partition and the events of 1984 and 2002, and one man's attempt to break free from the stranglehold of the past in order to usher in a brave new India. A work with especial relevance for the times we live in' – VIKRAM KAPUR, author of *The Assassinations: A Novel of 1984*

'A man's search for freedom from an imposed identity and forced displacement to an understanding of religion and finally a rejection of how the idea of God is marketed to billions in India. Lucid prose, deeply emotional, and scathing in its treatment of organized religion. Powerful!' – AMANDEEP SANDHU, author of *Roll of Honour*

PRAISE FOR THE AUTHOR

'Bobby Sachdeva has the rare talent to think of original stories. The stories move you, often question prevalent beliefs and expose shams of our society. There is a visual quality in the storytelling that makes the stories accessible' – BOBBY BEDI, film producer and director, Kaleidoscope Entertainment Ltd

'These stories of inhuman bondage, be it of blind faith, lust or exploitation, will hopefully shock the reader out of complacency to seek answers to the questions' – NIRUPAMA DUTT, poet, journalist and translator

'His short stories will give you more than enough fodder for understanding life. What better way to succinctly capture the lengths of moments in words' – KRISHIKA LULLA, film producer, Eros International

'These thought-provoking stories ... make us question many undesirable aspects of everyday life which we mindlessly subscribe to. A very readable, interesting book' – MITRA PHUKAN, author, translator and columnist

ONCE THERE WAS ME

Bobby Sachdeva is a storyteller by choice and a businessman by profession. He writes stories to highlight the problems with norms and standards in our changing society and believes that these perceptions can change. In all his writings, Bobby Sachdeva engages with the problems in the lives of common people and the ways to resolve these. In the last two years, he has written more than a dozen feature films, web series, and tele-serials and his popular book of short stories titled *Stories of Us*. Apart from writing, Sachdeva has produced nine short films in Hindi and three feature films in Punjabi and started a fully equipped studio, Ajab Productions, in his hometown Amritsar where he lives with his family. The production of his first full-length Hindi film will begin in 2021.

ONCE THERE WAS ME

Bobby Sachdeva

PAN

First published 2020 by Pan
an imprint of Pan Macmillan Publishing India Private Limited,
707, Kailash Building
26 K. G. Marg, New Delhi – 110 001
www.panmacmillan.co.in

Pan Macmillan, 6 Briset St, Farringdon, London EC1M 5NR
Basingstoke and Oxford
Associated companies throughout the world
www.panmacmillan.com

ISBN 978-93-89109-55-9

This is a work of fiction. All characters, locations and events are fictitious. Any resemblance to actual events or locales or persons, living or dead, is entirely coincidental.

1 3 5 7 9 8 6 4 2

Typeset in Scala by Manmohan Kumar
Printed and bound in India by
Replika Press Pvt. Ltd.

This book is for my father,
Late S. Jasbir Singh

1984

It was the shouting and the violent rattling of the gate that woke me up with a start. Loud voices yelled, 'Indira Gandhi *amar rahe*' (Indira Gandhi is immortal) and '*Tumhare kaatil nahin bachenge*' (Your murderers will die).

My father rushed into the room and urgently switched on the TV and the transistor radio. He yelled at my mother to lock the front door and shut the windows. Just the day before, 31 October 1984, Mrs Indira Gandhi, the prime minister, had been assassinated by her Sikh guards. Within hours, there was rioting and retaliatory killing of Sikhs in Delhi. News reports said that the mayhem had intensified and spread throughout the country. And a bloodthirsty mob was at our gate on which the nameplate said 'Sachdeva' – a surname that could be Hindu or Sikh – on top, followed by 'Jasbir Singh', my father's clearly Sikh name, below.

Mercifully, the mob did not break into the house. Before I could run with trembling legs to the window to see what was happening, the rattling stopped and the voices began to fade – the mob was moving away. When Papa was sure that the mob had left, he telephoned his two brothers and his brother-in-law. All three told him that there was carnage on the streets of Delhi, mobs lynching and killing Sikhs and even burning them alive. They were all huddled fearfully in their homes, hoping that no mob would come to their door, that they would be safe.

But a mob had brought the terror to our doorstep, and though it had left, there was no knowing if and how soon it would return. Our family was in danger. We had to get to a safe place. Papa frantically called his Hindu neighbours, but they were frightened too and refused to risk their own lives to help him. Finally, one neighbour hesitantly agreed to shelter my mother and sisters, only because they could easily be passed off as Hindus.

My parents quickly decided that my brother and I would be dressed in our sisters' frocks, our long hair tied in ponytails to pass us off as girls. The plan was that Mummy would go to the neighbour's house with all of us four children. But when I heard the plan, I flatly refused to go. I was fourteen and a half years old and had started sprouting a straggly moustache and beard. The very thought of wearing a frock, even in that fearful situation, was deeply embarrassing. Suppose one of my friends saw me? I'd never live it down! Besides, I didn't think that I could pass off as a girl. To add to that was the concern for Papa being left alone.

So Mummy left hurriedly with my two sisters and younger brother, taking neither cash nor jewellery with her. There was no time – our house could be attacked again any minute. Mummy called a couple of minutes later to confirm that they were safe in the neighbour's house.

Papa and I ensured that all doors and windows were tightly shut and locked and then huddled inside the house, tense and alert to every little sound. By 1 p.m., after 2 hours had passed and everything seemed quiet, we relaxed a little. Perhaps the mob had moved away from our locality and we were safe. We planned to go to my uncle's house at night. This uncle was my father's brother, and he lived in an area populated largely by Sikhs. We believed we would feel less threatened there.

As the tension ebbed, I felt hungry. I thought Papa had also not eaten anything since morning, so I went to the kitchen to make bread and jam sandwiches, the only thing I knew to make. I made one sandwich and took a bite, laid it aside and started making another one for Papa when a loud banging on the front gate startled me, and I dropped the slice of bread. The mob had silently made its way back! With my heart hammering loud, I ran into the bedroom where Papa had the TV on and had been talking on the phone to his brother and other relatives in Punjab. Papa too had heard the banging on the gate and he slammed the phone down. He ran to the almirah and picked up the Webley pistol and a double-barrelled gun that he used to shoot wild birds in the forest behind his factory. He grabbed my arm and made a dash to the staircase, locking the door behind it. The stairwell was the safest area in the house.

Ours was a single-storey structure, and from the outside, it was clear that the terrace held nothing but a water tank. So, there was a good chance that the mob would never go to the terrace in search of us.

As we hid there, even with the apprehension of death facing us, Papa asked me, 'Bobby, if they catch you and offer to let you go if you let them cut your hair, what will you do?'

'I will fire seven bullets into the mob and shoot myself with the eighth rather than let them cut my hair,' I said, without hesitation, although my legs felt like jelly and my heart was in my mouth.

I knew that the pistol held eight bullets. Papa squeezed my arm proudly even though he was not sure if I had spoken from my heart or out of bravado.

The mob broke open the back door within minutes. It looted and ransacked the house and set the car and scooter parked in front on fire. Then it came towards the staircase and tried to break open the door leading to the stairs. Papa and I quietly ran up the stairs to the terrace and used a wooden ladder kept there to climb right to the top of the water tank. I was carrying the heavy, wooden-handle, four-feet long, double-barrelled gun. Papa helped me up the ladder, and once I was up, he quickly pulled up the ladder and hid it along the boundary wall next to the 6,000-litre, seven-feet-high tank. He opened the round cast iron lid, and when both of us slid in, he quietly shut the lid. Fortunately, the tank was only half full. It was the beginning of winter and the water was cold, but all that mattered was that in the closed darkness of the tank, we were out of sight of the mob.

It had taken us three to four minutes to get into the tank from the terrace, and two minutes later the mob burst in. Harsh voices came in through the slightly open lid of the tank. Papa put his ear close to the lid to catch the conversation. 'The father and son must have escaped to a neighbour's house over the roof,' the mob was saying. Our roof was joined to those of our neighbours' houses on either side.

Someone in the mob said, 'That neighbour said that only the women left the house in the morning. Where have the man and his sons gone?' This statement broke Papa's heart. One of our own neighbours, with whom we had lived in harmony for so many years, had betrayed us. Now we knew why the mob was back and why our house was being searched so thoroughly.

The men left after a while, but before going they set the house ablaze. Papa and I remained hidden in the water tank. Below us, the house slowly burned, and in its heat, the water grew warm. We had already spent almost two hours inside the tank. Papa had tied the pistol to the top of his head with the thick, strong thread that he used to tie his beard from under the chin to the top of his head. We took turns to carry the heavy gun on our shoulders.

At around 3.30 pm, Papa pushed up the iron lid a few inches and warm sunlight and cool, fresh air gushed into the dark tank. There was an eerie silence – no traffic on the roads, no sound of children playing, not even birds chirping. I wanted to get out, but Papa reminded me that the neighbour who had given us away to the mob might be watching the terrace to see if we appeared from some hiding place. It was dangerous to put our heads out, even for a moment. But we decided to leave the lid half open for fresh air and as much sunshine as possible till darkness came.

We remained huddled there in the water, our hearts filled with fear and sadness. Inevitably the call of nature came, and I asked Papa where I could pee.

Papa smiled and said, 'Do we have any option? Slowly, in your knickers, as I have done twice in my pyjamas.'

I grinned, but also felt embarrassed at our plight. We had to drink the same water we were peeing in. It was 5 p.m., nearly five hours since we had entered the tank. We were hungry and cold. Our legs ached, and the skin on our feet was shrivelling up.

Finally, when the sun set and a dark, tense dusk crept in, Papa agreed to let me put my head out and take a look around. A double-storey gurudwara was burning and heavy black smoke rose from the Sikh-owned petrol pump outside our colony. There were many houses on fire, some nearby, some in the distance.

After making sure that no one was watching us, Papa put a foot on my shoulder to clamber out and then pulled me up. He reached down and picked up the hidden ladder, and we climbed down the tank and on to the hot terrace. We went downstairs and walked in dazed silence around our smouldering home. The furniture, curtains, mattresses were all burnt; the cupboards had been emptied of all valuables and then set on fire; even the fridge was a hot, molten mess. Fortunately, the mob had carried away the LPG cylinders before setting the house on fire. If those had exploded, the whole house would have been reduced to rubble.

My hungry eyes looked for the half-made jam sandwiches, but they were gone. All I found was a can of condensed milk and some roasted brinjals and radish in the burnt fridge. So, we spread the condensed milk on the brinjals and radish and ate them up.

With a bit of food in his stomach and the relief of having escaped the mob, at least for a while, Papa immediately began to plan our escape. The telephone wires had burned, so the phone was dead. The only option was to seek help from his closest friend, Ashok, a Hindu who lived nearby. There were Hindu neighbours around, but one of them had betrayed us, so we dared not trust anyone. I would have to dress up like a girl and go to Ashok uncle's house.

The fire had destroyed the drawing room and bedrooms, but the storeroom, which was to one side, had escaped the flames. In an aluminium trunk, I found my sister's frock. Some half-burnt hair clips on the floor in the bedroom helped make my hair look girlish. I took off the steel *kada* that all Sikh men and women wear as an article of their faith and hoped that in the darkness my faint moustache and beard would go unnoticed. Reluctantly, with a fearful heart, I left my father and the sanctuary of our burnt home.

Just outside the front gate, I saw to my delight the moped that Papa had bought for his factory staff, still leaning against the boundary wall. It had somehow escaped the attention of the mob. I climbed on, pedalled hard to start it and sped off, trying to reach Ashok uncle's house as fast as possible. As I turned a corner, I saw something burning on the road, and when I neared it, I was horrified to see that it was the half-burnt bodies of an elderly Sikh gentleman and a lady, perhaps his wife or daughter. My heart hammered, and I dared not look at them properly. What if they were people I knew? In the next lane, some houses and vehicles had been burnt, and I went past them at full speed, my eyes looking straight ahead, trying not to see the destruction around me. Ashok uncle's house, which was so close to ours, seemed very far away.

Suddenly, just as I was about to reach Ashok uncle's house, the moped stopped. There was not a soul around, not a sound. It was pitch dark, and I was petrified. I pedalled the moped furiously like a bicycle, unmindful of my aching legs and empty stomach. Five minutes later, I was at Ashok uncle's gate, but it was locked! For a moment I panicked, until I noticed that it was locked from the inside. I rang the doorbell and frantically hit the front wheel of my moped against the gate. I did not want to be alone in the dark, deathly silence outside the house for a moment longer than necessary.

Ashok uncle's daughter, Shilpa, came out and was surprised to see a young girl on a moped outside the gate. She assumed that the girl had lost her way and asked me who

I was looking for. I was frantic with fear. I insisted that she open the gate, not realizing that I was dressed like a girl and Shilpa had not recognized me. Shilpa hesitated thinking the girl was rather strange, hammering at the gate and speaking in a male voice. Only then did I remember how I was dressed and identified myself. Shilpa stared for moment and then started laughing. But when she saw the terror on my face, she quickly unlocked the gate and took me inside. The whole family had come out to the drawing room to see who had come calling at such a time, and they were bewildered to see this young girl. When Shilpa introduced me as Bobby Sachdeva version two, they all started laughing, except Ashok uncle, who urgently asked about my father and the rest of the family.

I told him all that had happened. Ashok uncle realized that I was in shock and starving. His wife brought some hot parathas, and the family offered me much sympathy and affection.

I ate quickly and asked Ashok uncle to come with me to fetch Papa. But to my dismay, Ashok uncle hesitated. A neighbour had betrayed our family. If that neighbour saw Ashok uncle rescuing Papa, he and his family would be in danger. So, like the other neighbour, Ashok uncle offered refuge to my mother, sisters and little brother, who could be passed off as a girl, but not to my father or me. Ashok uncle made it clear that he would certainly not go to our house. I couldn't believe my ears. Ashok uncle was my father's best friend, but now, when Papa needed him most, Ashok uncle was abandoning him.

I had written down the phone numbers of my uncles and of the neighbour with whom my mother and siblings were sheltering. I called up Mummy and wept as I told her about the attack on our house. Ashok uncle called Manmohan Singh, my father's brother, but there was no answer and our heart sank. With trepidation, he then called Paramjit Singh, my youngest uncle. To our relief, Paramjit uncle immediately answered. When Paramjit heard what had happened, he said that he would come out after midnight and take our whole family back to his own house in a Sikh-dominated colony. I was deeply relieved and touched.

'Blood is thicker than water,' I had often heard, but now I knew this to be true.

Both Ashok uncle and Paramjit uncle advised me to either stay on at Ashok uncle's place or go to my mother at the neighbour's house. Though I told them that I would go to my mother, I had no intention of leaving my father alone. Ashok uncle drained the petrol out of his scooter and filled the tank of the moped. I asked for two parathas to be packed, which I said I would eat later when I felt hungry. Feeling more confident now that my stomach was full and help was on the way, I rode off at moderate speed, straight to my father. I gave the parathas to Papa and told him all that had happened. For the first time in my life, I dared to advise my father – never trust any friend ever again.

Papa and I once again hid in the stairwell, in case another mob came and we had to go back into the water tank. It was pitch black, but the darkness made us feel secure. Papa told me that he had decided that once things normalized a bit, we would all move back to Amritsar. He was particularly afraid because he had two young daughters, and during riots, women and girls were molested and killed. He said that it was for the safety of our family that he had decided to move, not for fear of his own life. Amritsar is where Papa had come with his parents and siblings after the Partition, empty-handed, having left everything behind in Pakistan. We would be safe in Punjab, he said, the land of the Sikhs, our own state. Besides, the Golden Temple was also there.

Until that moment, I had no idea that my father's family were migrants from Pakistan. All I knew was that my father had lived in Amritsar with his parents and one older and six younger siblings. He was married there, his first two daughters, my sisters, were born there, and it was only in 1969 that he had moved to Delhi to establish his own business. I was born in Delhi in 1970. I had studied about the Partition in school, but I was shocked to learn that my own family had experienced those horrors first-hand.

Now it seemed that history was repeating itself. Papa wanted me to know how religion had made us victims before and how it was happening all over again. He did not know if we would be able to flee from Delhi or even survive the riots. It was apparent to Papa that such massacres could not happen without the complicity of the government. And if the government was killing citizens whom it should be protecting, it was going to be very difficult to survive.

Papa told me of the bloodbath that followed the Partition of India in 1947, in which more than a million people died and an equal number were injured. Ten million people were displaced and crossed the borders on either side. There is no exact record of the number of the girls raped or missing or forcibly married during the time. And there is no measure of the trauma that millions of people suffered, which haunts them to this day.

In that dark stairwell in the half-burnt house that had been our home, I listened in stunned silence as my father narrated the story of the Partition as he had experienced it.

***

I took a large gulp of the whiskey soda and leaned back in my seat. It was a long way to London from San Francisco, and I hoped that the alcohol would help me sleep through the journey. What had taken me back 10 years to that horrible day in Delhi? Was it the young American girl at the airport? Or was it because I was going back to New Delhi? Or both?

My flight had been delayed by an hour and I was whiling away time with a beer and a magazine when a young girl had come up to me. She had read my name, Singh Gurvinder, on the boarding card, that was sticking out between the pages of the magazine.

'Mr Singh, would you spare ten minutes to take a look at the work my NGO is doing?'

I had followed her to a desk placed near the boarding gate. (This was pre-9/11 and visitors could see off and receive travellers right at the gate.) A big projector showed pictures of the devastation caused by floods in Bangladesh. There were mud huts half washed away by the surging waters and poor, starving, orphaned children were crying for their missing parents. The girl gave me some pamphlets to read and asked for a contribution. I was not really interested. I felt sad for the hungry, homeless people, and somewhere at the back of my mind, I felt I owed something to America, which had sheltered me for three years and given me experiences that had expanded my horizons. But still I had hesitated, and she had said, 'You must be from India?' I had nodded. 'Then why can't you help your own people?' These words from the young American girl had somehow touched a deep cord in my heart and shook me up. I didn't know then that they would haunt me for a long, long time. I had told myself that this was my chance to contribute to this land and also help my people. The plight of the devastated Bangladeshis did not really affect me. I had seen a lot of poverty, death and destruction in India.

I had taken the receipt for the $20 I had contributed, slipped it between the pages of the magazine and gone back to my seat.

Soon after take-off, drinks had been served. I had thought that two large drinks would help me sleep all the way to London, where I had to change flights. But here I was, still wide awake. Something was bothering me, but I could not put a finger on it. I had picked up the magazine to while away time, and it had flipped open at the page where the receipt for $20 lay. I had gazed at the receipt and wondered why a young twenty-year-old American girl voluntarily worked for an NGO to help poor children whom she had probably never seen. And why do Indians, who have witnessed so many such disasters and deprivation and who are so proud of their culture and values, never care for their own underprivileged people?

'We Indians are humans, just like the young girl,' I thought, 'so why can't we understand their plight? Are Indians so hard-hearted that they cannot feel the pain of the poor and needy around them?'

'Yes,' my conscience had said, 'we are cruel and insensitive towards other humans and we are only spectators of their suffering.'

I had closed my eyes and from the depths of memory had come the fearful rattling of the gate on that horrible morning of 1 November 1984.

I took another sip of whiskey and recalled everything that Papa had told me in the stairwell that dark, fearful night.

THE UNTOLD STORIES

My father's grandfather was an educated man and the station master of Lahore Railway Station. It was a prestigious position then, since few men were educated enough to apply for the job. Lahore was also the biggest city in the large state of Punjab, which extended from Himachal Pradesh to Delhi and included Haryana and what is now Pakistani Punjab. My father's family lived in Gujranwala (now in Pakistan) and was well respected in the community. Mohinder Singh, my grandfather, was the second eldest in the family and had eight children. He and his family lived on the generous salary that his father earned, along with income from large tracts of agricultural land that they owned. My grandfather never held a job, but he looked after the family's farms.

When the Partition happened, the flames of communal hatred burned through the camaraderie the family enjoyed with its neighbours, and all the respect and the status came to nought. Hindus and Sikhs had to abandon their homes and land and flee from Pakistan, while Muslims on the other side of the border had to leave their homes in India and migrate to Pakistan. My father was just fourteen when he arrived in Amritsar with his family, penniless and homeless.

Papa told me that like him, his wife and my mother, Joginder Kaur, had also come to India with her family after the Partition when she was just five years old. Her father travelled to Panipat with his children because, fortunately, he and his brothers had exchanged large tracts of their agricultural land in Pakistan with Muslims who were migrating from Panipat.

Just before my mother's family left, a large Muslim mob was rumoured to be heading towards their village. Mummy's father had heard that Muslim mobs raped and killed women. Terrified that his wife would be raped and bring dishonour to the family, my *nana* in panic decided to slit her throat. He explained to her that he was convinced he had to do it. She agreed and with a quaking heart and shivering hands, my grandfather slashed her throat, left her body in the sugarcane field near his house and fled from the village with the rest of his family. But his reluctant, frightened hands had not done a thorough job, and my grandmother survived. A humane Muslim neighbour rescued her two days later from a pile of bodies of Sikh and Hindu wives, daughters and sisters who had been similarly killed by fathers, brothers and sons. She was hospitalized under the supervision of the army. Luckily for her, when she recovered, she could tell the authorities exactly where her husband had gone and was reunited with her large family.

I was shocked to hear these horrible stories. But my maternal uncles now lived in Thailand, and I wondered how and why they moved there from Panipat. And what happened to my nana? I had never met him.

Papa smiled sadly.

'Your nana was murdered,' he said.

Papa told me that my mother's father and his younger brother had settled down in Panipat. Since they had got a large tract of land in exchange for their own, they did not have to spend any of the money and gold they had brought with them. As a result, they became cash-rich Sikh landlords among a largely Hindu population.

A few Jaats, a community of Hindu landowners, became jealous of the rich migrant Sikh family and began to taunt and harass them. Saner voices in the community tried to make peace, telling them that Sikhs and Hindus are brothers. In fact, in many Punjabi Hindu families, the first-born son was often brought up as a Sikh, and Hindus and Sikhs married freely within the community.

My nana and his brother did not take the harassment by the Jaats seriously. Everything would soon cool down, they believed. But they were wrong. A rival landlord falsely accused them of diverting water from his fields into their own. There was a heated exchange of words and then something insulting about Sikhs was said. This was unbearable and the brothers beat up the lone Jaat. Sikhs are hot-blooded and quick to take offence, but so are Jaats, and the very next morning, when the brothers were on their way to their fields, they were attacked with knives and swords by a large group of Jaat men. My nana was killed on the spot. The younger brother was badly injured, but he recovered. He left Panipat and moved to Delhi.

My *nani*'s brothers had migrated to Thailand from Pakistan after the Partition in 1947. When my nana was murdered, they came down and took two of my nani's eldest sons with them to work in their tailoring business in Bangkok. They settled my nani and her five other children in a rented house in Delhi and regularly sent her money from Thailand. The two younger sons also moved to Thailand as soon as they were old enough, and my nani married off her three daughters one by one. My nani later moved to Thailand to live with her sons there. The sons married Thai Sikh girls. I had met my Thai cousins, and though they were Sikh, they spoke Thai and I could not converse with them.

A hundred questions raced around in my head after this story, but Papa was exhausted and fell asleep on the cold floor of the landing. Midnight was still four hours away, and only after midnight would Papa's brothers come to rescue us. But these disturbing and dramatic stories kept me awake. There was so much trauma in our family that I had been unaware of. And I recalled the earliest memories of my own life.

DILEMMA OF A SIKH BOY

My education began in a primary school close to my home in New Delhi, where many children of the neighbourhood studied. The mornings there began with English hymns and though I understood not one word, I soon knew them by heart. When I finished senior kindergarten, I was put in an all-boys, government-run, Hindi-medium school in class one. There the morning assembly began with patriotic Hindi songs. I understood these and loved them. I felt a great sense of pride and power in reciting them. Despite the mediocre standard of teaching and the not-very-well-to-do background of the students, I was very happy in the school. Everyone was friendly, spoke Hindi and shared tiffin boxes at meal times. Sometimes a couple of older boys would tease me, calling me 'Giani' – a Sikh priest and a name commonly used to tease Sikh boys – because of the white-scarf-covered bun on my head that marked me out as a Sikh. But my classmates would immediately confront the bullies and threaten to report them to the principal. The seniors usually backed off.

Though I was happy and secure in this school, Papa realized that I needed an English-medium education in a school that matched our family's social and financial status. My sisters were studying in a good English-medium school, the Kulachi Hansraj Model School, and the very next year, I was admitted there. The school was run by affluent members of the Arya Samaj. It was 6 kilometres away, and the school bus picked up my sisters and me near our home.

Lovey, my eldest sister, was a tough, confident and no-nonsense young girl. No one wanted to pick a fight with her, so on the school bus, I was protected. But in the classroom, things were different. I was the only Sikh boy. There were two Sikh girls, but they looked no different than all the other girls. As soon as I entered my class on the first day, there were whispers and giggles. I heard someone call out 'Giani'. Many of my classmates just stared at me. Only one boy walked over and introduced himself. He was new too, and he invited me to sit next to him.

The morning assembly in this school was different. Boys and girls stood in separate rows. I was tall and the teacher placed me at the back of the boys' row. We first had physical training, which I enjoyed, followed by recitation of the 'Gayatri Mantra' in Sanskrit. Sanskrit was mandatory in the school until class five. On that first day, however, the mantra made no sense to me at all.

The next day, in the middle of physical training, I noticed that an older Sikh boy, wearing a maroon scarf on his bun, was being constantly ragged by the boy standing behind him. At every opportunity, the boy would gently slap the Sikh boy's bun. Other students saw this and smirked, while the bully grinned as if he was a hero. I was angry and scared. Was this going to happen to me too?

Unfortunately, it did happen. I was teased and taunted so much that I became fearful and tense. Everybody laughed when a Sikh boy was ragged, except the Sikh girls. In the classroom, only five or six boys teased me, but during recess I was a target for many bullies. School became an ordeal, and I became withdrawn and depressed. Only one Sikh boy, Jaspal Singh, from class eleven was never ragged. He was tall, well-built and very confident, and I decided to seek his help.

I had never shared my fear and sense of humiliation with my sisters, because at home I was considered a tough young boy and was a hero to my cousins from Amritsar. But I gathered courage and approached Jaspal one day and told him how I was constantly ragged. Jaspal heard me out and said, 'Go home, little brother, or you will miss your bus.' He told me to not come to school the next day and that he would fix things.

The next morning, I pretended to be unwell and complained of feeling feverish. Mummy gave me a glass of milk and medicine and told me to get up, but I was adamant. Mummy had to finally give up, and I spent a happy day playing at home. The next day, I reluctantly went to school. When I entered my classroom, the boys who usually called me names came up to me. I was terrified that they had thought up some new form of torture for me. To my surprise, they declared that I was now their friend!

'You should have told us you were Jaspal's cousin,' one of them said.

Even during recess, the other bullies stayed far away from me. Jaspal's magic had worked.

Over the next two years, I learnt to handle the little bit of teasing that still came my way. I was growing up and I realized that most people were not bad, nor were they communal. The bullies needed a target and Sikh boys, who looked different from the rest, were easy to prey on. If religion had been an issue, Sikh girls would have been targeted too. But I also saw that very few people stepped forward to stop a wrong act. In fact, some of them quite enjoyed it from a distance.

THE SIGNIFICANCE OF UNSHORN HAIR

All festivals, Hindu and Sikh, were celebrated with great fervour in my family. I particularly loved Holi and Diwali. One Diwali night, my sisters and I had finished lighting all the firecrackers we had and were strolling down the colony lane collecting half-burnt crackers. During Diwali, kids were allowed to be up late, and the colonies were safe, so we could walk around without any worry. Lovey found a half-burnt *firki*, a spinning wheel, and gave it to me to light. The firki was damaged and would not spin, so I put it on the wall and poked it with a stick to make it go round. It wobbled for a bit, throwing out sparks intermittently; suddenly some robust part of it caught fire and it started spinning wildly and flew right off the wall straight into my hair. I was not wearing my scarf that evening because my mother wanted to wash my hair. She had tied it in a loose bun. All evening she had been calling me to come in and have my hair washed, and I had ignored her. The spinning firki got entangled in the loose bun and burnt my scalp and all the hair on one side of my head. I started screaming in pain and panic, and my sisters started shouting too. Mummy came running out. I started sobbing, afraid to cry loudly because I was sure Papa would scold and beat me up for being so careless and not listening to my mother when she was calling me in for a shampoo.

My mother quickly flicked off the firki and rushed me inside. My father, who had already gone to bed, had got up and came out to see what the commotion was about. He took one look at me and rushed me to the bathroom and held my head under the tap. The cool water was a relief, but the smell of burnt hair and flesh filled my nostrils.

To my surprise, Papa did not scold me, but rushed me to a compounder who lived nearby. Many compounders administer first aid and basic medical treatment. It was past 1.30 a.m., and we had to knock long and hard on the compounder's door to wake him. When he finally answered the door, he took one look at me and injected me with a strong painkiller and a sedative. Then he examined the burnt scalp. The burns were severe on one side, but not so bad on the other. My hair would have to be cut to apply medicine to the scorched skin. Papa was aghast. He absolutely refused to let my hair be cut. How could a Sikh cut his hair? It was against his religion. The compounder explained that it would be hard to reach the skin through the tangled, burnt hair and if not treated, it would get infected. But Papa would not budge. He was sure that a more qualified doctor would be able to treat me without having to cut my hair. The exasperated compounder gave up, but he took full advantage of the emergency and charged us an unusually huge fee. Goddess Laxmi had certainly blessed him that Diwali night.

The next morning, the smell of burnt hair was replaced by a new foul smell, but I did not say anything. Papa took me to a well-known doctor in the locality, who also said that the hair would have to be cut for any treatment to be effective. Papa went to a dermatologist and then to the special burns ward in a big hospital. Everywhere he was told that no treatment would be effective until the hair was cut. They assured Papa that the hair would grow back as soon as the skin healed. But he was adamant – his son's hair could not be cut; his religion just did not permit it. Finally, he took me to an Ayurvedic clinic almost an hour's drive from our house. The two Sikh brothers who ran the clinic examined my scalp. It was four days since the accident with the firecracker, and the smell of burnt flesh was now so bad that they had to cover their noses.

The Sikh brothers empathized with Papa's reluctance to have his son's haircut. They said that they could treat the wound by scraping off thin layers of skin every day and applying their herbal medicines on it. I would have to go to their clinic at 10 a.m. daily for at least twenty-five sittings. It would take another month after that for the skin to heal completely. I got a month's medical leave from school. Papa took me to the clinic every morning at 9 a.m. We returned around noon, and only then would Papa bathe, eat and go off to work.

Thanks to my father's efforts, I recovered from the accident. It was also deeply impressed upon me that a Sikh's hair is of the utmost importance and that I and others like me could never ever cut their hair.

A STEP DOWN

By the time I reached class five, I had settled down well in school, but there was no stability at home. Papa found it difficult to manage his business alone. His rubber factory was at one end of town, his home at the other, and he had to go to old Delhi to sell his products and collect payments. Besides, he rarely maintained accounts or inventory, making it very hard to run the business efficiently.

In Pakistan, he was in class eight in a government school when his family had to suddenly leave their home. He could not resume his education in India because they arrived penniless, and he and his elder brother had to find work to support their family. Papa's father had never worked or held a job in Pakistan and did not know what to do in India either. When they came to India my father, who was fourteen years old, and his brother Ranbir Singh, who was seventeen, started selling pens and optical frames to support their family. Papa spoke only Punjabi, his mother tongue, and Urdu, the medium of instruction in his school. Urdu was the language of that region, and it was only after the Partition that it became 'a Muslim language', because it was the national language of Pakistan. But Urdu was of no use to Papa in India. He did manage to speak Hindi, since it was similar to Urdu, and of course he spoke Punjabi with everyone in Punjab. He never learnt to write in Hindi. He could understand a bit of English, and even write a little, but could not speak. All his life, he read only Urdu newspapers and magazines.

Papa was a simple, honest and trusting man. Added to this was his inability to maintain financial records, and he became easy game for dishonest and cunning buyers and suppliers. Buyers refused to pay him saying that he had collected payments already and suppliers often collected payment twice from him, insisting that he had never paid them before. Since most transactions at that time were in cash and Papa kept no records, there was nothing he could do. As a result, the factory suffered enormous losses.

Small- and medium-sized businesses dealt mostly in cash at that time, especially in Delhi. Most of the businessmen had migrated there from Pakistan. They had begun their lives afresh and were not part of the old economic systems. They worked very hard, took risks, dealt in cash and avoided paying taxes. They wanted to settle down as soon as they could. Papa was no different. Ironically, he never could settle down completely and his life was filled with upheavals to the very end.

Finally, Papa's business suffered such losses that he had to sell our house to pay off bank and other loans. My siblings and I had examinations coming up, but we had to deal with it on our own. Our parents were busy trying to find a small house to rent and were dealing with their financial problems. Our house had to be renovated before it was handed over to the new owner, and my parents had to pack all our belongings and move out in four months.

It was a sad day when we moved to a small house with two bedrooms and a drawing-cum-dining room in a different locality. The four of us children had to share one room and bathroom, while my parents had the other. We hated it. It is easy to step up in life, but it is very hard to take a step down.

The money that Papa got from the sale of the house was fast depleting. Though the loans were paid off, the factory was still making losses. Somehow, Papa had to get his business on track again. As usual, he made an impulsive decision to send his three older children to live with his elder brother's family in Amritsar for at least a year, while he and my mother lived frugally and he did his best to turn his business around.

TO AMRITSAR AND BACK

My father's elder brother lived in the big family house and ran a successful business. He and his wife welcomed my sisters and me to their home. We had moved to Amritsar in the summer, but by the time we were admitted into a school there, the session had already been underway for two weeks. My sisters went to an all-girls school, while I went to the co-ed Shri Guru Harkrishan Public School, where my cousin Tarun studied. Tarun was one class senior to me, but we were good friends. A Sikh institution ran the school, and for the first time, most of my classmates were Sikhs, a new and happy experience for me. Even the morning prayers here were familiar – I had recited them at home since childhood.

However, in Amritsar, for the first time, I became aware of an undercurrent all-pervading caste system. Though they were all Sikhs, some were Jaat Sikhs, who considered themselves superior to the others. I had to face some light-hearted bullying about my caste, but I was unaffected by it. It was not just religion that divided people, I realized, but there were also castes within the same religion. It seemed that human beings just could not live together as equals.

All in all, those were happy days in Amritsar. Our grandparents lived in the same house, and we had our cousins to play with. It was a well-run home, with a driver, maids and other servants, and a gatekeeper at the gate. Besides, our other paternal and maternal cousins lived in Amritsar and visited often. Our uncle and aunt treated us with great affection, just like their own children.

Lovey had been put in charge of my second sister Daisy and me in Amritsar. She had to ensure that there were no complaints regarding our behaviour or our studies. She was a confident, tomboyish girl, and she had no difficulty in controlling Daisy and me – we knew that if we disobeyed her, we would not be spared a beating. Lovey had never hesitated to beat up even boys in school and on the playground.

One day, Daisy discovered lice in her hair. Daisy was tall and had beautiful, long hair down to her hips. Our mother used to regularly oil and wash our hair, but, in Amritsar, Daisy had to do it herself and she found it hard. When Lovey learnt that Daisy had got lice, she panicked. If anyone in the house came to know, it would be very embarrassing. So she wrote to Mummy asking for advice. Mummy responded by sending her a special comb that she had got from Thailand called the 'killer comb'. It was specially meant to comb out lice from hair. Everybody thought that Lovey had got a present from our mother and she secreted it away to the room she shared with us. After that, Lovey and I spent hours combing Daisy's hair with the comb every day until her hair was free of lice. It was a matter of great pride to us siblings that we had accomplished this in secret.

I enjoyed many things in Amritsar and food was the foremost. My school canteen had excellent snacks, the street food was delicious and it was much cheaper than Delhi. We received a decent amount of pocket money from Papa, and I spent most of it on snacking. Besides, I ate all the tasty, heavy meals that were cooked at home. The result was a rapid and considerable gain in weight – almost 8 or 9 kilos! My school uniform stretched tightly across my body, and I often came home with ripped seams in my pants and shorts. Once, to my great embarrassment, my track pants split open at the crotch! But I knew that there were only four or five months of school left in Amritsar before I returned to Delhi, so there was no point in buying a whole new set of uniforms. I decided to make do with the ill-fitting clothes.

March began and examinations were around the corner. The three of us studied hard. Our cousins were good students, and we had to be as good, if not better than them.

***

Papa had sent us away because the new house was too small for such a large family and school fees and living expenses were much higher in Delhi. He had given himself a year to revive his business, so that he could bring us back home. He looked for a partner to buy a share in his factory and help him run it. His friend Ashok introduced him to Roshan Lal, who bought a one-third share in the factory. Roshan Lal was a Hindu. He was smart and took over the management of accounts and inventory – areas in which Papa was very weak – while Papa worked hard on the production side, introducing efficient practices and cutting costs where necessary.

With the money he got from his new partner, Papa bought a large four-bedroom house near the factory and planned to bring us back in summer, at the end of the academic session. He also bought a brand-new Ambassador.

In mid-April 1983, Papa came to Amritsar to take us back to our new home in Delhi. We were very excited to return to Delhi. We would be meeting Mummy and our little brother after a long time. We would also go back to our old school and meet all our friends again. And then there was the brand-new house and a fancy new neighbourhood to discover.

When my sisters and I finally left with Papa in his new car, we were both sad and excited. We had spent a year in Amritsar in the loving care of our uncle and aunt. Our cousins had welcomed us with open arms. And, of course, our grandparents had lavished affection on us. Our bonds with the family were stronger than ever. Papa thanked his brother and especially his brother's warm and generous wife for looking after his children. We left for Delhi with me proudly sitting on the front seat with Papa, feeling very grown-up. My sisters sat at the back. Lovey did not object. Though she was the eldest and by far the bravest of the siblings, she had learnt that males, even if they were younger than her, always took the front seat.

We children thoroughly enjoyed the road trip back to Delhi. I had left Amritsar knowing that I would be back to visit my extended family, but I was sure that I would never again live there. I enjoyed the drive through the lush green land in the pleasant April weather. Every once in a while, I stuck my head out of the window to catch the breeze, despite being warned not to do so by Papa. Not many people had cars those days and only the super-rich had air-conditioned cars. Besides, there was no pollution. So the windows were always open to let the fresh breeze in. After a while, Daisy wanted to sit in front, and when we stopped for a snack at a roadside eatery, I reluctantly exchanged places with her.

We reached Delhi at 9 p.m. There was much excitement when we met Mummy and Gagan, our younger brother. We ran around exploring the new house. My sisters had one room and Gagan and me, another, while our parents had the main bedroom and there was one room for guests. My room even had a radio in it. Mummy had organized a lavish dinner for us. There were Chinese noodles, my favourite, ice cream for Lovey and even an imported Kit Kat chocolate for Daisy. Chocolates, watches and such stuff were often smuggled into the country those days for rich people to buy. Mummy had bought just one chocolate for Daisy for that very special occasion. Tired and replete, we children happily went to bed in our brand-new rooms.

The next morning regular routines set in. Papa went off to the factory, while Mummy got busy with housework. We kids had a two-week break before school started, and I went off to explore the local market and neighbourhood. I had to find the places that were of interest to me – the confectionery store, a video game parlour, the popular Chinese food stalls, and parks and playgrounds. Summer holidays were on, so there were many children out playing cricket or football. I struck up a conversation with some of them. I also came upon a small gurudwara, and I went in and prayed.

When I returned home two hours later, I saw a blue moped parked outside the house and a young man inside talking to my mother. I stood by listening to their conversation. I learnt that the man's name was Ramesh and he was a supervisor in our factory. He had come to collect some rubber samples that my father had forgotten to take with him in the morning. Mummy introduced me to Ramesh.

'He will be your boss in a few years,' Mummy said with a laugh.

Ramesh uncle smiled and shook hands with me saying, 'I will teach you all about the business when you join the factory!'

His friendliness put me at ease and I demanded to be taught how to ride the moped. Ramesh uncle taught me how to start it by pressing a lever and pedalling hard, so that the speed kick started the motor. After that it was just like riding a cycle with a motor.

I soon settled down in the new house, but had no friends in the locality. I had spent the past year with my cousins and other friends, and I found Delhi very lonely. 'Why have you bought this house so far from our old one?' I asked Papa. 'I have to make new friends everywhere – at home and in school. It's very unfair.'

Papa explained to me that he had bought this house because it was close to his friend Ashok's house and he would be able to visit him frequently and also because our school was much nearer from here.

I listened quietly and then burst out, 'Papa, I am not going to that school again.'

Papa was taken aback. He had thought things through before buying the house. It was large, in a good locality and all four children could go to the same school, quite close to the house. It was one of Delhi's good schools and he could not understand why I refused to go there. He was also surprised that I, usually quite obedient, had started arguing with him. Actually I had always been a little afraid of Papa's hot temper, but I was a teenager now. Papa too realized that I was in a rebellious phase.

The truth was that the thought of going back to my old school brought up all the trauma of my first year there, when I had been mercilessly teased and taunted. I dared not admit this to my father – how could I appear cowardly before him? Sikh boys are told from childhood that they are the bravest of men and can never show any sign of weakness under any circumstance. Sikhism was born as the militant arm of Hinduism, to protect the Hindu faith from the atrocities of the Mughals. Courage and strength were embedded in the very faith. Brought up on stories of valour and sacrifice, even very young Sikh boys dare not display any sign of even perceived weakness. So I could not tell Papa my real fears.

Amritsar had shown me how comfortable it was to be amongst my own kind, and I had no desire to brave the teasing in school again. So I made up a story about an imaginary friend, Ajit Singh, from Amritsar, who had moved to Delhi and joined the Sri Guru Tegh Bahadur School very close to our house, so close that I would be able to cycle to school. I had come upon this school while exploring the neighbourhood. I had seen a large building and discovered that there was a gurudwara on the ground floor and a school on the three floors above.

Papa was a regular visitor to this gurudwara and knew about the school, but it had never occurred to him to send his children to this small, unknown school. We were all admitted to a large, prestigious school and our school bus came up to a little gurudwara situated right behind our house. However, I was adamant and Papa finally gave in. I went with him to get admission in the school.

When we started filling the forms, Papa asked me in which section Ajit Singh studied.

'Section D', I said quickly.

That had been my section in the school in Amritsar. The form was submitted.

The cashier read the form carefully, then looked up and said, 'There is no section D in the eighth class. In fact, there is no section D in any class. There are only sections A and B.'

Papa turned to me.

I was rattled for a second but quickly gathered my wits together and said, 'I said B, Papa, not D. You heard wrong.'

Papa accepted this, made the necessary correction on the form and I was admitted to Guru Teg Bahadur School.

Before leaving the premises, we went to the gurudwara and I offered my heartfelt thanks to God for saving the day with a B instead of D!

THE GENTLE HARBIR

There was no Ajit Singh in my class, but one Harbir Singh joined class seven, section B, on the third day of school. The expression that I had seen on the faces of my classmates when I had entered class two in Kulachi Hansraj Model School now came upon my own face as I looked at Harbir.

Harbir was a Sikh, but that's where the resemblance with the other Sikh boys ended. He was very tall, had a thicker beard and moustache than the other boys, and his turban was tied differently. He was thin and had a girlish voice. His body language was very different – there was something unusual about the way he talked, walked, ate and looked at everybody. He sat alone by himself at a desk, very quiet and introverted. The rest of the boys started teasing him from day one, but he seemed to ignore it all. He just worked quietly.

Surprisingly, all the girls liked Harbir and soon became friendly with him. Perhaps they sensed the gentleness and sensitivity in him. I was intrigued by Harbir's different ways and impressed by his friendliness with the girls. I thought it would be a good idea to be friends with him and, consequently, with all the charming girls in the class. The seat next to Harbir was empty and I quickly asked if I could sit beside him. Harbir was happy to share his desk with me.

I soon learnt why Harbir seemed so different. He was not Indian; he was from Kabul. His family were third-generation Sikhs in Afghanistan. This was the first time he had visited India. The Afghan Sikhs had begun to migrate out of Afghanistan since the war with Russia because the locals had started looting the rich Sikhs to fund their weapons. Neither Sikhs nor well-to-do Afghans were part of the war, but the Sikhs were the first and easiest targets for the militants.

I felt a strong empathy for Harbir. I knew what it was like to be teased just because one looked different. It was just fun for the bullies, but I knew how traumatizing it was for the victim. Harbir and I soon became best buddies.

In a few weeks, I was well settled in my new school and new locality. I had many Sikh friends in the school and Sikh and Hindu friends in the colony. There was the large Chhatrasal Stadium near my house and many parks in which I played cricket and football with the neighbourhood kids. There is no religious discrimination among Indians in sports or business. It is only fanatics who try to divide people, who, left to themselves, will interact easily with each other. The Indian cricket team has players from across regions and religions, but they are all accepted as equals on the team.

Political groups often try to polarize Hindus and Muslims. India has a large Muslim population, and if they were not patriotic Indians, if they were anti-India, our country would have been a hotbed of terrorism and would have turned into a failed state.

There were only four Hindu boys in my class. One of the four had a Sikh name and wore a steel kada. I knew that many Hindus also wore the kada and worshipped at the gurudwara, because anybody can be a seeker. But only the 'true Sikhs' never cut their hair and had 'Singh' or 'Kaur' as their middle names. So it surprised me that my classmate was a Singh but did not have long hair. I asked Gurmeet Singh the reason and he told me that he was a Sehajdhari Sikh. Apparently, Sikhs are of two kinds – Keshdhari, those who never cut their hair, and Sehajdhari, those who cut their hair. I was surprised. In my school in Amritsar, I had learnt that even when Sikhs looked alike, there were castes that divided them, and now here were Sikhs who did not even look the same in the most important aspect!

Gurmeet told me that he had cut his hair, but his father had not. His father's brother, on the other hand, had short hair. But they were all Sikhs – they worshipped at the gurudwara and lived together in the same house. Gurmeet's father, despite the long hair, was not very religious. He only visited the gurudwara on major festivals. His short-haired brother, however, was very religious and went to the gurudwara every day!

Most Sikhs visit the gurudwara on the birthdays and the martyrdom days of the gurus. The martyrdom days are very important because most of the gurus died in some valorous, humane cause. None of the gurus sacrificed their life for a separate Sikh land or to protect their language or region. They sacrificed their lives for the well-being of humanity, not for any one particular creed. The message of Sikhism is equality and uplift of the underprivileged. But in the 500-year journey of Sikhism, this essence has been forgotten and the focus is somewhat more on highlighting the uniqueness of the community.

I wondered why my small community had so many divisions. How could Sikhs spread the message of unity if they were themselves so divided? Indians like to portray their country as a picture of unity in diversity, which was a sentiment proposed by the Sikhs' first guru, Sri Nanak Devji. But neither Sikhs nor Indians lived by this any more.

As the weeks passed, I was more and more impressed by Harbir's quiet and calm personality. The two of us spent a lot of time together and Harbir became a regular visitor at my house. We often spent the evenings in my room and talked about our past experiences. I spoke about my trauma at Kulachi Hansraj Model School, while Harbir shared bits about his life in Kabul before he came to Delhi. My trauma had ended, but Harbir's was still going on. I had found my troubles unbearable, but Harbir faced everything with his quiet, sad smile. How deeply he was affected was impossible to tell from his demeanour.

We met almost daily in the evenings. Every evening we planned to go out and play, but thanks to me, almost every time, we ended up at the Chinese food stalls to eat my favourite chicken and egg noodles or chicken fried rice. Harbir never ordered any food, but ate a few spoonfuls from my plate. In Amritsar, my cousin Tarun had been my companion in eating out every evening. He too had been small eater. But I loved food and ate far too much, consequently putting on serious amounts of weight. I did step out in sportswear every evening with the intention of playing in the park with the other kids, but the food was always too enticing. My mother gave me Rs 5 every morning when I went to school and Rs 5 in the evening as well. Indian mothers express love for their children by feeding them, and my mother was no different. She checked my pockets every night after I had changed into my nightwear. If the Rs 5 were gone, she promptly gave me more the next day.

Meanwhile, the factory and business completely occupied Papa. Though he now had better control over his business, he had to pay EMIs for his new house and share his profit with his partner. He never noticed that I was getting larger by the day.

Most of the girls in my class were friendly and comfortable with Harbir. Perhaps it was because of his slim build, girlish voice and gentle manners, things quite unexpected in someone from the harsh land of Afghanistan. Harbir was the opposite of the well-built, stocky Sikh boys with their loud voices and aggressive manners.

There was a girl called Jaspreet in my class on whom I had a crush. Since the girls were all friendly with Harbir, I asked him to tell Jaspreet that I wanted to be friends with her.

When Harbir told her that Gurvinder wanted to be her friend, she asked, 'Which Gurvinder?'

Another boy in our class was also called Gurvinder. Harbir told her that he had brought the message from Bobby, who was a good person, not the other Gurvinder, who was arrogant and not nice at all.

He pointed to me and she exclaimed, 'Who, Appu?' and burst out laughing.

Appu was the little elephant mascot of the 1982 Asian Games that were held in Delhi. Later an amusement park was opened called Appu Ghar. The park was hugely popular, as was Appu, the elephant, who featured on balloons, T-shirts, badges and posters.

Harbir came back to me with a sad face. His gentle smile was gone, and I knew that the news was not good. But when Harbir told me that the bubbly, tomboyish Jaspreet had called me Appu, I was devastated. I immediately blamed Harbir, saying that he had not properly put forward my case to Jaspreet, but in my heart, I knew that was not true. It was my round paunch, big bums and fat thighs that had earned me the nickname. I was petrified that the whole school would soon be calling me Appu.

Sure enough, the very next morning when I entered my classroom, three or four boys came up to me and one of them said, 'Good morning, Appu! Jaspreet is waiting for you outside the library.'

And they burst out laughing. I wished the earth would open up and swallow me. Luckily, Jaspreet was not there when this happened.

Harbir did not come to school for the next two or three days. He was back in school on Monday, but we did not talk about the incident. My classmates started calling me Appu, but then, many boys had been given nicknames in the school.

The new nickname upset me, but it did not stop me from eating my favourite food. I knew that I should lose weight, but I could never resist those egg and chicken noodles. But all this changed on 30 October 1984, when Prime Minister Indira Gandhi was murdered and I had to run for life, leaving behind my home, my friend Harbir and my favourite chicken and egg noodles.

One day, my mother asked me about Harbir's family and I realized that I knew nothing about them at all. All I had was his phone number. It was always Harbir who came to my house, not the other way around. I knew that Harbir lived with his family in a rented house in the colony next to ours, but I did not know his exact address.

So the next day, I told Harbir that I would go to his house in the evening instead of him coming over and we would then go to the park to play football. Harbir tore a page from his notebook and wrote down his address and drew directions to his house for me.

I reached Harbir's house at 4.30 p.m. and rang my cycle bell, which was our signal to each other to come out to play. Harbir didn't come out, so I parked my cycle and rang the doorbell. A tall, slim, pretty girl, about seventeen years old, opened the door. She had a beautiful pink complexion and the same soft, sad smile as Harbir. I couldn't take my eyes off her lovely face. She said 'Sat Sri Akal' and 'Welcome, Bobby' in her broken Punjabi with an Afghani accent, and I quickly turned my eyes away. I assumed that she was Harbir's sister, though Harbir had never mentioned his siblings to me.

The girl took me inside and introduced me to her two younger sisters and her mother. They were all very beautiful, like the prettiest film stars. The house was a little shabby and untidy. I sat on a sofa outside the kitchen. I was told that Harbir had gone out on an errand. I politely enquired about uncle, Harbir's father, and was told that he was at his shop and would return only late at night. We were making small talk when Harbir returned with two bottles of Thums Up, an Indian brand of cola, and a small plastic bag from which a delicious smell wafted out.

Harbir hugged me tightly, much to my surprise. He had never greeted me in that way before. But today, Harbir was in his true Afghani colours. He took me to his bedroom. His two sisters, who were sitting there, immediately left and his eldest sister went into the kitchen to help her mother. We sat on a mattress on the floor, since there was no bed. Through the door, I could see the whole house, which seemed to be filled with old things. I wondered why they had old Indian things, when they were new in the country.

Harbir's mother came in with two bottles of Thums Up and samosas and homemade roasted chicken legs. I was embarrassed at this hospitality. When Harbir came to my house, my mother at most offered cold water from the fridge! However, I enjoyed myself thoroughly. I loved good food and could think of nothing else when there was food before me. I had most of the samosas and half the chicken. I would have liked to eat it all myself, but I had to share it with Harbir. I finished the bottle of Thums Up, thanked Harbir's mother and sister and left with Harbir.

We went to the stadium, intending to play football. A group of boys were already playing and invited us to join the game, but I was too full to play. Harbir also declined. Instead, we sat in the stands. Harbir apologized to me for not being able to accord me the due honour that a first-time guest deserved. I was completely taken aback. I had never seen Harbir so emotional. Besides, I had been treated with enormous warmth and hospitality, more than I had ever expected. I told Harbir that I had eaten the best chicken legs ever in my life and there was nothing Harbir needed to apologize for. Instead I wanted to know all about his family and their life in Afghanistan, and for once, Harbir shed his reticence and told me his story.

Harbir's father and his two brothers had two big showrooms of western wear, an agency of Toyota cars and a transport business in Kabul. They were a well-to-do, renowned and respected family. Life was smooth until the Russian invasion of Afghanistan. America entered the fray to counter Russia and the war spilled over into the streets of Kabul.

The Afghans were fighting a guerrilla war, attacking their enemy on the streets and on the highway. There was massive destruction of property and many casualties. The Afghans had acquired shoulder-launched rockets from the Americans, one of which was aimed at a Russian convey on the highway but landed instead on Harbir's family-owned Toyota agency and destroyed it completely.

The war also led to the rise of radical Islam, which was opposed to anything western or modern. The showrooms of western wear were burnt down. The family's transport business slowed down because their trucks were looted on the highways. Even the gurudwara was shut down. One Jihadi group leader then threatened Harbir's family and demanded a large sum of money from them. They paid. But a few days later, another group made a similar demand for an even larger sum. That is when the family decided that it was time to leave Afghanistan for good.

Harbir's uncles fled with their families to Germany, but Harbir's father was conservative and did not want his daughters to grow up in a western country. So he came to India with his family. He now had a small rented shop selling imported electronic items in Ghaffar Market, where many Afghani Sikhs owned or managed shops selling all kinds of imported goods. Once a rich, well-established family, Harbir's family now could not even afford to stock a few bottles of Thums Up in their home and bought one or two bottles only when guests came.

I was shocked. I understood Harbir's silence better and felt very close to him.

A DIVISIVE POLITICS

In the following months, I became aware that there was a much bigger world outside my own little one. It was a time of uncertainty and upheaval in north India. The rise of terrorism in Punjab dominated the news, and I started listening to the radio every day. Punjabis were in the forefront all over the country – in business, in the government and in the film industry. In fact, Punjabi actors, writers, directors and producers dominated the film industry in Mumbai. Many of them were Hindus, but most Punjabi Hindus had great faith in Sikhism and regularly visited the gurudwara. They even kept Shri Guru Granth Sahib, the holy book of the Sikhs, at home.

Sikhism had been part of Hinduism until the tenth Sikh guru, Sri Guru Gobind Singhji, set it apart as a separate religion. Those who followed it were named Khalsa, and the men were given the middle name 'Singh'. None of the nine gurus preceeding Sri Guru Gobind Singhji, including Sri Guru Teg Bahadurji, the father of the tenth guru, had the middle name 'Singh', since they were not a separate religious community until 13 April 1699. The 13th of April is also Baisakhi, the harvest festival in north India. It is on this day that farmers start cutting their crops. Thus, the birth of the Khalsa and the annual commencement of harvest made Baisakhi a very important festival for Hindus and Sikhs alike.

When terrorism began to grow in Punjab, many Bollywood celebrities appealed to the Sikh extremists, the politicians in Punjab and the central government to work together to restore peace and harmony in the state. But it was all in vain. The extremists were adamant and politicians played their dirty games to polarize the community to gain votes.

In Punjab, Hindus were targeted and killed by Sikh extremists who wanted a separate Sikh state. But Sikhs were also killed in large numbers by the police and paramilitary forces. The police arrested young Sikhs suspected of militancy to extract information about their associates. Many of the youth were then killed in fake encounters. Human Rights groups are still fighting cases in Indian courts against the state of Punjab for large-scale violation of rights.

The radicals killed Sikhs who they suspected of being police informants or those who refused to give them shelter or money. In some rare cases, Sikhs were killed for not keeping long hair and beards, which the hardliners believed was an essential part of their identity. The Punjab Police force, which has more than 90 per cent Sikhs, killed Sikh extremists. Besides, terrorist groups often attacked police vehicles or even the families of policemen, resulting the deaths of large numbers of Sikhs. In rural areas, personal rivalry found 'suspected terrorism' a good excuse to kill enemies. Corrupt police officers were bribed to do this. The militants killed many liberal Sikhs who talked peace and tried to initiate dialogues or political agreements.

Despite all efforts, peace did not come to Punjab. In fact, the violence escalated. Finally, on 6 June 1984, the Indian Army fired upon the Golden Temple to free it from the militants who had holed up there. The order to attack was signed by the president of India, himself a Sikh. But everyone knew that the order actually came from the then prime minister, Mrs Indira Gandhi.

The Indian Army stormed the Golden Temple from all four directions. To its surprise, there was strong resistance from the militants inside, who were very heavily armed. The first few troops that entered faced heavy casualties. Then the army unleashed its might. Tanks and heavy guns were used in this Operation Blue Star. It took three days of fighting to kill the militants. Some innocent devotees and many soldiers also lost their lives.

Operation Blue Star caused heavy damage to the Golden Temple and deeply wounded the sentiments of Sikhs all over the world. The Sikhs in the army protested, as did Sikhs in the Indian Navy and the Indian Air Force, the Border Security Force and other organizations. Many Sikhs from the army marched in protest to Amritsar. They were arrested on their way and cases were filed against them in courts.

Other Sikhs protested by returning government awards and honours that they had received. Some resigned from senior government positions. There were articles and debates in the newspapers. The government action was questioned in article upon article in the media. Many believed that the Sikh militants could have been evicted from the Golden Temple without firing guns and causing bloodshed in the holy shrine. All kinds of questions were raised: Why had the government not explored other avenues first? Why were innocent devotees not given time to leave the shrine? Could the government not have cut off water and electricity and waited to see if that forced the militants out? Why did it not consult anybody before taking such a harsh step? But the blunder had been committed, and there were no satisfactory answers now. Criticism of the government action came not only from the Sikh community but also from all over the world. However, there were many who supported the actions of the government. They believed that harsh action was needed to rid the Golden Temple of militants.

Many senior officials who headed Operation Blue Star were Sikhs. Was it a coincidence that the order to attack the Golden Temple was given by a Sikh and carried out by officers, many of whom were Sikhs? General Arun Sridhar Vaidya, the chief of the Indian Army, was later gunned down in Pune, Maharashtra by the Sikhs hardliners. The president of India, who signed the orders to attack the Golden Temple, was provided enhanced security.

The terrorism in Punjab and then Operation Blue Star changed attitudes towards Sikhs all over the country. A huge haul of arms and ammunition was recovered from the Golden Temple, and it was learnt that the Sikh militants were being supported by Pakistan, which had attacked India twice and had trained and armed tribals in Kashmir to fight against India. The Sikh association with Pakistan destroyed the respect that people had for the community. Hindus and Sikhs, who had always been one, were now two different groups, thanks to the selfish motives of politicians. It was a deeply divided world.

Nevertheless, the efforts of some noble people were still on to end the killings of humans and restore peace. It was around this time that Sunil Dutt, a famous film star and member of Parliament dedicated to the welfare of his people, organized a march from Mumbai to Amritsar, a distance of 2,000 kilometres, to carry the message of peace to the people of Punjab. He appealed to Sikh hardliners to end the killing of innocent people. When Sunil Dutt reached Amritsar with his large group of Sikh and Hindu celebrities and common people, he went straight to the Golden Temple, the Sri Harmandir Sahib, the holiest Sikh shrine. It was feared that he would be attacked or driven away from the temple. But fortunately, the Sikh hardliners treated the film star and his group with great respect. They prayed for peace and harmony and then had *langar* in the kitchen with the other devotees.

UNPLEASANT CHANGES

In mid-June, Harbir and I had come out to play in the park, but were neither playing nor eating noodles. I was sad, so Harbir just sat quietly beside me, and we watched the sun go in and out of the clouds. It was not in Harbir's nature to probe; he was a silent observer. But I was restless because I wanted to talk about the thing that had disturbed me so much.

'People are not nice,' I stated abruptly.

'Why?' aked Harbir, giving me an excuse to unburden my heart.

The day before, Papa had to go to Hissar to buy a piece of machinery for the factory. Since it was a holiday, I decided to accompany him. Our car battery had discharged, so we took a bus. The bus was crowded. Many more tickets are sold than the number of seats on buses in India. Papa got only one confirmed seat. It was a long journey and I wondered what we would do.

'Don't worry,' said Papa. 'Someone will offer a seat when they see a young boy standing.'

There were two or three other Sikh men on the bus. Almost half an hour into the journey, I was still standing. No one had offered me a seat. The conductor suggested that I sit on my father's lap, but Papa took one look at my size and said that we would take turns to sit. So, I sat down and my father stood. No one offered Papa a seat either.

The bus stopped at a small town on the way to Hissar. Some people got down and many more got on. I had been the only one standing when the journey began. Now, there were at least seven to eight men who were also standing in the aisle. There were mostly men and elderly people on the bus. Two more men got on at another small stop. It was hot. Everyone was sweating. I was used to air conditioning at home and was miserable. I had two cold drinks and now I wanted to pee. Papa requested the conductor to halt the bus, and we got off. When we came back, our seat was gone. A gruff looking man was sitting on it.

When Papa told the man that it was his seat, the man retorted, 'Is your name written on it?'

An argument erupted between them, but nobody else spoke up. The conductor was called, but he refused to get involved.

'My job is to sell tickets,' he said.

When Papa protested, the conductor tried to pacify him by saying that it was only 15–20 kilometres to Hissar and he could easily stand for that short duration. There was no option but to stand for the rest of the journey, but the atmosphere in the bus became tense.

Suddenly, a loud Haryanvi voice said, 'We made these people sit on our heads for such a long time, and now they are killing us. Why should we cooperate with them outside Punjab when they don't want to be a part of India?'

Papa and I were shaken by the anger and hatred in this voice. There was complete silence on the bus – a tense, uneasy silence that continued until we reached Hissar. Not only had we not been offered a seat but also we had been insulted. The respect that Sikhs had earned through their valour and sacrifices throughout history had been wiped out by the actions of the militants in Punjab.

At the factory in Hissar, Papa examined the machine, negotiated the deal, paid an advance and fixed a delivery date. The seller was a Haryanvi, but he treated us with respect and offered us a hot lunch. His affectionate and respectful attitude was a balm after the rudeness we had encountered on the bus.

We returned to Delhi by taxi. The taxi driver was a Sikh who charged us a very high price, but Papa preferred to ride in his taxi rather than those of two other non-Sikh drivers who'd been available. We travelled back in silence.

Papa only asked the taxi driver one question, 'How is the environment in Haryana for Sikhs?'

The driver said that it was not the same any more.

I never asked Papa why we had taken a taxi back from Hissar or why he had chosen to pay 50 per cent more to a Sikh driver rather than going with one of the non-Sikh taxi drivers who had offered a cheaper fare. The anger and animosity in the bus had been palpable.

Harbir looked up at the sky and said that it should rain to bring relief from the scorching heat. I was nonplussed. I had expected some words of consolation or empathy. But what Harbir said seemed irrelevant.

School opened after a few days and regular routines set in. The only difference was that Papa now regularly watched the news on TV and listened to it on the radio. His calls to his parents and brother in Amritsar became more frequent.

I often watched television with Papa. I was interested in movies or in *Chitrahaar*, the weekly programme of Hindi film songs. But Papa held the remote and so the national news could never be missed. The headlines were always about the violence in Punjab, and later there would be details of how many militants had been killed and the number of deaths of policemen and civilians, Hindu and Sikh. Once one community in Punjab, Hindus and Sikhs had been irrevocably sundered into two separate entities. Even their deaths were now reported separately.

And so life continued for four months.

Until 31 October 1984.

***

And here we were – Papa curled up in uneasy sleep on the small landing, while I sat beside him impatiently waiting for midnight and for my uncle to come and fetch us. It was dark and deathly quiet. No dog barked, no car or scooter drove past, and no night watchman walked by with his stick dragging on the ground and his periodic calls of '*Jaagte raho!*'

THE RESCUE AND THE AFTERMATH

I did not know what the time was or how much time had elapsed while I was lost in old memories. The darkness and the silence were sinister. I moved closer to my father and laid my head on his chest.

Papa was startled and woke up in panic saying, 'What happened? What time is it? Where are your uncles? Why haven't they come?'

I said that nothing had happened. I had only put my head on his chest because there was no other place in that tiny space. Papa relaxed a bit and stood up to peer out of the ground glass window. Streetlights were on. There were lights visible in many houses in the neighbourhood, but some houses were dark. 'These must be the Sikh homes,' Papa said sadly. Just to pass the time hanging so heavy on our hands, I asked Papa what he would do in Amritsar.

Papa had the future all planned out. He would sell off this burnt house, repay the bank loan and use the rest of the money to buy out his partner. Then he would sell the factory building and land and use the money to buy a home and factory in Amritsar. He would transport his machinery to the new factory there.

Little did Papa know that his factory had already been looted and burnt down. There was a big four-feet high and three-feet wide mural of the first Sikh guru, Sri Guru Nanak Devji, on the front façade of the factory. It was customary those days to have such murals of religious figures on houses and factories. Below the picture was a fresh water tank with a tap and two steel glasses chained to the wall. Any passer-by could drink water there. This is a common Sikh practice. One of the basic principles of Sikh religion is unity, which is why Sri Guru Nanak Devji had introduced langar, a free common kitchen, and *piyau*, a fresh water tank from which all could drink. Papa had simply carried forward this charitable practice. But even the picture of the guru had not deterred the mob, and the water stored in the tank could not douse the raging communal flames.

Papa outlined his plans for a safe and happy life in Amritsar, and hearing them, I was excited about the future. Just for a few moments, we forgot the horrible situation in which we were caught.

After a while, I went off to get some water. It was so dark, I could hardly see. I roamed about a little and went towards the undamaged store, found a torch and came back. Back inside the room, all the steel vessels had been looted and the plastic ones had melted. The fresh water tap in the kitchen was burnt and jammed. But I found two empty glass coke bottles and filled them with water from the bathroom. Papa came and joined me. We estimated that it must be past midnight. Help would soon arrive, and we decided to salvage whatever we could from the house.

We hoped that some jewellery, cash and other expensive items had somehow survived. But there was very little that was undamaged. The cupboards were empty. The steel cupboards had been forced open, the safes and locker boxes in them broken and everything of value taken away. The only things left behind were a few items of religious faith lying on the ground. My steel kada lay where I had kept it when I wore the frock and went off to Ashok uncle's house. And engulfing everything was the strong, unbearable smell of smouldering mattresses. There also lay some photographs, many of them half burnt, in a small cabinet, which was still not that damaged.

We went back to the storeroom from where we pulled out a few clothes in trunks and some silver utensils used during the Diwali puja. That was all that remained in the house. Papa made up two bundles, one of the warm winter clothes from the store and another of the few photographs, a kada and the silver utensils.

And we waited – tense, impatient, fearful. At last, I went up to the terrace to see if I could spot my uncle's car coming. I was not so scared standing in the dark, still in my sister's frock. A pale moon hung in the sky, and I was visible in that feeble light. I had been standing there for ten minutes or so when I saw the headlights of a car coming towards our house. My heart lifted – it had to be my uncle coming to pick us up. But the car slowly drove past our house without stopping. Near the park, it suddenly made a U-turn and came right back. I panicked. Had the people in the car seen me and come back to kill me? Did they think I was a girl and were coming back to rape or kill me?

The car stopped outside our house and I realized that it was my uncle's car, but it was not my uncle who got down from it but two clean-shaven men. They entered the gate and I was immensely relieved to see them. I called out, 'Uncle, I am here.'

As soon as I called out, I felt foolish, because in that silent night, I could have been heard all over the place. But one of the men merely asked where my father was. I told them to wait and went down to call my father, and we left the house with the two small bundles of all that remained of our material goods.

Papa did not recognize the two men. They explained that they were his brother's neighbours. They did not want his brothers to risk driving around at night, so they had volunteered to come and pick us up. I was struck by this display of large heartedness and friendship. Ashok uncle was Papa's closest friend, but he did not help us. And here were two Hindu men going out of their way to pick up strangers in the middle of the night. There are no good or bad Hindus; there are only good or bad human beings.

We picked up Mummy, my sisters and Gagan from the neighbour's house. Papa hid in the boot of the car, while I sat on the backseat dressed as a girl. We drove fast silently and soon reached the safety of Paramjit uncle's house. What a relief it was to be with our family! I had never felt so happy to see my uncles, aunts and cousins before. We had been through a harrowing time, our house was burnt, but we were all alive and together.

The next morning, 1 November 1984, Roshan Lal called to tell Papa that their factory had been burnt down. Roshan Lal was present when the mob had attacked the factory. He had argued and pleaded with the mob and tried to stop it. He had tried explaining that the factory was no longer owned by a Sikh and that he, a Hindu, now owned the factory, but all to no avail. A local person in the mob told the others that Roshan Lal owned only a one-third share in the factory. The mob threatened him because he was in partnership with a Sikh and looted the whole factory, took away raw material, finished products and all the machinery that was not fixed to the floor – electric motors, switchgears and weighing machines. The attackers smashed the picture of Sri Guru Nanak Devji with whatever they were carrying. Roshan Lal tried to stop them, saying that Guru Nanak was not just a Sikh guru, that the Sikh religion was formed much later by the tenth guru, but they would not listen. They burnt down the factory before his eyes. Roshan Lal sobbed as he spoke.

Papa was devastated. He had nothing to say; there was nothing he could say. He remained stone-faced.

Roshan Lal called again the next day to give Papa an exact estimate of the losses. He said he had gone back to factory to take stock and found a man there who had taken away the weighing scales the day before. The man had forgotten to take the weights and had come back for them. The scale would be of no use without the weights, he said to Roshan Lal. Papa smiled. His house and factory were both looted and burnt, but he refused to give in to anger and despair. All around the city, Sikhs had been burnt and slaughtered in their homes and on the street. Our family was lucky to be alive and safe, and Papa was thankful for that. Factories and houses can be rebuilt. No one can be brought back from the dead.

The sheer relief that we were all alive brought the whole family closer. My cousins were like real brothers and sisters. The three ladies, who were sometimes jealous of each other, now lived together like sisters. The three-bedroom house seemed large enough to accommodate three full families. The kitchen ran like a langar, with hot food served to everybody. Two bathrooms were more than enough for thirteen people. No one felt inconvenienced or seemed to lack anything.

I remembered that only a year and a half ago, four children and two adults had not been able to manage in a two-bedroom house and three children had to be sent away to Amritsar for a whole year and a new larger house had to be bought. And now just because of their mindset, everyone was comfortable. I now understood how my grandparents had raised their eight children in a household of twenty people in Pakistan. If there's place in the heart, a place in the house can always be found.

Paramjit uncle's two Hindu friends provided mattresses, sheets and pillows from their own homes. Other neighbours also brought provisions and asked if there was any other help we needed. They even offered places to stay in their homes. This was another lesson for me – people imitate other people. When one person comes forward to help, many others follow suit. It is the first helping hand that is often difficult to find.

Our family was now together in one place, but the city was still on edge. There were rumours that our colony was going to be attacked and mobs were coming with arms and ammunition. The secretary of the colony set up a meeting in which one male member from each family living there had to participate. They had to chalk out a plan to defend our colony. Slums surrounded the colony on three sides, and the slum dwellers had been actively participating in looting and killing Sikhs.

A large number of Sikhs lived in the colony and because of their presence, the Hindus there also felt unsafe. The residents decided to go together to the local police station and ask for protection. But when they reached there, only one constable and a clerk were present. There was no senior police officer there. One of the residents was a minor politician of the ruling party, and he insisted that they be allowed to talk to the station in-charge. The constable called him on the phone, but the officer in charge of that police station told them that he was posted on duty elsewhere in the city for three days and he could not come back to the colony. The politician then called up another police officer he knew and they learnt the horrifying news – the police had been told to keep off and let the rioters have their way.

The government had abdicated its role, and instead of protecting its citizens, encouraged the bloodshed by holding the police back.

The residents of the colony now knew that they had to protect themselves; the police would do nothing. They divided themselves into groups and stationed one group at each of the entry gates into the colony. Each group would be on duty for eight hours. Even fifteen- and sixteen-year-old boys were part of the groups. I was not allowed to join them since my mother felt I was too young and she did not want me to be in any danger.

For two days, there was tension and fear. All kinds of rumours floated around. But our colony was not attacked, perhaps because of the constant guard that the residents had mounted. The mobs did not want to fight; they wanted to loot and kill. They had neither religious nor personal enmity with Sikhs. The murder of Mrs Gandhi by her two Sikh bodyguards had shocked the entire nation, but that was no reason to allow the murder of thousands of innocent people. After three days of complete mayhem, the army was finally called on the fourth day. There were flag marches through the streets and colonies of Delhi. I saw a Sikh colonel in the troop deployed in our colony and I felt a great sense of security, as if I was back in school and Jaspal Singh was there to protect me from the other boys.

The army disbanded the local protection groups and curfew was imposed in the city. There were shoot at sight orders, and the colonel made it clear that his soldiers would follow the orders implicitly – anyone who defied the curfew would be shot, irrespective of gender or age.

Peace was restored within the next three days, and Delhi limped back to some sort of normalcy.

Roshan Lal came to visit Papa and told him that the factory walls had collapsed. The cement sheets that formed the roof had fallen in due to the intense heat and what machinery had not been looted was burnt and reduced to steel scrap. He demanded his one-third share back. He did not want to continue the partnership. The factory had been burnt down only because it was owned by a Sikh, and he wanted to have nothing more to do with it.

The next day Roshan Lal came again with two friends and his brother and demanded his money again. Papa heard him out and told him to come after two days to take his money.

Two days later, Papa gave Roshan Lal his own two-thirds share of his factory. Now Roshan Lal was the sole owner of the land, the collapsed factory and the burnt machines, which had good scrap value. This was worth far more than his investment. But, as was his wont, Papa had taken this decision unilaterally and impulsively, as he always did. He did not consult his brothers. In any case, he would not have listened to them if they had intervened.

ANOTHER NEW BEGINNING

On 9 November 1984, our family left for Amritsar. Papa had hired an Ambassador taxi with a Sikh driver. I sat in the middle of the back seat with my mother on one side and Daisy and Gagan on the other side. Lovey sat by the window in front with Papa. There was no conversation in the car; nobody wanted to stop for snacks or food. I had no desire to stick my head out of the window and feel the cool air on my face. It was cold and there was a fire raging in my heart. The Sikh taxi driver recounted stories of the killings to my father, while I tried my best to shut them out.

We reached Amritsar at 10 p.m. It was only a year and a half since my sisters and I had left our uncle's house, full of joy and hope. This time we were sad and traumatized. We were greeted with affection and sympathy, and the sheer warmth of the family made us all feel secure and more hopeful. But there was an underlying sadness and sense of loss. We had a quiet dinner together.

Early next morning, Papa borrowed his nephew's scooter and went in search of a house to buy and a small shed with electricity to rent, in which he could set up a factory again. He intended to sell off his burnt-down house in Delhi to pay for the new one in Amritsar. Property was cheap in Amritsar after Operation Blue Star. From a golden state, it had been reduced to a failed state.

Papa managed to pay the advance for a large 2,600 square yards corner house on the main road in a fancy locality in Amritsar with whatever jewellery we were left with and the small amount that had been in fixed deposits in the bank. He also rented a small shed to set up a new factory. He no longer wished to become a big businessman like his elder brother; he just did not have the fire in him anymore. But he was well aware of his responsibilities. Lovey was eighteen years old and he wanted to marry her off and set his house in order as soon as he could. He was now acutely aware of how transient life is. He remembered the teaching of the first guru that human beings only own the one present breath: they have neither knowledge nor ownership of the next one. So all men are equally rich or poor, since they all own just the one breath that they are now taking.

The house in Delhi was sold to the first buyer who turned up, at 40 per cent less than the market value. Papa was in a hurry, and impulsive and impatient as always. He had to begin life anew in Amritsar and he wanted to get started. The only condition he set was that the money should be given to him quickly. That money paid for the new Amritsar house, which was nearly ten times bigger.

We moved to our new home. It was a very hard time for Papa. The house had to be furnished from scratch. We had lost everything in Delhi and had come to Amritsar literally with the clothes on our backs. We children had to get used to a far less comfortable life than we had in Delhi. We had to be admitted to new schools and business had to be re-established. But Papa still had hope. He had come to his own state, and he believed his trauma would be understood with sympathy and everyone would extend help. He expected his community to stand up and support him.

However, none of this happened. Nobody in the bureaucracy was willing to help him or even perform its routine tasks. Papa needed permissions and licences for all sorts of things – from getting a cooking gas connection to the registration of his property and loans for his new factory. Instead of extending a helping hand, he was treated like a milch cow that everyone wanted to milk. People assumed that he had come from Delhi with a lot of money. After all, Delhi businessmen were supposed to be rich. So bribes were demanded at every step, and Papa had to pay up. It was with great difficulty that he finally got all the required permissions to set up his small factory and get a loan from the bank.

My siblings and I had been at home since we came to Amritsar, because school sessions began in April and no school would take us in mid-session. I had nothing to do, but I no longer felt like playing or going out with my cousins. My cousins came over often to persuade me to play with them, but I always refused, and they slowly gave up. The terror of the riots had changed me. I started going to the gurudwara more often. I felt that Sikhs, and especially my family, were persecuted for their faith, first in 1947 and now in Delhi. Besides, the police and the CRPF killed Sikhs almost every day in Punjab. In my mind, the Sikh extremists became Sikh warriors fighting for their freedom from India.

I met Sikh radicals who were demanding a separate Sikh state. They did not seem to realize that more Sikhs lived outside of Punjab than in it. Sikhs have always considered India home and have lived in every corner of the country. But in my disturbed state of mind, I was deeply influenced by these radicals. I started dressing in the traditional Sikh kurta pyjama and *juttis*. I wanted to emphasize that I was a traditional, conservative Sikh and not afraid of the world. I was in search of my identity and dignity, which the riots had severely dented and the extremist Sikh movement seemed the natural path to regaining my self-esteem. The

Hindus around me seemed to me as different people with different mindsets. I had forgotten that they had once been my friends in Delhi's neighbourhoods. I only remembered the teasing and ragging that I had to bear in school and the horror of the riots.

Life changed drastically for Papa too. He struggled hard to get his factory started and to fulfil the basic needs of our family. Lovey, my eldest sister, was very young, but Papa had started looking for a groom for her. His only condition was that the boy should be from Amritsar. He did not want any member of his family to be far away from him. Besides, Lovey was his first and favourite child.

Papa's sister found a suitable match and Lovey got engaged. The tomboyish, confident Lovey, who never stepped back from a fight even with boys, did not demur. She was well aware of the changed circumstances of the family and quietly agreed to our parents' wishes.

Papa had always been a reticent man with very few friends, but after the riots, he stopped visiting anyone even for a casual drink. Most evenings he came home tired from the factory, had two large drinks alone and went to bed. He had no time to notice how his children or his wife were coping with their altered circumstances.

One day, Papa had to go to Delhi to get our school-leaving certificates and I insisted on going with him. I wanted to meet my friend Harbir and find out how he was. I had called him many times, but the phone was never answered. My father objected to taking me along. It was very cold and he had to go to many government offices and did not know how long it would take him there. But I was adamant. I said I would meet my friends and then come to the scheduled place at the given time. So Papa gave in.

When we reached Delhi, I went straight to Harbir's house. To my shock, the three-storey house had been burnt and was now a hollow shell. I asked neighbours about Harbir's family, but they were new there and didn't know anything. All they could tell me was that some Afghanis had rented the house, but three or four of them had been killed in the riots and the rest had escaped and never returned. I was stunned. I could not bear to think of Harbir murdered, and what had happened to his beautiful sisters? They had escaped the war in Afghanistan to come to this? I just sat there with a heavy heart, as if waiting for Harbir to walk up from somewhere, to reassure him that all was somehow well. But nothing was well; nothing was the same anymore. After a while, I slowly walked away.

In April, the new school sessions began. My sisters were admitted to the same all-girls school where they had studied earlier. It was now very close to the house. Lovey would be in school only for six months. She had not completed her last academic session, so she could not go to college but had to be readmitted to class twelve in school. Papa looked over her form before he handed it in and found that she had left the column for subjects unfilled. He asked her what subjects she wanted to study.

'Anything,' she said, 'how does it matter?'

Papa felt her sadness, but he did not know what to say. He filled in her favourite subjects and handed in the form.

Gagan and I were to be admitted to Apsara Public School, just half a kilometre away from our house. But nine-year-old Gagan wanted to go to the school where his cousins were studying. Gagan was too young to really understand all that had happened to the family. Besides, he was the youngest and had been the only child for a year while my sisters and I were in Amritsar. So he was pampered. My parents did not want to say no to him, and he was sent to the expensive school where our cousins studied.

I was already one year behind the rest of my classmates because I was born in May. Schools begin in India in April and everyone born after April is admitted the following year. The school principal refused to admit me in class nine, because I had not completed class eight. Board examinations were held in class eight, and they could not be bypassed. Papa explained that we had come away from Delhi after losing our home and all we had during the riots, but the principal said he could not legally admit me to class nine. The word 'legally' was the clue and Papa changed his tactics.

The principal knew that our family had moved to a large house in a fancy colony because he had read the address on the application form. He knew I was over age and had not passed class eight and my father was very keen that I be admitted to class nine. He said that the school was building a high-tech science laboratory for which they need scientific equipment and other materials. They were short of just

Rs 50,000. Papa understood. He had admitted his children to nearby schools in the hope that he would save a few hundred rupees in bus fees. Now he had to shell out a huge sum of money. He was late in applying for admission because he had been too busy trying to get his business going, and when he had the time, I was nowhere to be found. I was busy hobnobbing with Sikh radicals and preachers.

Papa wondered how the principal would bypass the eighth-class board exam certificate. The principal smiled and said that this is Punjab and anything can be managed with the help of Mr Gandhi, a reference to Mahatma Gandhi, whose picture is printed on every currency note. The next day, Papa handed over five large bundles of Rs 100 notes, assuming that it would take care of everything and my admission would be confirmed. But the principal smilingly accepted the money, locked it in a drawer and asked Papa to pay the admission and other fees. Papa was flabbergasted. He had just handed over Rs 50,000 that he could hardly afford. But that was for the science lab, explained the principal. The school fees were separate. No receipt would be given for the donation, he said. It was a secret donation, he added with a smile.

At that time, I did not quite understand what had transpired between the principal and my father. I wondered which Mr Gandhi helped people in Punjab. I wondered if I could ask this Mr Gandhi for help himself, but Gandhi was a Hindu name and I would never ever approach any Hindu for help.

Slowly but surely, I turned into a Sikh extremist. The radicals and preachers I spent time with impressed upon me that Sikhs were different, that we needed to fight against the oppression we suffered, that we needed to take revenge. I knew well that my religion taught that all human beings are equal, that they all came from the 'One Ray of Light'. But I had suffered in school because I looked different, my family had been targeted and traumatized during the riots, and my life had changed. I was now convinced that contrary to the teachings of the Sikh gurus, all humans were not equal. The Sikhs were different from the Hindus. I had been forced to acknowledge this.

Five days after the fees were paid, I joined Apsara Public School. Half the students in my class were Hindus and half were Sikhs. When I entered the classroom, all the boys and girls came up to talk to me. They asked me my name, where I had come from, and they were all very friendly. This was a surprise. In every other school I had attended, there had been some division – Hindus and Sikhs or different castes among the Sikhs or gender. For the first time, there seemed to be nothing dividing the students. For once, it seemed that there was Unity in Diversity!

I was made to sit in the front row with a sharp, intelligent boy called Sandeep Gupta, who was good in his studies, particularly in mathematics. There was another Sandeep Gupta in the same class and both the Sandeeps were friends. I settled down in school and things should have been back to normal, except that I was no longer the carefree teenager who loved sports and eating out and having fun with friends and family. My association with the Sikh hardliners had changed my perception. Despite this, I realized that I had mostly Hindu friends in school, and I wanted to ask them why my family had been targeted when we had never harmed anybody. But no Hindu had harmed me here. Besides, they were all just like me, except that I wore a bun and scarf on my head.

I tried to make a close friend in my class but found nothing in common with most of the Sikh boys. I got along best with Sandeep Gupta, who was simple and straightforward. Three students sat at one desk in this school. Earlier the two Sandeep Guptas used to sit together and whispered and fought and laughed during class. The class teacher, Mrs Manjeet Kaur, had been trying to separate them without success. Now that I joined the class, she immediately sat me between the two so that they could not disturb her during class.

I now had a Hindu on either side of me. In my mind, I wanted to take revenge on Hindus, but here I was, enjoying their company. One of them was quiet and studious, the other jovial and had a great sense of humour. I really liked them and spent all my time in school with them. I didn't mix much with the rest of the class.

I now lived a dual life – during the day, I was a normal student in school, but in the evenings, I spent time with young Sikh boys who were directly or indirectly involved with Sikh hardliners and was inspired by their ideology. I knew that the Sikh gurus had always preached Oneness and love for all, but I was unable to overcome the riots. The shocking revelation of all that my family had suffered during the Partition also deeply disturbed me. I was full of anger and hatred for other communities.

TROUBLES NEVER END

There seemed to be no end to the killings in Punjab. Militancy was at its peak. Hindus were killed by the militants, who were, in turn, gunned down by the police and paramilitary forces. Whether it was a militant or a policeman or an innocent Hindu, it was a human who died.

Papa had not expected such a situation in Amritsar. The violence showed no signs of ending. Though Operation Blue Star had curbed the activities of the hardliners, Sikh separatists were still fighting against the government. They were funded by Pakistan, which saw this as an opportunity to avenge the war that took away East Pakistan from it and turned it into Bangladesh.

The daily reports of violence and death agitated me. The dead Hindus reminded me of my friends in school and the two gentlemen in Delhi who had rescued my family and brought us to my uncle's house. In the dead Sikhs, I saw my own face.

Papa, meanwhile, worked very hard. His factory, which was 8 kilometres away from our home, had finally started production. He had to earn and save enough money for Lovey's wedding in November. All the money that he had got from the sale of the Delhi house and from bank loans for the factory had already been used up. Besides, he was squeezed for money on every pretext.

Lovey's wedding was in November. Indian weddings, especially Punjabi weddings, are lavish affairs. They are meant to showcase the status and prestige of the girl's family. Papa, too, felt obliged to make sure that his daughter's wedding was a grand affair. Our house had to be renovated, air conditioners installed and good quality furniture bought so that our standard of living looked as good as that of our relatives. Lovey's dowry was also supposed to be put together. Generally, dowry in Punjab includes jewellery, clothes, lavish parties and so on, which the girl's side arranges even if the groom doesn't demand it.

The whole vicious cycle of taking loans at huge interests began again for Papa. There was no income yet, but expenses were steadily mounting.

Militancy had badly affected business in Amritsar, which had the highest Sikh population, and many areas in and around it were strongholds of the militants. Buyers and suppliers from outside the state had stopped coming to Punjab, and even local traders did not travel to Amritsar because the hardliners attacked Hindus on buses and on the road, while the police stopped and searched every Sikh, in case he was a militant or had any connection to the hardliners. So, new businesses, like Papa's, were hard to take off and survive. Papa could not break even, let alone provide bread and butter for the family. On top of it, he had to pay rent for the factory shed and repay the interest on the loans he had taken.

Papa had a hard time meeting the day-to-day expenses of the factory. There were long power cuts and cheap labour from UP and Bihar had stopped coming to Punjab, leading to manpower shortages. However hard he worked; circumstances would not let Papa succeed. Mummy gave him an estimate of the cost of renovating the house and the wedding expenses, and he was shocked. Amritsar, a cheaper city to live in than Delhi, suddenly became the most expensive place on earth. As always, Papa reacted impulsively without thought and decided to sell off 1,000 square yards of the lawn at the back of his large house.

He called his property dealer and told him to sell the land immediately since he needed the money within a month. The dealer had helped him buy the house just a few months ago. He realized that a man who had just bought a house would not want to sell a part of it unless he was in dire need. He also knew that Lovey was going to be married in a few months. So, he told Papa that there were very few buyers in Amritsar, given the current violence in the state, and if he wanted the money in a hurry, he would have to sell at 25 to 30 per cent lower than the market rate. Papa agreed. The cunning broker probably earned a very good commission.

Lovey's marriage was a grand affair and all social appearances were kept up. Everyone was happy. Of course, no one had asked Lovey what she wanted or felt; she remained a mute participant in the events around her.

AND SO TO WORK…

The big new house was now only 1,600 square yards. The money from the sale of the back lawn had been spent on the wedding and in the factory. Papa still struggled to make ends meet. What he needed was a helping hand, someone reliable to help him run the business, but he could not find such a person. He was too proud to ask his brother for help. He felt that he had already taken enough favours from him. He and his elder brother, Ranbir Singh, were once the pillars of their family. They had worked hard and got their six younger brothers and sisters married and settled, ensuring that their parents never had cause to feel that the family was not looked after. Their father had managed the family's agricultural land in Pakistan, but he had never held a job or run a business, and he was unable to do anything much. But he was an affectionate man and had instilled all the right values in his children.

It occurred to Papa that I was fifteen and half, old enough to help him through this difficult time. I, however, had been unaware of my father's plight. I was treading a different path.

Deeply immersed in the company of hardliners, I was asked to become a baptised Sikh, an Amritdhari Sikh. If

I wanted to fight for the freedom of the Sikhs, this was necessary, I was told. Many young boys were doing this. But I was not sure if I would be able to conform to the strict rules and perform all the duties or live the lifestyle of a baptised Sikh. I had many Hindu friends, and in my heart, I knew that they were not to blame for what had happened to me. Besides, I wondered if it was really necessary for me to be baptised to fight for the freedom of Punjab.

The two Sandeeps noticed that I had become more and more radicalized, but they did not say anything. In the tense environment of Punjab and given the rift between Hindus and Sikhs, they probably thought it prudent to ignore it.

Though the agitation in my heart drove me to the hardliners, I did not find any peace there. I was being taught hatred, especially for the Hindus, but my best friends were Hindus and I just could not hate them. The Sikh religion teaches love and compassion for all living beings, but I was not being taught true Sikhism. I longed for peace and solace, but I was unable to find it in religion.

I was unaware of my father's plans for me, and Papa had so many troubles of his own that he had no time to notice that I had turned into a religious fanatic.

In February 1986, merely fifteen months after we had moved to Amritsar, Papa told Mummy that the money he had got from selling the land was nearly over and he was still unable to break even at the factory. He said he needed help and I could provide that reliable help. Mummy was not very happy, but she knew that there was no option. My examinations were just a month away and she told Papa that it would be better if I started working with him after my exams.

I learnt of my father's troubles from my mother only later. She also told me to study hard, otherwise I would have to leave school and join my father at the factory. I was horrified. I had no desire to work at the factory; besides I was deeply involved in religion. So I studied very hard and to everyone's surprise came second in my class. Even my teachers were pleasantly surprised to discover this unknown genius!

Papa was delighted that I had done so well. I expected my father to say that I should study harder in class ten. Instead, Papa was reassured that I was bright and would easily pass class ten. So, there was no problem in my joining work at the factory!

For the first time in Amritsar, I went to the factory. I was shocked to see how small it was, not even a quarter of the size of the Delhi factory. There were only about fifteen workers there. Within two weeks, I understood my father's financial problems and decided that I had to help him. I spent my summer vacations understanding and learning the work that went on at the factory. There was no manager, just some skilled and some unskilled labour. There was a supervisor who also kept accounts, checked quality and helped Papa in other jobs.

Neither Papa nor the supervisor had any time for me, so I started maintaining the attendance register and the cash expenses book. This only took about an hour, so then I wandered into the factory shed and started working with the unskilled workers, putting coal in the steam boiler, loading and unloading materials, packaging and assisting the skilled machine operators.

Papa noticed that I was working with the labourers in the factory, but he did not stop me. He felt it would be good for me to learn to operate the machines and do quality checks of the reclaimed rubber that was made by recycling old rubber tubes and tyres. Scrapped tyres and tubes were bought, shredded into pieces and crushed in machines to make crumb powder. This was devulcanized in steel chambers and made into rubber sheets called reclaimed rubber. When school reopened, I continued working in the factory after school hours. In six months, I had learnt to operate the chopping and crushing machines. Often when a skilled worker could not come because of curfew or unavailability of public transport due to violence in the city, I worked the machines myself rather than shut them down. By January, I had learnt the work of the supervisor as well. I could now do almost everything except keep accounts at the factory.

I was in class ten and the school-leaving exams were round the corner. All my classmates studied hard because the tenth board marks determine college admissions. Some schools went up to class eleven and twelve, but most, including mine, were only till the tenth. So students had to join junior college after passing from school.

The results of my class tests and mid-term exams surprised my teachers again – this time because I had done so badly. When asked why I had not studied, I told them that I was no longer interested in studying.

Sandeep Gupta, my friend, was observant. He realized that my family was probably not doing too well financially. He noticed that I never bought things in the canteen, nor did I go out after school like the other kids. Most of my classmates and teachers believed that I came from a rich family because I came to school on a new blue Suzuki motorcycle. Other students came to school on foot or in the school vans, while some had mopeds. The only other student who had a motorcycle came from a very rich family. No one knew that the motorcycle was for me to go to the factory after school, since public transport was unreliable.

The official age to get a driver's licence was eighteen years, but most teenage boys started driving two wheelers from the age of fourteen or fifteen. It was easy to find agents who would get them driving licences with forged birth certificates, and it was through one of them that I had got my licence.

FIGHT FOR YOUR RIGHT

In February, my classmates and I were asked to come to school neatly dressed to have individual photographs taken for the tenth class board examination entrance forms. The class group photograph would also be taken that day. One boy in my class, Mandeep Singh, came wearing a turban. In many schools, turbans were compulsory for Sikh students from class eight onwards, but this school had no such dress code. So it was a surprise to see Mandeep looking all grown up in a turban.

The turban is not just some ordinary headwear for Sikhs. It is an essential part of their religious identity and is worn with pride.

I congratulated Mandeep for wearing a turban. The photographer, however, asked Mandeep to take it off for the picture. Mandeep refused since the photo was for the Punjab State Education Board and not for school records. For the class photograph, the teacher insisted that he take off his turban. He was the tallest boy in class and had a beard and moustache, and she said he looked far too old with the turban to be a class ten student. Mandeep did not take off his turban and refused to be a part of the class photograph. There was palpable tension in the air, but nobody said anything. Harmony was fragile and no one wanted to disrupt it in the school.

The incident stirred up my latent fanaticism. In the recent months, I had been too busy working in the factory to spend evenings with the hardliners. After school, I used to change, eat lunch and rush off to the factory with lunch for my father. The factory was closed on Mondays, so I worked even over the weekends. My only free time was Monday evenings, and I usually just played with my brother and younger sister in the front yard at home. But the turban incident made me angry. It is the right of a Sikh to wear a turban. I called Mandeep and told him that for the next few days he and the other Sikh boys should wear turbans to school and nobody could stop them.

I called the seven other Sikh boys from my class and asked them all to wear turbans to school. Four of them agreed. The next morning, there were only three students in turbans – Mandeep, Dalbir and me. The others had backed out on one pretext or other. Our classmates were surprised and amused. Our class teacher ignored us; she was a Sikh herself. But the principal called us to his office and told us that the school policy was that only headscarves were allowed. I replied that the Constitution of India granted every citizen the freedom to practise his or her religion. The principal realized that this was a sensitive issue. He also knew that we would soon be out of school. So he smiled and told us that we looked very nice in our turbans, but we looked like uncles among the students, so it would be better if we wore headscarves. All three of us refused. We would wear the turbans for the rest of our school days, we insisted.

The next day, we all came in our turbans, but the day after, Dalbir was back in his headscarf. It took too long to tie the turban. Soon Mandeep also went back to the scarf, and I was the only one who wore the turban for the next three days. Then I too gave it up. But I had learned an important lesson. You can fight the system and win against it if you have support and the law on your side. People will fight for their rights if they are supressed. The cause is unimportant. What mattered was that we had fought for our rights, even if we chose not to exercise that right after a few days.

The board examinations were about to start and everyone forgot about the incident.

Despite living nearby, I rode my bike to school every day. It was nice to be thought of as a rich boy.

COLLEGE DAYS

The final class ten board examinations were close, and I studied hard so that I could do well enough to get admission to college. I worked at the factory after school and studied at night. Sandeep helped me with my studies. Another Hindu girl named Shikha, who lived near my house, also helped me sometimes. She was a rough and tough, tomboyish girl like Lovey. I liked her. She was friendly and sometimes talked to me about her family and friends. She was the only girl with whom I talked. Or rather, she was the only girl who spoke to me.

There was a farewell party organized by the students of class nine on the last day of the term. A big stage had been set up and there were plays, dances and, finally, a walk down a ramp by the students of class ten. Everybody wanted to be perfectly dressed for this. I decided to wear my turban again and I wanted to tie it perfectly – I was not very good at it yet.

All the students participated in some event on the stage except me, but I had to walk down the ramp with the rest of my class. I was the only person there in a turban since there was no male Sikh teacher in the school. I walked, not as a teenager trying to impress other students and teachers, but as a proud Sikh asserting my right to wear the turban. I had a point to prove and, consequently, I did not enjoy the event as much as the others who just wanted to look good.

I was backstage after my turn, watching the girls still walking down the ramp. I noticed that Shikha had trimmed her hair. I had whipped myself up so much with my Punjabi pride that the sight of the haircut made me furious. The moment Shikha returned backstage, I demanded to know why she had put a scissor to her hair. I had forgotten that she was a Hindu and could cut her hair any time she wished. Shikha was surprised and offended. She retorted that I had no business commenting on her hair and walked away.

I immediately realized that I had made a mistake. I had made an unwarranted personal comment and as a result had lost a friend. I felt very contrite, but the damage had been done.

I did quite well in the exams. I was pleased that I had been able to prepare well despite working at the factory. I often saw Shikha at the examination centre and wanted to apologize to her, but she was always surrounded by friends. If she ever looked towards me, it was with dislike.

It struck me that, for once, my own religion had let me down. I realized that religion was not for display.

True religion is a belief system to be internalized, not imposed externally.

There was a two-month break before the results were announced, and I spent the time working hard at the factory. A day before the results, both the Sandeeps came to my house with college admission forms. They were going to apply to the DAV College for Boys. They told me that all the boys from their class were applying to DAV and the girls to Government College for Women or to DAV College for Women.

There were two big co-ed colleges in Amritsar – Khalsa and Hindu. Khalsa College was once the best college in Punjab. It had beautiful Mughal-style buildings and huge lawns and grounds. It had well-appointed labs, a library and all other modern facilities. The DAV colleges did not have such facilities. But the Khalsa College had a huge number of Sikh students and it had now become the hub of Sikh hardliners. The Majha Sikh Students' Union, known for their active support of the Khalistan movement, had its roots in the college.

I was convinced that my Sikh classmates would go to Khalsa and the Hindus would go to Hindu College. I told Sandeep that I would apply only to Khalsa College even though the DAV colleges had both Sikh and Hindu students, and therefore, a more secular and congenial atmosphere. My cousin Tarun and his Hindu friend Munish Seth also studied there. But I was sure that Dalbir and Mandeep, who had joined me in wearing the turban to school and in asserting our Sikh identity, would certainly go to Khalsa. Without another thought I told Sandeep that I would apply only to Khalsa. Sandeep was shocked and went away disappointed.

On my first day at Khalsa College, I was very impressed as I walked through the plush lawns into the large building. I felt like a prince in a palace. I asked a student passing by for directions to the arts section. I spoke in English and the boy did not understand what I said. So I repeated my question in Hindi.

This the boy understood, but he said angrily, 'Can't you speak in your mother tongue? Why do you speak the language of the white man and the Hindu? Sikhs should speak in their mother tongue and I will answer only if I am asked in Punjabi.'

I was taken aback, but I repeated the question in Punjabi and only then did the boy answer my question.

On my way to my class, I passed through the medical section where I saw among the students some clean-shaven boys and a few girls. In the science and commerce sections, there were fewer girls and fewer Hindu faces. In the arts section, the small number of girls appeared to be from the villages around Amritsar and almost all the boys wore turbans. In my class, there were eight girls seated in one corner of the room near the wall. The sixty other students were all Sikh boys. I looked around and spotted a good-looking, well-dressed Sikh boy with a neatly tied turban and an expensive wristwatch. I knew the boy was a

Jaat Sikh because his beard was trimmed and his turban matched his shirt.

I went up to him and said, 'Hi.'

To my great relief, the reply came in fluent English. The boy's nickname was also Bobby and he was from St. George's School in Mussoorie. His brother, Jassi, short for Jaskaran, was also in the same college in class twelve.

During recess, all the boys introduced themselves to each other. I was asked my name and then the name of my village.

When I said that I was born in Delhi, some of the boys smiled and said, 'Oh, you are a *Paappa*.'

That is the name given by the Jaats to urban Sikhs, who they believe are of a lower caste than them.

I was dismayed. It had begun dawning upon me that I had come to the wrong college. There was no Sandeep here. And where were Dalbir and Mandeep? I should have found out more, thought things through before deciding to come here. Now, if I wanted to move to DAV College, I would have to forego the fees I had paid here for two semesters and pay a late fee plus the admission fees at DAV. There was no way I could afford that. Almost all my classmates were in DAV College. Because of my impulsive, thoughtless decision, I had lost the company of my friends, especially the two Sandeeps.

My only hope now was Deepkaran Singh Randhawa, my bench mate. Both our nicknames were Bobby, but nobody in class knew that. We stuck together because we soon realized that our upbringing was different from that of the rest of the class. Both of us had been raised in big towns and cities and had studied in good English-medium schools. The only difference was that I belonged to the urban Sikhs of the business community, while the other Bobby belonged to a rich Jaat landowning family. The two of us became good friends and much to the bewilderment of our classmates, who were unaware of our nicknames, we called each other 'Bobby'.

I soon learnt that there were no regular classes at Khalsa College. Since many students had joined the Majha Sikh Students' Union, which was at the forefront of the agitation for independence, there was always something that disrupted classes. An office of the union was located in the college and many boys from my class were permanent members. Most of my classmates had joined the arts section only to pass class twelve or to simply become graduates so that they could marry educated girls later on. I just wanted to get a degree. My real interest was in running the factory and reviving my father's dying business.

One day, a bandh was declared by the Sikh hardliners to protest against the killing of six militants in an encounter with the Punjab Police. No policeman was killed or injured, so it was believed that it was a staged encounter and the police had killed either innocent Sikh youth or illegally detained Sikhs. The college administration, however, refused to suspend classes and the members of the union were furious. Students, all members of the union, from the nearby Guru Nanak Dev University came in a large group to force the college to shut down and many Khalsa students joined them. They went on a rampage, shattering windows, breaking furniture in the administration block, tearing books in the library and smashing equipment in the lab. Professors and other staff helplessly watched the mayhem.

I stood in corner and watched as the boys ran amok. I felt terribly ashamed at what was happening and could not meet my teachers' eyes. They held masters' and PhD degrees; many had received awards and felicitations in India and abroad for their research work. They had chosen to stay back in their state and educate their youth, but the students had no respect for them. I hoped that they did not believe that I was part of this group, since most of the rioting students were from the arts department. To my surprise, I saw some Hindu students among the rioters. 'Truly, a mob has no religion,' I thought.

AN EXPLOSION OF TROUBLE

Things settled down in a week and my days fell into a pattern. I went to the factory after lunch every day. Only now it took me longer to get there. Security had been tightened in Amritsar, and since I was a young Sikh, 5 feet 10 inches tall, with a straggly beard and moustache, I was routinely stopped for checks on my way to college and to the factory. I could now operate most of the machines and often stepped in when the machine operator did not come.

During the summer vacations, my friend, Bobby Randhawa (BR) went to visit cousins in England, Canada and the US. I had lost touch with my school friends. I worked full-time at the factory and did all I could to help stabilize the business and make it profitable. The violence, power cuts, lack of affordable labour, shortage of funds and the absence of buyers and suppliers, however, made it an impossible task. I was more and more frustrated.

I started going to the gurudwara every evening, praying for divine intervention to pull my family out of its crisis. There had been no help from the children of God, except a few. But God was busy in some other part of the world, helping some other people, because my prayers remained unanswered.

Papa had not employed a licenced boiler operator in the factory because he could not afford one. The semi-skilled workers and I operated the boiler. All we knew was that we had to maintain the water level and the pressure of the steam in the boiler. Often I would work the boiler alone, shovelling in coal and starting the water pump whenever the water level receded.

Since I had learnt all the work at the factory, Papa decided I should also learn banking and financial management. So one day, he took me to the bank near the factory to open an account. While there, we heard a very loud explosio Everyone assumed that it was a bomb blast nearby. S explosions had become familiar since the rise of mili in Punjab. There was panic for a few minutes, then ev settled down and work continued. I was filling some forms when the factory foreman rushed into the bank, his clothes dusty, bruises on his arms and legs. He was looking for Papa and me. The blast we had heard was the boiler in the factory, which had burst! Many workers had been injured and a part of the factory building had collapsed. The foreman didn't know if anyone was dead, because the factory was full of dust and steam, and raw materials and rubble had scattered everywhere.

We ran back to the factory. People had already gathered there and were helping the injured. I was horrified to see many of the men I worked with hurt and bleeding. Sometime later, fire tenders arrived. Someone must have reported a bomb blast. But there was no fire, so they went away and reported to the Department for Small Scale Industries that it was an industrial accident and should be investigated.

By 7 p.m., most of the debris of the boiler section had been cleared with the help of workers from neighbouring factories. The mutilated body of Ram Lal, who had been operating the boiler was found. Papa and I were deeply distressed.

Officials from the Industries Department arrived and asked Papa to appear before them the next day. Papa asked for two- or three-days time to take to care of the injured workers and the family of the deceased. He also wanted to clean up the damaged portions of the factory. He was asked to leave the damaged machines and boiler untouched; he could clean up the rubble. The officials allowed Papa to appear before them after four days.

I was angry and bewildered. I had been taught that nothing in this world happens without God's consent; even a leaf cannot move unless God permits it. But God had killed an innocent man and injured so many others in the factory. Why?

When we went home that night, my mother thanked God for keeping my father and me safe. Many of our relatives also came to commiserate when they heard the news. They too said that it was the grace of God that had taken Papa and me to the bank or else we might have been injured or killed. I was in a state of shock. I could not understand why we were saved and Ram Lal was killed. He too was the son of a mother, the husband of a wife. One mother and wife thanked God for saving her son and husband, but another mother and wife wailed because God had devastated her world. Where was the justice in this?

Help came to Papa in the form of money from his brothers. This time, he accepted help from his younger brothers because he needed a large sum of money to restart the factory.

Four days later, he appeared before an officer of the Industries Department. When the officer learnt that Ram Lal had no licence to operate the boiler, he threatened to file a criminal complaint against Papa. A man had died, the building was damaged and the neighbours had complained, since they believed that the boiler and steam chambers required to vulcanize rubber were dangerous.

It was all settled with a bribe to the officers. The injured were given the best treatment in a private hospital and compensation was paid to the property owner. A large sum of money was given to Ram Lal's family. In spite of all this, the factory received a closure notice from the Industries Department because the neighbours did not want it to restart in that area.

A new location had to be found, as far from the old place as possible, where the new landlord had not heard about the accident. Luck favoured us this time, and Papa found a place to rent just a kilometre from our house – the rear portion of an old textile mill. A well-known Hindu family had set up the mill when there were no residential areas around. The posh Civil Lines had developed much later. The textile mill had run for five decades, but it was now the winter of 1988, and due to the violence in Punjab, the mill had run into losses. The Hindu family also became a target for money extortion. So they shut down the mill and spent most of their time in Bombay. They were our neighbours, so they were happy to rent the place to Papa, knowing that it would be in safe hands.

Papa bought a bigger and better steam boiler and had the other damaged machines repaired and painted. He applied for new permissions and licences to the various departments. The new factory was given a new name – Super Rubber Industries. But Papa's troubles were far from over. He had taken a personal bank loan and the machines were pledged to the bank. The bank now demanded repayment of the loan. Since he had no money, Papa pledged some of the constructed area of our home to the bank. Papa and I started work anew at the factory.

By February 1989, the machinery had been set up in the new place and the factory restarted. It was very close to home, but the bank was at the other end of town, near our old factory. I now did most of the bank work.

THE TRUTH ABOUT RELIGION

I had been unable to study after the accident, not only because of the shock but also because of all the work that setting up the new factory entailed. My father worked very, very hard, and I felt that I had to help him in every way I could. I went to college regularly, and then to the factory. But exams were near and I had to study hard. Whenever I had free time at the factory, I would read my books, and I woke up two hours earlier in the morning to study before college.

When the examinations started, the students of class eleven were divided into smaller groups and allotted different classrooms to prevent cheating. On the third day, a commerce student rode his scooter right on to the lawn at the back of an arts classroom and parked it by the door there. A senior arts student leader saw him and asked him to move it to the regular parking lot. The boy rudely replied that no one could prevent him from parking where he liked, upon which the angry senior arts student went up to the terrace, picked up a broken brick and dropped it on the scooter below.

This was a serious affront and the commerce student ran to his section and came back with around forty students, all armed with hockey sticks, iron rods and bicycle chains. The seniors from the arts section had anticipated this and a large group of them were ready, similarly armed. A vicious fight started. Luckily, the head of the local office of the Majha Sikh Students' Union arrived on the spot and stopped the fight. But many students were badly injured and had to be rushed to hospital. The police arrived and registered cases against the student leaders of both the departments. Exams were delayed that day. The injured students were allowed to reappear when they produced a medical certificate, while the students against whom cases had been registered were barred from entering the college for the next three months, which meant that they could not appear for the exams, losing a full year. All the students involved in the fight were Sikhs, mostly Jaat Sikhs.

I had never seen Sikhs fight amongst themselves.

'When a lot of Sikhs get together, they fight with each other over petty matters,' I thought, 'but in places like Delhi or even at the Apsara Public School, where there are many people of other communities, they are peaceful and hardworking.'

'So what will happen when Khalistan is formed,' I wondered. 'While Pakistan provided arms and training, it was the Sikhs from Canada, America, Germany and England who provided financial support for the movement. They would all come to live here when the state was formed. What would happen then?'

I had always believed that Jaats were aggressive, hot-headed and ill educated. But my preconceptions had changed after I met Bobby Randhawa, now my best friend. Though he was very rich, BR never showed off his wealth or acted superior. He treated everybody with respect, whatever his or her financial status or community. His only flaw was that he did not like anyone contradicting him.

When I joined class twelve, my belief about Jaats being ill educated also changed. Professor Maluk Singh Gill taught me history. Professor Gill was in his mid-forties, tall and handsome. He taught Sikh history in a way that made it easy to understand and it was utterly fascinating. I had only learnt about Sikhism from my mother. The Sikh hardliners and preachers I had associated with in my early days in Amritsar had their own version of the religion.

Professor Maluk Singh changed my understanding of my religion and gave me much to think about. I learnt that Sikhism did not believe in idol worship, but all Sikhs had pictures of the gurus in their homes and workplaces. Sikhs always bowed their heads, which must always be covered, before these pictures. The renowned artist Sobha Singh had painted many of these pictures. He made the portraits from his understanding and perception of the lives and teachings of the gurus. His pictures are accepted everywhere, but Sobha Singh was never allowed to enter a gurudwara because he did not wear a turban or cover his head. He had flowing long hair and a long beard that he never tied. He spent his life in a small village in Himachal Pradesh, living in harmony with nature.

It struck me that people who knew the true meaning of God and religion are not bound by the rules laid down by preachers.

A month later, I was shaken again when a story I had heard from childhood was turned on its head by the professor. The famous 'Saakhi' story of Guru Nanak Devji, as told by my mother and as written in religious magazines, was that once Guru Nanak was resting on a *manji*, a makeshift cot, under a tree. A Muslim clergyman passing by was appalled to see that his feet pointed towards Mecca and woke him up to tell him to move his feet to another direction. Guru Nanak said that he was very tired and could not move, but the clergyman was free to move his feet in any direction that he chose. When the man lifted his feet and started moving them, the popularly told story says, Mecca moved wherever his feet pointed, implying that Nanak was greater than Mecca. But Professor Maluk Singh told the students that while the first part of the story was correct, the second part was far deeper and more evocative than merely proving superiority. When the Muslim clergyman asked Nanak to move his feet, Nanak said he was very tired, but the man could move his feet wherever he wished. When the man lifted his feet, he told him, 'Make sure you move them where Allah is not there.'

Guru Nanak was secular and a true mystic. He had many Muslim followers. In fact, a Muslim named Bhai Mardaana travelled everywhere with him throughout his journey in all four directions for many years. He played the *rubaab*, a stringed instrument, when Guru Nanak sang his hymns. A few generations of Bhai Mardaana's family kept alive the tradition of playing the rubaab in gurudwaras. They were called the Rubaabi Muslims and they migrated to Pakistan in 1947. They were always directly or indirectly connected to gurudwaras despite their staunch faith in Islam.

Professor Mulak Singh changed my perception of Sikhism. I realized that if I wanted to really know my religion, I had to study its history and not just believe what the preachers said. I also had to give up on my preconceptions about Jaats. I learnt that the Jaat community had many learned men, authors, professors, doctors and engineers. They could be leaders in their fields, like Bobby Randhawa's father, who ran several successful businesses.

AN ENCOUNTER WITH THE POLICE

Summer vacations started and I worked all day at the factory. One day, on my way back from the bank, I picked up a spare part for one of the machines from a very crowded area of the city. It was a heavy metal part, packed in three layers of plastic. I hung it on the left side of the bike's handle bar. It was heavy and made the bike wobbly and hard to balance. A passing rickshaw brushed against it and the bike tilted to the right and, unfortunately, fell against a policeman on traffic duty, knocking him to the ground. I fell hard on the bike and my arms got badly bruised, but luckily the policeman was unharmed. However, his ego was hurt and he got up and angrily slapped me hard, not once but twice. Immediately passersby gathered around. A Hindu gentleman tried to placate the policeman saying that it was a minor accident and that it was me who was hurt and not the constable. But the sight of the seemingly well-to-do young teenager on a bike stoked his anger further and the policeman marched my bike and me to the nearest police station.

The policemen there asked me where I lived and my father's name and occupation. The moment they heard my address and realized that my father had a factory, the policemen wanted to extract money. A senior officer at the station asked me to call my father. I refused. I knew that my father could not afford to pay them money. I repeated that I had not done anything wrong, that it was just a minor accident that had not injured anybody except me. The police officer was annoyed. He asked two constables to take me to the interrogation room and make me call my father. I knew that I would be beaten up and I was very, very scared, but I remained adamant and refused to call my father.

The policemen beat me with wooden sticks and slapped me hard. The sticks used on my buttocks did not hurt much and the blows to my stomach and the slaps on my face inflicted deeper mental anguish than physical injury. But the fear I felt was very real. My turban came undone.

'You are Sikhs yourselves,' I said to the policemen, dredging up courage, 'and if you don't respect a fellow Sikh's turban, how can anyone else respect your religion?'

Whether this had any impact on them, I do not know, but they let me go with a warning not to file any complaint against them. They had already told my local police station that I had attacked a cop. They also made me sign some blank papers.

When I got home, I went straight to my room, locked the door, went into the bathroom and broke down. I had been brave at the police station, because I knew my father could not afford to pay off those policemen, but now the shock, fear and pain poured out in my tears. I felt that my soul was torn apart. After ten minutes, I managed to control myself, washed my face, tied my turban properly and went off to the factory.

The moment he saw my swollen face and bruised arms, Papa knew that something was wrong. He had been waiting for me for more than three hours. But I told him that I had hurt a poor man accidentally and had to take him to a doctor. The doctor had also given me an anti-tetanus shot for my bruises and my red face was just a reaction to that injection. I know Papa was not convinced, but I rushed off into the factory, and that night, instead to going home, I worked the night shift.

The experience at the police station disillusioned me even more about my own community. Before coming to Amritsar, my father had told me that we would be among our own people and we would get help. But the opposite kept happening. We worked very hard to revive our business, but nothing seemed to go in our favour.

The central government had launched various schemes to give benefits to those who had lost loved ones or property during the riots in Delhi. In the beginning, Papa was too proud to accept these handouts. He believed that he could rebuild his life with honest hard work. But after struggling for four years in Amritsar, Papa gave in. He went to Delhi to get a certificate from the government declaring that he was a victim of the 1984 riots, which would get him a yellow card in Punjab, making him eligible for various schemes of the Punjab government.

THE TRAGEDY OF SHAMBHU NATH

I had lost touch with the hardliners and preachers with whom I had spent so much time when I first came to Amritsar. Now what little free time I had, I spent with BR and sometimes with BR's brother Jassi Randhawa. They had all become very close friends.

In October 1989, the festival season had just begun with the Navratras. This is a Hindu festival in honour of their Goddess and people fasted for nine days, taking only liquids and fruits through the day. Shambhu Nath, a machine operator, strictly observed this fast. He worked on the rubber-mixing machine in the factory. The rubber was mixed with oils and chemicals and carefully fed from one side between two huge, continuously turning steel rollers. I could operate the machine, but rarely did so. I was always very careful with the machine, since the slightest mistake meant that one's hands could get crushed between the rollers. Only the trained operator did this job. Shambhu Nath was the most experienced operator and had done this job in our old factory too.

I was getting ready to go to college and my breakfast was laid on the table when the phone rang. It was the factory supervisor urgently asking me to rush to the factory in the car. Shambhu Nath had fainted at the machine, his hands had got trapped in it and were crushed. I was eighteen-and-a-half years old and had started driving the family's Fiat car. My father was in Delhi, and I was all alone and terrified. I had no idea what to do. I told Mummy to call Papa and tell him to come back immediately because a factory worker had met with an accident. I did not tell her anything more and rushed off. My breakfast lay uneaten on the table and I did not wait to tie my turban.

The factory was only a kilometre away, but it seemed to me as if it took a very long time to get there. Shambhu Nath lay on the floor in a pool of blood, his arms covered with another worker's shirt. There was no time for questions. We put him, moaning, semi-conscious, on the back seat with one worker beside him and Sukhwinder, the supervisor, in the front with me. I headed towards a private hospital, but Sukhwinder told me to drive to the government hospital.

Papa was not there to help Shambhu Nath get admitted into a private hospital.

As soon as we reached the hospital, Sukhwinder ran in and brought back two ward boys with a stretcher. We rushed Shambhu Nath to the trauma centre. One of the ward boys came out and told us that a surgeon had been called. The doctor on duty had not administered any first aid but declared the patient critical. He had examined his vitals and blood group so that blood could be arranged. A few minutes later, the doctor came out to tell me to inform the police, who would take the statement of the factory owner and workers.

Sukhwinder told me to pay the ward boys Rs 100. I was surprised. Government hospitals are supposed to be free.

'They are free,' Sukhwinder explained, 'but "services" have to be paid for. The treatment will cost thousands of rupees.'

I had only about Rs 150 with me. I went to a landline phone to call my mother and ask for more money. There was a sign above the phone that said it was free, but I had to pay Rs 2 to the person sitting beside it to make my call. In the next two days, I learnt that all the free services in the hospital had to be paid for – from parking to surgery.

I told my mother that Sukhwinder was on his way to collect Rs 5,000 from her. But she had only Rs 1,500. I went to a little shop outside to make an STD call to my father, who told me that bribes would have to be paid at every step and Sukhwinder would guide me on what to do. But Papa also warned me not to hand over money to the supervisor or else he would take his own cut from it. He told me to borrow money from my uncle, since I could not withdraw money from the factory account and my own account had zero balance. Papa had to appear before the committee the next afternoon and only then would he be able to leave from Delhi. Till then, I had to manage as best as I could.

Sukhwinder returned with Rs 800. My mother had kept some money apart for household expenses.

In the meantime, two police constables arrived. They recorded the factory workers' statements, then went into the trauma centre and took down a statement from Shambhu Nath, who had regained consciousness after being given painkillers. Only the police officers and the two doctors present inside knew what he had said. The police officers asked me to sign and authenticate the statements and give my own statement, but Sukhwinder intervened to say that I was just a college student and my family were riot victims and that my father was away in Delhi in connection with our riots case. The police officers were unsympathetic. Sukhwinder took them aside. They huddled in a corner of the trauma centre for a few minutes, while I watched them nervously. Then Sukhwinder came to me and said that for Rs 500 the police had agreed not to record my statement. He explained to me that the police could twist my statement around and make it go against the factory owner, so it was best that they spoke to my father after he was back two days later. I told him to get them to agree to Rs 300, but Sukhwinder said they would not accept that. So

I gave Sukhwinder Rs 400 and told him manage with that amount. The policemen accepted the money, and I learnt that there was scope for negotiation in every deal.

The doctor on duty told me that four bottles of the B+ blood group would be needed to prepare Shambhu Nath for surgery. I was B+ myself, as were some of the other workers, so four bottles of blood were arranged right there.

As I lay on the table while my blood was being collected, I wondered why the good and the poor always suffered. The Goddess had not come to the help of her devotee. But the corrupt and evil lived happily enough.

The chief surgeon examined Shambhu Nath and said that there was no option but to amputate his arms. I was horrified. It had not occurred to me till then that Shambhu Nath's arms would be cut off. For the first time, I asked the other workers how exactly the accident had occurred. They told me that Shambhu Nath was fasting, and being weak with hunger, he had collapsed on the machine and his hands had been crushed. The helper on the other side spotted his arms coming through and instantly stopped the machine. Then they reversed the machine and released his arms.

'As if being poor is not bad enough,' I thought angrily, 'the Gods had to snatch away Shambhu Nath's arms and make his life hell on earth. What will he do without his arms? Is there really a God?'

It was 3 p.m. and I had eaten nothing since morning. The blood donation also made me feel a little dizzy. The hospital staff had handed me a long list of medicines and supplies to be bought for the surgery. It was supposed to be supplied free, but they claimed that they never had any stocks. The junior doctor said that I would not have to pay for the hospital bed or the doctors, but without the required medicines, the surgery could not take place. I realized that I would have to pay at every stage.

The only person I could borrow money from was BR, and so I went to his house. BR took one look at my face and knew that something was very wrong. We went to BR's room and I told him the whole story, including the need for money. BR first got me lunch, then got Rs 15,000 from his father and gave it to me.

I called my mother and told her that I had got the money from my friend and asked her to call Papa and tell him that I had everything under control. At the hospital, Sukhwinder was sitting outside the operation theatre where Shambhu Nath's surgery had already begun. He had found a medical store owner who his cousin knew and had got the medicines on the promise of payment later. I breathed a sigh of relief when I learnt that the medicines had cost only Rs 4,600. I gave Sukhwinder Rs 5,000 and told him to get some food for himself and the workers with the rest of the money. But Sukhwinder had already paid more than Rs 500 for the X-ray and other required tests, which should also have been free of cost.

At 7 p.m., the chief surgeon emerged from the OT and told us that the patient was out of danger. He had lost lot of blood, but the doctors had managed to save his life. The junior doctor called Sukhwinder and me to his cabin and told us that Shambhu Nath's amputated arms would have to be buried somewhere. The hospital did not have the required facility to dispose them. I panicked, unsure about what to do. But the other workers were there and two of them went with the attendants and came back with a cardboard box covered with a white sheet. The supervisor led us to Company Bagh, the nearest local park. I trailed behind the others. I did not have the stomach to either look at or bury the amputated arms myself.

The workers found a spot where the mud was soft. It was winter and there was no one around. Two of the workers pulled down a couple of thick branches from a tree and with the sharp ends they dug a pit three feet deep so that dogs would not smell the flesh and blood. The faint light from a streetlight nearby gave me a glimpse of the arms as the workers took them out of the box. Some of the men started sobbing. One prayed to God to take Shambhu's life. How would the man survive? How would he feed his family?

I was too dazed to cry. 'A poor man could earn some sort of living,' I thought, 'but a poor man without arms was better off dead.'

Shambhu's accident, dealing with the hospital staff, the doctors and, finally, the surreal burying of the severed arms in the park at dusk, it had all exhausted me emotionally, mentally and physically. I went home and dropped into bed and slept dreamlessly till morning.

I went to the hospital early next morning and found Sukhwinder waiting for me with another long list of medicines. I wondered if there were medicines left over from the previous day. But the supervisor told me that he had given all the medicines to the nurses and nothing had come back. It was a one-way street of corruption – nothing came back.

When I went to buy the new lot of medicines, I learnt that the shopkeepers would buy back leftover medicines at 10 per cent less than the selling price. On questioning them further, I learnt that all the shopkeepers bought medicines from the hospital staff at a 20 per cent discount. They sold it at market price to their customers and took returns at 10 per cent off. There was no dearth of medicines supplied by the government to the hospital, but the staff sold it all to the shopkeepers and there were never any available free of cost for the poor patients. This was the case at every government hospital.

The next day Papa came back. I was relieved with his return and went to the college.

'DOES GOD REALLY EXIST?'

On Sunday, I went to visit Shambhu Nath in the general ward. The ward was packed. There were sixty odd patients lying on beds and on the floors. All of them had some family members looking after them. There was a foul smell everywhere. Shambhu Nath was on the last bed by the window. His wife and mother had arrived from Bihar to look after him.

As I entered the ward, I heard loud cries coming from within a door just outside the entrance. I peeped in to see who it was. A revolting stink assaulted my nostrils, but before I could withdraw, I saw a young man lying on a dirty bed, crying and moaning loudly. He was all alone. I turned around to some people sitting outside and asked them who the boy was. They told me that he was a Pakistani intruder who had been shot in the legs by the Border Security Force and brought to the hospital for treatment. The doctors had pulled out the bullets and put a cast on both his legs since the bones were broken. The BSF had asked that he be kept away from other patients, so he was put in this unused, dirty bathroom outside the general ward.

His name was Atif Hussain and he was from Gujranwala in Pakistani Punjab.

I looked in again and the Pakistani caught my eye and called out, 'Sardarji! Please, please help me.'

The boy spoke in Punjabi and I felt an immediate affinity with him. He told me he needed painkillers for the intense pain in his broken legs and his soiled pyjamas needed a change. He also said that he was terrified of the BSF officers who would come to interrogate him and perhaps torture him for information he did not have. He wanted me to somehow get a message across to Pakistani authorities to rescue him. Tears streamed down his face and my heart contracted as

I felt his terror, agony and despair; but I did not have the courage to overcome my horror and brave the stink and enter the room. I had not yet recovered from the shock of Shambhu Nath's accident and the trauma of dealing with the hospital and doctors. I lowered my eyes, backed away from the door and fled without visiting Shambhu Nath.

I went straight to the gurudwara. I was deeply distressed. A million questions jostled in my mind. I needed solace and answers from God, but it was Sunday and the gurudwara was crowded. There was no place for me to sit quietly and converse with God. So I bowed before the holy scripture and went home. Gagan had gone out to play with his friends and I had the room to myself. I tried to sleep, but I was too agitated and upset. Two hours later, my mother came in with my lunch on a tray. She sat quietly while I ate, watching the sadness and disquiet on my face. She asked if I had visited Shambhu Nath, but I could not bear to talk about my experience at the hospital. I said I had not gone there at all. I said I was just very tired because I had been reading a book and listening to music all night. My mother knew that I was very fond of listening to Ghulam Ali's ghazals and reading the poetry of Baba Bulle Shah, a Sufi mystic. She also saw that I was distressed and told me to take a sleeping pill from my father's beside table drawer and get a few hours of good rest.

I went to my parents' room, and instead of one pill, I picked up the whole strip of ten pills from the bedside table. I lay in bed and tried to sleep, but Atif's terrified, tear-streaked face would not go away, however hard I shut my eyes. He had begged me for help in my own language, but I had turned my back and run away from there. Now I was haunted by his terrified, pleading voice and my heart was filled with guilt.

'What is God doing sitting up there in the sky and watching such horrors being perpetrated on his children? No Sikh God helped the Sikhs when the Golden Temple was attacked, no Hindu God saved Shambhu Nath and now Allah is not around to rescue this Pakistani man crying for help. Perhaps God has just given birth to humans and has nothing more to do with them. But can God be so merciless? Does God really exist?' All these questions tormented me, as I struggled to sleep.

I took two more sleeping pills. I tossed and turned for twenty minutes and then took two more pills and finally dozed off. At 1 a.m., I woke up. My head was heavy and numb. The tension had eased, but I could not go back to sleep. I spotted the remaining six sleeping pills on my bedside table. I got some water and swallowed all six in one go.

Mummy and Papa shook me awake at 11 a.m. the next morning. I could barely open my eyes and my head felt very heavy. Papa immediately started scolding my mother, telling her that she should have given me one tablet herself. He told me sternly that it was stupid to take ten sleeping pills. I should have taken one, and if I still could not sleep, then two. But ten...? I could have died. I vaguely heard my father, but went right back to sleep. I finally woke up at

6 p.m. and had some food, and decided to go to the hospital and visit Shambhu Nath.

It was Monday, the factory was closed and it was also the festival of Dusshera. Papa offered to take me to the hospital, but I was afraid that if Atif Hussein saw me and called out to me again to ask for help, my father would want to know how a Pakistani intruder knew me and would scold me for talking to Atif. So, I quickly said that I had changed my mind and would rather go later. Papa went alone to the hospital with vegetable soup and fruits for Shambhu Nath.

I waited till my father had returned and then I too went to the hospital. I slowed down outside the door of the bathroom in which Atif Hussein was kept. It was bolted from the outside, but I could hear Atif saying his namaz. I quickly walked past.

Shambhu's wife was sitting beside him on his bed. I wanted to look at Shambhu, but I could not meet his eyes. After all, he had been injured in our factory. Shambhu Nath wept like a child. His wife ran out of the ward, unable to see her husband crying. Shambhu sobbed and asked me to make sure he got a good compensation, since that would be his family's only support. He would not be able to ever work again. I reassured him that I would ask my father to support him until his son was old enough to get a job. I would also ask Papa to educate Shambhu's son so that he could get a good job. Shambhu Nath thanked me and said that he was grateful to the Goddess that she had spared his life. It was to pay for the sins of his past life that his arms were taken away.

I was surprised at Shambhu's unshakeable faith in God.

On my way out, I stopped beside Atif's door and put my ear against it. He was still praying in Arabic.

I bought a strip of sleeping pills on my way home. After dinner, I lay on my bed and played Ghulam Ali's ghazals. The songs are all about love and separation and usually soothed me. But tonight, like the night before, they had no effect. I had seen too much tragedy and had to deal with too many things in the past week. I quickly swallowed five sleeping pills.

I got up late the next morning and found my father sitting in the lobby with a long list of names of relatives, neighbours, factory staff and government officials who all had to be given Diwali gifts. Then there was the compensation to be paid to Shambhu Nath. The only way he could think of to generate money for all this was to sell the car.

Papa did not want to sell the car himself. Amritsar is a small town and ours was a well-known family. It would soon be all over town that we were was in such a bad financial situation that we had to sell our car. So Papa instructed me to go and sell it. I went to two or three dealers to find the best deal and then sold the car for Rs 35,000. I repaid Rs 7,500, half the amount I had borrowed, to BR and gave Rs 27,500 to my father. The money was still not enough. So Papa sold half the stock in his factory at a discount to a dealer. Now he could pay a decent compensation to Shambhu Nath and do the Diwali shopping.

Papa had been worrying about Daisy's marriage for a while. In December, he found a groom and her wedding was fixed for February. Now he began to worry about the wedding expenses.

Meanwhile, I had become addicted to sleeping pills. Things that had earlier agitated me and kept me awake through the night, no longer bothered me. The sleeping pills deadened my sensitivity.

TRIMMED BEARD AND THE LIBRARY CARD

BR and Jassi Randhawa invited me to a party on New Year's Eve. I was asked to dress formally in a suit, but I did not own one. I called one of my school friends who I had not spoken to for more than two years and asked if I could borrow a suit. This friend was about the same height and build as I was, and had many suits. The friend asked no questions and loaned me his suit.

I went to the party looking handsome and well dressed and feeling quite confident. I was introduced to many girls, a couple of whom were my classmates from school. I danced with a girl I had never met before, but after a while, she left the floor and sat outside with some other girls. I followed her and asked her to come back to the dance floor with me. She refused and rudely said that when she wanted to dance again, she would do so with another boy. I felt very hurt.

I went to the bar and got myself a large drink for the first time in my life. I continued to drink till 4 a.m. and was so drunk that BR had to drop me home.

The next day, BR came to visit me. I poured my heart out to him.

'Girls are just not interested in me, even after I took the trouble of dressing up in a suit,' I said. 'The girl I was dancing with rejected me.'

BR told me that I had to improve my appearance. I needed to trim my beard and tie my turban smartly. I took the advice to heart. That evening I took a pair of scissors from Daisy's craft kit. I hesitated for a few seconds, assailed with religious doubts, then firmly trimmed three inches off my beard. 'I am not hurting anyone,' I told myself. And surely God would not punish me for something so small.

When my parents saw my trimmed beard the next morning, they were furious. Papa demanded to know how I had dared to cut my beard.

'I have cut my own beard, not someone else's,' I retorted. Papa glared at me, but then he noticed the slightly glazed look in my eyes and realized that I was under the influence of sleeping pills. So, he said nothing more and signalled to Mummy to say no more too. He pacified her by saying that I would one day realize the importance of unshorn hair for a Sikh and would then let my beard grow out again. I was surprised that there was no hue and cry. No one in my family, neither my uncles nor my cousins, had ever trimmed their beards. I wondered at the muted reaction of my parents. I went to meet my cousin Tarun after college and asked for his opinion. Tarun said that he did not approve of it, but it was my life and he had no right to raise a finger.

'Why has nobody said anything?' I wondered.

'They are scared this time,' Tarun said.

I was puzzled. Why scared? And, 'this time'? And then the story came out.

One of Papa's younger brothers had died in Bangalore, where he lived. I knew about this, but I did not know that the family had excommunicated this brother because he had stopped wearing a turban and cut his hair due to frequent headaches and swelling on the skull. The family did not consider this a serious enough reason to cut off one's hair and shave one's beard. The brother was very attached to the family and became very depressed. He grew his hair back and started wearing a turban again, but he could never overcome the severe depression, which finally led to his demise. It was a tragedy and Papa was deeply upset. But his own troubles were never-ending and he never had the time to properly mourn his brother.

I had three cousin sisters in Bangalore who used to visit us in Delhi. I particularly remembered the eldest, Navjot Kaur, nicknamed Jyoti, who was only two years younger than me and with whom I got along very well. I had very happy memories of the times we spent together as children. But once we left Delhi, there had never been time or opportunity to recall those happy days. The struggle was unrelenting.

I now knew why my family had been so gentle with me. But Tarun warned me that I better always keep the turban. There was only so much the family would tolerate and a clean-shaven, short-haired Bobby was not one of them.

January 1990 came and Daisy's wedding loomed large in February. Papa's financial situation was as bad as it had been during Lovey's wedding, but this time all his relatives were aware of it. Papa had sold his car and moved his factory, and his family knew about the losses he had sustained. So his brothers helped him and he sold whatever remained of his wife's jewellery. The wedding took place on a smaller scale in the colony park and went off gracefully.

***

The violence in Punjab showed no signs of abating but rather escalated. There were encounters between government forces and the militants, and Sikh youth were treated with suspicion. Many young Sikh boys cut their hair to hide their Sikh identity, as did those who were suspected of being militants or their associates.

I continued to work at the factory and attend college. Professor Mulak Singh had helped me get membership of the university library adjoining my college, and whenever I had a free class, I went there. I was interested in the history of religion. I could not understand the scriptures of Sikhism, Hinduism, Islam, Judaism, because the language and style of writing were not familiar. I believed that I could learn the truth about various religions only through their history. I learnt that Islam was a religion of love, peace and harmony, quite the opposite of common perception. Hinduism was the most liberal religion and the way of life in the subcontinent and Sanskrit was the root of many languages. But above all, I understood that in its true essence, every religion preached love and harmony, never division between people and communities.

My library membership card proved to be invaluable in a most unexpected way one day, in a completely unrelated situation. I was returning home from Jandiala, a nearby town, late in the evening. I had gone there to collect payment from a buyer and had Rs 8,000 in my pocket. Security checkpoints were set up along the highway those days and suspicious travellers were stopped and questioned. Sikh youth were always considered suspicious, and I was stopped and asked where I was coming from. I noticed that there was no senior officer there, only jawans. If they found money on me, they would ask all kinds of questions. They may even take away the cash. So I replied to them in English. The jawans were confused. Had they stopped a government officers' son or relative? One of them asked me my designation. I was stumped for a second, then took out my library card and presented it to the jawans. The two men looked at the card and then at each other. It was dark and they could not see the card clearly. Besides, they could not read English. They asked me to which department I belonged.

I replied in English, 'I am a student and belong to the history department.' They did not understand a word, but respectfully returned my card. One of them came forward and apologized to me saying that his colleague did not understand English and so did not realize that I was a government official!

I came back to Amritsar with my money intact, returned Rs 7,500 to BR and thanked him for his help when I was in need.

I was now completely involved in running the factory and had lost all interest in studies. But my father insisted that I should get my degree. He repeatedly reminded me that he himself could not get a degree and was therefore unable to succeed in business. I objected, saying that my uncle had no college education either, but was a very successful businessman.

'Some people have an innate ability and smartness,' Papa said, and he warned me that I certainly did not have it, so I should get a degree!

So I continued to attend college and study, but my focus was the factory. My father and I both worked very hard and slowly the factory started doing well. We began to break even and even make a small profit. For the first time, our labour bore fruit.

I was still addicted to sleeping pills, but immunity was setting in and I could not sleep despite taking them. One day, when I had a bad cough and cold, my mother gave me some cough syrup. That night I slept very well. So I started taking cough syrup, then strong painkillers and other medicines. I looked sleepy all the time and became quiet and withdrawn. My parents noticed this, but assumed that it was because of the pressure of work at the factory and studying for my exams. I appeared for the exams and did surprisingly well.

A PLACE OF OUR OWN

Papa's neighbour and owner of the factory space he rented called one morning to say that he had decided to sell all his property in Amritsar and move to Bombay. He was a Hindu and feared for the safety of his family in Amritsar. If he found a buyer who would pay cash for his house and mill, he would sell immediately and we would have to vacate the factory premises.

Papa advised our neighbour to stay where his roots were, arguing that it is not easy to re-establish oneself in a new place. But the experienced neighbour said that Papa had made a mistake in leaving Delhi and moving to Amritsar in a panic after the riots. Amritsar was a small town in the grip of violence. Delhi was a big city with many business opportunities. The value of property there had multiplied many times in the past four years. Foreign investors were coming in to invest in the metros and real estate was booming. The Sikhs who had lost their businesses during the riots were now well established again and doing very well, although those who had lost earning family members still lived in miserable conditions. Papa was quiet. Perhaps, he had made a mistake in moving out of Delhi in such a hurry.

'Isn't it surprising that rich Sikhs never help the poor in their own community?' Papa remarked to me.

'Rich Sikhs give big donations to gurudwaras, but not to people who are suffering,' I replied.

'I made a mistake in moving to Amritsar,' Papa admitted. 'I made life very hard for you.'

I was surprised. 'Bad times are over now and things will get much better,' I said.

At that time, I had no idea that the factory premises would soon have to be vacated. Papa was worried, but hoped that it would be impossible for our neighbour to find a buyer who would buy both the large house and a big factory together. Business had suffered in Punjab and who would want to invest so much money in property here? However, Papa applied to the Punjab government for an industrial plot under a scheme in which victims of the riots were given plots at subsidised rates.

The very next month, Papa got an allotment letter for a 1,500 square yards industrial plot at a very nominal price with a ten-year loan from the government. To assist the riot victims, the government would also give a subsidy on the central sales tax. We were delighted. The payment for the land was to be made semi-annually, beginning a year later. So we had one year to build the factory and start production.

However, a few days later, the neighbour called to say that he had a buyer for his properties and the factory would have to be vacated in three months. Papa was taken aback. Who could afford to buy such a large property in these turbulent times? The neighbour told him that he had sold his house and mill at half the price and the buyer had insisted that he would buy them both only if he had possession in three months.

Papa said, 'I can vacate the premises in three months, but I cannot build a new factory in that time. Please give me at least six months time. My lease agreement is for two years and only one year is over.'

'I have sold the property to a minister of the ruling party in Chandigarh. Why don't you meet him and request for more time? I will introduce you to the minister's personal assistant. He is a very helpful man.'

Papa explained the situation to me and we went to Chandigarh to meet the PA to the minister. The PA was a Sikh gentleman; the minister Hindu. Papa explained his situation in detail and the PA heard him out patiently. Then he went into the minister's office.

My father and I waited outside the PA's office till 5 p.m. We were offered tea and biscuits by the staff. Finally, the PA emerged and informed us that our problems were solved. We could run our factory for six months. He also asked Papa to bring all the papers and project reports of the new factory. We stayed overnight in Chandigarh since it was unsafe to drive back at night and the night buses had been discontinued.

A few days later, Papa returned to Chandigarh with all the papers. The PA assured him that he would get the required government clearances in a short time and he would also get a loan sanctioned at subsidised rates from the Punjab Finance Corporation, a subsidiary of the Punjab government. Papa returned to Amritsar a very happy man.

Two weeks later, we received all the required clearances and a cheque for the loan amount. The allotted plot was 15 kilometres away from our home, on the outskirts of the city, but at last, we had our own factory and a working capital to run it.

I suggested to Papa that we set up a unit to manufacture cotton canvas cloth, an industrial textile, under the same roof. Most of the rubber factories, which bought our reclaimed rubber, used this cloth in rubber transmission belts, rubber conveyor belts and rubber sheets. We would have two businesses under one roof and our overhead costs would be halved since there would be only one accountant and one set of gatekeepers. Our own time would also be doubly productive. Besides, a rubber factory uses inflammable materials, which are always a safety risk. A textile unit would be safer and easier to run. Papa liked my idea and he was familiar with this textile since all his brothers made transmission and conveyor belts and used the fabric.

The file for the textile unit was submitted to the helpful PA. He was the only Sikh who had assisted us since we had moved to Amritsar. He belonged to a village near our new factory and was influential in the area.

The work on the factory sheds began in full swing since there was no shortage of money now. We could now buy a new Maruti car. Papa had manipulated the project reports with the help of the PA to get 30 per cent more funds sanctioned from the Punjab Finance Corporation.

Four months later, the PA visited Amritsar and Papa invited him home for dinner. He wanted to gift him some money for all the help he had given us. For the first time, all our files had moved smoothly through government offices and no one had asked for a bribe because the minister's office had recommended our case.

A lavish dinner was arranged for the PA, with chicken and fish. Papa bought a bottle of Scotch for the evening. When they settled down with their drinks, Papa offered the PA an envelope with Rs 10,000 in it. The PA refused to take it. He said that money came to him from many sources; he did not need to take money from us. He was a big landlord himself and did not lack for anything. He said he was happy to help Papa and our family because we had suffered during the riots and lost all that we had. This put Papa at ease and so he brought up something that had been bothering him for the past four months – why did the minister, a non-Sikh, invest so much money in Amritsar in these turbulent times? I edged closer to hear the PA's answer.

The PA said he would explain it to us on the condition that we would never repeat this to anybody. The minister, he said, got a lot of money in bribes, so he had a lot to invest. He had enough security and did not think that he was personally at any risk in Punjab. Besides, more Sikhs than Hindus were being killed every day. He could buy all this property at half the market price, and the day the state and central governments decided to get together and end the violence, property prices would boom and make him a very, very rich man.

THE FIRST GIRLFRIEND

With money coming in, the lifestyle of our family improved. We had a new car, good clothes and even planned a holiday in the hills during summer. My hard work in the factory had ensured a good growth. I went to a gym in the evenings instead of studying and stopped going regularly to college. The production at the old factory had stabilized and the construction of the new factory was on at a good pace. I took care of production, while my father looked after the construction work. Papa received Rs 2 lakh as compensation from the Punjab government as a riot victim. He tried to get compensation for the burnt house from the Delhi government, but did not have time to make frequent trips to Delhi to chase it. He learnt that Roshan Lal had received compensation from the government for the burnt factory because he had managed to put together all the paperwork required for it. Papa went to Delhi and demanded half the share of the compensation amount, but Roshan Lal refused to give him any money on the pretext that my father had sold the factory and the burnt machines to him.

There was a lot of violence in the locality of our new factory. The villages around it were hubs of Sikh hardliners. Papa usually left early for work and returned home before dark.

Meanwhile, I tried to make up for the past four or five years that I had spent working hard at the factory. I wanted to live a normal life and enjoy myself like other young boys. I made an effort to revive old friendships. I went to meet my old school friends. Both the Sandeeps welcomed me and made me a part of their group of college friends. I knew some of them from school, but the others were new. It was a group of about a dozen boys, all Hindus except for two Sikhs. We met often, but not late at night since there was always the threat of kidnappings and shootouts. We met at each other's homes and often at my house, where we played cricket and badminton. Papa had put in floodlights in the large front lawn so that both Gagan and I could play there with our friends. He wanted to provide us with every luxury that he could afford. Mummy had new clothes and money for shopping and my sisters received gifts and money.

Some of my friends had girlfriends, but some had a hard time meeting girls since they studied in an all-boys college. I went to a co-ed college, had a car and a bike and was good looking, so my friends assumed that I had a girlfriend. I was too embarrassed to admit that I had none, so I pretended that I had one in college and had been talking to two other girls on the phone. I said that I would be meeting one of the phone girlfriends soon. The Sandeeps looked at me in disbelief. They knew that none of this was true. When I was asked for the name of my girlfriend, I said that I could not reveal her name without her permission. As for the phone friends, it was a casual friendship and I would disclose their names when something serious developed.

I had said all this in a fit of bravado, but now I was in a fix. I had to meet some girls. There were a few girls in my class but not anyone that I found attractive. One day, I went to Amritsar Club with my friends on Baisakhi. Many young and pretty girls had come there with their friends or families. Manbeen, a young girl, came up to wish one of my friends, who was her cousin. The friend introduced her to me and she smiled at me. I immediately asked my friend for her number, but he said that she was only sixteen and that I should consider other girls.

I had a lovely dimpled smile, but the dimples had disappeared under my beard. I managed to greet a few girls and flash my charming smile at them. My smile seemed to have done the trick, because the next day, my friend told me that his cousin had asked about me, and he gave me her number.

I started talking to the Manbeen on the phone. I soon realized that she was a serious sort of person and interested only in a long-term relationship that would end in marriage. I immediately backed off. I was not ready for commitment. I knew that life could turn upside down in minutes and I was not certain that my life was stable yet. I wanted a girlfriend just to be able to brag to my friends that I too had one. So I kept in touch with Manbeen over the phone, but I never discussed a long-term relationship.

One day a friend gave me his ex-girlfriend's phone number. He had broken up with her because he had fallen in love with another girl. I called this girl and was surprised that she was willing to talk to me even though she did not know me. I told her that I had been a secret admirer ever since I had seen her at a party. Now I wanted to meet her. She agreed and we decided to meet the next morning at 10 a.m.

I borrowed my father's car and had dark films put on its windows at a garage because some friends had told me that they made out with their girlfriends in cars and at home when the parents were out. I was really excited. I put on my new jeans, a black shirt, sneakers and a leather belt. To top it all, I borrowed my mother's perfume and used it liberally. 'It's a woman's perfume and I am using it for the benefit of a woman,' I told myself.

Lovers' Lane in Amritsar was a quiet back lane behind some bungalows, secluded enough to allow a modicum of privacy to young couples. I drove through the lane, decided on a spot where I would park and then went off to pick up my date. She was not at the appointed place and disappointed, I was about to drive off when I saw a tall, slim, dark Hindu girl with stylishly cut hair walking towards my car. I opened the passenger seat door and she slid in. I drove off immediately. I wanted to ensure that no one would spot us.

Then I turned to look at the girl. She had buckteeth and braces, was thin and not particularly good-looking. The first thing she asked me was who had given me her number.

'I have long been your secret admirer,' I said glibly, 'and I managed to get your number from a friend.'

She laughed and said, 'I know I am no beauty, so you better tell me the truth.' When I told her that it was her ex-boyfriend who had given me her number, she was very quiet for a while and then turned to look accusingly at me. I realized that she was no fool and apologized for lying to her. She smiled and started chatting with me. She had brought me some chocolates and a card, but I had not brought anything for her. I lied that I had brought her a perfume but had left it in my almirah.

'It is probably out on the table where you put it after trying it out on yourself,' she laughed.

I felt very embarrassed.

'Look,' she said, 'all I want is a casual relationship. I am not interested in commitment and all that. I don't want to be hurt again.'

That suited me fine and I asked her where she wanted to go.

To my surprise, she said, 'To Lovers' Lane, where else?'

I parked in the spot I had recced earlier and nervously reached out to hold her hand. I started talking to her about my interest in badminton and music, but she seemed uninterested.

After a few minutes, she interrupted me and said, 'Have we come here to talk?' I was taken aback. I did not have the courage to kiss her. I moved closer to her and she leaned forward and kissed me. I experienced my first kiss!

We met frequently during the next two months.

On my twentieth birthday, a big party was organized at home. Papa bought me a lot of gifts and a crate of beer for the party. A friend brought a bottle of whiskey and another brought a bottle of wine. We drank and danced all night. It was the best birthday I had ever had. The next morning, I received a special gift – my girlfriend invited me to her friend's place. The house was empty because the friend's parents had gone off to work.

That morning I was initiated into sex.

Later that summer, Papa took the family for a holiday in hills.

The minister took possession of the mill, and the machines had to be moved out from there before the construction of the new factory was complete. The walls had been put up, but there was no roof. The new textile machines were also delivered. The construction was speeded up and the factory was inaugurated in August. I was so engrossed in all this, that I lost interest in college, and after the second-year summer vacations, I gave up college completely.

The loan and compensation had made life comfortable for our family. My mother's niece's wedding was in August, and Papa decided to take us all for the wedding to Bangkok.

He had already applied for our passports. He felt his children had gone through hard times and he wanted us to enjoy ourselves now.

Sandeep Gupta got engaged and his wedding was in November.

A small function was organized for the inauguration of the factory on 15 August. Papa chose this date because it was a holiday and the minister's PA could attend. He invited all his relatives and I invited my friends. But many people did not turn up because the area was reputed to be unsafe. The PA arrived and cut the ribbon. The factory began production the next day.

The workers at the new factory were mostly Sikhs from nearby villages. Workers from UP and Bihar had stopped coming there because there had been an incident in which migrant workers in brick kilns had been killed by militants in the area. Only the old Sikh supervisor and some Punjabi workers moved to the new factory. Seventy per cent of the workers were now new, especially in the textile unit. The environment in the factory changed because the new workers were not meek and obedient. Punjabis find it hard to take orders; moreover, the workers from the villages usually had their own land and buffaloes, availed of free electricity and water supply, and harvested at least two crops a year. The factory job was not their only source of income. I sensed that a few of the workers were fanatic Sikhs; I recognized the same anger in them that was in me when I came to Amritsar in 1984.

My father and I were advised to leave the factory before sunset, since it was a long way from home and the area was unsafe. So I now had more free time to meet my friends. Even in the factory, when my father was away, I spent time talking to girls on the phone. My happy smile was back, and life seemed normal and stable after a long time.

THE AMERICAN VISA

By September, the factory overcame the initial teething problems and things began to run smoothly. We had a supervisor called Kashmir Singh in charge of the weaving unit. He belonged to the village outside which the factory was situated on the Amritsar-Jammu highway. One day, he did not turn up for work and two of the machines developed some snag. I had to go into the village to fetch Kashmir Singh.

It was really surprising that the village was divided into two parts – on the right side of the road were poor, mud houses, mostly single storey; on the left were bigger, double-storey houses with TV antennas and colourful water tanks on the roofs. A group of old people were sitting on a bench under a tree. I stopped to ask one of them where Kashmir Singh lived.

'Which Kashmir Singh do you want?' they asked.

I did not know. There were three Kashmir Singhs who lived on the right side who were a barber, a farm labourer and a washerman, respectively. But I didn't know my supervisor's caste. I spotted two gurudwaras, one on the right and one on the left. I realized that this was a divided village and even their God was divided. I explained to the old men that I was looking for the Kashmir Singh who was a supervisor in the rubber factory on the main highway outside the village. They immediately knew that I was referring to the Jaat Sikh who lived on the left side. But they also realized that I was the factory owner's son and the mood of the group changed. Some of them looked angry. They asked me to get off my bike and sit with them. I had no choice. I parked the bike and went towards them but did not sit down. One of them angrily asked me why the factory was inaugurated on 15 August. I said it was because the day was a holiday and all our friends and family could attend.

'It was India that got freedom on that day, not the Sikhs who had sacrificed so much in the independence movement. Instead our temple was attacked,' said one of them angrily.

'The firing was wrong,' I agreed, 'but how would they have flushed out the terrorists?'

This made the old men so angry that they shouted at me, 'It could have been done without attacking the shrine. They did that in Operation Black Thunder, didn't they? They got the militants out with just one casualty and Blue Star could have been carried out under a similar strategy. What do you have to say?'

Then one of them said to me, 'You and your father have made a huge mistake in inaugurating your factory on 15 August, and that too at the hands of a servant of the government that is killing Sikh youth in Punjab. Sikhs working in the government will not be spared. They are working against their own people.'

The atmosphere became menacing until one old man intervened to say that I was just a young lad from Delhi and I did not know how the Sikhs in Punjab felt.

I was shocked and frightened. Not only did they know that the factory was inaugurated at the hands of the PA on 15 August but they also knew that the owner was from Delhi. I told them that we were riot victims from Delhi. That cooled the anger somewhat. But one of the old men repeated that we would have to pay the price for our friendship with the PA. I apologized for arguing with them. The old man in the group then directed me to Kashmir Singh's house.

I set off in the direction the man had pointed out, but then made a U-turn and sped out of the village, past the group and back to the factory. I was tense and anxious and drenched in sweat. My father had gone to the bank and would go straight home from there. So I also left and went to the Golden Temple to listen to the *kirtan*, religious hymns from the Sri Guru Granth Sahib sung by trained *raagis*. Kirtan always soothed me. I got home at 7 p.m. in a much calmer state of mind and decided to say nothing to my father about the incident. I did not want him to worry unnecessarily.

Kashmir Singh was back on duty the next day, and I did not tell him that I had gone looking for him in his village.

A week later came the news that a neighbouring factory owner's son had been kidnapped for ransom. The owner was one of our buyers of reclaimed rubber. The ransom negotiations took time and the pressure by the police on the militants to release the hostage increased; the militants did not agree and they killed the boy. The kidnapping and killing of the son of a well-known family in Amritsar was shocking. My father and I were deeply disturbed.

A few months later, in October 1990, the PA came to his village near the factory to spend time in his ancestral home and distribute sweets and money to the workers who worked on his farm. This was a regular annual ritual and all the residents knew this, as did the militants, who had a strong network in the villages. When he was returning from the village in his Ambassador car, it was attacked just as it turned onto the highway. The PA, his driver and two bodyguards were all killed.

This news devastated Papa and frightened me. I now told my father about the incident in the village, to which my father told me not to mention it to anybody. Papa did not want to frighten the family. He got up to wash his hands and I said, 'I am not going to live in this country! I want to live in peace in a free country.'

Papa said in surprise, 'Free country?'

'Yes, America,' I replied.

I had a passport, but there were no visas in it. For the whole family to go to Thailand at this point was an unnecessary expense, so only my mother and Gagan were to go. Diwali came in the first week of October, but I felt no joy in it. The killings and the constant fear I felt for my safety and that of my father killed all the enthusiasm about the festival.

The impulsive trait of my father dwelled in me too, to some extent. I decided to get myself a US visa.

Papa laughed when he heard this. It was not easy to get a US visa. But BR and his brother Jassi had got theirs without any problem, so I saw no reason why I could not get one too. I told my father that though my friends had got tourist visas, they were not going to come back because of the militancy in Punjab. They were very wealthy and their father was often threatened for money. Papa told me that the militants were strapped for cash since the central government had tightened processes and it was no longer easy for Sikhs in Canada, the USA and England to send them money. As a result, Pakistan was no longer supplying arms and ammunition.

I went to Delhi to see off BR and Jassi. They left with their parents, but their parents would return, while they would stay on with their relatives in the USA.

I spent the night at my uncle's place and went early next morning to the American Embassy. I filled the visa application form, paid the fees and waited for my turn for the interview. At 3 p.m., I was called to the window. A white American lady sat there, turning the blank pages in my passport. She asked me why I wanted to go to America. I said I wanted to see Disneyland and Universal Studios. She asked me for my sponsorship papers and I said I had none.

She asked who was going with me to America and I said I was going alone. Then she asked for income proofs, but I had not brought any. I replied honestly that our factory was new and there was no income from it yet. The lady smiled, opened the last page of the passport and stamped, 'Application Received', which meant that the visa had been denied and the applicant could not apply again for six months.

She handed me the passport and said, 'Happy journey.'

I was bewildered.

'To where?' I asked.

'Amritsar,' she said with a mean smile.

I was very disappointed. I had told no one that I was applying for the US visa, so thankfully I could keep the embarrassment to myself. I left for Amritsar by the 9 p.m. train, for which I had no reservation, but a bribe to the ticket checker got me a sleeper berth, and since I was travelling in the second-class, air-conditioned coach, I got a sheet, a pillow and a blanket as well. But I had not been able to get a visa to go to America.

Life continued as usual with work all day at the factory and evenings spent with friends. In November, Sandeep Gupta got married and I met many of my old friends at the wedding.

The sun set earlier in winter, and I now returned from the factory by 6 p.m. I had more time to spend with my friends; but at the back of my mind was the constant thought that I had to get an American visa and go to the USA, away from the violence and terror of Punjab.

Five months after my visa application had been rejected, I called BR. I told him that I too wanted to move to America since life was getting more and more unsafe for me in Amritsar. BR explained to me that I would need a sponsorship letter, income proof and a return ticket, and I would have to prove to the officer at the visa centre that I was a tourist and would definitely come back to India.

I got very excited and the very next day I went about gathering the documents. I first went to the bank where we had our factory account and from where we had taken our loan. It was a small branch and I was a regular customer there, so the entire staff knew me. I withdrew some money for factory expenses and then went into almost every room to look for new blank passbooks and the files in which the bank filled in account statements. I saw these in the accountant's room, but the accountant was there with a colleague. I chatted with them briefly and left.

Then I went straight to the gurudwara. I still went there sometimes, especially when I was depressed or anxious, because I did not want to go back to drugs. Our improved financial situation and reconnecting with my old friends had helped me to slowly rid myself of my drug dependence. It was so much better to find my solace in the kirtans I so loved. I stayed there for a while and then returned to the bank around lunchtime. Most of the staff was in the lunch room, while a few clerks were attending to customers. I sneaked into the accountant's room, picked up two blank passbooks and one account statement file and hid them under the big loose T-shirt that I had worn specifically for this purpose. When I headed out, the guard, who knew me, stopped me and asked why I was leaving in such a hurry. I told him that I had left my passbook in the morning on the accountant's table and had come back to collect it. I gave the guard a Rs 50 tip and left.

The next morning, I went to Punjab National Bank. Gagan and I had savings accounts here, but there was not much money in them. I intended to steal a blank passbook from here as well. But this was an unfamiliar branch and I could not enter any of the rooms. So I deposited a small amount of money in my account and then hung around trying to find some way to get into the rooms. After an hour, I gave up.

The next day I returned to the bank and told the assistant manager that I had lost my passbook and so wished to close my old account and open a new one with a large deposit. The new account was opened with a deposit of Rs 10,000, dated 1991. I changed the handwritten date to 1988 and added the numeral 1 before the 10,000. So now my passbook was dated 1988 and had Rs 1,10,000 in it. I bought many different pens and made cash entries, mainly deposits and a few withdrawals in back dates. I used two kinds of handwriting to show that two different people had made the entries. I also copied the rate of interest from the old passbook and credited interest to make it look authentic. Finally, I rubbed the passbook on the ground and folded some of the pages so that it looked old.

I had already created balances of lakhs of rupees in both the accounts and big transactions for the factory on the stolen account sheets. I found out where the bank stationery was printed and bribed the staff of the press to get letter papers with the letterheads of the banks. I had fake rubber stamps of the banks made and finally went to an agent outside the civil court who specialized in providing false documents to litigants. I forged the signatures of the bank managers and printed certificates to confirm that the account holder had the mentioned sum on the given date in his savings account and the factory account.

BR sent me the original sponsorship letter that he had got from his cousin. I covered the date and personal details with white ink and filled in my own. I found the same quality of paper in a xerox shop and had the letter xeroxed. It looked just like the original. I also managed to make fake income tax returns with the help of our factory supervisor's brother, who worked with a chartered accountant. He used the returns of a wealthy Delhi-based businessman, which he got through a contact in Delhi. A travel agent got me a Thailand visa. I bought fully refundable tickets for four destinations – first Thailand, then America and on my return journey, Canada and England. Now I was all ready to apply for the US visa again.

The fear of violence continued to grow, since the militants seemed to have got an upper hand over the government. One night, there was a midnight raid by the police at the factory and they took away two young workers.

Papa rushed to the police station the next morning. He was told that the two boys were in contact with militants and had been taken away by the CID. He was warned that he should not try to locate the boys or a case would be filed against him for harbouring militants at the factory.

Nothing was heard of the boys again.

I rechecked with BR that I had all the papers that were necessary for a visa. BR warned me that it was nearly impossible for a young, single male to get a visa. The Americans had realized that such men never returned to their countries. I thought about this and came up with a brainwave. I had wedding invitation cards printed with me as the groom and the name of a fictitious bride, her parents and even their address. The wedding was to be held on 16 July 1991, three months from the date on which I planned to apply for the visa.

In early May, I went to Delhi. I first went to the Canadian and UK embassies where I picked up visa forms, filled them and attached a demand draft for the required amount to each form.

The next morning, I dressed up in black trousers, a white shirt and a black turban. On my wrist, I wore a heavy gold bracelet and around my neck, a thick gold chain borrowed from Sandeep Gupta, whose in-laws had presented it to him. I borrowed a diamond ring and some perfume from my uncle, and finally, I slipped on a fake Rado watch and zero-powered glasses. Thus dressed to the hilt, I made my way to the American embassy.

I filled out the USA visa application form and paid the fees. The purpose of my visit was to meet friends and as my marital status I had mischievously filled in 'engaged'.

Around noon, I was called to the counter and I appeared before the visa officer with all the documents in hand. All my papers were scrutinized – the sponsorship letter, the bank account statements, the wedding card, the certificates from both banks, the income tax returns and the passbooks. The return tickets and the application forms for the Canadian and UK visa were also there.

The officer examined my passport photograph in which I looked poor and scruffy and then looked at me and asked if I was the same person. I pointed to the scar on my left cheek, which was also visible in the photograph. I was asked why I had not brought the papers when I had applied the first time, and I replied that I had not read the requirements properly and therefore not brought any papers along. I was asked to wait.

I waited anxiously, afraid that my forgery was not good enough and I would be caught. I was called to the counter again at 4 p.m. The officer asked me why my income tax was filed in Delhi when I lived in Amritsar. I told him that my family had moved to Amritsar only after the riots, and we continued to file our returns in Delhi. When he asked me why I was getting married at such a young age, I said that I was having an affair with the girl and the families wanted us married before our affair became public knowledge.

Despite these convincing stories, I was sent away to wait nervously in the visitors' room again.

At 6.30 p.m., when only one other lady remained in the hall, I was called to the window. This time there was also another senior officer at the window.

'Why are you going on this trip just before your wedding?' he asked.

'Just to have the first and last bachelor holiday of my life,' I replied with a smile.

And why had I not applied for my Canadian and UK visas? Why the USA visa first? I explained that I wanted to go to Thailand since my relatives were there and from there to meet my friends in America. But when I bought my ticket, I was offered a very cheap rate to make a halt in Canada and the UK, so I decided to go there as well. Then the senior officer said that my income tax returns did not match my balances. I realized that I had made a mistake. But I thought quickly on my feet and said that I did not know how to evaluate balance sheets, but my chartered accountant must have made some error.

'We will check with the income tax department. If anything is wrong, you will be arrested,' warned the officer.

My hands were on the window showing off my diamond ring and Rado watch. I glanced at my watch and realized that all government offices would be closed by now and then it was the weekend. There was nothing the officials could do till Monday morning. So I said that they could certainly check with the tax department. The junior officer looked at his senior. The senior officer nodded slightly and got up and went away. The visa officer asked me to deposit the fees for a four-month visa and collect my passport the next morning.

I left the embassy happy and immediately called home. My father did not sound very happy at the news and my mother started crying and said she would never let me leave her. Feeling a little deflated, I went to a gurudwara and sat there quietly listening to the kirtan. I collected my passport the next morning and went back to Amritsar.

My parents would not hear of me going to America.

'If the violence worsens in Amritsar, you will go and live with your uncle in Delhi,' my father said.

'I will never go back to a place from where I have been thrown out,' I said. 'Would you go back to Pakistan?'

I went back to work at the factory, but I was not happy. I had gone to great lengths to create all the forged papers for my visa and had lied more than ever before in my life, and now it was all to no end. My mother took my passport and put it in the bank locker with her jewels.

TO AMERICA AT LAST

Two months later, Papa and I were sitting in our little cabin in the factory when three men forced their way in. They were dressed in traditional clothes and one of them held an AK 47 rifle, while another had a revolver. The leader carried no weapon. Papa was sitting at the table and I was in a chair in front of him. There were two other chairs in the room. I got up with a shock when the men entered and offered my chair and the two other chairs to them. They sat down, an armed man on each side and the leader in the middle. Papa recognized the leader from posters he had seen, offering reward money for information regarding his whereabouts. He respectfully asked the leader what he wanted. The militant demanded Rs 5 lakh. Papa explained to him that his factory was just beginning to make money and he did not have such a sum.

'Five lakhs is no big sum for a rich Delhi business man,' said the man angrily.

'I will try and get together whatever I can in ten or twelve days,' Papa said, placating him.

The leader agreed to wait, but said he would accept nothing less than five lakhs.

A few days later, Papa gave the militant Rs 1.5 lakh. The militant reminded Papa that Rs 3.50 lakh was pending and he wanted it soon. Papa had managed to put together the money by taking an advance from his buyers and offering them 10 per cent discount on the next lot of supplies. There was no way he could raise any more money. Papa and I started taking different routes to the factory every day and left at different times as a safety measure. But soon, the dreaded phone call came to the factory, demanding the rest of the money. This time the militant threatened to kill me if he didn't get the money quickly.

Papa was quiet for a moment and then said, 'Ok. Kill him. Because I do not have any more money.'

And he hung up.

He turned to me and said, 'Buy the first available ticket to America.'

I was thrilled that I was finally going to America, but worried about leaving my family in such a tense situation. But there was no other option. The visa would expire in less than two months. At such short notice, I had to buy an expensive Japan Airlines ticket to San Francisco via Tokyo. I called BR to tell him that I was finally coming over and called my phone girlfriend to tell her that I was leaving the country for good.

All the close relatives were told that I was leaving, but neither my friends nor anybody in the factory was informed. The money for the return ticket – the American immigration would want to see a return ticket – was raised by selling my motorbike and an electric motor that was lying unused in the factory. I bought gifts for BR and Jassi and some good clothes for myself. That took care of all the money.

In all the tension and rush of preparation, Papa and I forgot to get dollars and remembered only the night before we were to leave for Delhi. The banks had closed for the day. So Papa gave me all the rupees he had to buy dollars at the airport.

The next morning my sisters and their husbands, my uncles and aunts, and my cousins all came to the railway station to see me off. My parents and Gagan accompanied me to Delhi. We went to my uncle's house and despite the excitement of leaving for America, I called two of my old school friends to enquire about Harbir Singh, but nobody knew where he was. He had disappeared after the riots. No family member had come to school for his certificates or anything.

In the evening, five of my old school mates turned up and came to the airport to see me off. Papa said that they were excited that one of their classmates was going to America, a rarity for a young boy at that time. At 9 p.m., twenty people in four cars set off for the airport. Papa's brother-in-law had come with his family in his car and my friends had brought their own cars. I realized that people in Delhi had become very rich after the mid-eighties. For the first time, I acknowledged that my father had really made a mistake by moving to Amritsar in such a hurry after the riots.

At the airport, as everyone said goodbye to me, my mother wept, my father looked sad and my brother was excited. My friends and relatives all gave me little gifts. I waved to them all and walked in a little sad, but mostly very excited. The immigration officer carefully examined my passport and visa and asked many searching questions, which I answered quite confidently. I bought $20 for Rs 7,000 and saved the rest of the rupees to exchange for dollars with BR's relatives who often visited India.

There were many Punjabis on the flight, especially Sikhs and mostly older men. There were very few young men and women. They had all been made to sit together at the back of the plane and filled a quarter of the seats. When I went to the washroom, I noticed white and oriental people all sitting together in the front rows. Only the Indians had been segregated. There was discrimination here too.

The flight had a five-hour halt in Tokyo. At the airport, there were people of all races, but hardly any blacks, perhaps because most blacks were poor and could not afford international air travel. I felt very grateful that I was able to make this trip.

When the flight took off from Tokyo and the seat belt sign was off, a number of Japanese men and women got up from their seats and bowed to the ground. I was puzzled. I asked a Japanese girl what they were doing and she told me that they were paying homage to their motherland. I was very impressed. I had felt no such emotion when I had left my country. But then, my country had not given me a decent life and it was no fault of mine that I did not feel sad while leaving her.

During the long flight, many Punjabi men drank too much and made a nuisance by talking loudly and demanding more and more alcohol, and it became clear to me why all the Indians had been seated together.

After a long and tiring journey of almost ten hours from Tokyo, the flight landed in San Francisco.

There was a long queue at immigration, and mostly old Punjabi people stood in front of me. The officer seemed to be really slow. After a while, he stood up and asked if there was anyone who spoke English in the queue. I immediately raised my hand and was called to the glass booth. There was an old lady there who did not understand any English. I translated her Punjabi into English and vice versa and then continued to do that for the other Punjabi people. The queue began to move faster.

Most of the old people had been sponsored by their children who were US citizens. Finally, one drunk old Sikh man, obviously from a village, came up. I read out his name and type of visa and handed his passport to the officer. He was a Jaat Sikh and had only nineteen days left of a six-month visa. The officer asked him why he had come to America, and I translated. The old man said he had come to visit his nephew and niece.

'Why have you come when your visa has almost expired?' the officer asked.

He said, 'After I got my US visa, I found that my buffalo was pregnant. She would deliver in three months and I could not just leave her and go away. So, I waited for the calf to be delivered. Unfortunately during delivery, the buffalo died, leaving behind a healthy newborn calf. How could I abandon that motherless calf? It would not drink the milk of the other buffaloes, and I had to feed it with a bottle. After six weeks, it started drinking from the other buffaloes and then I could finally leave.'

I was in splits of laughter and had a hard time translating the story for the immigration officer. The officer also had a hearty laugh when he heard it.

'How long do you want to stay here?' he asked.

The old man told me, 'It does not matter for how long the visa is valid – even an hour is enough. I am going to my relative's farm, and I will tear up this passport as soon as I get there. I am not going back to India.'

I was in a fix but decided not to translate this. The old man was given a three-month visa.

Now I was the only one left and I was quite confident that I would face no problem after all the translating that I had done for the officer. But the officer opened my passport and saw the first rejection and the unused Thailand visa. I explained to him that my visa application was rejected the first time because I had not carried all the relevant papers with me.

'Why didn't you go to Thailand? You have a valid visa,' he asked.

I said, 'I got the visa without my parent's knowledge. When they came to know I planned to go to Thailand, they forbade me because of the sex industry in Bangkok.'

The officer smiled. 'And how are you going to pay for your stay and travel in America with just $20?'

'In India, when my relatives visit us from the USA, we never let them spend a penny. That is our culture. The same will be done for me here by my friends,' I explained.

The officer was not convinced. He put a red card in the passport and sent me to a room behind the immigration counters. There were two custom and immigration officers there, checking the luggage of an African lady. I was rather scared now. I handed my passport to one of them and my boarding card to the other, who called on an extension and asked for my luggage to be brought to the room. The black lady's bags were closed and she left. My large suitcase had arrived and the officers opened it and searched very carefully for anything illegal. They opened every gift and finally shut the suitcase, took away the red card, put a six-month time stamp on my passport and allowed me to go. One and half hours had passed since I had arrived at the immigration counter. I heaved a sigh of relief and rushed out.

FINDING MY FEET IN A NEW WORLD

I stepped out of the airport and took a deep breath. I looked around for BR and Jassi. But they were not there. There were two clean-shaven boys who were waving at me. I wondered who they were and turned away to look for my friends on the other side. But one of the boys who had a moustache called out to me in BR's voice. I turned towards him in surprise and discovered that the boys were indeed Jassi and BR! They were no longer turbaned Sikhs. And they looked nice, though BR looked a bit funny with the moustache! They hugged me warmly and led me to their car.

I was very impressed to see their brand new white Toyota Camry. BR had paid some extra money and got a number plate that read BOB 11. He said that now it really made sense because two Bobs had been reunited and one and one always means 11!

San Francisco mesmerized me. For the first time in my life, I saw the vast ocean. I loved the Bay Bridge and was delighted to get a glimpse of the famous Golden Gate. The six-lane freeway and the huge eighteen-wheel trailers running on them were fascinating. They were well maintained and looked beautiful in the sunshine. I had only seen Tata and Ashok Leyland trucks in India, which were often in poor shape and rashly driven. In India, there were only three kinds of cars – Fiat, Ambassador and Maruti Suzuki. Here, there were cars of all kinds in so many different colours.

I was surprised that Jassi and BR could afford such a big, expensive car so soon. Jassi laughed and told him that a Toyota Camry was considered a mid-sized car in America and was not very expensive in American terms. I realized that I had at last come to the right place, the true 'land of opportunity'.

We reached home, which was a two-bedroom flat on the second floor of an apartment block near a busy intersection in a town called Concord. I telephoned India. My father had gone to work and my brother was at school. I spoke to my mother who cried a bit when she heard my voice and then told me not to worry about the family but to concentrate on work. Then I called my father at the factory and told him to be careful while going to and from work. Papa told me not to worry and said that he was far more relaxed now that I was safe in America. Besides, the CRPF had put in a checkpoint on the highway close to factory and it was manned day and night, which made the area much more secure.

I had to settle in fast and find work and a way to get legal permits and papers. Jassi and BR said that they would train me in the grocery store they owned so that I learnt the work and picked up the American accent. About nine months earlier, the American government had come up with an amnesty scheme under which illegal immigrants, who had been working in the US for seven years or more, were given legal status. For $20,000, there were agents who could make fake papers showing that I was an illegal immigrant who had crossed over from Mexico seven years ago and worked on farms in California. There were farm owners who would issue an undertaking that I had worked on their farms and had been paid in cash. Immigration officers at one of the immigration centres in California accepted forged documents for a hefty bribe. I heard them out but all this information was of no use to me. I had only $20. Where would I get $20,000? I told Jassi that we would have to find another way.

The first step, BR told me, was to cut my hair. I was taken aback, but I was told that neither the staff nor the customers would be comfortable with someone who looked so strange. I knew that I had no professional qualification, and it would not be easy to find a job. I would have to look acceptable to find a job. So, reluctantly I went to a barber and had my hair cut. I kept the beard because it hid my dimples, so that I did not look like a cute young boy. When I stepped out of the shop, the fresh air blew through my hair. It was a very pleasant feeling!

That evening, the three of us planned a little party to celebrate our reunion. We went out to get some beer and were walking past the exit door of a large store when a lady came out. I stopped to peer inside and BR gave me a little push into the store. The door shut behind me and I panicked. I didn't know what to do and BR and Jassi laughed at me from outside. Some people nearby also started laughing at my bewildered face. I then stepped towards the door and, to my delight, the door opened automatically. I had never seen anything like that before. I grinned and came out. We went into the store through the right entrance, and I was amazed at its size and the variety of products on its shelves. I wondered if it was the biggest store in America, but I was told that it was just mid-sized.

'It is at least 200 times bigger than any grocery store in India!' I exclaimed.

I had not yet seen Walmart or K Mart or Safeway. Jassi and BR bought a lot of their stock from wholesale mega stores like Costco and Trader Joe. America had large, mid-sized and small retail outlets.

We had a happy time that evening. I enjoyed my drinks with Jassi; BR did not drink whiskey and had just one beer.

BR and Jassi owned a store in partnership with their uncle, Simarjeet Singh, generally known to everyone as Sam. Sam was an American citizen. The store was called Village Market and was in a nearby town called Clayton. Clayton was a rich, mainly white town with a population of about 5,000 people. It was a close-knit community and had only three coloured families – one black, one Mexican and one Indian. I was introduced to Sam at the store. Like me, Sam had cut his hair but kept his beard. He greeted me warmly and immediately set me to work.

The Village Market had liquor, meat, groceries, sandwiches and other counters. A German lady called Doris, two American girls named Keeta and Amy, and an American boy called Robert worked in the store with BR, Jassi and their uncle. The Americans seemed to have accepted my friends as equals in a short time and did not discriminate against them. I felt that America was truly 'A Free Country'.

I started work at the store by stacking groceries and doing other chores at the back where I did not have to deal with customers. In the evenings, I used Jassi's old Toyota Corolla to learn to drive on the right side of the road and get familiar with the rules of driving there.

Within two weeks, I was driving confidently and speaking in an American accent. I was familiar with it because I watched American TV shows and movies and listened to American music, and I had practised the accent before my visa interview.

There was no vacancy in the Village Market for a regular job for me. I had to find a job elsewhere. But I had neither a work permit nor a social security number. Jassi gave me his work permit to use. Jassi's photo on it could be passed off as mine, and anyway, Americans were trusting people. They could not imagine that one person would use another's work permit to get a cheap job, so they never looked at it very carefully. I could also use Jassi's social security card, which had no photo on it. Jassi lent me his old car to go job hunting, but warned me to be careful. If I had even a minor accident, the police would demand to see my licence and then Jassi would be penalized for lending his car to a tourist.

I thanked Jassi and drove around looking for a job. Wherever I saw vacancy signs, I stopped and went through the tedious process of filling in forms. But more than a week later, having applied at over fifteen places, there was still no job. Feeling a little desperate, I now started going to the owners of stores and enquiring about the status of my application. Many owners brushed me off or showed a clear bias against me. Some said the vacancies had been filled. One white man was downright rude and said there was no vacancy for Arabs in his store. I did not bother to correct him, since he was clearly a racist.

One night, BR and Jassi's uncle, Sam, invited all three of us home for dinner. Sam explained to me that Iraq had attacked Kuwait and America had rushed to help Kuwait because it did not want Iraq to control the oil reserves in Kuwait. But many Americans saw it as unnecessary assistance to Muslims at the cost of American lives. So they hated anybody who looked like an Arab to them. He advised me to shave off my beard.

For the first time, I realized that not all Americans were nice and religion was a cause for discrimination even in this 'free country'.

THE DIGNITY OF LABOUR

I shaved off my beard and moustache. With my dark brown hair and fair skin, I could pass off as Mexican or even European.

On BR's advice, I spent time on improving my accent and learning American English. In India, British English is taught and spoken, and I had to learn American idioms and usage. I spent a lot of time with the staff at the Village Market and picked up their accent and language. Jassi sold me his old car, for which I had to pay him $100 a month as soon as I got a job. Now I was independent and felt far more confident. But I still had no job.

Sam told me that it was easier for immigrants to get jobs at fast-food restaurants, gas stations and convenience stores like Seven Eleven. I applied to such places wherever I saw a vacancy ad. I also met the owners and mangers to ask for jobs. Four days later, I got a job at a McDonald's outlet at $4.50 per hour. It was basic pay, but I had been warned that most of these places did not pay a lot. I had converted almost all my Indian rupees into dollars and spent it on food, gas, beer and snacks. My haircut had cost a lot of money. I was happy to get a job, even at the most basic pay.

The white American manager at McDonald's checked the work permit of Jaskaran Singh Randhawa, looked at my face for a moment, went into his office and came back with a photocopy of the card. He returned the original, and I forged Jassi's signatures on the forms. At last, I had a job.

I had to work the evening shift, 4 p.m. to midnight, and two extra hours on the weekends for which I would get 50 per cent extra for the overtime and food at 50 per cent discount. I was happiest about the food discount – I had developed a great love for burgers and colas.

On the first day, I was shown training videos by the store manager. Then I was introduced to the rest of the staff. There was Ram, an Indian; Sarfaraz, a middle aged Pakistani lady, who was the assistant manager in the evening shift; and Rania, a pretty young Egyptian girl. All the other staff was white and I assumed that they were Americans. But Ram told me that one of the girls was Polish and one boy was Romanian, both immigrants like me. The rest were Americans. Ram's job was to flip burgers, since he could not speak good English.

I introduced myelf as Jas to the staff. I got a uniform, a cap and a trainee badge to wear on my T-shirt. On the first day, Ram told me all about the outlet and then I spent three hours at the cashier's desk. I was very excited because I stood next to the pretty Rania and learnt from her how to greet customers and take and fulfil orders. I stood close to her. She was really very pretty with long curly hair, fair skin and a very good figure.

I was given a personal locker in the staff room and a job card with Jassi's name on it. The card had already been punched in at 16.00 hours, which meant that I was being paid for the hours of training as well. At the end of eight hours, I had made friends with most of the staff, especially

Rania and Sarfaraz. Sarfaraz spoke fluent Punjabi and even enquired about my family back home. She was from Lahore – only 38 kilometres from Amritsar – and in America, it felt as if we were neighbours. I did not get along very well with Ram, who was from central India and spoke a different kind of Hindi and very little English.

At 12.02 a.m., I took my job card to Sarfaraz's room to punch out, but Sarfaraz stopped me. It was Friday and I had to work two extras hours. The store had closed for customers and I wondered what I would have to do. I would have to clean the dishes, Sarfaraz informed me. I was shocked. 'I was hired as a cashier, not a dishwasher,' I told her. Sarfaraz laughed.

'There are no separate cleaners and dishwashers in fast-food chains. The staff does all the work,' she explained. 'Today you will wash dishes, tomorrow you will clean glasses and windows and doors, the day after you will sweep and mop the floors, and finally you will dismantle the machines, wash them and reassemble them. On some days, you will also dispose off the garbage in the big steel drums outside the store.'

I was really upset. These were chores servants did in India. I had been cleaning my toilet, doing the laundry and vacuuming the house just like Jassi and BR, but that was home and I had been prepared for that. I didn't know this would be part of my job as well. It felt very demeaning. But I had no choice. I went and joined Ram, who was waiting for me, and was given yellow rubber gloves and a long plastic apron. There was a big rubber pipe with a nozzle for hot water. Ram started washing the grills, hot plates and the back trays where uncooked or overcooked food was thrown. I dried it all with a big cotton cloth. At the back of the store, we washed the plastic trays in the sinks, dried them and lined them with paper liners, all ready for the next day. By the time we finished, it was 2 a.m. I went to Sarfaraz's room and politely asked her in Punjabi if I could now punch out.

She smiled and said, '*Ja, mere puttar* – go, my son,' and added that now I had become a man. I sheepishly smiled back at her, though I was not amused at all.

BR was waiting up for me. I told him all about the day at work and also that I had a Big Mac, French fries and a large coke for lunch, all for just $2. My dinner of chicken nuggets and burgers was free because they were leftovers and would have gone into the garbage. Then I also told him angrily about the dish washing.

BR smiled at me, patted my hand and said, 'Jassi and I have invested $2 million in our business and are owners of the store, but very often we have to sweep and mop the floors when a staff member is absent. We do all the chores in the store. This morning, we filled the freezers and cleaned the sandwich counter since one person was on leave. We do every chore here. Get used to it.'

I realized that in America, all work was equal, no job was big or small, and there was no shame in doing any kind of work. BR also told me that some of the rich clients in his store worked in the counties cleaning sewers and building roads. They were very well paid. I excitedly asked if I could get a job like that and earn a lot of money, but learned that those jobs were for trained people.

I quickly settled into the routine at McDonald's. I really liked Rania, but though she was friendly, she maintained her distance. Her brother picked her up after the shift every night. She could drive but was not allowed to do so alone at night. She and her brother lived with their relatives who were US citizens. Their parents were still in Egypt. Rania still had an Egyptian accent and I found it very cute.

Rania was declared the employee of the month and given a golden star to wear above her name badge on her T-shirt. I took the opportunity to congratulate and hug her, but she did not hug me back. A few days later, we were alone in the restaurant while she waited for her brother to pick her up. We were sitting at a table by the window, watching young couples walk hand in hand down the road and even kiss each other. I looked at Rania. I was sure that she was also attracted to me, but she would not meet my eyes. I told her that I liked her a lot and wanted her to be my girlfriend. Rania was not surprised, but she looked at me and said that the she could not be my girlfriend because I was a Hindu. I had never expected this, especially in America, and I said I was a Sikh, but it made no sense to her. She smiled softly, laid her hand on mine and said that she could be my friend, but never my girlfriend. There was complete silence after that. The headlight of a car showed up in the parking lot and Rania's drunk nineteen-year-old brother walked towards the entrance of the restaurant.

I burst out, 'Your little brother is allowed to stay out late at night, probably with a non-Muslim girlfriend and drink, but you cannot have a non-Muslim boyfriend?'

Rania looked at me sadly, said goodnight and walked out. I sat there feeling very depressed.

Religion had created a chasm between the one I really liked and me.

POLITICAL ASYLUM AND AMERICAN LESSONS

I had a weekly pay cheque, but it was way below what I had calculated. I had forgotten that taxes would be cut from my salary. The cheques went into Jassi's account, as did the refunds. I now shared the house rent, electricity and water supply bills with my friends. I also paid $100 every month for my car. As a result, I had no savings and very little money left over. I decided I needed another job during the day. Besides, I needed to get my work permit, social security card and driving licence.

Sam recommended an expensive Sikh lawyer in San Francisco who had helped two of his relatives get political asylum in the US and I went to meet him. I was just about to get on to the freeway when I saw a small accident on the roadside. Two cars had crashed into each other. A police car and an ambulance were parked beside them. The victims were obviously getting first aid in the ambulance, and a policeman was cleaning the shattered glass on the road with a broom and a flat plastic sheet. As I passed this site, I remembered Shambhu Nath and the insensitive behaviour of the policemen in India. And here, a policeman was cleaning the mess and an ambulance was providing immediate aid to the injured. A happy and warm feeling engulfed me. I was in the right land. I would never have to face another situation like Shambhu Nath's again.

The Sikh lawyer was an American citizen who specialized in political asylum cases, especially for Sikhs. I paid the $120 consultation fees that I could barely afford and went in. The lawyer asked me if there were any registered cases against me in India or if I had any marks of police brutality on my body. I replied in the negative to both questions. I said that I had been slapped by a policeman and punched in the stomach and hit with a stick on my bums. The lawyer laughed. He showed me photographs of Sikh youth who had been tortured in custody. He then explained to me that he could file my case and when the court accepted it for hearing, I would be given a work permit, a social security number and a driving licence that would be valid till the end of the case. If an applicant wins the case, he gets a white passport that is proof of his refugee status and he is never allowed to go back to his own country. In my case, the lawyer said, he could drag the case on for two years, but he was unlikely to win it. His fees were more than $15,000. There was no way I could pay such a sum, so I said I would think about it and left.

I enjoyed the dual identities of Jassi and Bobby. At work, I was called Jas and at home people called me Bob. During the day, I did laundry, washed the car, cleaned the house and, whenever I could, called my parents.

I also answered calls that came in usually from BR's or Jassi's girlfriends. BR had a white girlfriend who often visited the store, but he usually just talked to her over the phone. He was not ready for commitment. He believed girls showed an interest in him only because he had a nice car and owned a business at a very young age. Jassi had two girlfriends who often called on the landline. Their numbers appeared on the caller id and I soon recognized them. When I was alone at home and one of Jassi's girlfriends called, I would talk to her pretending to be Jassi or even as myself. The talk would soon turn from fun to sex talk, and I thoroughly enjoyed it. One day, a sweet new voice called for Jassi. I answered as usual and tried to initiate a seductive conversation, but the girl only answered in monosyllables. Finally, she told me that she was Kathleen Swinder from the immigration department. I got the shock of my life. I quickly put the phone down, feeling sure that I had been caught using Jassi's work permit and the immigration department was going to arrest me. I did not go to work the next day and wandered around town instead of staying at home. Finally, with trepidation, I went to the store to tell Jassi what had happened. Jassi laughed heartily and told me that the lady had called the store and all she wanted was to confirm his correspondence address so that she could send his renewed work permit and other papers required to file for a green card. I heaved a sigh of relief and swore never to fool around on the phone with anyone, especially girls.

I now applied for day jobs in other restaurants. I got a job at a Subway, but the Sikh owner looked carefully at my work permit and knew that I was using someone else's permit. He still offered me a job, but taking advantage of my illegal status, at only $3 an hour. The shift here was from 8 a.m. to 4 p.m. My shift at McDonald's started at 4 p.m. The distance between the two restaurants was only 400 metres and at both the places I had to wear black trousers and black shoes. Only the T-shirts and caps were different. If I punched out a couple of minutes after 4 p.m. from Subway, it would take me at least three minutes to reach MacDonald's and punch in my card. There was a traffic signal on the way, which could delay me further. I had an idea. I quietly reset the timer on the Subway machine to three minutes ahead of the McDonald's clock. So now I was punching out of Subway three minutes ahead of the actual time, which allowed me to change my T-shirt in the car and reach McDonald's on time.

I now had two jobs and worked continuously for sixteen hours without sitting. On weekends, it stretched to eighteen hours. I got a fungal infection between my toes and ingrown toenails. One big toe had to be drained of pus. But nothing deterred me from continuing to work regularly.

I went to Sam again for advice about political asylum and learnt that I did not need a lawyer to file an application in court. So I typed out a letter, attached a copy of my passport, made out a bank draft for the court fees and submitted the documents through a human rights organization.

A few days later, I was called before the judge. Pretending to be far more confident than I felt, I stood before him while he read my application and then asked me to call my lawyer. I told him that I could not afford a lawyer, so I was given a list of government lawyers who could assist me. The reader gave me a receipt for my application, which meant that I could now apply for a work permit and other papers. I went to the office of one of the lawyers on the list and explained my case to him. The lawyer told me that there was no way I could win the case, and I would be deported from the US in a year or so. He insisted on being paid to tell me how to apply for a work permit. So I walked away and simply went to the help desk and got the relevant information.

On the way back, I had to go to the Department of Motor Vehicles (DMV) at Walnut Creek. I passed through a small, peaceful town called Rossmoor. There were luxury cars in the parking lots and on the road, mostly driven by elderly white men and women. I also spotted a Safeway store with a vacancy sign in the window.

In Walnut Creek, I could not find the DMV. I found myself in a residential area and stopped to ask two white men for directions. One of them told me to go back to my country and learn English first. I felt humiliated and angry. I retorted that I had spoken perfectly correct English, upon which he told me that my accent was as fake as me. I drove away angrily and managed to locate the DMV where I found out that I would have to first pass an oral test and then clear the driving test. In Amritsar, my driving had never been tested. An agent had brought my licence home and charged Rs 300 extra for it.

Two weeks later, I had my work permit, social security number and driving licence, and I immediately gave up the Subway job. I could now work legally and deserved to get the legal pay. I did not want to leave McDonald's because of Rania. I really liked her.

My meals consisted almost entirely of burgers, chicken nuggets and colas, and I rapidly gained weight. I now worked in the drive-through section of McDonald's. I sometimes deliberately punched in the wrong order and when the order was cancelled, the cook gave me the new burger as per the amended order. I kept the wrongly ordered burger and ate it later. I was alone at the window, so nobody knew what I was doing. I also ate a lot of chicken nuggets by stealing a couple of pieces from several orders. I knew that unlike Indians, Americans would not count the nuggets they got. They took honesty as a given. I threw all the wrappers from the burgers and nuggets under my seat, which created a foul mess. One day, Sarfaraz saw the mess and lost her temper.

'Even a dog cleans the place he is going to sit in with his tail,' she said angrily in Punjabi. 'You have no business being so dirty.'

I was embarrassed and ashamed and apologized to her and kept my surroundings clean after that.

Sarfaraz was promoted as manager and moved to another branch of McDonald's. In her place came Becky, a tall, white, plump and pretty thirty-year-old. Rania told me that she was a divorcee with a three-year-old daughter. I often picked up and dropped Becky to her apartment because she did not drive. We got familiar with each other and sometimes kissed, but Becky never let me go any further. For me, it was a chance to show Rania that other girls found me attractive. I was hoping she would get jealous and respond to me. But Rania paid no attention to Becky and me.

One day, Becky invited me into her house for coffee when I went to drop her home. I was sure that since I had been invited home; it would lead to other things. I sat on the sofa sipping my coffee and holding her hand. Then we started kissing and my hands moved all over her body. When I reached her breasts, she caught my hand and told me to stop, but I tried to move my hand again. Becky stopped kissing me, looked angrily into my eyes and told me again to stop, but I tried to move my other hand to her breast. A stinging slap stopped me short.

'No means no!' Becky said.

Becky was a strong lady and the impact of the slap brought tears to my eyes. I felt very small, said sorry and left. In India, my experience had been that when girls said no, they didn't really want you to stop, but obviously, in America, a no meant no!

A HAPPY TIME AT ROSSMOOR

After the horribly embarrassing incident with Becky, I didn't want to work at McDonald's any more. I was afraid that she would tell Rania, with whom she was very friendly, what had happened. And the thought of Rania laughing at me, or even looking at me with dislike, was unbearable. I remembered the vacancy sign in the Safeway store window in Rossmoor, and the very next day I went there and put in my application. Safeway was a union store and I knew that they would pay $6.50 per hour.

That evening riots broke out in San Francisco and many other cities in America. A video showing two white policemen mercilessly beating up a black youth whose car they had stopped to check was aired on all TV news channels. People protested strongly and the black community took to the streets, rioting, burning and looting stores. No one could raise a hand on another in America. Even parents could not hit their children. In India, on the other hand, physical punishment was a part of the upbringing of children. The riots brought home to me the fact that even America was not without its discrimination and divisions. Here the reason was race and colour rather than religion. It was not a perfect society, as I had believed in the beginning, but had its own problems, I felt, though far less than India.

The next afternoon, I was called to the Safeway at Rossmoor for an interview. The manager, Mr Little John, was a very polite white man in his mid-thirties. He told me to start work as a trainee. I would be observed and then given a suitable job according to my abilities. I would be paid $6.50 per hour. If selected for the cashier's job, I would get $8 per hour.

I joined immediately and for the next few days, I worked in almost all the departments. Finally, Little John gave me the job of helping the elderly customers carry their groceries to their cars and sometimes delivering them to their homes. I was surprised. I had not heard of this kind of job anywhere, but Little John said that he had seen me interact with the elderly in a way the other staff members did not. He said the old people would tip me generously for helping them and for delivering their goods home. But I would have to use my own car.

I resigned from McDonald's and joined Safeway. My job included all kinds of work, from assisting cashiers to packing groceries in plastic or paper bags. In fact, a large part of my time was spent in asking 'Paper or plastic?' I carried groceries for the elderly to their cars. On the instruction of Little John, I had calling cards printed with my name and gave it to those elderly people who had trouble coming to store for their shopping. They could call and ask for me to deliver groceries to their homes.

The government had developed Rossmoor as a retirement community for the rich. The residents all lived comfortably on pensions. I was amused to see that some of the old women had young boyfriends and many old men had pretty young white girls with them. I guessed that most of the young people were with the elderly for the money. It was a materialistic society, but then, money did buy them happiness and companionship.

Nearly two-thirds of the clients of the store were elderly, retired people and most of them were single, in the middle of a divorce or widowed; there were very few couples. Almost all of them had pets and one-third of the store's sale was of pet food.

I now met many different kinds of people. I talked with the customers in the store, who had a lot of time to chat; I visited their homes when I went to deliver groceries. I realized that they often came to the store only for a change from their dull and monotonous lives. I was often late in getting back to the store when I went out for deliveries or to put bags in the cars, because the elderly were lonely and liked to talk.

I met an old German lady called Dorothy. She was almost ninety years old and had blue eyes, short, curly hair and sharp features. She must have been beautiful in her youth. Dorothy told me that she had been an interpreter for the Americans during the Second World War. She fell in love with an American soldier and when the war ended, he brought her to America and they got married. But just a year later, he died in a car accident. Ten years later she remarried and had a son, who lived in New York, and a daughter, who was settled in Los Angeles. Her second husband had also passed away three years ago, and she lived alone in Rossmoor with her two cats. I often visited her because she was the only person who showed any interest in me. She asked me about my life in America and in India before that. When I told her that I had to leave my home because of the threat of violence, she was full of sympathy. I really liked her and also had a faint hope that if she got fond of me, she might help me in some way to become a permanent resident. Getting a legal status in America was most important for me at that point.

I also met Natalie, an active sixty-year-old, who came regularly to the store and bought a lot of wine and Dunhill cigarettes. She drove a convertible and sometimes brought a boyfriend along. One day, she bought her stuff at the store, but instead of carrying it herself requested Little John with a twinkle in her eyes to have it delivered to her home. Little John called me and with a mischievous smile told me to deliver her parcels home. I wondered why Natalie had not carried her stuff with her as usual, but I looked forward to getting a good tip.

The door was open when I reached her house and Natalie was lounging on the sofa in a gown, a glass of wine in one hand and a cigarette in the other. She offered me a cigarette, which I refused (Sikhs don't smoke), and then invited me to have a glass of wine. It was 6.30 p.m. and my shift finished at 7 p.m. Half an hour could be passed off as time taken in making deliveries. So I accepted. I sat beside her and sipped my wine. I had finished two glasses when she asked me if I had any girlfriends and I remembered Becky's sharp slap. I told Natalie that I had a girlfriend, but she had cheated on me, so I dumped her. It soothed my ego to tell this lie. Natalie inched closer to me and asked if I would like a new faithful girlfriend. There was lust in her eyes and I got nervous.

I said, 'No!' and got up and walked out of the door. Within minutes I returned. Natalie smiled and began to unbutton her gown, but I simply leaned over the sofa, reached for the table beside it and grabbed my car keys, which I had left there. I ran towards the door. Natalie started laughing. I didn't know whether she was laughing at me or at herself.

Little John was standing right behind me when I turned after punching out. With a knowing smile he asked if I had received a good tip from Natalie. I said the tip was too big for me to accept. Little John shrugged and said that I should have accepted the tip; it would have helped my career. I had no idea what he meant. We smiled at each other, and I left for home. But I wondered what Little John meant.

I was now curious to know all about Little John and I asked my colleagues about him. I learnt that Little John used to be a cashier at a Safeway branch. He was close to his boss and got promoted as the manager of this branch.

The Safeway at Rossmoor was running at a loss when Little John came here. He collected population data from government offices, interacted with the people who came here to shop and concluded that most of the clients were rich retirees with pets. So he introduced all kinds of pet foods and related items and increased the variety of cereals and packaged foods that old people liked. Very soon, the store started making a profit. I realized that making me help old people carry their groceries to their cars and making home deliveries was another of Little John's clever strategies to make the store popular.

A HANDFUL OF EARTH

BR had a cousin called Ken, who was an IT engineer in Silicon Valley. He was only three years older than Jassi but very successful. He drove a Lexus and was always dressed in formal suits. On one of his visits, he asked me how I was doing. I told him that I was an assistant manager at the Safeway in Rossmoor and would soon be made manager. I did not want to appear small before Ken.

A few days later, a client dropped a bottle of ketchup in the aisles and I was cleaning up the mess. I had swept up the broken glass and was going to mop the floor when I noticed a pair of polished black leather shoes walking up the aisle. I was about to caution the person not to step into the mess, when I looked up and saw that it was Ken. I felt terribly embarrassed and very small. But Ken smiled and told me that he knew how difficult life could be in America. He said he had gone through all of this when he first came here eight years ago. He told me to be proud of myself and that no work is too small; it is only hard work that matters. This made me feel so much better about my work and myself that I vowed never ever to lie about my job again. Ken walked away, and I never learnt why he had come to Safeway.

My respect for Little John began to grow when I saw how hard he worked and how smart and observant he was. I wished to learn all I could from him. Little John was a friendly person and very willing to answer all my questions. Often, I sat in his office and asked him about work and money and other things. Little John told me that he was not a big planner; his basic theory was 'take it as it comes'. I learnt a lot about my boss. I had never felt nor suffered any racism from him or anyone else in Rossmoor. I concluded that if the majority of people in a community are good, the bad ones do not get a chance to express their negativity.

One day, when I went to Dorothy's house to deliver her groceries, I found her lying in bed with fever. There was an old white man sitting beside her. She introduced him to me as an old friend from Germany who had come to visit her. She said that this was his third visit to America in forty years, just to see her. This time she had asked him to come because she felt that she was not going to live very long. I noticed that there was a bottle filled with what looked like mud on her bedside table.

Dorothy noticed me looking curiously at the bottle and said, 'I would have liked to die in Germany, but my family is here. So, I asked my friend here to bring back a little bit of my own country to be put on my coffin when I am buried.'

I was deeply moved. I had landed in America and plunged into work. I was desperate to earn enough and find a legal status so that I could help my family back home. The homesickness I had had no time to acknowledge suddenly surfaced and I drove home through a haze of tears.

***

Little John had a drinking problem. Every once in a while, he would go on a bender, drink too much and come late for work the next day or even miss work for a few days.

Once he did not turn up for five whole days. He sent a letter to the assistant manager asking him to inform the head office that he wanted a week's leave because he was getting divorced. The news leaked out and soon all the staff knew that Little John's wife had left him because she found out that he was gay and she was already fed up with his alcoholism. I recalled that Little John had a friend, a balding gentleman, obviously gay, who visited him at the store regularly and spent time in his cabin.

I was shocked to hear of the divorce and, as a friend, felt that it was my responsibility to help Little John. So I went to his house and found him drunk, watching TV. After some small talk, I said I would like to give him some advice. Little John turned off the television and turned towards me.

'You should quit drinking. Or, if you can't do that, you should have only two small drinks a day,' I told him.

Little John heard me out in silence and then yelled, 'Nobody tells me how much I drink! I will fire you if you interfere in my personal life again!'

Hearing him shout, Little John's friend came out from the kitchen and stood quietly by the door without saying a word.

I was shaken. This was not what I had expected. In India, friends are expected to step in and help when one is in trouble. Their advice is received with warmth and gratitude. Here, I had been humiliated and almost thrown out of the house. I could not understand this.

Little John came back to work in a few days and talked to me as if nothing had happened. He told me that Dorothy had passed away two days ago, and we went to her funeral together that day, though we reached late. The coffin had already been lowered into the ground and relatives and friends were throwing handfuls of earth on it. Dorothy's old German friend sobbed as he emptied the bottle of German soil on her coffin. A few close relatives were in tears too, but the rest of the crowd was calm and quiet. I, too, felt sad. 'This way of mourning is so very different from India,' I thought. In India, people wailed loudly and beat their chests and fainted. Nothing was quiet in India!

Six months later, Jassi bought a new store in Fresno. He asked me to come with him and work there as manager.

I could not refuse. I resigned from Safeway and moved in with Jassi at Fresno. I recalled the lessons I had learnt so far in the USA: first, personal space is very important and should not be invaded, a concept unheard of in India; second, people may live their lives in any country, but when death is near, they wish to go back to their own homeland; and finally and most importantly, no work is big or small and ego is man's greatest enemy.

FRESNO

Jassi and I soon settled down in the new duplex apartment in the heart of the city. We had taken over a running grocery store called Carter Hanson. The store was twice the size of Village Market. Fresno had a mixed population of Mexicans, black Americans and Indians and a relatively smaller number of white Americans.

I was introduced as a friend and partner who held a small share in the store. We had seven employees – four Mexicans and three white Americans. I soon settled down and worked twelve hours a day, from 7 a.m., when I opened the store, to 7 p.m. My evenings were free, and I had plenty of time to explore the city. Many Sikhs lived in Fresno and I found three gurudwaras there.

Meanwhile, I fought my political asylum case myself, having convinced the judge that I did not need a lawyer. I had learnt how to ensure that the case dragged on. The court allowed a four-to-five month gap between hearings, so I was quite at ease. My work permit was renewed for another year. I now had a regular income, but not so much that I could spend it on luxuries like taking girls out. I did, however, meet many older women at the store for whom I became a young good-looking companion. We would wine and dine, dance and have sex, and I was always dropped back to my apartment.

Back home in Amritsar, my father's business was floundering. He could not work late because his factory was in a violence-prone area, and on many days, he could not go there at all and the factory remained shut. I spoke to my father regularly and became even more determined to get political asylum and bring my family to America.

I sold my old car and used the money for a down payment on a new Toyota Corolla. I lived on junk food and kept gaining weight because I did not know how to cook. I often went to an Indian restaurant called Bombay Cuisine run by a Sikh. The captain there was an Indian girl called Preeti Patel. Preeti was always dressed in a salwar kameez and was gentle and friendly. I normally reached the restaurant after work at 7.15 p.m. The dinner rush began at 8 p.m., so I was usually alone there at that time and could chat with Preeti. Preeti was twenty years old, studied at the university and worked part-time at the restaurant. She was born and brought up in America. Her parents owned two motels outside the city, and she had an elder sister and a younger brother. She knew me as Bob, part owner of a store and obviously well-to-do since I drove a new car and dressed well. My fine Hindi, clean-shaven look and the surname 'Sachdeva', a surname common to both Hindus and Sikhs, all this added to her not even having an idea that I was a Sikh.

Preeti introduced me to another Indian boy called Rakesh, a twenty-three-year-old student who sometimes ate at the restaurant. Rakesh told me that he missed his family and had no friends in America. He had a very good childhood friend, Aslam, who had also come to America to study. They lived together until the demolition of the Babri Masjid and the subsequent riots in India. Then, things changed. Aslam was so disturbed by these events that he broke off his friendship with Rakesh and got ransferred to Berkeley. Rakesh was heartbroken and could not understand why Aslam had moved away. After all, they had been friends for years, and neither he nor his family had personally demolished the masjid or supported its demolition. Rakesh wanted to be friends with me, but I did not have any time to spare for him. I knew that Rakesh was looking for a Hindu friend and I had not told him that I was a Sikh. Religion, I had learnt, was a strong divisive force.

I had been to a gurudwara in Fresno when I first came here, because a gurudwara was always a place of solace for me and, besides, Jassi had sponsored the langar for the day. After the prayers, Sikh hardliners took over the stage and started talking about a separate Sikh nation and the need for funds to fight for it. The poison of hatred was being fed to the Sikhs here. I was very upset. I had read and learned from childhood that Sikhs always lay down their lives for the protection of Hindus and other innocent people, but here appeals were being made for money to kill innocent folk. I was so disturbed that I resolved to stay away from any kind of religion.

The next hearing for political asylum came up, and I was asked questions that I found very hard to answer.

'Why did you not move to another part of India?'

'I lived in New Delhi and was attacked there.'

But I was given hard data of the number of Sikhs who lived outside Punjab and who were at the top of their careers and services in all kinds of fields. The President of India was a Sikh, as was the ex Air Chief Marshal, the ex Chief of the Army Staff and many others. I had no answer. I lied to the court that I would need some time to get proof from India that my life was in danger there because I was a Sikh. I was asked to appear with evidence in four months. I knew then that my case was weak and I was unlikely to get political asylum without very strong evidence.

A few weeks later, Ranbir uncle, my father's elder brother, called to say that he was coming to America on a business trip and I was delighted. I made all kinds of plans to entertain him and show him around. My parents called and insisted that I grow my beard and wear a turban when I went to meet Ranbir uncle two weeks later. They knew that I had cut my hair, but the rest of the family did not know. Reluctantly, I started growing my beard.

The day came when I had to receive Ranbir uncle at the Los Angeles airport. With my beard fully grown, I stood in front of the mirror with the 6 metres long black turban. I tried to tie it many times but couldn't do it properly. The turban, which was once a part of my daily routine, seemed such a struggle.

'Why am I doing this?' I wondered. 'I have not committed any crime; I just did whatever was needed to survive in a foreign country. Are my beard and turban more important than believing the real, inherent principles of my religion?'

On an impulse, I put away the turban and shaved off my beard.

My uncle did not recognize me at first, but after the look of initial shock, he made no remark at all on my clean-shaven appearance.

When I apologized for it after a while, he simply said, 'While in Rome, do as Romans do.'

I was so relieved. Ranbir uncle had travelled the world and understood the compulsions of immigrants.

A SIKH, BUT NOT ENOUGH

Ranbir uncle spent three days with me. I made the best of efforts to give him a good time, took him to several places of sightseeing and entertainment. I also drove him to San Francisco and to Concord to meet BR.

On the day of my uncle's return, while driving back to the airport, I told him that I was going to lose the political asylum case and the only way I could stay on in the US was to marry an American citizen. Ranbir uncle had many Sikh friends in America and wondered if any of them had a daughter of marriageable age. Immediately, he called some of his friends on my mobile phone – I had borrowed BR's mobile phone to show off to my uncle – and a friend in Atlanta said that another friend of his, who ran a big showroom of formal Indian clothes in New York, was looking for a match for his daughter. I could go and meet them in New York. Uncle's friend provided the contact details and a brief about the family.

After Ranbir uncle left, I called Mr Gurjeet Singh Bhatia and introduced myself. Mr Bhatia invited me to New York on the following Wednesday to meet him and his wife. If they found me suitable, I could meet their daughter.

On Wednesday, I flew to New York. I wore a smart leather jacket and Jassi's branded watch, and carried BR's mobile phone. As I entered the store, three Sikh men and two women were attending to Indian, Pakistani and Bangladeshi customers in the store. An old Sikh man sat at the billing counter. I approached a lady behind one of the counters and she asked me what I had come to buy. She was friendly and asked my name and details of my family and business. I said that I had come to meet Mr Bhatia. She was surprised and called out to her husband and I realized that she was Mrs Bhatia.

'How may I help you?' asked Mr Bhatia.

I told him that I was Bobby Sachdeva, who had spoken to him on the phone. Mr Bhatia looked surprised.

'I was expecting one Gurvinder Singh Sachdeva,' he said.

'That's me,' I smiled. 'Gurvinder Singh Sachdeva.'

Mr Bhatia's face turned red with anger.

'Sorry, this meeting is over,' he said, abruptly. I didn't know what had happened. I looked at Mrs Bhatia and then back at Mr Bhatia.

'There is no question of meeting my daughter; she will only marry a Sikh,' said Mr Bhatia angrily. 'Had I known that you are not a proper turbaned Sikh, I would not have asked you to come. You should be ashamed to introduce yourself with a Hindu name like Bobby Sachdeva!'

Mrs Bhatia looked on sympathetically and her pitying expression made me even more uncomfortable. I apologized for wasting their time and left.

I was furious and felt terribly insulted. I went straight back to the airport. I had planned to spend two days in New York meeting the girl and sightseeing in the city, but now I just wanted to get out of there. There was no flight to Fresno that day, so I went to San Francisco and spent two days by myself, mostly sitting on the shore near the Golden Gate Bridge. I visited Alcatraz, the site of an erstwhile military prison, and felt that I too was a prisoner of circumstances, especially of my religion.

When I returned to Fresno, I told Jassi that I had met the girl but did not like her. I had no desire to recount my insulting meeting with the Bhatias.

I started spending a lot of time at Bombay Cuisine talking to Preeti. She also seemed to like me. One evening, she told me that she wanted me to meet her elder sister, Himani, who was a bookkeeper at a JCPenney store. Balli madam, the owner of the restaurant had been watching my interactions with Preeti with interest. She told me that this would be my first vetting. Himani was going to get married to a Gujarati boy a month later, and her parents were keen to find a match for the younger daughter too. My heart filled with hope. I really liked Preeti, and if we got married, I would become a bona fide citizen of the USA and all my problems would be solved.

Preeti hinted to me that I should dress smartly to meet her sister. So I bought a new pair of jeans, a black shirt and new shoes. It was a sunny day, so I wore sunglasses and borrowed Jassi's sports car for the day. I felt so smart and stylish in my new clothes and the sports car, that when I went to pick up Preeti from her college, I did not get down to open the door for her. I did not wish to spoil the picture I presented! Preeti settled in and we drove to the JCPenney. I waited in the car while Preeti went in to fetch her sister. I was surprised to see that Himani was very stylish, unlike Preeti who dressed simply in Indian clothes. I got out of the car and started walking towards them. Himani was smiling mischievously.

She came close and instead of hello said in a low voice, 'Your zip is down.' I did not understand and looked at them, puzzled. They were both giggling. I said, 'Pardon?'

Himani said loudly, 'Your zip is down!'

I looked down quickly and horror of horrors, my fly was open. I had to salvage my dignity somehow and I immediately concocted a story that Jassi had challenged me to go to a public place with my fly down. I had done it and won $20. The girls laughed, and I pulled my zip up.

The three of us went to a coffee shop and Himani asked me a lot of questions about my interest in music, sports, movies and business. Then I dropped her back to the store and Preeti to her large house in a fancy part of Fresno. The meeting had gone well and I was very hopeful.

Two days later, Preeti invited me home to meet her parents at 7.30 in the evening. I reached early. Preeti, her parents and grandmother, Himani and Himani's fiancé were all there. I bowed to the elders and shook hands with the fiancé. Preeti looked nervous. Her father offered me a drink, which I refused, saying that I did not drink.

Her father smiled approval and said, 'Same here.'

He asked me about my education and I lied again, saying I was a graduate of Amritsar University. He enquired about our business in India and in America and I lied again, saying that we had two factories in India and I was a major partner in the store in Fresno. Preeti's dad looked impressed.

Then, he asked my parents names and I said, 'Jasbir Singh and Joginder Kaur.'

There was a sudden tense silence.

'But your name is Sachdeva, not Singh?'

I said, 'My full name is Gurvinder Singh Sachdeva.'

'So you are a Sikh,' said Preeti's grandmother.

'Yes, but a clean-shaven one,' I said.

'It doesn't matter,' said Preeti's father, getting up. 'You are not a Hindu. You cannot marry my daughter.'

I could hardly believe my ears. I was really angry with Preeti. Why had she put me in this situation? But she was furious with me and accused me of hiding my religion. She had no idea that I was a Sikh. She was considered the most cultured girl in her family, keeping up all the traditional values despite being born and brought up in America. And now I had embarrassed her before her whole family.

I could not understand how being cultured and keeping traditions alive prevented one from loving a person who prayed to another God.

LAS VEGAS WITH MARDA

I stopped going to Bombay Cuisine. I started thinking of other ways to get a green card. One was to have a contractual marriage with an American citizen. There were girls who charged money for this sort of thing, and many Indians had got green cards in this way. I had three older girlfriends with whom I went out after work. One of them was thirty-seven-year-old Marda, a divorcee with two teenage children. She was quite attached to me, and if I pretended to be in love with her, perhaps she would marry me. But I did not know whether such a marriage with the huge age difference would pass the scrutiny of the authorities. Besides, I did not like the idea of being committed to a tall, bulky lady, fourteen years older than me. I was still in touch with the girl in Amritsar, my phone friend, who wanted to marry me and live in America with me.

All my relatives now knew that the Bhatias in New York had rejected me because I was clean-shaven. Papa was worried because this meant that many Sikhs would not accept me as their son-in-law. He told me to find an American girl and marry her to become a citizen. I could not tell him that I was going steady with a lady whose son was of Gagan's age. So I kept Marda as a reserve option.

Marda decided to take me to Las Vegas in the middle of the week. I needed a break after the Preeti episode, so I took leave from the store and went with her to Sin City. I drove Jassi's sports car and Marda sat beside me, looking very different from usual. She had dyed her hair blonde and wore blue contact lenses and a little black dress. She looked young and sexy and behaved like a teenager, jumping and singing in the car. She had saved $1,000 for this trip. I had no money. I had to pay rent, car insurance and spend on food and gas. When I went out with Jassi, I always shared the bill with him. So I had no money to spend on luxuries. Marda knew this and never allowed me to pay for anything when I was with her.

Marda and I went to Hotel Mirage. It was too expensive for us to stay there, but we went to the hotel's casino and started playing on the 50-cent slot machines. It was the middle of a working week, so the casino was almost empty, with more staff than customers. After a while, we moved to the next aisle where there were machines with bigger stakes. We expected to win some money; instead we won two bottles of beer. The more money we spent, the more complimentary gifts we received – food coupons, wine and, finally, two nights at the hotel.

Vegas sleeps during the day and wakes up at night. So did Marda and I. During the day, we frolicked in the bedroom and slept, and at night we stepped out. We had planned to leave on Friday, but we were having so much fun that we both extended our leave by another day and stayed on.

We moved to another hotel and in the evening went off to play at another casino. This time, we decided to split up and play separately, since we had had no luck playing together. I finished off my money at a roulette table and went in search of Marda, a glass of whiskey in hand. At a flash table, I saw Harpreet Singh, a classmate of Preeti's, whom I had met once or twice. Harpreet was a student in America, and belonged from a conservative Sikh family in Chandigarh and his parents were unaware that he had cut off his hair and shaved off his beard. He was at the casino with his white girlfriend, who was sitting on his lap while he held a glass of wine in one hand and a cigarette in the other. He was startled when I greeted him. He had not expected to meet anyone he knew in Las Vegas. He knew I was a Sikh and looked very embarrassed to see me because here he was doing everything that was considered a sin in our religion and society. He introduced his girlfriend, a waitress named Diane. She appeared to be a very sharp young woman.

Marda came up and I introduced her to Harpreet and Diane. We got together as a group and spent the evening together. The next day we watched a movie, had lunch, wandered around the city and then left together in the car in the evening. We stopped for dinner on the way back and Harpreet stepped out for a smoke. I followed him, and Harpreet asked me not to tell anyone that he smoked. If his parents heard, they would be devastated. He was a bright student and after his degree he wanted to settle down in the US. I asked him how he had managed to find a white girlfriend. Harpreet said he spent a lot of money on her. 'America is a materialistic society,' he told me. 'Spend enough money and you will find a girlfriend.' I laughed. The older women who befriended me were spending money on me! I told Harpreet about my failing the political asylum case and Harpreet said he would ask Diane if she had any friend who would agree to a paper marriage.

THE AMERICAN SYSTEM OF JUSTICE

The next morning, it was back to routine in Fresno. Jassi had fired two of his white employees for insubordination, and he and I had to work fifteen to sixteen hours a day until new workers were hired. Sam told Jassi that there were two clean-shaven Sikh boys, working at a gas station in Bakersfield near Fresno, who were looking for better jobs. Jassi offered to arrange accommodation for them, provided they worked free for two weeks while they learnt the job. If he was happy with their work, he would hire them. The boys agreed. They were cousins and told the garage owner that they were going to India for their sister's wedding. The garage owner believed them because he had not learnt that Indians lie. Within two weeks, the boys had learnt to do their jobs, and Jassi hired them at a lower salary than his white workers.

Ten days later, Jassi was issued summons from the Labour Court in Fresno. His two ex-employees had filed a case of racism against him, saying that he had fired them because he wanted to hire Indians. Jassi had to appear in court five days later. He was very worried. He would be heavily penalized if found guilty.

Sam advised Jassi to collect all evidence and ask his other staff to give testimony. Jassi was afraid that the white judge would be biased against him, but his uncle assured him that judges in America were never biased. Its system of justice was fair and that is what made it such a great country. I advised Jassi to present the case himself rather than hire a lawyer. I told him that I had been fighting my asylum case myself and was confident of having my work permit extended for another year by presenting fake evidence of criminal cases in India and forged proofs of membership of the All India Sikh Students' Federation. Jassi warned me that I would be deported when the court learnt that my proofs were all forged. But I said that before that I would contract a fake marriage with an American citizen, take back my asylum case and apply for a green card. Jassi was impressed. He agreed to take my help and present the case himself in court.

I scanned the security camera footages of the past two months and put together a tape showing the two employees being negligent in their work, ignoring customers and arguing needlessly with Jassi. Our two Mexican employees agreed to testify in court because they had witnessed the carelessness and bad work of the two ex-employees.

When Jassi, Jassi's girlfriend Amy, the two Mexican employees and I reached the court, the two ex-employees were there with their lawyer. When they saw their old colleagues, they turned pale. Twenty minutes later, a handsome white man came out of the courtroom and called Mr Jas Randhawa. He asked him to come in with his lawyer. Jassi said he would be presenting the case himself with the help of his friend, Bobby, who had all the evidence. The judge invited the two of us inside.

It was large hall with a rectangular table in the centre and chairs around it. The judge gestured us towards the chairs and pulled out two chairs for us. I was amazed. I had never known any judge to be so polite. In India, even the peon of a judge would not give you the time of day, leave alone pull out a chair for you. After seating Jassi and me, the judge moved to the only chair on the other side and sat down. He read out all the allegations to Jassi, who pleaded

'Not guilty'. The video with the evidence was submitted. Jassi made it clear to the judge that he had fired the white workers for bad work. He was not a racist.

'In fact, I am in love with a half-white, half-Mexican girl and I am going to marry her next year,' he said.

This was news to me. I did not know that Jassi had proposed to Amy. The two Mexican employees were called in and their testimonies were recorded. Finally, Amy was called in for her statement. The two ex-employees and their lawyer looked beaten. They knew that the case was not going in their favour.

Two weeks later, the judgment came in favour of Jassi and the case was dismissed.

I compared the judicial system in America with that in India. In India, cases go on for years on end. Sometimes complainants die before the judgment is delivered. I was now more confident and prepared to fight my asylum case. I had got in touch with a broker working at the court in Amritsar, who provided all sorts of forged documents to litigants. For a large sum of money, he sent me forged police reports, letterheads and identity cards of the All India Sikh Students' Federation. Papa had paid the broker and collected the sealed envelopes with the documents and mailed them to me. He asked me what was in the envelopes that cost so much money, but I told him that they were documents Jassi required for his green card.

I lied to my father, but I told myself that it was just to survive and save my skin in a difficult situation.

I submitted all the forged proofs to the court. The old judge had retired and a new one had taken over. He was unfamiliar with my case. He allowed a year's extension of my work permit and set a date three months later for the next hearing, so that the American Embassy in India could verify the documents I had submitted.

Meanwhile, things were looking up in Amritsar. Papa told me that the state and central governments had together declared that they would end terrorism in Punjab. Mr K. P. S. Singh, a decorated IPS officer was appointed as the inspector general of Punjab Police. He had requested and received modern weapons, bulletproof vehicles and specially developed bulletproof tractors to fight terrorists everywhere, even in the fields. He refused the help of any paramilitary forces and said that the Punjab Police would handle the task without any outside help. He did succeed in bringing militancy under control, but a lot of innocent people died at the hands of corrupt policemen. It was a simple matter to bribe a policeman to settle land disputes by killing off a rival. All kinds of enmities were resolved this way by rich landlords.

Papa told me that much to his relief, the militant who had threatened us at the factory had been killed. But he had to shut down one of the factories because he could not handle the pressure of running two of them. I asked if the other factory was doing well. There was a brief pause and then my father said that it was breaking even. I sensed that something was amiss – my father was not telling me everything.

The next evening, I called Mummy and learnt that the factory was working only one shift and that too at a loss. Their financial situation was bad. Militants had snatched their car at gunpoint from Gagan when he was waiting for Mummy outside the doctor's clinic. I was shocked to hear this. Then it struck me – why was Mummy at the doctor's? But she said it was just a mild fever, nothing much. I immediately called my sister Lovey. She told me that Mummy had fibroids in the uterus, which were so large that they could burst any time. The doctor had advised immediate surgery; if the fibroids ruptured in the body, it could be fatal.

I felt terribly guilty. I had forgotten Diwali, Holi, birthdays and anniversaries of my family in India. I had not even bothered to ask about their physical and financial well-being. I was totally engrossed in my work and women and fun. I felt even more strongly that I needed to somehow get my family to America. The only way open to me now was to marry an American citizen. I remembered that Harpreet had promised to ask Diane if any of her friends would agree to a paper marriage. But when I called Harpreet, he said angrily that Diane had dumped him as soon as he had stopped spending money on her.

I thought quickly. On an impulse, I dressed up, put $200 in my wallet and went to the restaurant where Diane worked. It was a nice Italian restaurant and I got a table by a large window. I gave a waitress $10 to send Diane to my table and Diane came with a smile. She said that I needn't have given $10 to the waitress to call her; I could have gone to the captain and asked for her. I said that I needed to speak urgently with her. But Diane was on duty and could only meet me for drinks after dinner. She served me dinner, smiling and flirting all the while. I thought it would be easy to make her my girlfriend. I gave her a $20 tip, half my dinner bill.

A DIANE DEAL

Diane happily went out with me after dinner and took me to a restobar, where I ordered a Jack Daniels and Coke for myself, and Diane had a seafood platter with a glass of red wine. It was an expensive place and I hoped I wouldn't run out of cash.

Diane said she lived only 2 kilometres away from where we were, but 7 kilometres away from her place of work. She did not own a car because she could not save enough money for the down payment. Cars were cheap in America, but she said she preferred to spend on expensive clothes and perfumes that she loved. A year ago, she had sold her car to fund a trip to Paris with her friends. Now she planned to buy a second-hand convertible, but hadn't saved the money yet. She also complained that Harpreet was a loser who didn't know how to take care of her and her needs. I listened quietly to all this talk. I wanted to know her well before I broached the topic of marriage. I asked if Harpreet had told her of my problem.

She said, 'Yes. You want to get a permanent residency here by marrying a citizen. And you are willing to pay for it. Is that right?'

I nodded. She immediately wanted to know how much I was willing to pay. I had been uncertain how to broach the topic with Diane. But when she asked me outright, I had to come up with a number. The lowest figure I could think of was $20,000.

'No girl will be willing to do this for less than $40,000,' said Diane. 'After all, the girl will have to marry you before filing for the green card, and immigration officers will keep a watch on both of you for six months to check whether the marriage is real or not.'

I tried to negotiate. 'The girl will have free accommodation and no domestic expenses during the period.'

'That is taken for granted.'

I imagined how wonderful it would be to have my family here. Gagan was now eighteen, and I dreamt of finding a Sikh girl in America for my brother and getting him married. Gagan was not clean-shaven, so that would not be a problem. I was so taken up with these dreams that without figuring out where the money would come from, I agreed to $40,000. Diane's eyes brightened. She ordered another drink and told me that my work would be done. I eagerly asked who the girl was.

'She is sitting before you,' said Diane with a smile.

I was stunned. I shook hands with her.

'It's a deal!' I said.

I could not wait to tell Jassi the news when he got home. Jassi was delighted, but told me to be very careful and not give the girl all the money in one go.

'Twenty five per cent in advance, 25 per cent when she moves in, 25 per cent after the marriage and 25 per cent when you get the green card,' he advised.

I had to find the $40,000 first and the only way was to ask my father for it. I told him that there was no way I could win the political asylum case. My father said that a lawyer could do it for me. So I had to confess that I had been representing myself and the agent that he had paid in Amritsar had supplied forged documents for me.

'You lied to me?' Papa was furious.

I apologized profusely and Papa cooled down, but when I asked for $40,000, he said that he could not even give me $4000. For a whole minute, we were both silent.

Then Papa said, 'Ok. The money will be arranged soon. I will call you.'

I was excited, but at the back of my mind was the niggling worry about how my father would find such a sum. I told myself that Papa would borrow from his brothers or take another loan. Once I had the green card, I reassured myself, I would repay all the debts. Then I called my friend to tell his cousin – Manbeen, my phone girlfriend – that I would soon get my green card and she should wait just a little longer and we would get married.

A week passed by. Diane called me nearly everyday to say that she was planning to move to Miami and would delay it by a year only if my money was going to come through. I told her to wait for ten days.

I was very tense and found it hard to concentrate on work. It was the fourth of July weekend and the store was crowded. There was a long queue at the billing counter that I was manning. I punched in a six-pack Budweiser, peanuts and chips for a customer and the bill was $7.50. I put it all in a plastic bag, took the $10 note and returned $2.50 change. The client demanded $90 more. He said he had given me a $100 note. He called me a cheat and started shouting. Jassi was not at the store. The customers in the queue got impatient and other staff stopped work to see what was happening. There was nothing that I could do except give him $90 and diffuse the situation. The customer left, everyone got busy with work. I had very little money left after the Vegas trip and the money I had spent on Diane, but I knew that I had to repay the $90 into the till. Now, my pockets were empty.

After that, every time I worked at the cash register, I stole $2–3. At other times, I took some groceries home. In this way, I recovered my $90, but I felt very guilty. I had never done such a thing before. I was stealing from a friend who treated me like family and always helped me. I felt guilty and angry, irritable and very helpless.

A few days later, an unshaven man in dirty, stinking clothes put a 1-litre bottle of milk, a loaf of bread and a small jar of jam on the counter. The bill was $5. He took out pennies, nickels and dimes and put them on the counter.

I counted the change found it $2 short. I yelled at him to leave the stuff and get out. The man begged me to give him as much as his money would cover or to let him pay the balance the next day, but I was unmoved. The customers in the queue were watching. Two of them broke the queue and came forward. They demanded that I apologize to the man. One of them paid the $2 and told me that I had no right to speak to any human being like that. I felt embarrassed and ashamed. I apologized to the customers and to the man and gave him his groceries. I realized that the tension of getting the $40,000 was taking a toll on me.

The two incidents taught me that Americans could also cheat, but most of them were compassionate people who would fight for the dignity of a poor Mexican beggar.

The next day, much to my relief, my father called. He had arranged for $40,000 to be delivered to me in Fresno through an agent. He had raised $55,000 by selling the 1,000 square yards front lawn of our house. It was sold very cheap, because the money was needed in a hurry and there were few buyers in Amritsar.

'Bobby, be really nice to the girl you are marrying. She will fall in love with you and then it will be a real marriage and she may not accept the money,' Papa told me.

I was struck by my father's naivety. Diane was a greedy, materialistic girl, as was much of the world.

I helped Diane move in with me. I was amazed at the number of clothes, footwear, cosmetics, fashion magazines and music CDs she had. The next day, the money arrived.

I did not want Diane to see all the cash, so I stuffed it into a pair of socks and put them in a suitcase in the store. I told Jassi that I had received $20,000 and that I would give Diane $10,000.

Diane was furious.

'Such deals work on 100 per cent advance payment, and only then does the girl get married and apply for the green card for her spouse,' she said angrily. She spoke like a professional and after much argument, it was settled that I would pay her 50 per cent in advance, 25 per cent after getting the marriage certificate and 25 per cent after getting the green card. I immediately went to the storeroom and brought out another $10,000 and gave it to Diane. It did not occur to me that Diane now knew that the money was in the house.

I took Diane to the office of the residential complex to register her as a resident, so that there would be proof that we were living together before we got married. Diane carried all her relevant papers since she knew what would be required. A neighbour engaged me in conversation, so all I managed to see of her papers was her full name on her driving licence, Diane Sanders.

That evening, Diane ordered a large pizza and energy drinks for supper without asking me and made me pay for it. We could not finish the pizza or the drinks even after Jassi shared them when he came home. Diane went off to her room, and I complained to Jassi that she had ordered too much food and I could not afford such waste.

Jassi smiled, 'This is just the beginning, my friend. Diane will try to extract money from you on every little pretext,' he cautioned me. 'The whole deal will cost you at least $50,000. You have done a background check on her, haven't you?'

I had not even thought of it. I decided to meet Harpreet the next day.

Later that night, I went up to my room and found Diane lying in bed with her headphones on. I sat next to her.

She stared angrily at me, took off her headphones and demanded, 'What the hell are you doing in my bed?'

'It is my bed, not yours.'

She switched off her music and ordered me out of the room.

'Remember, no sex,' she said very firmly.

This was unexpected. I picked up my pillow and sheet and knocked on Jassi's door.

Jassi said, 'Come on in,' as if he had been expecting me and moved to one side of the bed.

I slid into the other side and pretended to sleep.

I was usually up at 6 a.m. and dressed and at the store just before 7 a.m. But, that night, it was 4 a.m. before I finally fell asleep. I woke up with a start at 6.45 a.m. and had just enough time to brush my teeth, dress and rush off to open the store.

That evening, I went to meet Harpreet. I told him about my deal with Diane. Harpreet listened to me in silence.

'You should have talked to me before rushing off to see Diane,' he said. 'She is mercenary, selfish and shrewd, and she is into drugs.'

He told me that Diane was a divorcee with a two-year-old daughter, who lived with her mother. Her ex-husband paid maintenance for her and the child, because she declared only her salary as a waitress, not the considerable amount that she received as tips. Harpreet said that it was his good fortune that he realized the truth about Diane and stopped spending all his money on her.

'Forget the $20,000 that you have given her and ask her to leave the house immediately,' he told me. 'Diane is a huge mistake and the sooner you get rid of her, the better.'

I was horrified. All the way home, I regretted that I had not spoken to Harpreet before rushing to Diane. I decided that I would return the balance $20,000 to my father and concentrate on the asylum case. If I could get another year's extension, I would find some other way of getting a green card.

Diane was in her room when I got home, but I did not want to see her. I sat before the TV in the living room, feeling very upset. I did not even eat any dinner. Jassi came home at 10 p.m. I could not bear to meet his eyes. But Jassi told me that he had run a background check on Diane and found that she was a divorcee with a two-year-old daughter. I then told Jassi everything that Harpreet had told me. Jassi agreed that I should get rid of Diane, but he told me that it would have to be done cleverly. A girl like her could accuse me of sexual assault or forcible sex. He also said that I was lucky I would get rid of her for just $10,000. I was filled with guilt and remorse. My father had to sell a part of their house, just because I had been so impulsive and impatient and not paused to think before acting. Then there was the guilt of lying to Jassi about the actual amount I had given to Diane.

Jassi, BR and I thought of several plans to get rid of Diane, but none of them seemed fool proof. Meanwhile, Diane had given up her job and spent all day at home. In the evenings, she went out with her friends. Sometimes, she borrowed my car. She often asked me to join her, but I knew that she only wanted me along to pay the bills, so I declined. I reluctantly gave her whatever money she asked for.

One day, Diane asked Jassi for his sports car to drive to Yosemite National Park. Jassi refused. Diane said that she was only asking to borrow it for a few hours not taking it forever. Jassi understood the threat behind the words, and for my sake, he let her take the car. That night, Diane came home drunk. The next morning, Jassi saw his favourite car parked askew with the front bumper and right headlight broken. I had already seen the car when I had gone to open the store. I had pulled out $1,000 from the suitcase, and when Jassi got there, I offered him the $1,000 for the repair of the car. Jassi refused to take it, since insurance would cover the repairs.

Now, I had had enough. I decided to tell Diane to leave right away. Jassi warned me again to be careful. But when I reached home that evening, Diane had disappeared. All her things were gone. I breathed a sigh of relief and went to the store to return the $1,000 to my suitcase. To my utter shock and dismay, Diane had got there first. All my money, $17000, was gone. Almost in tears, I called Jassi, who simply laughed and said, 'You are lucky. You saved $1,000!'

I was devastated. It was by selling off a part of my home that the money had been raised. My father had assumed that the American girl was a nice human being who would fall in love with me. I always had faith in human beings and believed every situation could turn positive. How would I ever tell Papa about Diane and the loss of the money?

I decided I had to find Diane and get my money back. Her old building society did not know where she was, but they gave me her ex-husband's address. I met him, but he only sent cheques to her bank account every month; he had no idea where she was. I went to Harpreet, who gave me one of Diane's friend's telephone number. The friend sounded like a drug addict. She knew all about me and also that Diane had run away with my money. She did not know where Diane was, but she offered to marry me and get me a green card for only $20,000. I banged the phone down.

Three days later, there was a call for me from Miami. A heavy male voice warned me not to chase Diane or else she would lodge a complaint of rape and drug possession against me. I was terrified and said that I was not interested in getting my money back and disconnected.

Finally, I had to accept that the money was gone, but I was weighed down with guilt. I could not bring myself to tell my father that I had lost such a large sum of money. I avoided my father's calls and made Jassi answer the phone and make some excuse to my father for not talking to him. However, I kept in touch with my mother. The guilt ate away at me and I could hardly eat or sleep. I finally decided to leave Fresno and go back to Concord. I needed some major change to shake myself out of the Diane-inflicted depression. Jassi tried to reason with me, but I was adamant. Two weeks later, I was packing all my stuff to take back to Concord, when the phone rang. It was my mother. She said that they had a good marriage proposal for me, because she had let it be known that I was returning to India.

'Why are you saying that I am coming back?' I asked angrily.

She said that it was her gut feeling. And she started crying.

I was quiet, listening to her sobs, when I heard my father's voice. Papa had taken the phone from my mother. I didn't know what to say, so I just said hello and kept quiet. Papa said, 'Bobby, don't worry about the money and the betrayal of that *daayan*.'

I started laughing. My father could not pronounce 'Diane' and had used a word that meant 'witch' in Hindi. It was just so apt! Within minutes, my father had consoled me and lightened my burden of guilt.

When I had started avoiding his calls, Papa had first got upset and then concerned. He had rung Jassi, who had told him the whole sorry story. I was greatly relieved that my father knew what had happened.

'Money is just a thing; it comes and it goes,' he said to me. 'There is no point crying too much over it.'

Normalcy was returning to Punjab now, and the business was bound to improve. Papa told me to come back to India. But I said I wanted to make one more attempt to get a green card.

A DIFFERENT AMERICA

The next day, my friend from India called to say that he had learnt that I was returning to India and so his uncle had sent a proposal on behalf of Manbeen to my parents. I realized that it was this proposal that my mother had received. I told my friend that I was not coming back and his cousin should accept another proposal and get married. I immediately called my mother and shouted at her to stop spreading rumours of my return.

She said, 'My heart says you are coming back.'

I just hung up. I left Jassi and Fresno with a heavy heart.

I generally drove fast and had received three tickets for speeding till now. But that day I drove as slowly as I could. I was in no hurry to reach Concord. I was so depressed that I did not want to go anywhere. My American dream was in tatters, and I was tired of living like a gypsy. I wished I had a home and a family. BR was waiting for me. I finally reached late at night after losing my way and spending nearly an hour trying to find BR's new house.

BR was worried. The distance from Fresno was just about four hours, but I had taken eight hours to get there.

I was unusually quiet. BR asked me why I was so late, but I simply said that I had stopped for a lazy lunch. Actually, I had just picked up a sandwich from a gas station.

The night too, I slept badly and woke up late. BR had already gone to work and left a note asking me to call at the store. I called and BR told me that the fridge was full of frozen food and I should help myself to it.

That afternoon I went out to look for work. I saw a lot of job placement signs outside stores and offices. The Gulf War was over and the economy was picking up under Bill Clinton. The anger against Arabs was not so visible any more. I applied for seven jobs. I no longer faced the kind of bias that I had encountered when I first came, probably because I no longer had the look of a new immigrant. I had a confident, American body language. But I did not get any good job that paid at least $8–$9 an hour. I was being offered only $5–$6 per hour, which was not enough to meet my expenses.

I received a call from a large store for the job of a cashier and was asked to come for an interview at 10 a.m. I reached at 10.15 a.m. because I got up late. The receptionist refused to send me in, even though I made all kinds of excuses.

'Sorry,' she said. 'Try again next time.' I learnt that unlike India, punctuality was non-negotiable in America. I decided to apply for night jobs, the graveyard shift, because I was sleeping so badly and it was hard for me to wake up early in the morning.

Kaiser Hospital was recruiting security guards for their new branch in Oakland in the San Francisco Bay area.

One of the conditions was that the selected candidate should be willing to move to a different town in California. Without much thought, I applied. I was called for an interview, and I made sure I was there well before time. The manager was a tall, strong black man, who scrutinized all my papers and asked me to come in a tracksuit the next afternoon for a physical test. I did not have a tracksuit and did not want to spend on an expensive one. There were no clearance sales on, but I spotted an ad for a flea market in a town nearby.

The next morning I drove there, but since I could not read maps and my sense of direction was poor, I could not find the place where the flea market was being held. But I spotted a garage sale being held at a house I was passing and stopped to look in. I found a tracksuit, a size small, but it stretched over my large body. Though I had lost 10 kilos in the past couple of months, I was still bulky. I also found a good pair of sports shoes that fit me comfortably. I paid for the clothes and shoes and also asked the man where he was moving. The man said that he was recently divorced and was now moving to a new town with his new girlfriend.

As I headed for the security company office, I reflected on the American way of life – getting divorced, having affairs, changing jobs, moving from place to place – Americans seemed to get bored very easily. They always wanted excitement, new things in their lives.

I reached for my test just in time and had two minutes to get into my tracksuit. It hugged my body, especially the tummy and bums, but enhanced my height. I easily passed the physical fitness test and was handed a book, *Duties of American Citizens and Bylaws for Security Guard Officers*. I had to read it and pass a written test based on it.

I learnt a lot from the book. The American Constitution gave every citizen the right to self-defence and security officers could act as law officers under special circumstances. I passed the exam and the drug tests and medical examination for communicable diseases. According to the manager, many young boys failed these tests because they used drugs from a young age.

On the following Monday, at 7 p.m., I drove down to Oakland – known for its street violence and drugs – to start my first day at work. I received a uniform, a badge, a baton and a flashlight, and was directed to start work at the back gate of the hospital. I had expected to work inside the hospital, but my duty was to prevent intruders from entering the hospital from the back gate. I was warned that there were a lot of drug addicts around at night and they often tried to enter the hospital grounds from the back gate to find a secluded spot. I was also warned that they could be violent. I was scared, but duty is duty and off I went to do my job.

The uniform, badge and baton made me look like a policeman, but I was uncomfortable in this role, that too in the insecure environment of Oakland. It was not the America I had known so far. This was a crime-infested area, and in the hospital, I saw drug addicts, victims of drunk-driving accidents and stabbing, and people injured in gang wars and domestic violence every night.

One night, while I was on duty, two drug addicts tried to break open the back gate and enter the hospital grounds. I ran towards them and shouted that they should immediately go away or I would charge at them with the baton. The two young boys looked at me and laughed. I felt helpless. What would I do with my little baton? I called the security in-charge, Mr Miguel, on my walkie-talkie. Mr Miguel came running and yelled at the druggies to leave at once. And they did.

Mr Miguel was a tall, muscular, bearded man. He looked imposing in his uniform. He told me that I needed a more aggressive body language and a rougher tone of voice to scare intruders. I felt that it was Mr Miguel's beard that made all the difference and I decided to grow one to get a more commanding look. Mr Miguel agreed that a beard would help. He also said that many security officers gave up the job because it was a tough and scary area. He had recommended to his company that two guards should be posted at the back gate.

Even after three weeks at the job, I was always tense and afraid. Throughout the night, I heard police sirens and ambulances speeding through the streets, indicating some accident somewhere. I often saw gangsters, prostitutes, drug peddlers and other low life roaming the streets outside the back gate. It just added to my sense of anxiety and unease.

'I'M COMING HOME'

The next court date came up. I had to appear before the judge and record my final statement. After that, at the following final hearing, the judge would give his verdict. I had nothing new to say and no new documents to submit. I knew that the documents I had submitted earlier would prove to be forged and I would be deported. My hearing was at 10 a.m. in San Francisco, very close to Oakland. So, I decided to drive there straight from work. I had my turban, headscarf and some pins in the car. After duty, I showered and then requested Mr Miguel, who happened to be there, to hold one end of my 6-metres long turban. I told him that I had to go to a wedding where a Sikh boy was marrying a white girl. Mr Miguel had worked in Yuba City in California, which had a lot of Sikhs. He was familiar with them and told me that he had been witness to many fights at Sikh weddings. One clean-shaven Sikh groom, who was marrying a white girl, had attacked a guest with the ceremonial sword that was part of the formal dress of a Sikh groom. The guest had made some comment about the groom's family back in Punjab to which he took umbrage. The groom was arrested, but got bail in a couple of days since the guest had to withdraw the case due to pressure from his family. He even had to apologize to the groom, in spite of the fact that he was the one who had a 14-inch cut down his arm!

I was impressed with Mr Miguel's knowledge of my community and also embarrassed that he had such a bad impression of it. But Mr Miguel said that he had selected me for the job because I was a Sikh, and Sikhs were always courageous and kind-hearted. That made me proud. It was whiskey and inflated egos that were the bane of Sikhs, I concluded.

I reached the court well before time. I was tired and fell asleep in the chair in the waiting room, until an old lady woke me up just before 10 a.m. and told me that I was in court not in my bedroom. I apologized and went to wash my face. I was called into the courtroom soon after.

Once again, I told the judge that I was presenting my own case and had no lawyer. The report from India about my documents had not come. The government attorney told the judge that even if the documents were genuine, there was no case for granting me political asylum. The state of Punjab was almost normal now and the government had announced special packages to help revive the economy. The Punjab administration had a majority of Sikhs in it. I might be attacked here for wearing a turban, the attorney said, but not in Amritsar. I had nothing to say, except that my family had suffered religious violence from 1947 to 1984 and continued to do so. The judge said that he sympathized with me but the law of the land must be upheld and justice delivered. He would give his verdict after two months.

I was now sure that there was no way I could continue to live in America. I had tried to marry Preeti, but her family had refused because I belonged to a different religion; the

Sikh family in New York had rejected me because I did not wear a turban; and then there was Diane...

I consulted BR, who offered to lend me money for a paper marriage and even offered to find a girl, but I had already lost my father's money; I did not want to risk my friend's money as well. Sam said that I could appeal to the higher courts after the lower court rejected my case. That would certainly buy me another year or two. Meanwhile, I could find a Sikh girl willing to marry me, especially since I now wore a turban again. I was not convinced. Sam told me that I was smart and good-looking and an American girl would fall in love with me and I could marry her and solve my problems. Or the American government might reintroduce the immigration scheme for illegal immigrants and legalize those who had been living here for a long time. And if all else failed, I could just live under the radar as an illegal immigrant.

None of these ideas appealed to me. I was homesick. I wanted to be with my parents, celebrate Holi and Diwali at home, and attend the weddings of my friends and cousins, many of whom had got married while I was in America. I was making good money but was always tense and fearful. If anything happened to me, my family would be shattered. The ugly face of America that I had seen in Oakland had deeply disturbed me.

I called my father and told him that my political asylum case would most likely be rejected. Papa asked me to return to India. Punjab was almost normal again and the few militants around would also be arrested. But I told him that I would go to Canada, which legally accepted immigrants. Papa did not argue.

'Do whatever you want to,' he told me.

I could not decide what to do. A week later my mother called. She asked how I was, and I could not hold myself back. I poured my heart out. I told her that I was unhappy with my job, it was unsafe and I had to drive a long distance to work since Oakland was no place to live in. Mummy started sobbing. She said that I should return to India immediately. She told me that their business was almost defunct, and they were living on the money left over from the sale of the lawn. When that money finished, there would be nothing because the bank had a lien on the factory and the house. She was inconsolable. With a sinking heart I listened to her sobs.

I had made up my mind and said, 'I am coming back,' and Mummy stopped mid-sob.

But I had disconnected.

Now I had no uncertainty or tension. I had decided on a course of action and I knew in my heart that it was the right and the only thing to do. I immediately resigned from my job. Mr Miguel was furious. I had signed a one-year contract. He threatened to sue me.

'Ok, sue me,' I retorted and cut the call.

I called BR and told him I was going back to India. BR was astonished, but he knew my penchant for sudden, impulsive decisions. Jassi told me that they would find some way for me to stay on in America, but I just wanted to go home.

I called Papa at the factory, but there was no answer. My mother called back, weeping tears of happiness and wanting to know when I would be back.

'In ten days,' I said, without thinking.

I asked why my father was not answering the factory phone, and she told me that there were no orders and since three days the factory was closed. I spoke to my father who asked if I needed money for my ticket and to buy gifts for people in India. But I believed that I could raise enough money from selling all my household stuff. My mother told me that I had to bring gifts for every member of the extended family because I was returning from America and that was the done thing.

I needed a garage where I could hold a sale of all my things – car, TV, music system, electronics and furniture. BR lived in an apartment, but Sam lived in a large house. I asked him if I could hold the sale in his garage and Sam agreed but wondered why I was selling all my things. When he heard that I was leaving, he was shocked.

He said, 'But Bobby, I have told you so many ways in which you can stay.'

'My family needs me more than America does,' I replied.

Almost all of my things got sold, except my car and some used clothes and other small things. I loaded it all in the car and donated it to a charity at a church. Then I drove the car to a used car dealership and sold it for $6,500. I had hoped to get $7,500, but I had no time to show the car to buyers and took what the dealer offered.

On Monday morning, I called a travel agent. It was close to Diwali and tickets to New Delhi were very expensive, nevertheless I bought a British Airways ticket for $1,650. Now all that was left was to buy the gifts. I spent more than $2,000 on them over two days. Then I treated myself to a full body massage at a spa. It was as if I was getting rid of all the aches and tensions of my life in America. In the evening, I went out for farewell drinks and dinner with BR.

The next morning, just as I was getting ready to leave for the airport, my friend from Amritsar called. He had learnt from my mother that I was returning and he was furious. Just a month ago, I had told him that I was never coming back, and so he had advised his cousin, Manbeen, to accept one of the many proposals that she was receiving. She had got engaged only a week ago. I tried to explain to him that it had been a sudden decision, but my friend did not believe me and disconnected.

I was not bothered by the news of Manbeen's engagement. I was excited about meeting my family and bringing the factory back to life. The only thing I was sad about was leaving BR and Jassi. They had been the truest of friends to me; in fact, they had been my family for three years.

BR and Sam dropped me to the airport. They gave me gifts. When BR hugged me and said goodbye, we both had tears in our eyes.

AMRITSAR REJUVENATED

The overhead lights came on and the announcement that my connecting flight from San Francisco to New Delhi via London was about to land at Heathrow broke into my long reverie and reminded me that I was halfway home to India, to my parents, to Amritsar.

There were many Sikhs, turbaned and clean-shaven, working at the airport. They were immigration officers, security staff, customs officials, cargo handlers and sanitation workers. There were many Indian travellers as well.

I was surprised to see that the Indians worked in complete harmony with the English. It was only forty-seven years since the British had left India after ruling there for 200 years. Only one new generation had grown up since then, and they had managed to change their mindset and accept those they'd once ruled as their equals.

When perceptions change, then mindsets also change, I realized.

I finally fell asleep on the flight to New Delhi and woke up only an hour before landing. I had to put on my turban, because I could not land in Delhi without it. My family and relatives knew that I was clean-shaven now, but I couldn't present myself to them without a turban. For the same I had grown my beard to fake my identity. Besides, fingers would be pointed at my family and I didn't want that. So, I pulled out the turban from my handbag and went in search of a Sikh who would help me put it on. An elderly Sikh gentleman was fast asleep and his wife refused to help me, saying she could only help her husband and not a stranger. I thought it was a very backward mode of thinking for a lady who was flying from London to Delhi. Another Sikh man in the front row would have helped me, but the seat belt sign flashed on just then and he apologized and refused to get up and come to the back of the plane. Finally, a white airhostess, who came up to ask me to go back to my seat understood my predicament and agreed to help me. Her husband's best friend was a Sikh policeman in England and she knew how much pride Sikhs vested in their turban. She held one end of it and I tied it quickly, though not very neatly, and I returned to my seat.

When I reached New Delhi, the immigration officer kept turning the pages of my passport. He had found a four-month US visa, but I was returning after three years.

'Did you stay there illegally?' he asked belligerently.

I took out my wallet, showed him my work permit and told him that I had got a job and my employer had applied for my work permit. I had lived and worked in the USA legally. The officer was not convinced, so I showed him my social security card and driving licence, and only then did he allow me to go.

I was overjoyed to see Papa, Mummy, Gagan, Paramjit uncle and his daughter waiting to receive me. It was an emotional reunion. Gagan was now more than 6 feet tall, had a moustache and beard, and was wearing a turban! Mummy looked the same, but Papa was thinner and looked older than his age. My cousin had grown into a beautiful young lady.

Even Delhi had changed in three years. Wider and better roads, flyovers, new buses, bigger and better cars, and it was much cleaner than before. Papa and Uncle told me that it was because of the opening up of the economy and all the foreign investments coming in. Besides, it was the capital city of India and so it received the maximum benefits of growth. Restrictions on import and export had been lifted and business was booming. But there were also beggars and slums, and I felt that they just did not fit into India's growth story. The rich were richer, but the poor still remained in their hovels.

A lavish dinner was served at Uncle's house. Paramjit uncle offered me a drink. I looked questioningly at Papa; he smiled and I accepted the drink. Mummy noticed and immediately objected, but Uncle told her that I was now a grown man and must have been drinking with girlfriends in America. Everyone grinned; I just focussed on the scotch.

The next morning, on the new, super-fast 'Shatabdi' train to Amritsar, I sat with Mummy, while Papa and Gagan sat across the aisle. Mummy told me about all the problems that Papa had faced. One of the factories had to be closed down, while the other was on the verge of closure unless revived immediately. There were neither trained staff nor labour and no orders. Almost $4,000 of the money from the sale of the lawn had gone in routine day-to-day expenses. And, much to my amazement, they were building rooms on the first floor for me.

'What is wrong with my old room?' I asked.

'You cannot live in your old room when you are married,' Mummy said with a smile.

I explained to her that it was imperative for me to get the factories up and running, only then would I think of marriage. But she said that business and marriage were two different things and should not be confused with each other. The conversation ended there.

The train rolled into Amritsar and imagine my surprise and delight when I saw the station platform full of relatives and friends! Ranbir uncle and his family, my sisters and their families and many of my friends were all there. As I got into a car, I asked Sandeep Gupta why everyone had come in the middle of a working day to receive me.

'Because you are now "America returned",' he said with a smile.

It made no sense to me.

As we drove home, I saw how much Amritsar had changed. There was no CRPF anywhere and the police barricades were all gone. The air of tension and fear had disappeared. But the city looked worn and dilapidated. The roads were in a bad shape, traffic signals did not work and garbage was piled up in many places. Heavy vehicles occupied most of the roads and left little place for cars and scooters. It was a complete contrast to Delhi. Peace had enabled progress in Delhi. However, the people of Punjab were hardworking, and now that violence had been rooted out, they would certainly prosper.

Home looked different too. A 10-foot wall separated the house from its lawn. The main gate had a big lock on it and the entrance had been shifted to the side lane. The house looked much smaller. The car that Gagan drove had been borrowed from our uncle. With a hard shock, I realized that my dream of becoming an American citizen had cost my family very dearly. I felt terribly, terribly guilty. But no one blamed me. They were just happy that I was back home. My sisters had prepared a lavish lunch and my cousins joined us.

That evening I went out with my friends. Some of them were married, some engaged. Only a couple of them and I were single. We all had drinks and dinner together and talked about wives, fiancées and business. The city was coming to life again. We stayed out late, which itself was a sign that the city was now safe.

I woke up at 7 a.m., had breakfast and left for the factory on Papa's scooter. It was difficult to ride because for three years I had only driven cars, and that too on the right-hand side in America. The dusty and potholed roads were hard to bear. On the way, I saw a new Maruti car showroom and stopped to ask the price of a basic model. I could get a discounted price since it was almost the end of the year and the year of manufacture would change in January. But even the discounted price was much higher than the cost of luxury cars in America. However, I calculated that if I put together the money that I had brought back and the sum that was left over from the sale of the lawn, there was enough money to buy the car, finish the construction of the rooms on the first floor and invest in the factory. I signed the required documents and ordered a brand-new car without consulting Papa. To be honest, it never occurred to me to ask him. I had been making my own decisions for three years now. I was going to drive home a new car that evening.

At the factory, I was shocked to see that besides the gatekeeper, supervisor and accountant, there were only five workers. The gatekeeper was new and stopped me at the entrance, but the supervisor saw me, came running up and escorted me into the factory. My heart sank when I saw that more than half the machines were rusting and covered with cobwebs. Obviously, they had been out of use for a long time. There wasn't enough raw material to feed even the few machines that were running. I checked the quality of the fabrics on the weaving machines and found lots of defects. The supervisor told me that there were only nine workers left and only five were on the job because there was not enough raw material for nine people to work with.

With a sinking heart, I went into the rubber factory. It was in a far worse condition. It had been shut down, and the roof had holes and pigeons and sparrows had made nests in the walls. Insects and rats ran on the floors and over the machines. There was a foul smell everywhere. I could not stay there for long and went into the office. There too, paint was peeling from the walls, the furniture was scratched and shabby and the windowpanes dirty. How had the business deteriorated so much?

The supervisor had been with us for a long time. He told me that after I left for America, Papa found it hard to handle the pressure of running the business. There was shortage of finance, threats from militants, power cuts, unavailability of raw materials. Besides, he could not stay at the factory for long because of the unsafe situation. Consequently, the quality of the reclaimed rubber deteriorated and their biggest client stopped buying from them, and soon the rubber factory had to be closed down. But the supervisor hoped that now that I was back, the business would soon be revived.

I reassured him that not only would the textile factory be revived but also that I intended to restart the rubber factory. I told him to hire more workers and start cleaning the machines in the rubber factory.

Papa called to say that he would soon be there with lunch for me. He had borrowed Ranbir uncle's car. But I asked him to go to the bank instead and reopen the rubber factory account. He agreed without asking any questions.

I spent the whole day at the factory and took charge of things. I called a mechanic and a technician and asked them to fix the machinery that required repairs. I told the supervisor to get forms for the reinstatement of the electricity connection to the rubber factory and to resume the old sales tax number of the rubber factory. I called Gagan and gave him the number that unlocked my briefcase and told him to take the dollars from it and convert them to rupees at one of the money changers near the railway station. Gagan converted the dollars and handed the Rs 2 lakh to the supervisor who brought it to me at the factory.

In the evening, I picked up the new Maruti car and drove home with difficulty. I was no longer used to driving on the left. The supervisor rode behind me on the scooter that I had driven to the factory that morning. When we reached home, I gave him a gift of Rs 200 and Rs 20 for his fare back. It was 7 p.m. and everyone was inside the house. No one had seen me come in the new car. Mummy had made fried snacks and sweets for me, but I just had a piece of fried chicken and refused the rest. I had to lose weight. Mummy, of course, felt that I did not need to lose any weight. Indian mothers express their love through food!

We were all having tea when I gently put the beribboned car keys on the table. Gagan and Mummy first looked puzzled, then looked at my face and exclaimed in delight, but Papa was furious.

'I know you can't manage without a car now, but I had a second-hand car in mind,' he said. 'It would have cost so much less.'

I explained to him that a new car would be maintenance free and last for at least five years. Papa cooled down, though he was not convinced. And we all went for drive in the new car.

That evening my cousins came over for dinner. They wanted to know all about my experiences in America. I did not tell them that I had worked as a dishwasher or a guard.

For Indians, these are menial jobs for the lower castes. I told them instead that I started my first job as ADC and was then promoted to DC. My cousins did not understand what this meant but were impressed. However, Gagan asked that night what these terms meant.

I said gravely, 'I was the additional dish cleaner and then dish cleaner in McDonald's!'

We both burst out laughing.

I WILL ALWAYS BE THERE FOR YOU

The next morning when we reached the factory, Papa was very surprised to see the mechanic and the technician working on the machines. In the rubber factory, too, there were workers sweeping and washing the floor and walls. The supervisor had got the forms for the electricity connection and the sales tax registration, and I started filling them out. Papa looked on in complete silence. I knew there was a storm brewing. At lunchtime, he demanded to know who had ordered all this restoration work. He yelled at me for spending so much money on the car and the factory. He said he had far more experience and could have done it all for half the money that I was spending. I lost my temper.

'I have used my own money to buy the car and am spending my own money on the two factories. Only when I run out of it will I touch your money,' I told him. 'And it is because of your disorganized way of running the business that one factory had to be closed and the other is on the verge of closure. You just don't know how to be professional. You should have concentrated on maintaining accounts and stock registers and selling your products at good prices and buying raw materials at low cost. Instead, you waste time on all kinds of petty things that should be delegated to your staff.'

I had never ever spoken like this to Papa and he bristled with anger.

'I am still the man of the house,' he said, 'and you better remember that and obey me.'

'I am already doing you a favour by growing my hair and beard and wearing a turban, which I now find very uncomfortable,' I retorted. 'But the factories, I will handle them my way. My priority is to revive the business. You should concentrate on the construction of the first floor and the renovation at home.'

I had drawn the battle line, but Papa calmed down and we finally agreed that this was the best way to go forward.

My grandfather had prostrate cancer and the doctors had warned the family that he might not survive for more than six months. When I went to see him, I found him very weak, but he was happy to see me after such a long time. I spent the next few days meeting all my relatives and basking in the affection showered on me.

My cousin Tarun's factory was close to mine and he helped me hire good staff and workers. He was also able to help me get the best technology and the people required to restart the factory. I put all my money and borrowed some more to get both the factories running in a single shift. I set aside the money required for the construction at home, and took the rest from Papa for the factory. I managed to get raw materials at a low price, improved the quality of our product and packaged it well. That soon brought me more customers and better prices. My 'America Returned' tag was a big draw, since people were still impressed by someone who had lived and worked in the USA. Even girls were attracted by it.

In the beginning, many girls called me at home and at the factory. But I brushed them all off, and slowly they stopped calling. I had realized that money was very important for a dignified life. On the other hand, I found religion and religious ceremonies a total waste of precious time. However, I kept these views to myself because I knew that in India, religion was intrinsic to daily life and no one would give up their daily prayers or their visits to their shrines, certainly not the Sikhs.

I no longer prayed. Even on religious holidays, I was at the factory. I knew that no religion would help me in a crisis – only money would. If I managed to make enough money, many problems could be sorted out. The rest could be solved through contacts with the right people. And those contacts could be developed with money.

I had both the factories up and running smoothly in the day shift. The construction work at home was almost done, and Papa started coming regularly to the factory. But

I was most unhappy with Papa's interference in the day-to-day work. He was used to old-fashioned ways, whereas I wanted a professionally run unit and had hired a full team of technical staff and accountants, and a separate supervisor for the rubber factory. Papa gave his own orders to the staff, and they were confused about who they should obey. I gave instructions to the staff in the morning and then asked for results at the end of the day. Papa worked with the staff and also stood around watching them work, instead of leaving them to it and sitting in the office. The tension between us grew.

On 1 January 1994, I woke up late after a very enjoyable New Year's Eve with my friends. I was especially happy because BR was returning to Amritsar that day for good. He had never adapted to the American way of life and just wanted to come home.

My new year's resolution was to get rid of all the old machines from both the factories and buy modern new ones with a bank loan. Papa disagreed. He did not want to take any loan. He said he could modify the old machines to produce the kind of quality that I wanted. A cold war had started between us.

I placed an order for a new machine for the rubber factory and paid an advance for it. When Papa heard this, he went straight to the manufacturer, cancelled the order and took back the advance money without saying a word to me. I came to know this only when I went to check if the machine was going to be delivered as per schedule. I felt like a fool enquiring about my machine when my own father had cancelled the order. I came home in a rage and refused to talk to anybody. Papa tried hard to explain to me that he had cancelled the order only to save our hard-earned money. He had already bought steel with the money he had taken back and would modify the old machines. I said nothing.

The next morning, I did not get out of bed till 10 a.m. Gagan went to college and Papa was all dressed to go to work. Finally, Mummy came to wake me up. I went into the bathroom and did not come out for an hour. My breakfast was cold. Mummy came to call me again, and I said that I would not go to the factory. She said that Papa was waiting for me.

'Tell him that it is his factory; he can run it,' I said. 'It is not my factory; I will not work there.'

Papa went alone to work that day and the next. I spent the days at home and evenings with the two Sandeep Guptas and with my cousins.

On Monday, the factory was closed and Papa decided to talk to me. I tried to avoid meeting him by keeping to my room, but in the afternoon I had to come out because Mummy had refused to serve me breakfast in my room and now I was very hungry. Lunch was laid out on the dining table and Papa was waiting for me. Mummy served us hot chapatis. I kept sitting sullenly and refused to look at Papa.

Finally, he asked, 'What do you want me to do?'

'I respect you and appreciate all the hard work you have done,' I replied, 'but my way of doing things is different from yours. I cannot work with you, and I do not want you to interfere in my work or my decisions.'

'You should have consulted me before ordering the new machine,' Papa said.

'I consulted a technical person.'

'So, what do you want from me?'

'I will not go to the factory with you. It's either you or I – only one of us can work there. If I am to run the factories, then you have to stop coming there.'

Papa was quiet for a minute. Then he said that he would tell me his decision the next morning. We were both tense all day.

The next morning, he came to the breakfast table and told me that he would no longer go to the factory and that I could run them both. I had been feeling rather remorseful for being so blunt and rude to him the day before, but I felt it was necessary to tackle the issue head on.

I just nodded my head. After about fifteen minutes, I said gruffly, 'I will go to the factory. But I intend to start the night shift soon, and I will need your support.'

Papa smiled. 'I will always be there for you.'

That day neither of us went to the factory. We needed to digest and come to terms with this major decision. The next day I went alone to the factory. I missed Papa, but I knew that this was one tough step that needed to be taken. I wanted to run the business in a new, professional way. Like Papa, I liked to make my own decisions myself. And two people with the same headstrong nature could not work together.

I decided to immediately increase productivity by running the factories for twenty-four hours in two shifts. I also reordered the new machinery. I had many orders in hand now. I knew that it was the right time to expand the business. Militancy had ended in Punjab and the Indian economy was growing. The quality of our rubber and cotton canvas cloth had improved, and I now supplied to many new clients including my cousin Tarun, who gave me regular orders. My business was growing rapidly.

WEDDING BELLS

Grandfather's cancer had spread and he was in the last stages of the disease. My older cousins were all married and Tarun was engaged. Tarun was very attached to Grandfather and wanted him to be there for his wedding, so his marriage was preponed. The family was keen to fix my marriage too, but I had made it clear that I would marry two years later, by then I hoped my business would be well established. My parents, of course, disagreed.

Paramjit uncle came to Amritsar to visit his ailing father. As was our custom, the whole family got together for a family dinner. Grandfather was not very well that day, but was happy to have his five sons and two daughters and all his grandchildren around him.

He addressed us all and said, 'You must stay together, all of you, in good times and bad.'

'There can be no bad times when the family is together,' replied his youngest son.

We all wondered why the old man was so sentimental and whether he had realized that he did not have much time left.

'Bobby, you should get married soon,' he said suddenly to me.

I said I would marry after two years.

Grandfather ignored me and said to Papa, 'I want to participate in Bobby's wedding. You should get him married in two months.'

'Two months? You don't need two months,' replied Paramjit uncle enthusiastically. 'Just two days is enough. I already know a girl in Delhi, my daughter's friend's elder sister. She will be perfect for Bobby.'

Mummy jumped in excitedly and agreed that I should be married soon. Everyone had something to say, and I could not get a word in. I tried to say that it was wrong to bring home a new bride when I was still struggling to establish my business. But nobody listened to me. I said the girl would complain that I worked all the time and had no time for her. But Paramjit uncle said that he knew the girl and she was not so silly. At the end of the evening, it was agreed that I would soon be married. I lapsed into silence, which was taken as my acquiescence.

Two day later, I left for Delhi with my uncle. I had to go there to check out new machinery for my factory at a Tools and Machinery Exhibition at Pragati Maidan, a huge exhibition centre in Delhi. We boarded the second-class, air-conditioned compartment without reservation, since tickets were not available, and sat on two seats reserved for passengers who were to board from the next station. Paramjit uncle had just opened a box of kebabs, placed a bottle of whiskey on the tray table between the seats and was cleaning a glass with his handkerchief, when the ticket collector came and asked to see our tickets. Paramjit uncle told him that we did not have reserved tickets since none were available. He offered the TC a drink.

'You are not allowed to drink on the train,' the TC admonished him.

'I have been travelling on the night train for twenty years and I have never gone without my evening drink,' Paramjit uncle said. 'Please find us two berths in this coach. I really can't move around with my food and drinks.'

'You have to pay a fine and go to the unreserved compartment,' said the TC sternly.

'Please find us two seats,' said Paramjit uncle with a friendly smile.

'There is no place and I cannot find you a berth even if you give me Rs 10,000.'

Paramjit uncle smiled, opened his briefcase, took out two bundles of Rs 10,000 each and said, 'How about Rs 20,000?'

The TC smiled, told us to enjoy our drinks and said he would join us later.

A couple got on at the next station and were politely escorted by the TC to berths in the next coach. He joined us in a while and spent two hours chatting and drinking and eating. He left without taking any money. At 12.30 a.m., Uncle and I went to sleep. At 6 a.m., we alighted in Delhi and took a taxi home.

JASMINA

The next morning, Paramjit uncle sent his daughter, Jeva, to her friend Sheena's house. The plan was that I would go to Sheena's house in the afternoon on the pretext of picking Jeva up. Jeva had to ensure that I got enough time to get a good look at Sheena's elder sister, Jasmina. She was very excited. She really wanted me to marry her best friend's sister.

I went to pick up Jeva at 3.30 p.m. Sheena lived on the top floor of a four-storey apartment block in Punjabi Bagh in west Delhi. The lift was out of order, and I had to climb up the stairs. For the third time in my life, I was going to meet a girl with the intention of marriage. This time though, I was not meeting her parents formally and whether I decided to marry the girl or not was my call. Besides, religion was not an issue this time – she was a Sikh girl and I was a turbaned Sikh.

A sophisticated lady, obviously Sheena's mother, opened the door.

'Sat Sri Akal, Auntyji,' I greeted her.

'Sat Sri Akal,' she smiled back.

'I am Bobby Sachdeva, Jeva's cousin from Amritsar. I have come to pick her up.'

She welcomed me into the house and asked what my real name was.

'Gurvinder Singh.'

'My name is Mrs Rani Harjit Singh Banga.'

I was impressed with the long title, though, of course, her name was Rani and Harjit Singh was her husband's name. Her heavy-duty name was illustrative of the patriarchal Indian society, where the woman's identity is either her father's or her husband's name. Her own identity is irrelevant.

Mrs Rani Harjit Singh Banga led me to Sheena's room where Jeva and Sheena were chatting together. Jeva immediately jumped up and introduced Sheena. I liked the gentle and soft tones of the mother and daughter. But my eyes searched for Jasmina. She was not around. I looked questioningly at Jeva and she indicated that I should be patient. So I sat down and looked round the room. There were happy family pictures on a soft board on one side and cosy furnishings. A half-eaten plate of food sat on the bed. Jeva asked Sheena to call her sister so that she could say bye to her before she left. Mrs Banga offered me a choice of tea, coffee or juice. I asked for plain water and she went off to the kitchen. I turned my head around idly to look through the door and there was Jasmina skipping along happily towards the room. She saw me but did not slow down to a normal walk. She simply entered the room and looked with questioning eyes at Sheena.

'This is Jeva's cousin, Bobby,' said Sheena.

'Hello,' she said.

'Hi,' I said with a smile.

And she sat down on the bed, picked up the plate that she had obviously left there some time ago and started eating her rice and curry. Her attention was focussed on the Charlie Chaplin movie on TV. She had curly brownish hair and wore a crumpled school uniform. Even her socks and tie were still on. She must've been hungry. I noted that she had beautiful eyes and a lovely smile.

Mrs Banga came back and I quickly took my eyes off Jasmina, but not before Mrs Banga noticed. She had brought me a glass of juice.

'I just wanted a glass of water,' I protested mildly.

'It is just healthy water with a bit of sugar,' she smiled.

I liked her sense of humour and easy way of conversing.

Mrs Banga sat on the bed next to Jasmina. Jeva, Sheena and I sat on the couch in front of the bed. Mrs Banga asked me what I did and what had brought me to Delhi.

'My Bobby *bhaiyya* runs a business in Amritsar and is "America Returned" and is not married yet,' said Jeva in one excited breath before I could answer.

Mrs Banga was a sharp lady and she guessed that I had not come just to pick up Jeva and that I was there to see her elder daughter. She asked about my family and I told her everything, including that I was born in Delhi but had moved to Amritsar after the 1984 riots. Jasmina remained oblivious to our conversation, focussed on the food and Charlie Chaplin.

I finished the glass of juice and got up to take my leave. Jasmina casually looked towards me and I said, 'Bye. Nice meeting you.'

'Bye,' she said and turned back to the TV.

We left the room but Jeva was not done. She was feeling so important to be part of this boy-cousin-sees-girl-who-is-best-friend's-sister event and wanted to play her part in it. She said to Sheena's mother that her Bobby bhaiyya would like to meet Harjit uncle and Dadiji, Sheena's grandmother. Mrs Banga smiled and took us to her mother-in-law's room, where Harjit Singh sat on the bed in his ironed white kurta pyjama and a neat white turban. He had big eyes, a broad face and an impressive personality. Unlike his wife and daughters, he did not have a smile on his face. He was an interior designer and handled large projects, remodelling and designing corporate offices. I wondered why he was home on a weekday. He offered me a seat, but it was late, so I simply said hello and goodbye and went to meet Dadiji, who was listening to Gurbani in the drawing room. I touched her feet and she asked her daughter-in-law to take me to the prayer room to take blessings of the Sri Guru Granth Sahib. We had to take off our shoes, and I thanked God that I had worn new socks and put anti-fungal powder on my toes. The fungal problem that had started in America continued to bother me in India. I bowed before the Sri Guru Granth

Sahib, which is like a deity for the Sikhs, and placed an offering of Rs 100. This is a custom, and the Rs 100 marked me as a rich man. The offering was often a way of showing off the monetary status of a person.

Finally, we left the house. Jeva could hardly wait until she got into the car to ask me what I thought of Jasmina.

She made excuses for her: 'Bobby bhaiyya, when her face is washed and her hair is combed and she wears nice clothes, she looks very beautiful. Much better than in her school uniform.'

I smiled and told her that I liked Jasmina very much and, in fact, I liked unselfconscious, tomboyish girls because they had no pretensions.

I dropped Jeva home and went to meet a business associate. On the way, I thought about the Sri Guru Granth Sahib. At one time, it was commonly found even in Hindu households. Hindu Punjabi women often recited Sikh prayers and lived by the Sikh scripture. But after the violence and hatred spread by the separatists, many Hindus returned the holy book to gurudwaras, saying there was no one to read it and its sanctity could not be maintained in their homes. The Sikh hardliners had built a wall between Sikhs and Hindus, and what was part of one religion had now been irrevocably separated. The first Sikh guru spent his life trying to unite Hindus and Muslims. Nowhere in the scriptures does it say that unshorn hair and the turban make someone a Sikh.

It is the truth and the spiritual power in the Sikh scripture that still brings so many Hindus to gurudwaras.

The simple language and the message of unity in one God keep the connection alive.

That evening, I told Paramjit uncle and my parents that I liked the girl. The next step was for my uncle to send a formal proposal to the girl's family. I returned to Amritsar. The next day, my aunt called to say that Mrs Banga, who was her friend, had called to ask why I had come to their house. She was sharp enough to know that I had not come just to pick up Jeva.

A formal proposal was sent to the Bangas, but they were not inclined to accept it. Harjit Singh felt that his daughter was too young. He wanted her to go to college and get a degree. But Paramjit uncle was very persuasive. He told them that I was hardworking and would do well in my business and my family was also good and appropriate for their daughter. He said Jasmina would be very happy with my family and me.

Harjit Banga was not too keen but still made some independent inquiries and eventually a week later, seven members of the Banga family descended on Amritsar. Ranbir uncle hosted a tea party at his house since construction work was still going on at our home.

There were twenty people in the drawing room, seven of the girl's family and thirteen from my family. I had to walk into the drawing room – an act that would normally be performed by a girl. Traditionally, the boy's family goes to the girl's house and it is the girl who enters the room with a tea tray for the guests. Tarun's wife, Hariti, teased me saying that I could take the tea tray in! It was awkward, but I walked into the drawing room, minus the tea tray, of course! Twenty pairs of eyes turned towards me. I greeted them all with 'Sat Sri Akal' and sat next to Jasmina's family.

Harjit Singh looked at me searchingly. He had not taken much notice when I had gone to their house. I looked at Jasmina seated beside her aunt. For a moment, I thought it was some other girl. This Jasmina was dressed in a formal salwar kurta, wore jewellery and make-up. She looked beautiful.

The awkwardness was lifted a little when Jasmina's aunt told her to go to another room with me so that we could have a private conversation. We both walked out.

'Ask me anything you like,' I said to her.

Jasmina was shy.

She had only two questions: 'Will you let me study?' 'Will you keep me happy all my life?'

I immediately replied, 'Yes, of course.' The answer came from my heart.

She smiled radiantly. Then I said there was something I had to tell her. She looked at me anxiously.

'You don't need to wear any make-up,' I said.

She grinned and we walked back to the drawing room. Jasmina discretely indicated her consent to her mother and father who were sitting side by side. Harjit Singh politely showed his concern that Jasmina was too young and needed to continue her studies, but Papa assured him that she could do so happily after marriage. Jasmina's mother asked my grandparents to bless us, and we were engaged.

THE JOY OF TRUE LOVE

This newfound happiness put a sheen on all of my life. I realized that life sometimes had good things to offer as well.

When I went to Delhi a few days after the engagement, Jasmina came to receive me at the railway station. She was dressed neatly and wore no make-up, but there was a glow on her face. Once more, she was a different girl. This time, her real beauty shone through, and I was enchanted.

She drove her own car, which her father had gifted her on her eighteenth birthday. She had been given four hours to spend with me and she asked me where I wanted to go. I appreciated the rules set by her father and her obedience of them, but I had no idea where to go or what to do. I hated free time since it only brought back old traumas. Now I didn't know what to do. So I said we could have lunch first.

Jasmina believed that I was a rich man. The visit to Ranbir uncle's luxurious house had strengthened that idea, especially the sight of the expensive diamond jewellery and solitaires that all the women wore that day. Even my mother had borrowed jewellery from my aunt for the occasion. So Jasmina immediately drove me to a five-star hotel. I had no desire to spend my hard-earned money on an expensive lunch, but we were still to really know each other and I didn't know how I could say what I felt. In my heart, I really hoped that she was not a spendthrift with expensive tastes that I would have to fulfil. I scanned the menu, more the right side than the left, and found that the cheapest dish was *rajmah* at Rs 450 I immediately said that rajmah *chawal* was my favourite food. Jasmina smiled and said it was her favourite too, but we could always eat rajmah chawal at home. I insisted that since we both liked it, that's what we would have. Jasmina gave in, ordered a Coke for herself, while I just had plain water. Even a bottle of mineral water cost more here than a glass of beer in Amritsar! Over our pretended favourite meal of rajmah chawal, we discussed hobbies. Jasmina was fond of craft, interior designing and music. I knew she could sing, but was delighted to know that her favourite music was old Hindi film songs of the sixties and seventies and Punjabi folk songs, both of which I also loved.

She asked me what my hobbies were and I looked into her eyes and said, 'I had never found anything that held my interest, but now I have.'

She blushed.

Jasmina enjoyed her rajmah chawal, but I merely pecked at my meal. The combination of kidney beans and rice always created a havoc of gas in my stomach. The last thing I wanted to do was fart on my first outing with my fiancée!

For dessert, I ordered nothing though I loved sweets. I said I was on a diet. Actually, I was horrified at the prices.

Jasmina ordered a chocolate ice cream, and I watched helplessly while she ate it with great enjoyment.

The bill was paid and we went out. I took over the driving seat. My male ego could not accept that an eighteen-year-old girl would drive while I sat in the passenger seat. As soon as we were settled in our seats, I gave her a gold chain that Mummy had sent. Jasmina was happy to receive it, but handed it right back saying that it would be more appropriate that I give it to her at the family dinner that evening. I was struck by her maturity. I decided right there that I would tell her everything about my financial position.

'I am not really used to five star hotels. I was not comfortable there,' I said hesitantly.

I told her that my business was still in the early stages and I did not like to spend lavishly.

'Why didn't you stop me?' Jasmina immediately asked. 'We hardly eat out at all because Papa does not like it.'

She added that she hated spending money like this, too, but since I was 'America Returned', she thought that I would only eat at a five-star hotel.

'My dream is to be a rich man one day. But at the moment, I am just a struggling businessman,' I confessed.

This honest confession and Jasmina's ready acceptance of my circumstances punctured the formality and brought a sense of closeness. She suggested that we go to Lodhi Garden and walk there for a while. Lodhi Garden had its fair share of courting couples, some holding hands and others kissing and snuggling together. I was surprised.

Amritsar was far more conservative in its public spaces. Jasmina felt very embarrassed. She had brought me here because a friend had told her that it was a 'cool' place to go to. She had not expected it to be full of courting couples. But I quickly found a secluded spot behind a bush and we sat down. I sat close to her, held her soft hand and touched her thin, perfect fingers, topped with red nail polish on short nails. Gently I put my arms around her and embraced her. Jasmina hugged me back shyly. Her fragrance wafted around me and I felt her breath on my ear. I brought my lips close to hers and Jasmina closed her eyes. We kissed for a long time and I felt a tenderness and warmth for her that I had never felt for any woman before. After a few minutes, we moved apart and were quiet for a while. Then Jasmina turned to me and hugged me again, and we kissed again.

I had kissed many women and lusted after them, never loved them. For the first time, I was filled with love, and the experience moved me deeply.

Later, Jasmina dropped me to my uncle's house and went home. Her fragrance lingered in my clothes and I could feel her warm breath on my face long after she had left.

I borrowed my uncle's scooter and went to the hardware market to buy some spare parts for my machines and check on the status of the new machines I had ordered. At 9 p.m., I went with Paramjit uncle, aunt and the cousins for dinner to Jasmina's house.

The Bangas greeted us warmly. Manmohan uncle was already there with his wife and children. Drinks and snacks were offered and I accepted a drink from my father-in-law. My aunt gave me an angry look. She did not want me to drink in front of my in-laws.

But Manmohan uncle came to my rescue saying, 'Bobby has been drinking for a long time. No wonder he became so fat in America!'

Everyone laughed. On his request, Harjit Singh and Jasmina sang a duet. I was surprised and delighted to hear them both sing so beautifully with so much emotion. It was quite late when we finally had dinner.

I had only two small drinks, but it was the dinner that caused me a serious problem. Jasmina had told her mother that I loved rajmah chawal and that is what she had made for me. I was forced to have three servings of it and my stomach rebelled with swirling gas. I tried to make some excuse to go out to the terrace where I could fart without being heard, but Jasmina walked out with me. It was a cold evening and a romantic full moon shone down on us. She hugged me tight and I almost groaned out loud. She was pressing against my distended belly! I kissed her perfunctorily on her forehead to show her that my love had not faded in the few hours that we had been apart. Then I said I had to go to the washroom. Jasmina didn't know what to make of my behaviour, but she took me to the washroom and waited outside, thinking that I was feeling unwell. I was desperate and irritated and told her to leave the room and shut the door behind her. Hurt and confused, she left the room and I finally let go of all the gas bottled in my stomach and farted loud and long. What a relief it was!

I went back to the drawing room smiling happily, but Jasmina looked at me angrily and turned away. Luckily, she could not hold her anger for long when I looked at her so lovingly, and when I left, she saw me off with a warm and affectionate smile. I received a gold bracelet and Rs 3,100 from my in-laws. It embarrassed me, but it was tradition and I could not refuse. My aunts also received gifts.

The next evening, I returned to Amritsar. I started going to the Public Call Office to call Jasmina everyday. It was embarrassing to talk to her from home because the phone was in the lobby, right in the centre of the house, and people walked around all the time. Jasmina missed me already. She cried and wanted me to come back to Delhi; she was lost without me. I realized there was a childlike side to Jasmina. She sent four or five cards to the factory every day. They came in bright coloured envelopes, and the manager brought them to me with a twinkle in his eye. My image of a serious and tough boss took a real beating!

I had never given a gift to any girl, and it never occurred to me that I should buy a gift for my fiancée. My cousin, Sonia, came to Amritsar to visit our grandfather. She was going to return via Delhi and asked me if I wanted her to take back something for Jasmina. I looked at her blankly, so she told me that I should send her a gift and a card. I had no clue what to buy so I told her to buy whatever she thought appropriate. Sonia bought three gifts, one of which was a white teddy bear. She gave them to me to pack assuming that I would want to put in some special message. I wrote 'With Love' on the card and added a note saying, 'Missing you. Always yours, Bobby.' I found an old plastic bag in the kitchen and stuffed everything in it and took the bag to Sonia. She took one look at the bag and pulled all the gifts out of it. The bag had obviously carried onions at some point and still smelt strongly.

'Oh God, you are impossible,' she exclaimed exasperatedly and told me to go away. I was quite relieved.

Two days later, Jasmina called to thank me for the gifts. She especially praised the beautiful packaging.

WORK COMES FIRST

My grandfather's health deteriorated and the doctors declared that he would survive, at the most, for a couple of months. The family decided to bring forward my wedding to April. I wanted it to be a year later, but, as usual, I was ignored. This urgency was conveyed to Jasmina's family, and they were told that the wedding need not be lavish, given the constraints of time.

The wedding was fixed for 16 April in Delhi. The whole family came to Delhi, including Grandfather, who was brought lying down on the back seat of a big sedan. BR and all my other friends from Amritsar also came. There were three days of ceremonies and functions, and it all went off with joy and gaiety. The arrangements were perfect and even my cantankerous brothers-in-law had no cause for complaint. Grandfather blessed us and was taken back to Amritsar by ambulance. Jasmina and I, along with the rest of the family, got there the next day, and a reception was held to welcome the bride and groom.

Two days later, Grandfather passed away. The family went from celebration to mourning. However, he had died at eighty, having lived a full life, and because of his illness, we had been prepared for his passing. So we recovered quickly. I had only seen dead people during the riots in 1984. This was the first natural death in my blood relation that I had ever witnessed. I had never been to the cremation ground before and all the people there mourning their loved ones made me very sad. Rituals were being performed at pyres, and it struck me that religion did not leave a person alone even after he was dead. Religion even divided the dead into Hindus and Sikhs – the Hindu cremation ground was just next door. What was ironic was that at the entrance to the Sikh cremation ground was a picture of Guru Nanak Devji, the first guru who preached 'Oneness', the principle on which Sikhism is based. What a chasm there is between the soul of a religion and its outer, ritualistic manifestation!

I fell ill after returning from the cremation ground. I had spent many nights after work looking after Grandfather; then there was the strain of the wedding ceremonies and immediately after that Grandfather passed away. I was physically and emotionally exhausted. I had to spend five days in bed before I was well enough to go back to work. It was the first time in my life that I had been away from work for so long. So despite Mummy and Jasmina's protests, I went to the factory. Things were in a mess there. There was a shortage of raw materials and an excess stock of finished goods. There had been quality problems and many clients had rejected and returned materials. The supervisor had obviously been slacking.

I realized that this one-man show could not run for long. I needed a helping hand. I regretted that I had not sorted out issues with my father. Papa would have been of enormous help.

I worked very hard and stayed late at the factory every night. Jasmina spent her time alone. She had no friends in Amritsar and the family was still new to her. Mummy knew this and suggested that I involve Gagan in the running of the factory. Gagan was nineteen and had just joined college. He was keen to start work with me, but I refused. I wanted Gagan to get his degree. I knew just how important education was and what a difference it made to have those growing years free from the pressures of earning money.

Jasmina could not get admission to college because during the rituals and other ceremonies after Grandfather's death, we missed the last dates for application. I knew that Jasmina was lonely. We had not even had a honeymoon. But, apart from occasionally bickering with me, Jasmina did not complain. She knew that work was my priority.

A couple of months later, Tarun and his wife, Hariti, planned a long weekend at a hill station and insisted that Jasmina and I come along. Hariti was pregnant, and on the way back, we had to stop the car because she was feeling sick. She and Tarun got out of the car, and I asked Jasmina if she had enjoyed the honeymoon.

'Honeymoon?' exclaimed Jasmina, angrily.

She looked at Hariti *bhabhi* throwing up by the side of the road.

'Is this what you call a honeymoon? Three days at a nearby hill station with your cousin and his wife?'

I was taken aback and felt embarrassed and guilty all at once. I had been so busy at the factory that I had not given a thought to what my new bride expected or would have liked. I immediately declared that I would take her abroad for Christmas and New Year. Jasmina was thrilled.

When Tarun and Hariti came back and we were on the road again, Jasmina told them of my plan. Tarun gave me an accusing look. Why was I fooling my wife? He knew I could not leave my factory long enough to go abroad, neither did I have the money to spend on a foreign trip. I shrugged helplessly.

Jasmina soon made friends in Amritsar. My sisters took her under their wings and introduced her to three kitty parties. My friends had couples' kitties and we became members of two of them – one was a group of my school friends and the other, Tarun's, in which I had included BR.

Life seemed stable. Business ran smoothly, so did our social life. But I was still unhappy. The knowledge that Papa had to sell our front lawn for me gnawed at my heart. The wall in front of the house reminded me everyday of my folly. I wished I could buy that land back. But the new owner had divided it into three parts and sold it to three different people who would build their houses there. One of them had already started construction. So I had to accept that I would never be able to buy it back.

THE TYRANNY OF TRADITION

One day, I had to go to a village for the cremation of the foreman at my factory, who had died in a road accident. I was shocked to see three separate cremation grounds there: one for Sikh landlords, one for Brahmins and one open ground for Scheduled Castes and other lower-caste Sikhs and Hindus. I noted again with sadness that even in death, religion divided people.

With the factory running smoothly, I was able to get home by 8 p.m. This gave me time with Jasmina and the family. I had promised Jasmina that she could join college the following year, and she had already started studying for her entrance exams. But all her plans had to be abandoned when she discovered that she was pregnant. We had decided to start a family only after her graduation, but a couple of slips and life took a different route altogether.

My family was delighted with the news, but Jasmina's father was unhappy. He had wanted Jasmina to get her degree. Jasmina was very disappointed initially, but she soon accepted the situation and started looking forward to the arrival of her baby. I was very excited.

For the next nine months, I lavished attention on Jasmina. I had already decided on a name for the baby, whether a girl or a boy. In fact, I had decided on them long ago. 'Angad' was a name I had loved ever since I saw the movie *Vijeta*. It was the story of a brave young Sikh air force officer. It was the only Hindi movie in which the hero was a turbaned Sikh, even though his father had cut his hair and his mother was a south Indian Hindu. The hero falls in love with a Christian girl. I loved this confluence of religions and Angad's fight against his own fears. Yes, my son had to be named Angad.

On 9 March 1996, my wish was fulfilled and a son was born to Jasmina. The family insisted that the name would be finalized as per tradition after a Sikh priest found a letter from the Sikh scripture.

I was really angry and for the first time declared to the family, 'I do not believe in religion.'

My wise grandmother said, 'I know that Bobby, but I also know that you believe in the Sikh scripture.'

'I will call my son Angad; you all can name him whatever you wish after the ritual.'

The following Sunday, the family gathered in the prayer room in our house, in which I had once placed the Sri Guru

Granth Sahib with my own hands. I was all prepared to fight for my son's name. But fate decided to take my side and the letter that came up was 'A'!

Angad was a happy child, chubby and sweet looking. He became everyone's favourite, especially Papa's, who had found time hanging heavy on his hands after the construction in the house was complete.

I learnt to manage my time, and though I worked very hard, I no longer neglected my friends and family. I still aimed to be a rich man, because I knew that money smoothened the rough path of life. I sold my small car and bought a bigger one. My father-in-law had gifted me a small car, but I felt that was Jasmina's car and should be reserved for her use. Jasmina, on the other hand, differed and said that it was a car for the use of the family.

My business flourished. With money to spare, I began to invest in small plots of land. My plan was that in five to seven years, all the land I bought could be sold and I would buy a large house. The house I lived in was by no means small – it was a 625-yards, double-storey house with eight bedrooms, a lobby, a porch, drawing and dining rooms, a storeroom and servant rooms. But I felt so very guilty that the large lawn had been sold to fund my adventures in America that I felt it was imperative that I replace this house with another that had a large garden as well.

I had now turned completely against organized religion and was a confirmed agnostic. I could not find answers to the questions that rose in my mind and heart anywhere.

Following my example, Gagan too, started trimming his beard. My relatives, particularly the husband of Papa's elder sister, tried hard to bring me around. This uncle was a baptised Sikh, and he could not bear the thought of anyone in his family going against his religion. One day, he came to my house with his family and talked, cajoled and harangued me to accept his religion. When none of it worked, he tried to scare me with the karma theory, telling me that rejecting his religion would bring the wrath of God upon me, if not in this life, then surely in the next. He said that good deeds done by me in my past life had ensured that I was born a Sikh in a good home, but I was frittering away this advantage.

This theory of karma has been strongly entrenched in the minds of Indians and allows all sorts of godmen to manipulate them. We never question preachers and so they get away with anything.

I heard my uncle out quietly. The rest of the family agreed with everything he said. Finally, I asked him, 'This circle of birth and death, it has a beginning somewhere doesn't it?'

'Yes, there is a first time for everything,' said my uncle.

'So, the first time, it is God who decides where a human being will be born?'

'That's right. God has sent us all on this earth.'

'So, God is solely responsible for where we are born and what our religion will be?'

My uncle looked confused and asked me to continue.

'If our first birth is in the hands of God, and the environment He puts us in decides whether our deeds are good or bad, how can He then punish us for the bad things we may do by giving us birth in a bad place the next time?'

Uncle was speechless. He finally told me that it would be best for me to recite the religious verses every morning and evening so that my corrupt mind could be enlightened.

'I will pray to God to pardon you and bless you so that such doubts about God never arise in your mind,' he said angrily.

'I have read a lot of religious books and found the essence of the teachings. It is Oneness and humanity, not divisiveness,' I said.

Uncle walked out. I smiled, but Mummy and my aunt were furious with me.

Later I tried to explain to Mummy that I had only asked a simple question, not insulted Uncle, but she would have none of it. My aunt was very angry and told me that there would be social consequences to face.

The damage had been done, but I was now quite confident that I could ask questions of even staunch believers. Mummy warned me never to do it again, but Papa just smiled.

I read the histories of various religions and found that most events were quite different from the way they were preached. Since the original texts were in Sanskrit, Persian, Arabic or Latin, people depended on preachers to interpret them and a whole lot of discrepancies crept in there, unknowingly or wilfully.

Out of respect for Mummy and in deference to Jasmina's wishes, I stopped raising such questions before elders. Besides, I felt that no one had the answers to my questions anyway. Mummy followed the daily rituals and read as much as she could from the holy book in order to reserve a good place for herself in her next birth. Jasmina did the same, but for peace of mind, rather than rewards in the next life.

Jasmina had turned our house into a beautiful home. She upgraded the family's standards and lifestyle, including our way of dressing. Before this, we had neither the means nor the time to think about clothes and the finer things of life.

Jasmina and I decided that since she was looking after Angad and could not study, we should have another baby. On 15 August 1999, a daughter was born to us and we named her Aashna. This time the family raised no objection because they knew that I would not listen to them anyway. Aashna means one close to the heart, and I had come across the word in a book of Urdu poetry.

I loved my children and looked forward to weekends and holidays, so that I could spend time with them. Though I worked as hard as ever, now it was without pressure or tension. But I still did not feel financially stable. This feeling was exacerbated by the financial crisis that hit my father-in-law.

UNETHICAL DOCTORS – THE FIRST ENCOUNTER

Harjit Singh had suffered from depression for a long time, but now it had increased greatly. He often did not go to work and his business suffered. The losses at business made him more depressed and he started drinking more and more. I realized that he had no one to talk to, since he had no brothers and his father had died. He was an introvert and tried to drown his frustrations and worries in alcohol. His younger daughter was yet to be married, their house needed renovation and a lot of money was needed to support their rather lavish lifestyle. I knew this and was worried too.

To make things worse, Sheena, Jasmina's sister, fell ill and had to be admitted to hospital. She suffered from severe, uncontrollable headaches. The doctors could not diagnose her ailment, but the hospital bills rose alarmingly. Harjit Singh had to sell a flat he owned to pay the bills. After three weeks and bills of lakhs of rupees, her reports were sent to the USA and the UK for expert advice, but since they showed nothing wrong, there was no diagnosis. Finally, the hospital simply sent her home. She had been treated with huge amounts of steroids and had put on a lot of weight. Most of the money from the sale of the flat had all gone in paying medical bills, but her family continued to live in the same style and Harjit Singh even bought a new car because the old one was giving trouble.

I wondered how they managed without a regular source of income, but Harjit Singh had three other small properties and he believed that if he sold them as and when needed, he would manage. Sheena's health was the real cause of worry. He had made it clear to the doctors when she was admitted to the hospital that he would spend any amount of money on her treatment. The doctors took him for his word and extracted all they could. He paid a hefty amount, but Sheena was not fully cured of her headaches.

Jasmina was very worried about Sheena. When Sheena was discharged from hospital, Jasmina decided to bring her to Amritsar. She believed the change would do her good.

She took Sheena to our family doctor, Dr Sunil Arora, in Amritsar and showed him all her reports. He asked for some basic pathology tests and a chest X-ray, all of which cost a few hundred rupees. After studying her reports, he concluded that Sheena suffered from digestive problems that resulted in flatulence, and the gas, rising upwards, caused her headaches and too much coffee gave her migraines. She also suffered from hypothyroidism, which slowed down her metabolism. She was advised to avoid all junk food and eat simple, light food at home. He prescribed Eltroxin, which cost 25 paise per pill, and charged a fee of Rs 100. The total cost of this treatment was less than Rs 1,000.

For three weeks, Sheena stayed in Amritsar and was pampered by everyone. She returned to Delhi in far better health. The whole episode was an eye opener for me as far as doctors and hospitals were concerned. Doctors went against their oath just to feed their greed for money. There was no concern for the patient who depended on them for his very life.

I also realized that I had to have serious savings. My father-in-law had survived this crisis in his life only because of the properties he had invested in. I decided to put every penny I could into buying land or property. This became a hidden pressure for me. To add to this, there was the unfortunate incident of Graham Staines, which occurred early that year, and was constantly troubling me at the back of my mind. This Christian missionary who was working in the villages of Odisha, was burnt alive in a van with his two small sons. He had left his native country Australia to spend his life bringing education and good health to people in remote villages. But Hindu fundamentalists belonging to the Sewa Dal accused him of converting the poor tribals to Christianity and set fire to the station wagon in which he and his sons were sleeping. His wife took over his mission and, over time, even forgave the murderers of her husband and sons. She hoped that they would one day repent their gruesome deed and be reformed. 'Forgive them oh Lord, for they know not what they do.'

I was deeply distressed by this event. It exemplified to me how depraved religion could make people.

GODHRA AND THE RESURGENCE OF OLD TRAUMAS

In 2000, Gagan married Sofia, a girl from Amritsar and the celebrations were lavish. We could afford them now. In 2001, Sheena married a boy from Delhi. Harjit Singh sold one more flat to fund the wedding. He was now left with just one property as a safeguard against any financial problems.

My life was finally stable and happy. My factories were doing well, I spent a lot of time with Jasmina and the kids, and we had a busy social life.

Then in 2002, I came home one afternoon to collect some papers. I was eating lunch in my bedroom and had switched on the TV. As I surfed the channels, I saw some 'breaking news'. I tuned in and, to my horror, saw that a train coach had been set aflame at Godhra station in Gujarat, burning alive more than fifty people. It was said to be an attack on Hindus returning from Ayodhya where the Ram Temple was to be constructed. The police and administration suspected that local Muslims had set the coach on fire. The burnt bodies of the victims were clearly visible. I felt sick and set my plate aside. The memories of 1984 came rushing back. Papa had come into the room to say something to me, and he stood at the door staring in horror and despair at the images on the screen.

He closed his eyes and his voice trembled as he said, 'No, no. God, not again, not again '47 and '84. Why can't we live in peace? Why?'

He left without looking at me and went straight to the prayer room.

Jasmina was not home. Angad had just come back from his nursery school and when he saw me, he jumped in delight on to my lap. I immediately switched off the TV. Aashna was asleep in her cot and the kids' maid sat in the dressing room. Jasmina had told her that the children were never to be left alone. I hugged Angad, looked at my daughter's innocent face and told the maid sternly not to switch on the TV without my consent. For good measure, I pulled the plug from its socket.

I left home to go to the bank, but I was troubled and agitated. I drove around aimlessly for a while until my eye caught a flag flying high, signifying the presence of a gurudwara. It was 3 p.m. I went in, bowed before the Sri Guru Granth Sahib and sat right in front of it, as if I wanted to have a conversation with God. I was an agnostic but felt a connection with the spirit of my religion. The Gurbani always gave me peace and quiet. There was no one in the gurudwara except for the Sikh priest called Bhaiji, who was silently reading the holy scripture. He indicated to me to take *prasad* from the bowl kept on the side. I folded my hands and shook my head in refusal. Bhaiji was surprised. No one refused prasad; it was considered a blessing from the Guru. He went back to his reading. I sat there, a storm raging through my mind and heart.

Suddenly the storm burst out and I shouted loudly and shrilly, 'God, please stop this hatred if you can.'

Bhaiji looked up, shocked. I simply got up and walked out.

I drove straight to Sandeep Gupta's shop and asked him to come with me as I had some urgent work. Sandeep left all his work and got into my car. I drove straight to Amritsar Club. I told Sandeep I had to meet someone there. Sandeep was a member there; I was not. We went to the bar and I ordered two large whiskies. Sandeep was surprised.

'You are drinking in the day?' he asked.

I said nothing.

'Who is this drink for?' he asked again indicating the second glass.

'For the person I am waiting for,' I replied.

I gulped down my drink. Sandeep told me to call this person, and I picked up my cell phone and dialled Sandeep's number. When his phone rang, he thought that I was teasing him. But he knew me well enough to realize that something had upset me deeply. I finished the second drink, paid the bill and dropped Sandeep back to his shop.

He asked me what was wrong and I said, 'Watch the news.'

I drove to the factory with my heart full of fear. I knew that now there would be a backlash against Muslims in Gujarat. Many innocent Muslims would be killed just like the Sikhs in Delhi in 1984. If the government wished, they would be protected and nothing much would happen. But knowing politicians, I did not have much hope.

All my fears came true that very day. Riots broke out all over Gujarat and the police seemed to stand by like spectators. Men were chased and killed, shops looted and burnt, women raped and children massacred.

Outwardly, I kept calm. I did not want my family to be upset. But inwardly, I was tormented. On the third day of rioting, I read in the newspaper that a pregnant Muslim woman had been raped, then a sword pierced into her womb and her almost fully developed foetus pulled out, both murdered heartlessly. I broke down.

Jasmina heard me sobbing and rushed to the room, but then stopped. She knew that my scars had not healed and the Gujarat riots were like boiling oil being poured on my wounds. She waited for me to calm down and come out. I emerged after two hours. She looked searchingly at my face, but I said nothing. She knew it was no use trying to talk to me when I was in such a mood.

THE FIRST PIL

The Gujarat riots had brought me to a decision about something that I had been thinking about off and on. I drove straight to the district court and went to the chambers of the biggest criminal lawyer. I told him that I wanted to file a public interest litigation (PIL) demanding protection for people who did not belong to any religion. I said that I had come to a criminal lawyer because I believe it is a crime against humanity to kill innocent people because of their religion.

The lawyer told me that PILs did not come under the purview of criminal laws but were under civil laws. He gave me the reference of a senior civil lawyer. The senior civil lawyer advised me to save my time and money. He said that no judge would ever approve my application for hearing. But I insisted that I wanted to file an application for identity cards to be issued to all atheists, so that they would not be harmed during any religious riot. The lawyer was irritated. He told me that my application would not go to the Supreme Court on behalf of all the atheists of the country but merely to the sessions court in Amritsar. I said I wanted identity cards for all my family members. The lawyer was surprised.

'Your parents and siblings are all atheists?' he asked.

I realized that my parents, Gagan and his wife were very religious. So I asked the lawyer to file the case on behalf of my own family – my wife, my children and me.

The next day, affidavits were prepared stating that Gurvinder Singh and Jasmina Sachdeva testify that they are atheists and should be given special identity cards so that they and their children never fall victim to religious bigots.

The PIL was filed in court. The Sikh judge read the application and looked at me in disbelief.

He said if the applicant was an atheist then why had he kept a turban and beard, to which no one had an answer. He shouted at the lawyer, 'Mr Verma, you are a seasoned lawyer, how can you bring such an absurd, baseless PIL?'

He handed the file back to the lawyer. The orderly called the next litigants.

I was deeply disappointed and angry. I went to the factory and flung the file into the steam boiler. Jasmina called but I did not answer; instead I simply sent a message – PIL rejected.

BLIND FAITH

After his marriage, Gagan joined the business and worked hard. He was ambitious and wanted greater growth in the factories. He was a commerce graduate with a degree in accountancy. I had ensured that he completed his studies so that he could handle administrative and financial matters. There were eleven government departments and a number of banks with whom we dealt. A lot of time was spent in dealing with these. Once Gagan took over the accounts and all the financial and administrative matters, I was free to concentrate on production, sales and marketing. As a result, the quality of our products improved, as did the marketing. The business steadily grew.

Two years later, Gagan had a daughter and a year after that Sheena gave birth to a baby boy. A celebration was held on the fortieth day, and Jasmina, the children and I went to Delhi. There was to be a religious ceremony in the day and a party at night. I tried to avoid the religious ceremony, but the family would have none of it.

The usual rituals were performed and a letter from the holy scripture was picked out for the baby's name. Lunch was in a park opposite their house. Jasmina's parents and Sheena's in-laws were followers of a guru, and he was to come and bless the baby. A huge crowd, called *sangat*, had gathered uninvited in the park to seek the blessings of Guruji. There were nearly 200 people there. The guru owned a big *dera*, a large bungalow on the main road in an upmarket colony. The devotees called themselves *premis* – lovers of their guru.

I was very uncomfortable. I had no faith in these gurus and *babas*. The Sri Guru Granth Sahib says that there is an answer to every problem within the scriptures, if only it is sought with a clear mind and heart. And yet, educated and uneducated people followed such godmen.

After a religious ceremony, langar is traditionally served to all who are there. The langar, consisting of vegetarian food and sweets, was served and everyone had started eating when a fleet of luxury cars arrived. Guruji's Mercedes-Benz S-class was in the centre, with two pilot cars in front and two at the back. People abandoned their meals and ran to greet him. Only my father-in-law, who had cirrhosis of the liver and was running a fever, and I kept sitting on our chairs. Jasmina asked me to come with her to receive Guruji's blessings, but I frowned and glared at her without a word. She realized that it was a mistake to have insisted on my presence at this event. She quietly took Angad and Aashna and received Guruji's blessings.

A special table and chair were arranged for Guruji for the langar. When he was seated, Sheena asked me to help her father, who found it difficult to walk because of swelling in his feet, to go and take Guruji's blessings. I had no choice and did as I was asked. My father-in-law bowed before Guruji. Guruji put a hand on his shoulder and told him to come to the dera on Baisakhi. A special puja would be held there to cure him of his illness. Jasmina's family was delighted and filled with hope. I wondered how Guruji, who was neither a doctor nor a magician, could so confidently say that he would cure such an ill man.

Jasmina's mother was unhappy that I maintained a distance from Guruji. She asked me to take his blessings.

'I am in good health and high spirits. I don't need any blessings,' I immediately replied.

There was a shocked silence. I was usually never rude. Even Guruji looked surprised.

'Everyone needs blessings, whether in good health or not,' said Jasmina's mother, trying to ease the tension.

'In that case, he should go to the poor people in backward areas like Bihar and Jharkhand where they really need his blessings. But he won't get any money from them. So he only visits fancy colonies with rich people who support his dera.'

Guruji was speechless. His devotees saved the day by declaring that Babaji had to leave because he had another function to attend. No one said a word to me. In India, sons-in-law cannot be ticked off.

Jasmina was furious with me, and when I left for Amritsar the next day, she refused to go with me. I was not bothered. I had done what I felt was right and what I firmly believed in my heart.

A week later, Jasmina returned. Her anger had cooled off, but she told me never again to embarrass her like that.

'Well, don't invite me to meet any guru or baba and things will be fine,' I said.

But nothing important happened in Jasmina's house without the presence of Guruji. So the matter remained unresolved.

On Baisakhi, special prayers were held at the dera for Harjit Singh's good health. I had to attend. This time, I sat right at the back, hoping that Guruji would not notice me. Jasmina's family, including Sheena's husband, sat in the front. The prayers were conducted by a baba who specialized in curing sick people. He was sight to behold – he had a huge paunch, like a nine-month pregnant woman, and long, skinny legs. He wore a *kacchera*, a kind of long-legged boxers. I was very amused at the sight of him.

At the end of the prayers, each family member was given a *siropao*, a special, holy long cloth, as a blessing and some prasad. My name was called out – I was the eldest son-in-law – and I had to go up to receive my offering. I went reluctantly and smiled at Guruji, who promptly turned his face away and pretended not to notice me. I found Babaji even more amusing up close, but I stifled my laughter, received the siropao and prasad and sat down with the rest of the family. Guruji never looked towards me.

That evening, I asked my mother in law, how Babaji, who himself seemed ill, could cure anybody else?

'He suffers from an incurable disease,' she told me. 'But it is because he takes on the illness of each person he cures.'

I could not believe that an educated woman like Rani Banga, who had a master's in English literature, could be so irrational. But faith seems to override intellect.

THE CHINA CONNECTION

I started developing a new quality of reclaimed rubber. This meant that I had to spend five to six hours every day in the hot factory shed, where the steam boiler and steam chambers added humidity and heat to the already uncomfortable atmosphere. Besides, my head was coved in six metres of turban. When I took it off at home, my scalp would be chaffed and red, and Jasmina had to apply calamine lotion on it every day. It made me very irritable. I asked Papa if I could just cut my hair and be clean-shaven like I was in America. But Papa categorically refused.

'This is not America; Amritsar is a small town, where society will boycott us if you cut your hair again.'

I tried to explain my problem to him, but to no avail, and I continued to suffer the discomfort.

There was a lot of competition in the industrial raw materials market because of an influx of cheap imports from China. The Chinese rubber and industrial fabrics were of good quality. Many big rubber factories had stopped buying fabrics in India and imported them directly from China. Big traders became importers and supplied material to small factories, which could not import directly. Many of my clients shifted to the better and cheaper Chinese products and my business took a hit.

Gagan and I thought over the situation and decided to explore the possibility of becoming importers. We studied the Chinese systems and the Indian market closely and finally approached two Chinese companies. I fixed meetings with them and went to China.

I was picked up at Shanghai airport by Melissa, a Chinese girl who was an interpreter. The manager of the company and a driver had come with her, but she was only one who spoke English.

The factory was a four-hour drive from the airport. Melissa sat at the back with me. I was struck by how confident and comfortable she was with three males in the car. I wondered when men would treat women as equals in India. All three men in the car were well dressed, and it was impossible to say who was the manager and who the driver.

I was very impressed with the progress so visible in China. There were six-lane highways and high-rise buildings – all gleaming and looking as good as their US equivalents or even better.

We stopped midway for lunch and sat together at a round table. I was uncomfortable with the driver sitting next to me. In India, hierarchies are firmly demarcated, and a driver and a manager never eat at the same restaurant, let alone at the same table.

We reached the factory at 5 p.m. I was put up at a five-star hotel, and Melissa asked me to settle in and then meet them and the owner of the company for dinner at 7.30 p.m. Business would be discussed the next day.

'Why not start the business discussions tonight? That is what I have come for,' I asked.

'Sorry Sir, we don't talk business while eating,' she smiled back.

I had a cup of tea in my room, rested for a while and got ready. Sharp at 7.30 p.m., Melissa called from the lobby. Melissa, the manager, the driver and another pretty lady of my age were waiting for me. They all got up as soon as I came there and shook hands with me, including the driver. I would not have shaken hands with the driver, but he held out his hand and there was no way to avoid it. The lady, Shirley (Chinese name, Xu Hong Mei), was the owner of the company and spoke fluent English. We walked across out to the latest model of an Audi car, and I sat at the back with Shirley on one side and Melissa on the other. I felt like James Bond with his girls!

A lot of people had stared and smiled at me ever since I landed in China. I asked Melissa why this was so and she told me most people had never seen a hirsute man with a turban before! Most Chinese men have scanty facial hair.

A special room had been booked at a big restaurant for ten people. Two more women and three men from the factory joined us. None of them spoke English, but they all shook hands with me and sat at the table. Melissa introduced me to them: one lady was the supervisor on the night shift, the other was the lab in-charge; the men comprised a PR manager, a weaving master and a dipping technician. It was the weekly day-off at the factory, which is why they could all come for dinner.

Shirley ordered an expensive red wine and the four bottles were beautifully presented. We all started eating and drinking. It was a full banquet with more than fifteen dishes being offered in 2 hours; six bottles of wine were consumed. Everybody talked and laughed, and they were all very comfortable with each other. I found it hard to accept that the driver could share a cigarette with the dipping technician. There seemed to be no barrier between them, though they worked at different positions in the company.

I asked Shirley a question that had been bothering me for some time. I had not seen any sign of a temple or a religious structure anywhere in China. Why was that?

Shirley explained that China was a communist country with very few numbers of people with religious affiliation. Though there were a few Buddhists, a few Christians and some Muslims, people were generally discouraged from following any religion by the state.

'If you don't have any God, whom do you believe in?' I asked, surprised.

'We believe in ourselves,' said Shirley simply.

She told me that they had doctors to take care of illnesses, lawyers to take care of disputes and a strong government to help businesses in financial distress. Besides, there were always families and friends to help tide over personal problems.

I was impressed.

The next day I visited the factory. It was huge. There was massive machinery that produced various goods of different qualities. To my great surprise, more than half of the workers were women.

I liked the quality and the prices, and I figured out that I could make a profit of 7 to 10 per cent if I bought the goods from China. I placed large orders. I also visited a yarn factory because I had heard that Chinese yarns were high in quality and low in price. I could trade in yarns and also use them in my factory. I ordered a container load.

At dinner that evening, I asked the owner of the yarn factory how China had progressed so much so quickly. China had been a poor, underdeveloped country not so long ago.

'It has been possible because of good leaders and their policies,' he said. 'Chinese people can have only one child and they cannot buy property. The government funds industrial projects at low interest rates.'

He added that most Chinese people had no religion. A lot of problems were eliminated because of that. Most of the country spoke one language and the country had only one political party. There was only one skin colour and the Chinese preferred to employ their own relatives and friends in their businesses.

I wondered how relatives and friends worked together without jealousy. In India, it is often friends and relatives who are most jealous of each other's success. But in China, friends and relatives become the support system of the company because they are all equally respected.

'No wonder,' I thought, 'that the driver is treated at par with the manager.'

I had a night flight from Shanghai to Delhi. All through the journey I kept thinking about all that I had seen and learnt in China. Just a few years ago, there was not much difference between China and India, but now, China was way ahead. Its urban infrastructure was as good as any western country. It is true that the rural areas were not as well developed, but that was because it was so densely populated, with a majority of the population concentrated in the rural areas. I was most struck by the fact that there were no riots or strikes in China and no attacks on the public or the government. The Tiananmen Square incident, when students rose up against the government was a blot on its image, but after that no such thing has ever happened. The standard of living has been continuously on the rise.

The most important thing, I felt, was that there were few followers of religion there and those few practised their religion in the privacy of their homes. There was no public display of religion at all. Why could the Indian government not learn from this? 'It is because the religious divide means captive vote banks for Indian politicians,' I thought. But I could not understand why people thought their Gods were so weak that they needed humans – and politicians – to protect them.

I landed in India with new ideas, new energy and a lot of business. I now knew that I could survive and flourish in my own country, as long as I kept away from religion and concentrated on work and the well-being of my family.

I read a lot of socialist and communist literature and learned that many leaders in many countries had banned religion. Once preachers are banned in a country, its citizens soon stop practising any religion. I finally concluded that the human brain is like the hard disk of a computer. It is blank until information is fed into it and then, it can only work with what has been put in. So if religious preachers are banned, then the next generation will become atheist since no one will feed it with religious propaganda.

***

Two months later, the consignments from China arrived. The products were good and well packaged. I replaced the Chinese labels with those of my own factory because many people still believed that Chinese products are of poor quality and also because I did not want my customers to know that I was not supplying products made in my own factory. Soon, the business recovered. I started getting lots of orders because my quality and rates were both very good. Besides, I delivered on time. I now focussed my energies on importing from China rather than producing in our own factories.

I soon realized that technology had made major advances and the new machines I had installed were already on their way to becoming obsolete. The cost of production on them was far higher than on the Chinese machines. But I kept the factories going because I wanted my customers to believe that the products came from our own factory. People still believed that Chinese goods were inferior.

THE HORRORS OF THE MEDICAL SYSTEM

Jasmina called at 5 p.m. one evening to tell me that her father was seriously ill. I wound up my work quickly and went home. When she saw me, she came running and clung to me like a child, sobbing. She calmed down in a while and brought me some tea and snacks and then told me that her father had developed breathing problems and his feet were so swollen that he could not walk. She wanted to go see him, so I booked air tickets for her and the children. I could not leave immediately due to work.

Jasmina spent a week with her parents and returned when her father's health seemed stable. But it was a temporary respite. Ten days later, her mother called me to say that Harjit Singh had developed serious breathing problems and had been admitted to the ICU in a hospital. She had not told her daughter, because Jasmina was deeply attached to her father and would panic. I took the first flight to Delhi on the pretext that I had some urgent work there.

I went straight to the hospital and found Sheena, her husband and Jasmina's mother all there. Sheena's husband was a great support to the family and had spent the night outside the ICU. Three days passed without any improvement in Harjit Singh's condition. Jasmina used to call me every morning and night, and now she began to sense that something was not right. So, I asked Sheena to tell her to come to Delhi to see her father. I told her to say that he had been admitted only last night and I had just come to see him.

By the time Jasmina reached that evening, Harjit Singh had been shifted to a new multi-speciality hospital since the doctors at the first hospital said they could do nothing more. During the next five days, Rs 4 lakh were deposited in the hospital, but his condition did not improve. He was put on a ventilator. The doctors and nurses kept reassuring us that he was in a 'semi-coma' and he would come out of it in a few days.

The ventilator charges were Rs 25,000 per day. Besides, there were other sundry expenses. The family could not afford this, but they paid because the doctors kept telling them that he would recover. Jasmina's aunt, Harjit Singh's sister, arrived with her family from Bombay. Other cousins and relatives all visited the hospital. One distant cousin went up to the doctor as he was leaving the ICU and in an emotional fit told him that the best possible treatment available in India should be given to Harjit Singh. If necessary, medicines and doctors from abroad should be brought. The doctor immediately took out a pen and paper from his pocket and prescribed two injections to revive the patient's liver. I went down to the chemist with the prescription to buy the injections. The two injections cost Rs 67,000! There wasn't enough balance in the patient's account to cover the cost. I was asked to deposit the money first.

I suspected that the hospital and its doctors were exploiting the family. I had seen a similar exploitation in the case of Shambhu Nath in a government hospital and again when Sheena was treated in a fancy private hospital for no serious illness. I didn't know what to do. I knew the family would not agree to take another opinion from a decent and honest doctor. They had faith in this big hospital. So I called Dr Sunil Arora in Amritsar and read out Harjit Singh's medical history to him. He advised me to find another doctor, who was not affiliated to the hospital, for a second opinion. He also said that the family should take Harjit Singh home. There seemed no hope of any recovery. When I mentioned the injections to him, he laughed and said these were useless on a patient who could not even breathe on his own. And he now suspected that the hospital had put a dead patient on the ventilator just to make money from the family.

I was horrified. How could I, a layperson, find out if the patient was dead or alive?

'Just raise the eyelid to check the pupil of the eye for more than a minute. If it is still and there is no movement at all, the patient is dead.'

When I returned to the ICU and told the family that the injections would be of no use, they were very angry with me. Even Jasmina said that they would do whatever it took to save their loved one. There was nothing I could say. I gave the prescription slip to Sheena's husband and left the hospital saying I had some work.

When I returned to the hospital at 9 p.m., only Jasmina and her mother were there. I went into the ICU and looked carefully at all the equipment my father-in-law was hooked on to. The pulse machine beeped every five to seven minutes. The beep signalled that the pulse had fallen and another machine connected to it immediately pumped a fluid into the patient's body and the pulse returned to normal. I realized that the blood pressure, sugar, pulse and cardio readings were normal because the patient was on artificial life support. I turned on the torch in my cell phone, lifted my father-in-law's eyelid and flashed the light into his eye for more than a minute. There was no response. I lifted the other eyelid and flashed the light on it for more than two minutes, just to be sure. There was no response at all.

I came out, took Jasmina aside and explained the situation to her. She could not believe what I was saying, but she knew that I would not say this without being very sure. She broke down and asked me what she should now do. The family would never believe me. I told her that it was her duty to convince them and save her father from further exploitation at the hands of the ruthless doctors. He could no longer feel any pain because he was either brain dead or dead. In either case, there was no chance of survival.

Jasmina explained all this to her shocked mother. They decided that they would consult the family in the morning. But when the family was told this the next morning, they started shouting at me and told me not to interfere in their family matter. Jasmina came to my defence and said that they could get a CT scan or an MRI done to confirm if her father was dead or alive. The family had to agree.

When the consultant came, the family told him that they wanted a CT scan done to ascertain the exact condition of the patient's brain. The doctor was shocked and asked who had recommended it.

'The patient has been dead since last night or earlier,' I said to him softly.

'The patient is still breathing,' the doctor replied.

'Only because he is hooked to the ventilator!'

Finally, the doctor agreed to do a CT scan. For some time, the ventilator was removed and Harjit Singh was shifted to a handheld respiratory system to be taken for the scan. The CT scan was done only at 4 p.m. because the doctors said it was not free till then. But I knew they were passing time to raise the bill.

Jasmina's relatives all rushed to various religious places. Five groups were formed, which visited five different temples and performed all kinds of pujas. One group even went to the baba at the dera who had done a special ceremony for Harjit Singh's health. They asked the baba to come to the hospital to bless Harjit Singh, but he refused citing another engagement. He said he would send his blessings to him.

When Sheena told her mother this on the phone, I said, 'Send how? Through bluetooth?'

The report of the scan came at 8 p.m. and the consultant arrived an hour later. The report showed no activity in the brain; in fact, there was some internal bleeding. The consultant examined Harjit Singh and declared him brain dead and in a vegetative state. Now Jasmina told her mother that he must be taken off the life support system. Some family members disagreed, but I went in and told the doctors that the family wanted to sign the LAMA (leaving against medical advice) form and take the patient home. They were surprised that I knew about the form, but Dr Arora had given me good advice. The doctor on duty told the family that the patient might bleed from the mouth or his skin might rupture because vital organs would fail when he was taken off the ventilator. They were frightened, but I stood firm. I told Jasmina to convince her mother and aunt to sign the LAMA form. Some of the relatives were very angry with me, but I ignored them and handed the form to Jasmina and walked off. I didn't want Jasmina's aunt and mother prevented from signing the form because some of the family had ego issues with me.

When I returned, the form had been signed and Jasmina walked up to me with the doctor. Not one of the relatives wished to go in and witness Harjit Singh being taken off the life support. I went in with the doctor. We stood by the bed and the doctor asked me if I wished to reconsider my decision. I said that once I made a decision, it was final. The doctor started switching off the machines and taking off the wires. There was no response from the patient. Finally, he switched off the ventilator. The cardiac monitor immediately showed a straight line.

The sight of that straight line broke all my defences. I came out of the ICU and looked at Jasmina, telling her silently that her father was gone. I walked over to a corner, away from the relatives, and then the tears flowed.

I had to get a grip on myself soon and, as the elder son-in-law, take charge of things. Harjit Singh was cremated the next day and other rituals were conducted three days later. Everybody went back to their daily lives, except the immediate family that still grieved. The anger against me had dissipated. In fact, many of the relatives appreciated my bold and firm handling of the corrupt hospital system.

The final prayers for the departed soul were held at the dera and Rs 31,000 was donated to it. This was a good business, I thought.

If a person is born, the dera gets money.

If a person dies, the dera gets money.

If a person is sick, the dera gets money.

If a person recovers, the dera gets money.

I was amused to find a parallel with alcoholism:

If an alcoholic is happy, he drinks.

If an alcoholic is sad, he drinks.

If an alcoholic is with friends, he drinks.

If an alcoholic is lonely, he drinks!

However, I had to keep this amusing thought to myself, because no one would appreciate it but rather be offended.

Jasmina grieved deeply for her father. It took four months of medicines and counselling to get her out of the depression. I was very busy at work. My business had really picked up with the Chinese imports, and now I regularly visited China to buy materials and negotiate prices. I sometimes thought that it would be a good thing to move to China and escape the religions of India. But the Chinese thought I was an Arab because of my beard and turban. My suppliers, of course, knew that I was a Sikh by birth but an atheist by choice.

Shirley was an atheist, too, but she was turning towards spirituality. She had started meditating for her peace of mind. I figured that an atheist could be spiritual. After all, it was important to control the mind and meditation helped you do that.

My family was now financially secure, but buying a large house was still just a dream. Prices had risen and continued to rise so that the cash I saved and the small pieces of land I had bought were just not enough to pay for the kind of house I wished to buy.

THE FIGHT TO SAVE PAPA

Papa went to have a tooth extracted and the dentist found a growth in the jaw under the tooth. The doctor was well known to our family, so he called me to the clinic immediately. He scraped a bit of the tissue and I took it to the best pathologist in town. The pathologist confirmed that it was an abnormal growth and a good doctor should be consulted. I immediately went to my trusted family doctor, Dr Sunil Arora. He told me that it was most likely cancer in its third stage, nearly incurable, and recommended an oncologist.

Dr Neerav Goel was a young oncologist with a three-year-old practice in a small clinic in the old city. He carefully examined all the reports, heard the symptoms I described and said that the cancer was already in an advanced stage. There was no hope of any cure. The carcinoma was in the jaw and was spreading towards the left eye, from where it would travel up to the brain. It was an area hard to operate upon. I asked him to recommend a line of treatment or a hospital anywhere. I would take Papa wherever the best possible treatment was available.

'Any standard treatment will only cause physical, mental and financial suffering to him and to all of you,' said Dr Goel. 'Besides, your father may not be able to bear the effects of chemotherapy and radiation.'

Despite this clear and honest opinion, I was not convinced. I paid the Rs 150 consultation fees and thought that I should go to a senior doctor, someone better aware of the latest developments and research on the disease, who might be able to cure Papa. I was not ready to accept that Papa could die.

Mummy, Gagan, Sofia, Jasmina and Papa were all waiting to hear what the doctor had said. I took one look at their worried faces and told them that it was cancer but the disease was in the initial stages and only a part of the jaw was affected, so it could be cured. Mummy, Sofia and Papa heaved a sigh of relief, but Jasmina and Gagan knew that it was not the whole truth. Gagan asked to see the reports. I told him to get them from the car, where I had left them. He and Jasmina went out and I followed them. Jasmina read the reports carefully. She was well versed with medical terms and could approximately understand them. She realized that the problem was serious and incurable. I told them what the doctor had said and also that I wanted to consult a senior doctor, even the best doctors in India. If necessary, I would take Papa abroad. They both agreed.

I told my uncle the real diagnosis. My uncle immediately found the best doctors in Delhi and got appointments with them. Papa and I took the first flight to Delhi the next day. My mother-in-law received us and drove us straight to the Rajeev Gandhi Cancer Hospital, where my uncles were already waiting.

At 10 a.m., Papa and I entered the doctor's room. I handed over the medical file with a note pinned on top on which I had written, 'Please do not reveal the actual position before the patient. He is not aware of the stage of the disease.' The doctor acknowledged the request with a little nod. He read the reports, examined the jaw and then sent Papa with the nurse for some blood tests. He then turned to me and told me that there was a small hope of recovery, but Papa would have to take chemotherapy and radiation along with oral medication and it would all be very expensive. I anxiously told him that we could afford the treatment, but I needed to be sure that my father would be able to tolerate the treatment and its side effects. The doctor said that it would depend on how his body responded.

I had paid the Rs 1,000 consultation fees in advance, and I now paid another Rs 2,500 for the unnecessary blood and urine tests, done just to get Papa away from the doctor's room. The doctor had asked for the tests on this pretext just to extract money, I thought, otherwise he could have used any other excuse to send Papa out. The doctor estimated that the treatment would cost about Rs 15 lakh and the chances of recovery were slim.

I assured Papa that he would certainly recover, but I wanted to see other doctors so that the best treatment could be provided for him.

The next specialist that we visited told me that the disease was curable. He said there would be six cycles of chemotherapy and twenty-four cycles of radiation and the cost would be Rs 10 lakh.

Now I was confused. The doctors in Amritsar had both told me that the cancer was at an incurable stage. I told my uncles what had been said and they decided to see yet another doctor who was the head of the oncology department at a multi-speciality hospital.

That night Papa asked me why we were seeing so many doctors when the disease was not serious and was curable. I told him that we wanted the best and the most modern treatment.

The next day, we met the head of the oncology department.

He examined the reports and then asked, 'What is the annual income of the family?'

'What is the connection of income to the disease?' I asked, surprised.

'That will determine the line of treatment. We need to know what he can afford.'

'I can spend whatever is necessary for my father's health.'

The doctor's eyes lit up. He said that a renowned surgeon would take out my father's affected jaw and left eye. Then chemotherapy and radiation would be given to kill the cancer cells. Six months later, a plastic surgeon would reconstruct his jaw and fix an artificial eye. The total cost: Rs 75 lakh.

The doctor's mercenary motive was clear to me. I got up to leave. The doctor immediately offered a 10 per cent discount since Papa was a senior citizen. I looked the doctor in the eye. There was no shame there. I walked out.

The last option was a doctor at a newly opened, large, multi-specialty hospital. I went there alone because travelling to hospitals and seeing doctors had exhausted Papa. I was amazed to see that this new hospital looked more like a five-star hotel. I went to the OPD and paid the consultation fees of Rs 2,500 to see an oncologist. I was told that I would have to wait for three hours to see the doctor. I wandered around the hospital and had lunch at the cafeteria, which was rather like a coffee shop in a luxury hotel. The hospital was full of people who had come with ill relatives in the hope that doctors would cure their loved ones. Doctors are next to God for the common man.

Finally, my turn came and I went to see the doctor who offered me a Rs 90-lakh package with the assurance that the patient would certainly recover. I heard him out and then asked if the hospital would give a written guarantee on stamp paper that my father would recover and would not die of cancer for at least five years.

'There are no such guarantees,' said the doctor, irritated. 'Ultimately everything is in God's hands.'

All the visits to hospitals and doctors, who were clearly out to extract as much money as they could, had exhausted me and left me tense and angry. I didn't know who to trust and what to do.

'You and your God only exploit vulnerable people, giving them false hopes. Stop this unethical business and have mercy on these people who come to you in distress. You don't care about their suffering and only want their money!' I said.

The doctor angrily told me to leave his room.

The next day, we returned to Amritsar. I told Ranbir uncle about our experiences in Delhi. He then called everyone he knew all over India and abroad to suggest a good oncologist to treat his brother. My cousin, Sonia, from Bangalore, was married and lived in Mumbai. Her father-in-law had been cured of first-stage cancer of the stomach. She recommended his oncologist.

Papa's reports were sent to Sonia. She consulted the doctor who told her that the cancer was curable, but he needed to see the patient first. The next day, Papa and I flew to Mumbai. Before leaving for Mumbai, I emailed the reports to Jassi in America and Ranbir uncle sent them to a hospital in London through a friend.

Papa, Sonia and I went to see the doctor. We had a long wait because the clinic was very crowded. The doctor was famous for his ability to cure advanced stages of cancer and people came from all over the country to consult him. His consultation fee was higher than that of any doctor in Delhi. I had decided that he was the last doctor we would consult. After that, we would follow the recommendation of the young Dr Neerav Goel in Amritsar, whom I had first consulted.

The doctor in Mumbai was handicapped and his assistant did all the necessary work for him. He read the reports and asked his assistant to photograph the growth in the jaw with his mobile phone and show it to him. The growth was much worse now, but the doctor was not bothered. He smiled happily, and ignoring my note on the file, told Papa that there was no cause for worry. He had cured many patients in a worse condition and they were all healthy now. He discussed the treatment in Papa's presence. He said all that was needed was six cycles of chemotherapy, done every third week, followed by twenty-one cycles of radiation. No surgery was required. The treatment should be started immediately, that very day. It would be under his personal supervision. He was so confident and reassuring that I was impressed and agreed. The doctor wrote a note and sent me to the oncology department to make arrangements for admission.

The junior doctor wrote a note for the cashier and there I was asked to deposit Rs 80,000. I paid immediately. The treatment here seemed far cheaper than Delhi. I had brought only Rs 1 lakh in cash with me. Our return flight had been booked for the same night, but it had to be cancelled now. I called Gagan and Jasmina and informed them of the developments. The whole family was relieved. They believed that Papa would now recover.

On the first day, all the tests were done. When the reports came in the next afternoon, the doctor read them and wrote out a prescription for the medicines to be used during chemotherapy. The doctor on duty got the medicines from the hospital pharmacy, with my permission. In twelve hours, three bottles of medicine were given intravenously. There were no complications and things went smoothly. Late in the evening, the doctor on duty told me that two injections had to be given intravenously and asked me to sign a form giving permission to get them from the hospital pharmacy. I signed it. The injections were brought and administered.

It was late at night and I dozed off. Sonia arrived at 11 a.m. I told her that everything had gone off well, but the consultant who had promised to personally supervise the treatment had not even seen the patient. Sonia went to see the doctor in his room with the reports and the hospital file. Just then, the nurse came to tell me that the patient would be discharged and the room should be vacated by 12 p.m. I had Rs 18,000 with me and I was sure that it would cover the expenses since I had already deposited Rs 80,000. To my complete shock, the cashier asked me to deposit Rs 2.95 lakh. I was stunned. I thought that there was some mistake. But the cashier explained to me that Rs 80,000 was just the initial deposit. The two injections for which I had signed the consent form cost Rs 85,000 each! They were imported from Europe. I asked the cashier to recheck the price in case it was Rs 850 and he had read it wrong. But the cashier impatiently assured me that there was no mistake. He told me to stop holding up the queue and come back with the money. I felt humiliated and left.

I sat in the hospital lobby and examined the bill. The charges for visiting doctors, room rent and medicines were high, but this was not what bothered me. It was the two injections that were of concern. I went back to the room to look for the boxes on which the price is printed. But they had been thrown away. Sonia came back and I showed her the bills. She was shocked. She had not met the doctor, but had got a token number and had to wait for her turn. We both sat outside the doctor's room. Meanwhile, Sonia called some people she knew to find out about the cost of the injections. She learnt that there was no fixed price as very few licenced agencies imported these into India. They could cost anything from Rs 50,000 to Rs 70,000. I called Jasmina and told her to find out the cost in Delhi as her cousin owned a hospital pharmacy. She got the same information as Sonia.

Our turn came and the doctor smiled as usual when we walked in. I asked him why he had not visited the patient, and he said that he only diagnosed and prescribed treatment for patients. Other doctors carried out the treatment and gave him feedback twice a day. I asked about the exorbitant cost of the injections and he said that he was neither the seller nor the importer of these, but his patient would require twelve of these injections during the six sessions of chemotherapy. He said that the injections could be bought at a cheaper cost from other sources, but they could be fake, so he insisted that his patients get them from the hospital itself.

'Instead of being concerned with the cost of the treatment, Bobby, be happy that your father is being cured,' he said with a smile.

I had to agree.

Sonia managed to get the required amount of money and we took Papa home. He was happy and hyperactive from the steroids that he had received and was sure he would soon be cured. I did not tell him the cost of the treatment. As soon as we reached back home, I sent back the money Sonia had lent and thanked her.

Meanwhile, Jassi called to say that the oncologist in America who saw the reports said that the disease could be treated, but there was no cure. Deep in my heart, I now knew Papa could not be cured, but I could not let go of the faint hope that he might just be cured, and besides, I did not want to go against the sentiments of the family. The Bombay doctor had given us false hope and we were caught in the trap.

When we were away in Delhi, Dadiji, my father's mother, had been hospitalized with health complications due to old age and was finally put on life support. Once we returned, I visited her daily and was reminded of my father-in-law. She lay unconscious in bed, while nurses had to change her diapers and wash her. I felt it was an insult to her dignity. She had lived a hard life bravely, bringing up eight children and taking care of her husband through very difficult times. It was painful to see her, old and shrivelled, lying in bed with all sorts of tubes running through her body. I decided that if Papa was ever in such a condition, I would keep him at home surrounded by his family. I would make sure that he died as peacefully as possible.

For two weeks, Dadiji battled for her life. She developed bed sores, squints in her eyes, had seizures and loose motions. It was only on the sixteenth day that she found release. The family came together for the last rites and rituals.

'I DON'T BELIEVE IN GOD ANYMORE'

I took Papa to Mumbai for his second session of chemotherapy. He had started losing hair and his beard and moustache had become scanty. The loss of hair on his head did not bother him as much since the turban covered it all, but losing facial hair was like losing his identity. He began to lose confidence. After the fourth session, almost all his facial hair was gone. At the Mumbai airport, the security officer at the entrance could not tell that it was the same Jasbir Singh whose photo was on the identity card. Instead of a tall, well-built man with a thick beard and moustache, there stood before him a weak, shrivelled man who wore a headscarf instead of a turban and had almost no facial hair. I explained that he was a cancer patient. The security officer was sympathetic but nonetheless asked Papa to remove his headscarf so that he could see the birthmark on his forehead. Papa was embarrassed and very hurt.

The next day when I returned from the factory, I found Papa watching TV in his room with a glass of whiskey and a plate of snacks before him. His facial hair was back and he was wearing his turban. Suddenly, he looked good. I was puzzled by this miracle. Papa simply smiled at me and turned back to the TV. I sat beside him, looked closely at his face and started laughing. Papa had painted on a moustache and beard with an eyeliner. Almost immediately I realized that he did not like being laughed at. I hid my amusement and started talking about how I would increase business with China. I wanted to close down the rubber factory and turn the shed into a big warehouse for imported Chinese stocks. Papa agreed. He had stopped working at the factory for a long time now, and he believed that whatever his sons did was for the best.

Jasmina asked me if I liked Papa's new look.

I smiled and said, 'I am happy that he is happy.'

She told me that she had found him looking for something on her dressing table. When she learnt what he wanted, she took a thick eyeliner and painted the moustache and beard for him.

Papa's health, however, started deteriorating. The heavy doses of chemotherapy supressed his immune system, and he began to suffer from low grade fever, loose motions, cold and cough, and pain in the joints. The doctor advised him to use a walking stick, but he hated the idea.

After the fifth chemotherapy, Papa took to his bed. He was weak and afraid that he would fall if he walked around.

Gagan spent more time at the factory, while I looked after Papa. I slept in Papa's room to help him to the bathroom twice or thrice during the night.

After the last chemotherapy session, Papa was so weak that he just rested on the hospital bed. Our return flight was cancelled due to rain in Mumbai, and I decided to keep him in the hospital for another day instead of going to Sonia's house. He had very little energy. He was restless and just wanted to go home. He did not want to talk or watch TV, so I went in search of an Urdu newspaper for him to read. I asked a Muslim doctor where I could find an Urdu magazine or newspaper, but the doctor had no clue. I wandered around and found myself in the general ward. There were around twenty patients in the ward, each accompanied by one relative, and there were just two nurses and a junior doctor to attend to them.

I had come to find some old person who might have an Urdu newspaper, but I found patients of all ages, even children as small as two years old. I saw a young Sikh boy and went up to the middle-aged lady accompanying him in the hope that she may have some Urdu reading material.

She saw me and said, 'Sat Sri Akal.'

'Sat Sri Akal,' I responded.

She told me that she was also from Amritsar. Her only son was suffering from spinal cancer and had undergone bone marrow transplant. The treatment was so expensive that they had to sell their house to pay for it. The boy was born after four girls, fifteen years of marriage and long prayers. And at such a young age, he was fighting for his life.

Most doctors had told her and her husband that bone marrow transplant often does not work and that the body may reject the transplant. Only this doctor had assured them that their son would recover and be free from cancer all his life. So they had admitted him here at an exorbitant cost. But just four months after the transplant, the boy had developed complications, and they were back in hospital.

I was surprised that the doctor had said exactly the same thing to this poor mother as he had to me. He was either a greatly talented doctor or a liar who gave false hope to desperate patients just to make money.

The poor lady poured her heart out to me. She said she prayed regularly and was sure that God would not take away a child He had Himself given to them. Her hopes were kept alive by her faith in God and doctors. I felt even sadder when she said that she would now sell her jewellery for her son's treatment and, if necessary, even the jewellery they had bought for their daughters' dowry.

I wanted to offer financial help, but felt that it was the wrong moment. She needed emotional support. She had broken down before a complete stranger simply because he belonged to her religion and her hometown. I noted her address in my phone and walked back to Papa's room.

Papa was fast asleep, so I, too, lay down on the couch. But I could not stop thinking of the poor lady and her son and felt very depressed.

We left the next day. I paid the huge bill for the chemotherapy and was relieved that we would not have to come back. The radiation could be done in Amritsar.

While the medical file was being completed, I went to the general ward to see the young boy. I found another patient in his bed. The nurse told me that the boy had picked up an infection from the other patients and had to be shifted to the ICU.

In Amritsar, Papa seemed to recover with a good diet and regular medication. He even gained some weight. The radiation treatment started at a hospital there. Hundreds of patients from villages and towns around Amritsar came there for treatment. On the last day of radiation, I noticed a young boy with his middle-aged mother and was reminded of the boy in Mumbai. I checked my phone for the address and decided to visit the family as soon as I had dropped Papa home.

I found their house in a very narrow lane in a middle-class colony. I rang the doorbell and a beautiful young girl opened the door. I explained to her that I had met her mother and brother in the hospital in Mumbai. She asked me in, said her mother was resting and went in to call her. I wondered why her mother was sleeping at this time of day. I sat in a small room where another young girl was doing her homework. She left the room as soon as I came in. The house and furniture were in a very bad shape. I felt sad and anxious, I didn't know why. I waited impatiently for the lady. Suddenly it struck me that this house, with the two pretty young girls, and the fourteen-year-old boy, was just like my friend Harbir's house in Delhi in 1984. Harbir and I were also fourteen then. I felt even more uneasy and depressed.

The lady came into the room looking sleepy. She was surprised and happy to see me. I touched her feet. I felt a connection with this family, even though I didn't even know their name. I believe it was a connection of grief and sadness.

I enquired about the boy's health and she told me that he was unwell. He had fever and body ache and was restless all night. She had spent the whole night by his bedside. I told her that I wanted to help financially for the boy's treatment, but she refused. She just wanted me to pray for her son. She believed that the more the prayers, the greater the chance of his recovery.

I told her that I could not pray, but took out an envelope with Rs 25,000 in it and put it on the table.

'Why can't you pray for my son?' she asked. 'I want your prayers, not money.'

'I will tell you, but only after you accept this,' I said, indicating the envelope.

She reluctantly agreed. I got up, touched her feet, ready to leave. But she was still looking questioningly at me.

So I said, 'I don't believe in God any more,' and I walked out.

Two weeks later, Papa was tested again and the results showed that he was now free of cancer. I took the reports to a general practitioner (GP) and then to the young oncologist Dr Neerav Goel. Dr Goel studied the reports in detail and told me that the cancer cells were no longer visible, but it was a temporary respite. Sometime after radiation, they begin to grow again. I was bewildered. I didn't know what to think. I told myself that both the GP and the oncologist were pessimists. The Mumbai doctor had been optimistic and had cured my father. The family was happy and my uncle wanted to throw a party to celebrate. But I wanted to show the reports to the doctor in Mumbai.

When I called for an appointment, I was told that the doctor was in Delhi visiting one of the large hospitals there. I made an appointment to see him there and went to Delhi. I paid the Rs 2,000 consultation fees in advance and went in to see the doctor who congratulated me and asked me why I hadn't brought any sweets. I returned to Amritsar a happy man and threw a big party to celebrate. I was not bothered about the large sums of money spent on the treatment. Papa was cured and that was all that mattered.

A month later, I visited the young boy again. The lady and the boy had gone to Mumbai, but I left another envelope with Rs 25,000 in it with the young girl. She told me that their father was in his shop; he had to earn a living.

Papa's hair started growing again and with it his confidence returned. But he was not very healthy. His appetite was poor and he developed a low-grade fever that would not go. Despite this, we were not really worried. We thought that once he started eating well, his health would improve.

I was haunted by memories of Harbir, and I went again to visit the boy who was suffering from cancer. This time, however, nobody opened the door, though I rang the bell several times. A neighbour heard me and came out. She told me that the boy had died and the family had moved to another house. I was shocked. Tears filled my eyes and for a while I could not say a word. Then I asked for their new address, but the neighbour did not know. She said they probably moved to a cheaper area because they had spent all their money on their son's treatment and could not afford to stay in that house any longer.

Then she added, 'It is all God's will.'

I wanted to shout, 'What kind of God gives so much suffering? Why does He just look on mutely?'

I told myself that God made humans suffer so that they would pray to Him and satisfy His ego. Those whose suffering was mitigated became votaries of their own God. But those whose prayers were never answered still continued to pray because they were afraid that they would be punished. They believed that everything was predestined and had to happen. But if it was predestined, then why pray? I was convinced more than ever before that there is no God, and even if He exists, He is not a good God. He cannot feel the pain of His devotees.

'PAPA, WHERE HAVE YOU REACHED?'

Gagan and I were busier than ever at the factory. I went to China again to see if I could get a better quality of conveyor belt fabric for the rubber industries. I saw a huge scope in industrial fabrics. This time I stayed for four days. Shirley helped me develop a better quality of dipped fabric in the factory.

We worked all day, and in the evening, Shirley and the senior staff of the factory came to my hotel for dinner. We usually discussed India and China and the socio-economic scenarios of both the countries. I learnt a lot about China. One of the factory supervisors told me that China had progressed so much because of its leaders. I told them that India was left behind because of its leaders! I told them that I was already an agnostic, but the frequent visits to China had turned me into an atheist. If China had made so much progress without any help from the Divine, then I was sure India could survive without Him too.

When I returned, I found that Papa had fever and body aches. Our family doctor suspected that the cancer was back. Tests confirmed his suspicion. The cancer cells were back and growing rapidly in all directions. Now there was no chance of recovery. We told Papa that the aggressive treatment had caused a severe infection and it would take a few weeks for him to recover. He was not convinced, but he didn't know much about cancer and believed us. The GP made a home visit and told Papa that there was nothing to worry about. He did not charge any fees for this visit. Jasmina and I thanked him profusely.

My uncles would not accept that the cancer had recurred. They insisted that I go to Mumbai with the reports and show them to the doctor there. So I went there, paid the Rs 2,000 consultation fees and waited till afternoon to see the doctor. He examined the reports. His usual smile was missing. I stared at his face anxiously. Without looking at me, he said that the problem had recurred in the same area and it would need a stronger dose and longer treatment to cure Papa.

'There is no new problem, doctor,' I said. 'It is the same old problem that had been supressed with strong medicines. There was never any cure then and there is no cure now.'

The doctor was annoyed.

'Why did you come to me if you knew there was no cure?' he asked

'Because my family insisted. And because you are a very senior doctor and you had assured us that my father would be cured. Human beings look for a ray of hope and when that ray of hope comes from a doctor like you, people are ready to believe,' I said. 'But you are probably only concerned with the commission you earned on the twelve injections that you gave my father.'

The doctor was agitated, but I was not done yet.

'I am not bothered about the time and money I have spent. But what about the young boy from Amritsar? You gave his parents false hope and treated an untreatable spinal cancer. They are now facing financial ruin and don't even have a home to live in.'

The doctor had nothing to say. He returned the file to me and said he was sorry for my father, but added that the cancer could still be treated. I asked him if he believed in God.

'Yes, of course,' said the doctor.

'Then, doctor,' I said, 'you better be very afraid of God and have mercy on your patients. Don't exploit them. Don't give them false hopes.'

I walked out. I saw the doctor call his receptionist, who stopped me and tried to return the consultation fees. I refused to take it back. I told her to keep it for some poor patient who could not afford to pay the doctor's fees. I also told her to ask the doctor not to misguide poor people into expensive and unnecessary treatments.

Everyone was worried about Papa. He was getting weaker by the day. Mummy started visiting some babas on people's advice and performing rituals on their instructions. All I was concerned with was that Papa should not know that he was now terminally ill, so that he did not get traumatized and depressed.

I went to Dr Neerav Goel and showed him all the reports. Dr Goel told me that there had never been any scope for a cure either earlier or at present. I requested him to visit Papa at home, not as an oncologist but as a GP treating him for some common ailment.

Papa's muscle control became very weak and he had to use diapers. He was very embarrassed when I first put one on for him, but there was no option. I told him that it would be a matter of just a few days; he would soon be well again.

Dr Goel made a home visit. He checked Papa, asked some innocuous questions and left the room. He told me that Papa had just a few weeks or maybe just a few days left. The cancer would soon reach the brain and he would go into a coma. He told me that the disease could block his food pipe in the next few days, and he would have to be put on a liquid diet. I listened to him carefully.

Then I asked, 'If it is certain that he will not survive for long, what can be done to end his suffering as soon as possible?'

'The patient can be kept sedated most of the time, so that he is unaware of his pain,' said Dr Goel.

I asked him how much were his fees, and Dr Goel said, 'Rs 150.'

I insisted that he accept Rs 500 since he had come all the way and spent nearly an hour here.

Jasmina and I then went to Dr Sunil Arora. He refused to see any reports; he just wanted to know the current situation. He told me that there was nothing he could do, and I said that I knew that.

'All I want is that my father should die peacefully without being aware of his condition.'

Dr Arora was a good family friend, but his ethics demanded that he do whatever was needed to cure a patient. I understood his dilemma and reframed my question.

'Can you explain to me how the human body works and how it shuts down?'

The doctor told me that the brain sends signals to the body to perform all its functions. It is also the brain that lets the body feel pain. If the brain sleeps, the signals to the body become so minimal and weak that the patient can hardly feel anything. He suggested that morphine patches could be used on the patient's back to relieve his pain. He also said that dehydration causes the brain to slowly shut down, resulting in a peaceful end for the patient.

Over the next few days, I used all my ability to cook up stories to tell Papa how his health was getting better and better. Whenever he was awake, Papa asked whoever was around why he was dizzy and nauseous. We all told him that he had an infection that had robbed his appetite and that as soon as it was cured, he would be able to eat better and regain his strength.

'For once,' I thought, 'my storytelling abilities are being put to good use.'

Soon, Papa's oesophagus was blocked and he could swallow only very soft food or liquids. This worried him and I had to come up with another innovative story. I told him that the infection was slowly leaving the body and it had come up to the throat. Soon it would be in the mouth and then out. As always, Papa believed me. He was sedated, but now the nausea was so strong that he could not sleep. So I put a morphine patch on his back. He was immediately at ease and went to sleep.

Relatives started pouring in to see him. They prayed for him and some came daily to perform all kinds of pujas for the sick soul.

A week went by. Papa now slept most of the time. When he woke up, he was unaware whether it was day or night. Then he slipped into a semi-coma and stopped responding to anything around him.

His brothers invited a senior oncologist from Delhi to visit him without telling me. The doctor examined him and said that there was nothing that could be done at home. Papa needed to be in hospital. This was a real test for me. I had to stand up against my uncles, who I had respected and obeyed all my life. I tried to explain to them that doctors could only prolong my father's agony for a few days. Papa had been a proud, independent person all his life, and now to find himself dependent on others for the most basic needs would be humiliating for him. But all my pleas fell on deaf ears. Finally, I said that I was following medical advice not for his recovery but to make the end peaceful for him. They were not convinced and one of my uncles was furious. But I was adamant and they had to give in.

The oncologist from Delhi charged my uncles a large fee, air tickets and stay at a five-star hotel and left. I was relieved that he had not misguided them.

Now the care of Papa was completely dependent on the family. I moved him to a small room near my own. We gave him drops of glucose water with a spoon several times a day so that he got the required calories for the body to function. After some days, that too stopped and he had to be given drops of water through a cotton swab just to keep his mouth and tongue moist. Breathing, too, had become difficult.

I called Dr Goel and Dr Arora. They came at different times but said the same thing: Papa had just a couple of days left. I asked them again and again whether he was in pain. But they both reassured me that his brain was no longer sending too many signals to the body. The vital organs were fighting to work on their own and this would last for a very little time. He was not in pain.

I told Ranbir uncle that Papa had very little time left. He told Paramjit uncle, who had come from Delhi, to stay on. Jasmina checked Papa's pulse and blood pressure regularly. It was low but steady. During the day, the ladies of the family performed prayers outside Papa's room. I had forbidden them from going into the room for fear of infection.

A baba was called to perform a special prayer one day. A lavish lunch was served to him and his followers. There were just people and more people in the house. I was extremely irritated by the spectacle of the godman being served by the ladies and the men all standing before him with folded hands. I hated this, but it was being done in my own house and I was helpless.

Babaji left in the evening and so did all the relatives. We were all tired and decided to sleep early. I lay down in Papa's room, but sleep eluded me. I kept looking at him in the dim light of the night lamp. At 1 a.m. I noticed that his lips were dry and cracked and I moistened them with a piece of damp cotton. Everything was quiet, but something was keeping me awake. At 4 a.m., Papa was breathing normally. I covered my eyes with my arm. My eyeballs felt as if they would burst and my body ached. Another 15 minutes passed.

Next I know, it was 5 a.m. and Mummy was shaking me out of a deep sleep.

She finally said loudly in my ear, 'Bobby, your father is gone.'

I sat up with a jerk and it took me a few seconds to realize that Mummy was really standing there, that I was not dreaming. I immediately turned to Papa. His mouth and eyes were open; he was no longer breathing.

We both stood beside him quietly, almost emotionless. Then I shut his eyes and mouth and covered his face with a sheet. I turned to Mummy. She was calm. She told me to call Ranbir uncle and went to wake up Gagan and Jasmina.

By 6.30 am, all the relatives were there. By noon everyone from out of town had arrived. The cremation was fixed for 2 p.m. The factories were shut for two days and all the workers came to pay their respects, as did all our friends and business associates. At 1 p.m., the male relatives bathed the body, while the women sat in the outer room praying. I heard Mummy finally break down. While every family member was in tears since the morning, I had remained quiet, participating where necessary and just watching things unfold. Phones rang and people answered them. They referred to the 'body', which I found particularly cruel. Jasbir Singh Sachdeva had lived a full life, and now he was just a body.

When the body was ready to be taken for cremation, I covered the nearly bald scalp with a black cloth. But the priest who had come to perform the last rites pulled it off and used an orange cloth instead.

'He has to be covered with an orange cloth, as permitted by our religion,' he said to me rather rudely.

Even after death, religion and priests hold sway over people, I realized. I decided to write in my will that no priest would perform any rites over my dead body.

As we were about to leave, I realized that Papa looked different. I knew what was missing and I rushed to get the net and the eyeliner. I painted in the moustache and beard and put the net around his chin and then stepped back to look at my handiwork. Papa now looked like the brave Sikh man that he had been, never defeated by the vicissitudes of fate. My numbness dissolved; the tears flowed at last.

The grandchildren were brought in to pay their last respects.

The body arrived at the cremation ground after stopping at a gurudwara on the way. More than 500 people had gathered there. The last rites were performed and I, still weeping, lit the pyre.

We came home. Someone sent us food; for three days, no fire would be lit at home. I had lunch, switched off my phone and slept through the afternoon and the night. I woke up early in the morning. I had to collect the ashes from the cremation ground and disperse them in the river, which was 40 kilometres away. Papa's sisters and brothers, Gagan, my sisters and Mummy, all of us went to the cremation ground. The pyre had burnt out and Papa's body was now just ashes. We were given a gunnysack to put the ashes in. Gagan and I filled it, and I carried the 10–12 kilograms sack to the car. My uncle unlocked the boot, but I walked straight to the front, opened the passenger door and put the sack on the front seat and tied the seat belt around it. I took the car keys from my surprised uncle and climbed into the driving seat. Mummy and Jasmina sat at the back. Seven cars followed me. Our driver, Kulwant, drove Gagan's car. He was still crying. He had been Papa's driver and had developed a deep affection for him and for the family.

The ashes were immersed. Life resumed its routines. I got busy again with work, so busy that I did not get much time to think of the one who was gone.

About fifteen days later, around 9 p.m., when I was on my way back from Jalandhar, I remembered that whenever I was late getting back home, Papa would call at 8 p.m. and ask, 'Bobby, where are you? Where have you reached?'

No one called me today, but I heard Papa asking, 'Bobby, where have you reached?'

'Papa, I am here. Where have you reached?'

MUD, MIND AND THE MEANING OF LIFE

The Internet connected me with many businessmen and opened up avenues to expand and grow. I worked harder than ever. I did not make many new friends because, after a certain age, it is hard to adjust to new people and one becomes more class conscious. But my business circle expanded rapidly because there were monetary considerations there.

Technology had changed rapidly and the fabrics produced in my factory found few buyers now. Others had better fabrics at cheaper rates. Other factors too made running a small-scale factory very difficult, so I decided to shut it down. I gave my staff a thirty-days' notice, so that they could find other jobs. At the end of the period, I cleared all dues and the staff left, almost satisfied. The next step was to sell the machinery, but there was no buyer for them. I had to sell it as scrap metal.

The scrap metal dealer sent his men to dismantle the machines. The metal went to steel mills to be melted, the wooden parts were sold as fuel, the plastics went for recycling and the leather parts went to rural areas to be turned into packing materials for agricultural machinery. Nothing was wasted, though I got only a fraction of the money I had spent on them. Gagan and I now had one factory less to run and we focussed our energies on trading.

I bought an SUV, a Fortuner. I had never had such a powerful car before, and I decided to take the family on a holiday to Shimla to try it out. Some distance into the hills, all traffic came to a standstill because there was a landslide a little ahead. We were told it would take at least two hours to clear, so we decided to have a picnic nearby in a grassy clearing. Jasmina spread a sheet on the ground and took out all the food that she was carrying. From where we sat, we could see our car and the landslide ahead. Several men were lifting the mud into trolleys to be trundled away.

'Papa, what will they do with all this mud?' asked Angad.

'Mud has value, because people buy it for different reasons – some use it to level their land; good quality mud is used to make pottery; and in villages, people use it to plaster their walls. There may be other uses that I don't know about,' I said. 'This mud has some value, but our mud, this mud we are made of, it has no value at all. It is a total waste and no one even wants to touch it when we are dead.'

Angad looked confused and Jasmina stared at me in disbelief.

'Why are you saying all this to Angad', she whispered angrily. 'Why are you talking about death when we are on vacation?'

It struck me that Angad was too young to understand what I was saying. But I explained to Jasmina that this thought had been on my mind ever since I sold off my machinery and found that every piece of it would be put to some new use.

'Everything has some value, even the mud from the landslide, but what about us? Are we of any value once we stop breathing? No one keeps bodies at home beyond a day or two. Some of us are buried, some turned to ashes. In either case, we are of no value to anyone. Then why do we feel that we are superior to some and inferior to others? The fact is that we are all the same – just mud.'

Jasmina was surprised, but didn't want to prolong this conversation on a holiday. She told me that I was better off doing my 'busy-ness', since that didn't give me any time for such philosophizing. I smiled and Jasmina changed the subject.

The traffic began to move slowly and we quickly gathered our things together and ran to the car.

We spent three happy days in Shimla. I spoke to Gagan every day, but other than that, I did not make any business calls. On our way back, when we were nearly home, Angad spotted a pile of mud from an under-construction house.

Excitedly he asked, 'Papa, how much is that worth?'

Jasmina burst out laughing. I grinned. But my new theory had changed the way I saw human beings around me.

I was now financially quite stable. I realized the worth of money – once there is no need to worry about basics like food and clothing, money gives one freedom to pamper oneself a little. I still wanted to be a rich man so that my family was secured against the unforeseen future. Gagan and I both agreed that we should buy a bigger house to enhance our worth and our standard of living. We started putting some money aside regularly in a separate account.

I visited China again to attend the China Rubber and Tyre Exhibition in Shanghai, the biggest such exhibition in the world. I still marvelled at the progress China had made in such a short span of time. It seemed like a miracle, except that the Chinese did not believe in miracles, they believed only in hard work. There was corruption in China, but the government arrested many of the corrupt bureaucrats and politicians. Even members of the judiciary had been arrested. They had a 98 per cent conviction rate. In India, many crimes are not even registered. Besides, the judicial process is so long and cumbersome that at times, litigants die before their cases are resolved. The rich and influential manipulate the system and almost always get off scot-free.

'India could also flourish like China,' I thought. 'If only we could get past our jealousies and hatred and religion and caste and language.'

My mind worked in overdrive, but I got very little physical exercise and had put on weight again. I had also developed piles that led to iron deficiency and low haemoglobin. My doctor advised me to undergo surgery immediately.

At my own request, I was given full anaesthesia instead of a local one. Under its effect, I spoke to the doctors in fluent English in the operating theatre before I passed out. I did not utter a single word of Hindi or Punjabi. The surgery took two hours. I partially came out of the anaesthesia as I was being wheeled out of the operating theatre and found myself in acute pain. I abused the doctors and nurses in fluent English. I was given sedatives to relieve the pain and slept through the night, but the next morning the pain was back. Jasmina was standing beside my bed and I told her, again in fluent English, that I was in pain. When the surgeon came for the morning rounds, I complained to him.

The doctor had a great sense of humour and said, 'You have abused me and my staff so much since yesterday that God is punishing you with this pain. Other patients who don't abuse their doctors don't suffer so much pain.'

Jasmina was embarrassed and did her best to stop me from talking, but I would not shut up. The doctor gave me more sedatives with painkillers to settle me down.

On the third day, I gained full consciousness and the pain had lessened. Jasmina was very angry with me. It seems I had abused every doctor and all the staff – that too in fluent English, with no grammatical errors! I did not remember much, but I was amazed to know that I had spoken such good English. Normally, I hesitated to speak in English and made many mistakes. I wondered where I had learnt to speak so well. I remembered that Papa constantly recited the Gurbani when he was semi-conscious and my father-in-law abused his servant and driver in Hindi when he was in hospital.

I had read that humans have a conscious mind and an unconscious one. The conscious mind has filters and keeps out things that are inappropriate, but the unconscious mind has no such filters. No wonder when I normally spoke

English, I was so concerned with how I sounded that I hesitated and made mistakes. But when unconscious, I did not care what anyone thought of me and so I spoke easily and clearly. The power of the subconscious mind is definitely greater than the conscious mind.

With my piles cured, my haemoglobin improved and the iron deficiency slowly reduced. But I was still overweight, felt bloated and had cramps in my legs and feet. I was sluggish, irritable and depressed. My blood pressure was low. Tests showed nothing wrong. Finally, my GP recommended the TSH test and I was diagnosed with extreme hypothyroidism. I was put on medication for life, but my metabolism had slowed down, which weakened my digestive system and made me feel very hot or very cold, depending on the weather.

Slow metabolism meant that I had to spend at least an hour on the pot every morning. I turned that into my 'me time'. I read two newspapers, one English and one Hindi, and perused every word in every column. I enjoyed the detailed analysis and got particularly fond of some columnists. The more I read about the lives of the underprivileged in India, the more I wanted to help them.

'But what can one person do for people who constitute more than half of the Indian population?' I wondered.

But then, the gap between the super-rich and the poor is so vast that one rich person can help millions of poor people in India. I wanted to help, but I was very attached to my hard-earned money. I did not want to simply throw it around; it had to be spent meaningfully. I started donating every month to two orphanages, one Christian and the other Sikh. I disliked this division of aid based on religion, but that is how things functioned in India.

'Money should be taken from corrupt and unethical people and distributed to the needy,' I thought.

Life was routine and uneventful, but I was changing. Besides newspapers and news shows on TV, I watched documentaries on Discovery and National Geographic channels and learned about the latest research on life on earth, space and the universe. I had no interest in science in school, but now it fascinated me, especially astrophysics. The idea that the earth is but a speck in a galaxy and that there are dozens of galaxies out there was new to me. I had read about it in school, but then it had no impact on me. The fact that millions of stars are born and dying every day, swallowed up by black holes, gave me a new perspective on human existence. Here we were, tinier than ants on a miniscule planet, but we live as if we are the only important things in this universe. Our egos grow rapidly, and based on mere material possessions, we consider ourselves superior to all those who have less things. Ego, I believe, is man's biggest enemy. If earth is a mere particle in the universe, what is the worth of a human who will live on this particle for just a few years?

I decided that I would try my best not to live at the level of the ego. It would be very, very hard because we are conditioned from childhood to act from our ego. I had to deal daily with people with very inflated and fragile egos. I also realized that all humans are the same. It is only their circumstances that mould them differently.

All the reading and contemplation brought its rewards – I felt much more at peace. My mind was clear – I was a traveller on earth and I had to make my journey as peaceful and as meaningful possible.

NO CASTE IN SIKHISM, YET WE ARE DIVIDED

I decided to spend my thirty-ninth birthday at our favourite hill station. Jasmina made all the arrangements, and we planned to leave early on the morning of 25th May. I skipped the usual morning routine of watching news on TV and reading newspapers. The family wished me with hugs and kisses. Jasmina too, hugged me tightly and kissed me. Whenever she is happy, she hugs and kisses me passionately, which delights me.

By 8.15 a.m., we were on our way, passing through the residential and commercial parts of Amritsar. None of us noticed that the streets were unusually empty and quiet. We reached the outskirts and had just turned onto the highway when I saw a group of men hurling stones at passing vehicles. Some of the men were clean-shaven, some turbaned, and they carried swords, sticks and stones. We were about 200 metres away, when I saw vehicles turning back and speeding towards us. The children were terrified. Angad immediately ducked on to the floor, trying to hide. He had just entered his teens and he could recognize a dangerous situation.

The cars passing us had managed to turn back before the crowd could reach them. I didn't know why this crowd of Sikhs and Hindus was attacking innocent people. I turned my car around and sped back into the city. Vehicles with broken windows and windshields raced past us at very high speed. There were injured people in them and faces full of panic. I drove fast but not recklessly and only now did I notice that all the stores were closed, even the small grocery stores that opened very early in the morning.

Mummy, Gagan and Sofia were surprised to see us back, looking so frightened. I asked Gagan if he knew of any incident in the city. He said that all he had heard was that a guru of a Sikh sect had been critically injured when a Sikh shrine was attacked in Vienna, Austria. He had not paid much attention to it.

I searched on Google and found some shocking news. Some Sikh hardliners had attacked these gurus and shot them and injured many others in a gurudwara in Vienna. The accused had been arrested. There were no other details available. The local Punjabi channel, however, had much more information. Some upper-caste Sikh hardliners had accused the gurus, who belonged to a lower caste, of not following the basic principles of Sikhism by the book. The gurus preached their own ideology along with teachings from the Sri Guru Granth Sahib. The upper-caste Sikhs objected to their way of teaching and attacked them. The followers of the lower-caste gurus were now out on the streets, agitating against the murderers. The violence spread rapidly all through the state and then into the neighbouring states, which had large Sikh populations.

Gagan and I locked the gate of our house and stayed at home.

The lower castes are defined not only by religion but also their power as a vote bank. Politicians promise them special benefits, which remain mostly on paper. Nothing has changed for them in so many years since independence. Instead their basic dignity is taken away by labelling them as Scheduled Castes.

When Angad learned that the lower-caste Sikhs were attacking the higher-caste ones, he was bewildered. He knew he was a Sikh, but he had no idea of his caste. He asked me what our caste was. I didn't know what to say. I did not want to teach my son about caste and the divide that it brought among people. So I told him that we belonged to a middle caste, neither upper nor lower. Angad wanted to know who else belonged to this middle caste and how would the rioters distinguish them from upper or lower castes. I had no answer and was irritated. I told Angad not to bother me with such silly questions.

For the next three days, Punjab remained in the grip of violence and rioting. Major damage was done to properties of upper-caste Sikhs. Mercifully, only a few lives were lost.

I called Angad to my room. He came with a host of new questions.

He had read up on Sikh history in his textbook and he asked, 'There is no caste in the Sikh religion. Our gurus said that there is no caste system and we are all one. That is why they had the name "Singh" for men and "Kaur" for women. So why do we have "Sachdeva" after "Singh" in our name?'

I knew that caste was a divisive factor that lived within the shell of religion.

'It is true that there is no place for caste in Sikhism. But in India, we carry our traditions and old belief systems from generation to generation. We call it "keeping the tradition alive". But we don't think of what we are really doing. Our ancestors converted to Sikhism for a good cause, but they took their caste along with them and continued to pass it on.'

On the fourth day, Punjab returned to normalcy. But I was too shaken to just resume life as before. I was haunted by the fact that my birthday could have been fatal for my family if we had started on our journey just a little earlier. It was Sikhs against Sikhs here. I now knew that the clean-shaven men in the mob were the lower-caste Sikhs. I decided to protect my family in the only way I knew. I went to Chandigarh to see a lawyer.

AN ATHEIST IDENTITY

The high court lawyer listened in surprise as I explained to him that I wanted something that identified my family as belonging to no religion.

'Aren't you a Sikh?' he asked, looking pointedly at my beard and turban and noting my name, Gurvinder Singh Sachdeva.

'I do not believe in God or caste. Society and my family have given me a particular name when I was born. I had no choice in it. I now want a legal document saying that no one can harm me or my family on the basis of caste or religion.'

The lawyer told me that there was no chance of such a case being accepted in court unless public discourse or the media backed it. He said that it would be best to file it as a PIL and hope that the media took an interest in it at some point. I agreed but asked the lawyer to keep the case discreet. I did not want to attract the attention of hardliners to my family or to myself.

Within a week, I completed all the paperwork and sent it to Chandigarh with the court fees. The lawyer was well known and respected in the Punjab and Chandigarh courts. He did his best to present the case in such a way that the judge would accept it for hearing, but he did not succeed. The judge found it irrelevant and unsuitable for judicial intervention. Nobody wants to interfere in matters of religion in India. I was disappointed. This time it was two subjects – caste and religion – and I had thought the court would take cognisance of it.

I immersed myself in work again. I started developing a new product in the factory. It required me once again to spend many hours in the 45 degrees Celsius heat and humidity of the steam boilers in the shed. My headaches recurred and I was unable to bear the pressure of the turban. The bone at the back of my skull was over grown and my headaches became so severe that I could not work. It was a problem I faced throughout the long summers every year in Amritsar. Doctors advised me to wear a light cloth or a cap during summer instead of the turban, but I decided that a permanent solution was needed. I cut off my hair and stopped wearing a turban. I kept the beard since I would have to wear the turban during family functions.

I kept myself very busy – work all day, badminton in the evening for fitness and a few hours with the family before bedtime. I liked this routine. The work satisfied my soul, the play eased my mind of the day's tensions and tiredness and ensured that I slept well. In the morning, I had enough time to read the newspapers and the informative magazines I liked.

I came to the conclusion that there are a few people who are generous, kind and intelligent. They make people's lives better and work continuously for the betterment of mankind and other living beings. They are concerned not only about other humans but also about the environment and other creatures. They are the people who are actually happy and content, because they spend their whole lives working for others. They have exposure to education and to the world around them through travel and, in modern times, also through computers and new technology. Education and technology are keys to greater knowledge in the modern world.

I regretted not getting a good education in school and college. My use of computers was limited to Google searches. I did not have the physical or mental space to take classes and study computers, even though I had the interest. I read a lot, particularly biographies of people like Mother Teresa, Stephen Hawkins and Einstein, who made a difference in the world. I was particularly impressed by the efforts that Mother Teresa had made. But given the magnitude of poverty and unhappiness in the world, I felt that one Mother Teresa was needed in every city and every village of underdeveloped nations.

I wished to have the courage and conviction of such people. I heard about many young people who had given up jobs and homes to work for the underprivileged. They found real peace and happiness.

I understood that real happiness comes from this kind of selfless dedication to the good of others. The happiness of making money is transitory. There is always someone who has more money and one is chasing a mirage. It is a never-ending rat race.

UP IN THE SMOKE

My first cousin, Manmohan uncle's son, got married. The wedding was celebrated in a five-star hotel in Delhi and family, rich friends and business associates were put up there. Lavish lunches and dinners, late night parties and drinking and dancing carried on for three days. For the first time, this extravagant display of wealth bothered me. I had spent the last few years reading and learning about poverty and suffering in India and the world. The plight of these half naked, hungry, homeless people did not awaken the conscience of the government or the rich to do something for them. This insensitivity deeply disturbed me. I admired Bill Gates, who used his wealth for the benefit of the poor and inspired so many others to do the same. Famous film stars and others in the western world have adopted children from poor countries. They are the few who give back something to the world, which has given so much to them. But the majority, I thought, are asleep. They cannot see the suffering of the underprivileged of the world.

In Sikhism, there is a tradition of giving 10 per cent of one's income, called *daswandh*, to the needy. But few Sikhs follow this, and among them, most people simply contribute to the local gurudwara. Of course, the gurudwaras always have a free langar, the meal served to every person who comes there, irrespective of caste or creed or social status. But the Sikhs comprise 2 per cent of India's population; even with all their devotion and efforts, how many hungry people can they feed? Equal distribution of wealth is the answer, but in this capitalistic world, it is impossible to implement.

After three days of partying, my cousin got married in a gurudwara. The next day was the reception, which was attended by family, friends and even some politicians. The three-day event finally came to an end and it was back to routine and back to reality for me.

Two weeks later, the wedding album and wedding CDs were sent to Amritsar for the family to see. Jasmina was excited and brought out our own wedding albums. The whole family got together and examined both the albums. Everyone remarked on how they had grown older over sixteen years. Many who were kids during our wedding were adults now. Many of the elders were no longer there. My grandparents and father were not there, nor was Jasmina's father. Many were too old to attend the wedding. Some had died young.

That night, as I sat before the TV, it struck me that many of those who had passed away would not have been missed if it had not been for the albums. People came and went, but the world kept spinning on. Other than a few who were close to them, nobody was affected by the absence of the dead.

'What will happen when I die?' I wondered. 'What will change? Who will be most affected?'

Jasmina will be the most affected because we are very, very close and she will find life hard without me. My children will be affected if I die when they are young. If I die in old age, it won't affect them much. As for the extended family, it will not affect them at all. And the other 770 million people on earth did not even know of my existence, so my death would be of no consequence to them at all.

Only if I can do something meaningful in my life, will it affect more people. But what can this meaningful thing be?

***

The rubber factory had started doing well again with the better-quality product that had been developed. I went back to China for meetings with our suppliers. I had a late dinner and drinks with them and was in deep sleep when my phone rang at 6 a.m. It was from the factory. I was really groggy and did not want to answer it, but suddenly it struck me that it must be 3.30 a.m. in India. A call from the factory at this hour meant trouble. I snatched up the phone. It was my terrified gatekeeper telling me that a massive fire had broken out in the factory. It had started in the boiler area and spread everywhere, including the sheds where raw materials and finished good were stocked. I told him to call Gagan and the fire department. He said he had done both, but Gagan's phone was switched off.

The gatekeeper told me that there were no workers in the factory to help extinguish the fire. Only the boiler man and his helper were there. They were running the boiler at night to catch up on two days of work because the boiler tubes had been under repair. The supervisor had also been informed of the fire and was on his way to the factory. I could do nothing. I waited impatiently for the fire tenders to reach. The gatekeeper went off to disconnect the electricity to the factory from the mains. I called the fire station but could not get through; the number was continuously busy. I kept calling until someone answered and told me that three fire tenders had rushed to my factory.

I called the factory landline, but there was no answer. The gatekeeper did not answer his phone.

Finally, at 8.15 a.m., China time, the gatekeeper called. He told me that the factory had burnt down to the ground. Two fire tenders had reached there, but they were too late. The first one had only a quarter tank of water. The second one tried hard to douse the fire, but the flames were too strong because of the rubber burning inside.

'What about the third fire tender?' I asked.

The gatekeeper said only two had come. He handed the phone to a fireman.

'What happened to the third fire engine?' I yelled, angry and frustrated.

The third fire engine had broken down half way to the factory. I could not believe my ears. I abused the fireman, who disconnected the phone.

I took the first flight back, and when I landed in Amritsar, I went straight to the factory. The factory that I had built with my blood and sweat and hard, hard work had burnt to ashes. It took all my effort not to wail at the sight of the burning ruins. I was shattered.

To claim insurance, I had to get a certificate from the fire department stating that the fire had been reported on time and the fire tenders were paid for their services. Another certificate was required from the fire safety inspector.

The fire station in-charge had no sympathy for me because I had abused one of the firemen.

'My men put their lives at risk to save your houses and factories. Instead of being rewarded, they only get abused,' he said angrily.

I apologized to him, but it was not apology that he wanted. So I asked him how much I should pay. I was told that I had to pay for three fire tenders and the fifteen men who had gone to put out the fire. I told him that only two fire tenders had come, of which one had hardly any water in it. But the officer showed me the ledger, which said three fire tenders had been dispatched.

So I paid double the fees for all the services, since my factory was technically outside the city limits. I also paid an extra amount to the officer for the certificate, and some more for having used abusive language with the fireman.

Three days later, the fire safety inspector came to the factory. He looked around and told me that the factory did not have the mandatory fire safety equipment. He could not issue the certificate. I turned around and walked into my office. The inspector followed. He told me not to worry and there were ways to show on paper that every regulation had been complied with. He would take Rs 1 lakh to do it.

I knew that after I got the certificates, I would have to deal with the insurance company, wait a long time to get my claim and then rebuild the factory, which would take more time and money.

I looked straight at the inspector and said with a smile, 'I don't need the certificate.'

The inspector was surprised.

He said, 'I am really sorry for your loss and I can make some concession for you – I will take only Rs 75,000.'

'Would you like tea or coffee?' I asked him politely.

'I can take Rs 5,000 less. I do want to help you.'

I smiled. I picked up the phone and called Gagan in the next cabin and told him that I had decided not to restart the factory, so I did not need to claim any insurance. I would simply build warehouses to store rubber materials for trading. Gagan paused and then asked me if I would give it a second thought. I said I did not need to think again; I didn't want to change my mind. Gagan agreed and there was no further discussion. The fire safety inspector walked away.

I told the supervisor to put up a one-month closure notice for the staff. I assured him that he would be rehired as the supervisor of the warehouse. I would also hire four or five of the better workers as loaders and unloaders at the warehouse. I worried about those who I could not reemploy, but there was no way I could run the factory again.

The factory shut down. The burnt machines were sold as scrap. The sheds were renovated to turn them into warehouses. From an industrialist, I was now a full-time trader. My uncles were not happy. They felt it was degrading to come down from being an industrialist to a trader. But I was happy and Gagan supported me fully.

WHERE THERE'S MONEY, THERE'S A GURU

The warehouses were soon ready and our trade picked up. I tried to put the loss of the factory behind me and move on. Hanging on to the past is a hindrance to future progress. Trading was more mental work than physical. I had faced so many difficult situations in life that I now had the ability to take risks. Coupled with a strong instinct, it helped me to grow much faster than my competitors. Sometimes, hasty decisions brought a backlash of losses, but that did not make me change my way of functioning. I worked in a small city near the border of the country where few buyers or sellers came. Lack of suitable opportunities was my biggest disadvantage and I believed that I had to take these risks to grow. My product quality, reputation and long-credit facilities to clients helped my business grow rapidly. It spread all over India. I travelled a lot and met many people from all over the country, who spoke different languages, ate different kinds of food, looked and dressed differently and followed different faiths. None of these was a hurdle in business.

What struck me in all my interactions was that most people had some kind of guru who they followed. Sometimes it was a religious preacher, sometimes a spiritual guru. Most of these gurus had large followings and many had branches abroad. Jasmina told me that many of my close relatives also followed gurus who had set up deras. This shocked me, because the last Sikh guru had clearly stated that there would be no more gurus and all the knowledge and guidance needed could be found in the Sri Guru Granth Sahib.

During my travels in Punjab, I saw many large deras that had come up all over the state. They were lavishly constructed. The babas there had fleets of luxury cars and travelled only business class with full security. If they were spreading the message of peace, why did they need security?

Every day new TV channels promoting these gurus and religious sects came up. These channels had a surprisingly large number of viewers, mainly women and the elderly. Huge hoardings announced the events of the gurus in many cities and large towns and newspapers advertised their upcoming talks. I had previously seen such big public gatherings only during political rallies in India.

One such event was planned in Amritsar. A famous Hindu preacher was to come here from a town in central India. Seventy thousand people were expected to attend and arrangements had been made for them on a big piece of empty government land. One of my friends was part of the organizing committee and approached me for a donation. He said he needed funds to build a hut for the guru. Apparently, this guru believed in living a simple life and did not stay in hotels or people's houses. He preferred a hut where he could meditate quietly.

I told my friend that I was an atheist and would not donate for any religious cause.

'Why don't you simply build the hut with your own money?' I asked him.

His answer was shocking. The guru did not live in the kind of simple hut that I had imagined, the kind that children draw or the poor live in. This hut had to be air-conditioned, have fire alarm systems, CCTVs, the works. It would cost half a million rupees to set it up. I refused to contribute. My friend was annoyed.

'You are an atheist and will never understand the meaning of spirituality,' he said to me. 'You will never get the blessing of the guru.'

I smiled and quietly walked him to the gate of the building.

A week later, I watched the live telecast of the guru preaching. I wondered what it was that drew so many people to him. The grounds were packed and people had to be turned away from the gates. Devotees climbed up trees and fences to get a glimpse of their beloved Guruji. What he finally said was just a rehash of the same old theories: he talked of karma and of the four yugas. He told his followers that we are now in Kalyug, the darkest of times, and only good deeds would save them from going to hell.

I had no faith in devotion instilled due to such fears. But people were impressed and followed such gurus with blind devotion.

Besides gurus, I also noted during my travels that slums had spread rapidly all over urban and semi-urban India. The gap between the rich and the poor had widened – the rich were becoming richer and the poor poorer. The poor cannot meet their daily needs and have no means of earning respect. Respect depends only on the amount of money one has. I wondered why all the great gurus did nothing for the poor. Would we all go to paradise just by listening to these gurus? Would I not attain heaven by adopting a homeless orphan or helping the desperately poor to build toilets in homes, or bearing the expense of educating their children? Was God so egoistic that He had to be praised every day and only then would He reward his children? I reminded myself that I was an atheist and need not think of God so much. But these were questions to which I needed answers.

The rise of self-proclaimed gurus and babas disturbed me because most of them did not do anything for the poor and needy. Though there were a number of Christian missionaries who worked for the uplift of the downtrodden, their activities were mainly directed at Christians. The government had schemes, of course, but these were rarely implemented properly and the poor never got their full benefit. Conmen, quacks, black magicians, everyone took advantage of the poor. The poor have no money, so the gurus and babas have no use for them.

THE LOST BANGLES

My trade flourished. I had regular clients and my supply chain was now stable. I travelled less and worked daily from 10 a.m. to 7 p.m., followed by badminton. I spent the weekends with my family, going out for dinners and movies.

However, life is never perfect, and worry came into my life from my sisters. Both of them had been in financial difficulties for a long time. Mummy worried about them all the time. Gagan and I did all we could to help and had became their support systems. In my heart, I still carried the guilt of the lawn of the house being sold off for me when I was in America. My family lived in a small house because of me. I wanted to buy a bigger house or at least something the same size as this house originally was.

I had been hunting for a suitable property for some months when I learnt that the house just opposite ours was up for sale. An old lady lived there with her daughter-in-law, and they found the house too big for their use. When the real estate agent told her that I was keen to buy her house, she approached me. I was delighted. I thought one brother could live in the new house. The old lady reduced the price a bit for me, but I still found it too high for the 800 square yards house. Before I could decide what to do, she sold the house to another buyer. I now regretted that I had not made a quick decision.

Four months later, I came across another house that was on sale. It was located on the main road, right in front of the land Papa had to sell. It was a well-built, corner property, open on three sides. It was 4,000 square yards, five times the property I had lost the opportunity of buying. Gagan also liked this house. The problem was how to put together the necessary funds. But my mind was made up. With Gagan's financial and administrative abilities, we would manage to find the money.

We sold the small plots of land we had bought and paid the token money. The deal was done. I missed Papa. I wish he had been alive to see that his son had got back what we had lost.

With proper financial planning, we got some money from bank loans and some from lenders. My credentials in the business world were put to the test. Many people agreed to lend us money when they learnt that most of the sum was paid and only a fraction was required.

'Nothing succeeds like success,' I thought. 'If you are successful, many will come forward to help you. But if you are in distress, no one comes to your aid. No wonder, people find it hard to recover from financial distress.'

Owning a 4,000 square yards house in the best part of the city was a big thing in this materialistic world. I found myself the recipient of greater respect, even from unknown people, just because I had bought a large property. They were not interested in knowing me; it was my possessions that earned me their respect. My friends introduced me to new people as 'the Bobby Sachdeva who has bought that big house on the main road'. Many people now knew my address, but few knew me. They never asked what I liked, what I thought or what I wanted to do in future. It was just the wealth that impressed them.

More respect flowed in when I bought the Mercedes-Benz E-Class Sedan, although my reason for buying it was safety on the highways, given the number of road accidents that occurred every day. Jasmina bought me sophisticated, branded clothes. She had always chosen my clothes and I simply wore whatever she laid out on the bed for me. Shoes, accessories, watches and pens increased the respect with which the world viewed me. All this was a very big deal in small-town Amritsar. I was now a well-established, successful businessman at the peak in my mid-forties. Many people wanted to know me.

I stuck to my old friends and cousins.

My successful and stable life made me much calmer. I continued to read and watch documentaries and other educational programmes on TV. The socio-economic changes in India raised many questions in my mind. The statistics did not show a truly developing nation. On the one hand, the number of millionaires and billionaires was growing rapidly, and on the other, the poor remained poor. Every rich, fancy colony in the city had an adjoining slum next to it, and the slums were growing bigger every day.

In the rural areas, only a few people, the landlords, had big houses, while the remaining lived in poor shanties. People were also divided on the basis of caste. The upper castes could not live together with the lower castes. At least in the cities, the caste divide was not so stark, and anybody who could afford it could buy a fancy house to reside.

There was a large slum very close to my house. Most of the people living there were painters, masons or other daily wagers. My domestic staff, including my driver, came from there. I passed this slum every day on my way to and from work. Once I had a reason to go inside and see what the place was really like, and I was shocked.

Jasmina's set of four gold bangles was stolen and she was certain that our new maid, who had worked for us for just two weeks, had taken them. I had questioned the maid and though she said she had not touched a thing, her body language convinced me that she was the culprit. The day after I accused her, she stopped coming to work. There had been minor thefts of food, accessories or some small change left on tables, which Jasmina never bothered about. But this was a big thing, and she and I both believed that we had to deal with it to send a message to the rest of the staff.

So, I went with Kulwant, our driver, to find the maid's house. He took me to the house of our washerwoman, who had worked for us for twenty years. She had brought the new maid to us.

The washerwoman was surprised and apprehensive when she saw me with Kulwant. She immediately invited us into her house. The 'house' was a shanty with a dilapidated door. Within was a 10 by 12 feet room with a low roof. There was a TV and a mobile phone, but no kitchen or toilet. Through a tattered cloth covering an opening in the back wall, I saw a small, enclosed area with a tap. A few clothes hung on a rope above it and a stove and some utensils lay nearby. A piece of tin formed a sort of roof over the stove and the utensils.

The woman asked me to sit on the bed and offered me tea, which I declined. She then got me a glass of water from the tap, and unable to refuse it, I took a tiny sip and gave the glass back. Kulwant asked about her family and she told us that her two daughters had gone to school and her husband had gone to look for work. He was a daily wager.

'Does he find work every day?' I asked.

'No, only on days when God is kind.'

I was amazed. Living in such desperate conditions, they still believed in God! They all worked in the wealthy colonies nearby and even that did not make it clear to them that they were being exploited. Instead they believed that it was their karma for bad deeds of their past lives.

Kulwant asked for the new maid's address, and when she asked why, he told her that she had stolen gold bangles. The woman was horrified. She knew the location of the maid's house and led us there.

We were led through narrow, stinking lanes. There was no sewage system and open drains ran along the houses. No wonder these people suffered bad health. And they had no money to get proper medical aid.

The new maid's house was worse than the washerwoman's. She was not at home, but an old lady with thick glasses through which she could barely see was washing clothes. A paralysed old man lay on a tattered bed and a small girl was crying in a corner. The washerwoman went in and talked loudly to the old lady, who was hard of hearing.

The old woman said, 'My daughter-in-law's brother died in a car accident. She has gone to the village for his cremation.'

'She has stolen gold bangles from the house she worked in,' the washerwoman told the old woman.

The old lady looked terrified. She shivered and started crying and looked beseechingly at me with folded hands. She did not have the courage to come near me or invite me in. I realized that these poor people felt like thieves even when they were simply being asked the whereabouts of the accused person. I felt mean and small, as if I was assaulting their dignity. But it was not a crime I could ignore.

I said, 'Ask your daughter-in-law to return those bangles, otherwise she will be arrested.'

Kulwant led me out of the slum through a different route. This was a much cleaner lane. I saw a gurudwara and a church in the lane. Indians keep their Gods in better conditions than they themselves live in. The Gods are the privileged ones in India.

THREE BANGLES DO NOT MAKE A SET

I went straight to office. Jasmina called at lunchtime. She had heard what had happened from the washerwoman and the driver, and she was not happy that I had not taken stricter action. She wanted me to file a report at the police station. I didn't want to humiliate the poor people any more. At the same time, I could not let my staff feel that I took such incidents lightly. I called Bobby Randhawa and asked for his help. BR had contacts in the police force. He referred me to the Station House Officer (SHO) of the second-largest police station in the city. All the Civil Lines areas, which were the wealthy areas of the city, and the slum near my house, called Nai Abadi (new settlement), were under its jurisdiction.

The SHO was very polite and offered me tea and biscuits. Thanks to BR, I was not treated like a common man. I told him about the theft, showed him a picture taken at a wedding in which Jasmina was wearing the bangles.

There was no one else waiting to meet the SHO at that time, and he chatted with me asking me where I lived and how I knew BR. We talked for half an hour. I had only been to a police station once before when I had been dragged into it as a young boy. I wanted to see the lock-up and the interrogation room. But the SHO told me that the interrogation room was out of bounds for civilians. He took me to the lock-up. There were separate rooms for men and women. The women's section was empty since women can't be kept in custody overnight; they have to be presented in court on the same day. But in the men's lock-up, there were eight men, one of them a teenager. All of them looked poor and two of them looked very distressed and in obvious physical and mental pain. Most of them ignored me.

The SHO assured me that he would do his best to recover the bangles and asked me to file a report so that the police could arrest the maid. I had no desire to do that and become embroiled in a long court case. I told the SHO to just recover my property without arresting or harming the maid. The SHO said he would help me, but BR should not be told of the deal. I did not understand what this deal was.

The SHO said, 'What are you offering me to do this?' He added, 'My wife has long wanted gold bangles. I cannot afford them with my poor salary. So if I recover the bangles, I will keep two of them as a gift from you for your bhabhi.'

I refused. I said he could keep one and return three.

'Three bangles don't make a set and neither does one,' said the SHO. 'I will take two or none.'

I used my trump card – BR.

'You can take one or you can talk to Bobby Randhawa.'

The SHO gave in.

The next day, he called me mid-morning and said he was outside my house. I found him dressed in his uniform, waiting in his jeep outside the gate. He pulled out three bangles from his pocket handed them to me and left.

When Jasmina got the bangles, she immediately wanted to know where the fourth one was. I explained to her what had happened and told her to get the fourth one made. But she said that was impossible, because these were specially designed and made in Kolkata. She could either wear only two or she needed the fourth one. The SHO was right: three bangles did not make a set.

I asked Jasmina the cost of one bangle, and then called the SHO and offered to buy the bangle from him or sell him one.

He was delighted and asked, 'What does one bangle cost?'

'Rs 25,000,' I said.

'In that case, I will buy all three from you,' he said.

I told him that I definitely would not sell all three; in fact, I wanted the one he had. But the SHO refused. I had to agree to sell one bangle to him for Rs 25,000. I was amazed that the man who had told me just a day earlier that he could not afford to buy his wife gold bangles was now willing to buy all three of them.

Jasmina was unhappy with the decision, but she knew that there was no other option.

On Sunday, the SHO arrived early. I had Rs 30,000 in my pocket. I first offered him Rs 5,000 extra for the bangle, but the SHO refused and instead offered to give me the extra money. So I gave him the bangle and he handed me a plain-white stapled envelope.

When he left, I opened the envelope and found only Rs 20,000 in it.

I immediately called the SHO, who said angrily, 'Don't call me about this unregistered case. I had to handle it properly, otherwise I would have lost my job."'

'What do you mean?' I asked.

'I had to give Rs 5,000 to the maid for treatment at a private hospital. She could not take the interrogation.'

The SHO disconnected the phone.

I was shocked and speechless. I realized that I should never have involved the police in the matter. When dealing with the poor and helpless, policemen have no mercy.

Jasmina saw my face and knew that something was wrong.

'They interrogated her at the police station. She had to go to a private clinic for treatment.'

Jasmina started crying. She wanted to go immediately to the maid's house to find out where she was admitted, but I stopped her. The maid's family would not welcome her.

Jasmina asked the washerwoman about the maid, but she looked frightened and said she didn't know anything. The next day, Kulwant was sent to the maid's house. He came back and told me that the family was frightened and refused to say anything. They were afraid of further police action. She and her husband were the only bread-earners in the family and they had a paralysed father, an old and nearly blind and deaf mother, and a two-year-old daughter to look after. She had stolen the bangles to give them to her parents, because her brother, the only earning member of the family, had died.

I felt very sad and guilty. The maid was a mother, wife, daughter-in-law, sister and daughter, and she tried to fulfil all those roles in the most trying of circumstances. The bangles would have meant bread and butter to two families. Now they would be showpieces on the wrists of two ladies.

Jasmina wanted to give away the bangles to the maid. Kulwant was sent to her house again the next day, but the family had left Amritsar and gone back to their village for good. Jasmina never wore the bangles again, and finally sold them and donated the money to an orphanage.

MONEY FLOWS IN, WORDS FLOW OUT

I had noticed a gradual but steady rise in the number of godmen and shrines and temples of all religions all over India. The proliferation of godmen both intrigued and disturbed me. They were everywhere – on hoardings, in newspapers and magazines, and on TV channels devoted to them. They were in social clubs, in government offices and even in educational institutions. Every Indian seemed to follow some godman or the other.

Many of the gurus are richer than the most corrupt politicians. Temples and other religious shrines have also amassed great wealth because people donate more and more money, jewellery and land to them. The domes of many deras and temples are plated in gold and silver, while the roofs over the poor are full of holes.

Why did God accept such materialistic devotion? And why did religion not give people the clear message that being kind to other human beings was more important than donating riches to temples?

Jasmina and I returned from a wedding in Ludhiana late one night. I had a court hearing the next morning at ten. I had filed a case against a client who owed me Rs 35 lakh and his cheques had bounced. I could not afford to overlook such a large sum. Like my father, I too have faith in human beings. I believe that they are essentially good;

only circumstances make them behave badly. So, I give goods to people on long credit and often incur debt. But this time, I had decided to get my money back. I did not want to give the impression that I never bothered about my money.

We reached home at 3 a.m. and Jasmina went straight to bed. I tossed and turned and finally got out of bed, switched on the TV and started surfing channels, national, regional and international. To my utter surprise, I found more than 50 gurus, babas, astrologers, preachers, numerologists, tarot readers and what not on various channels even at that hour. For more than an hour I watched them with the sound muted. Many addressed huge gatherings, others preached from TV studios. My curiosity piqued, I went to another room and put on the TV there with the sound on. On one channel, I saw an ordinary-looking moustachioed man in his mid-fifties, dressed in kurta pyjama and slippers, addressing a large gathering. There were security men all over the hall. People would tell him their problems and he would provide an answer.

When I first heard the questions and answers, I thought it was a comedy show, a rip-off on modern-day gurus. But the audience never laughed. Was this serious?

A man from the audience introduced himself as an engineer in a government-run refinery at Panipat. He wanted to know why he was not promoted despite his seniority and hard work.

Babaji: Do you eat dosa?

Engineer: Yes, Babaji.

Babaji: What kind? Plain? Masala?

Engineer: Masala.

Babaji: Potato and onion mixed masala?

Engineer: Yes, Babaji.

Babaji (smiling): No more onions in the filling. Eat dosas on every Friday for lunch for the next 10 Fridays. No onions, remember. Blessings will start coming to you from above.

The audience cheered loudly.

Engineer: 'Jai Babaji!'

Babaji smiled and raised his hand to bless the audience.

I could hardly believe what was happening.

It was the turn of a lady next.

Lady: Jai Babaji ki. I am Kamla Mehta.

Babaji: Where have you come from?

Lady: From Surat.

Babaji: By air?

Lady: Yes, Babaji.

The audience clapped as if Babaji had solved a mystery.

Babaji: I see an old lamp in your house. Do you have one?

Lady (surprised): Yes, Babaji.

Audience clapped.

Babaji: So, what is your problem?

Lady: My son has failed his class twelve examinations again.

Babaji: What is his name?

Lady: Mukesh Mehta.

Babaji: Do you go to a Krishna temple?

Lady: Yes, Babaji.

Babaji: What do you offer there?

Lady: Some money?

Babaji: How much money?

Lady: It varies depending on my mood.

Babaji: Ah, I know that. That is why I asked. Because you offer different sums at different times, Lord Krishna's blessings to your son are blocked.

Kamla Mehta looked as if she had committed a major crime.

Babaji: Don't worry. Offer Rs 101 regularly for one year until your son completes his examination. He will pass with very good marks and make you proud.

Lady (shouting): Jai Babaji ki!

I watched the unbelievable show till 6.30 a.m. and then switched to other channels. Most of the godmen had disappeared, except on channels that were dedicated to them. On the news channels, astrologers held sway on the breakfast show. I switched off the TV and went to get tea. Later I learnt from the Internet that Babaji was a Sikh from a Punjabi business family. He had amassed Rs 300 crore in short span of time.

I told Jasmina about the funny Babaji show.

'But how did Babaji guess all kinds of things about the lady?' she wondered. I explained it to her, 'The lady had come from Surat, so she was most likely a Gujarati. She had travelled by air so she was from a well-to-do family. Most Gujaratis worship Krishna, so it is most likely that she went to a Krishna temple. If she had said that she did not go to a Krishna temple, Babaji would have said that is reason why her son failed.'

'Why don't you become a babaji?' Jasmina asked me, laughing. 'You can read people well. And you would become a rich man in no time. There are no bad debts in this business. Money flows in and fake words flow out.'

THE WAYS OF GODMEN

I reached the court on time. The other party did not turn up for the third time in a row, and the judge set another date for the hearing. I was fed up with the rounds of the court, waiting till my case was called up for hearing and then finding out that the other party had not turned up.

I returned home, had a late lunch and went to sleep. I got up only at 4 a.m. the next morning. I had been dreaming all night, but the one I remembered clearly was a nightmare.

I was in a television studio and a row of babas sat on chairs before an audience for a talk show. I was among the audience. I raised my hand and asked a question, which no one could answer. The producer intervened and took a commercial break. He asked me to leave the studio because he was a devotee of one of the godmen and did not like me questioning him. No one stopped me. I left in my car, feeling frustrated and humiliated. The car was on the highway and I asked the driver to speed up because I wanted to reach home quickly. I googled 'rich and famous gurus in India'. Within seconds, all the gurus who were present in the studio were displayed on my phone screen. I then googled 'criminal cases against Indian gurus'. But before the results could be displayed, my Internet connection broke. I saw that the driver's phone showed full connectivity and I asked the driver to lend me his phone. Kulwant gave me his phone, which was an old Samsung Galaxy Note 2 that I had given him. But the phone was locked. I asked Kulwant for the password, but he gave me the wrong one. I asked him again and he refused. He said it was his personal phone and he had private information on it. I felt offended. How could my driver deny me the use of his phone? I started trying all kinds of passwords to unlock the phone. I was engrossed in this when there was a loud crash. An oncoming truck had hit my car with full force. Both the vehicles had been speeding. The car flew up in the air and crashed down on the road. I was dead on the back seat; the driver's seat was empty. Kulwant had never been there.

I woke up drenched in sweat. My heart was hammering. It took me a few minutes to calm down. It was 4 a.m. I had slept for nearly twelve hours. Jasmina was asleep beside me. I went over the dream again. It was very vivid. I wondered where Kulwant had disappeared during the accident, but then shook my head and reminded myself that dreams were only dreams. There was no logic to them.

I made myself some tea, went to another room and looked for another interesting baba on TV.

After surfing for a while, I zeroed in on two channels and alternated between them. One featured a very famous south Indian guru in his mid-fifties. He was short and thin, wore a white kurta and lungi and chappals, and had a long white beard. He always had a sweet smile on his face, as if he was at complete peace within himself.

The TV channel was airing a recorded show that had taken place in north India by the banks of a river. More than 50 thousand people had attended it, squeezing themselves into every inch of space. The show started with prayers before the arrival of the guru. Soon Guruji arrived in a Hummer, a bullet-proof car worth Rs 2 crore or more. He had such Hummers in most of the big cities of India and even abroad, where he had many followers.

The south Indian guru claimed to have 50 million followers – corporates, industrialists and politicians among them. At the mega event, Guruji gave a speech about the sanctity of maintaining our environment and respecting nature. Three hours later, the event ended. The ecosystem of the riverside had been destroyed and piles of garbage lay everywhere. A billboard announcing 'Cleanliness is next to Godliness' floated down the river.

The other channel that I watched had a hirsute sixty-year-old guru on it. His following, which he claimed was 5 million strong, was largely in west and central India. He was known to have a direct connection with Lord Krishna and claimed that Lord Krishna Himself had bestowed wisdom upon him. The rich Gujarati community gave him lots of money, while the not so rich formed his audience. His sermon that day was based on the *vastra haran* episode in the Mahabharata in which Dusshasan tries to disrobe

Draupadi in King Dashrath's court, with all the elders looking on. Krishna comes to Draupadi's rescue and her sari becomes infinitely long, which Dusshasan cannot pull off. The message was that women should be respected and protected. The audience comprised mostly women, including a few white women. The camera kept focussing on them, as if their presence lent greater credibility to the guru. The show ended with Guruji dancing to a *bhajan* based on the tune of a Bollywood number.

At 8 a.m., breakfast shows started and the astrologers came on. I listened with interest to what was said to be in store for me that day: 'Geminis will have some kind of financial gains today.'

For Sagittarian Jasmina the forecast was: 'You will have a good day and will be appreciated by your loved ones.'

That evening I got a call from one of my transporters that a truck carrying an outgoing consignment of fabric rolls had overturned and the entire consignment had fallen into a paddy field full of water. Cranes and labour to pull it out would only be available the next morning, by which time all the material would be ruined. Goods worth nearly Rs 30 lakh were destroyed.

When I reached home, Jasmina was ready and waiting to go to the mall with me to buy a birthday present for Aashna. I refused to go and Jasmina was disappointed and said that I never had time for her and always let her down at the last minute. I yelled back saying that she was getting too demanding and left the house to go to the park for a walk.

An hour later, I returned much calmer and told Jasmina about my bad day. It was only as I lay in bed at night reading the astrology column in a magazine that I remembered the predictions for us that morning. Neither of them had come true!

I turned to the gossip columns about movie stars. Maybe they had more truth in them.

THE CURSE OF UNQUESTIONING FAITH

I was obsessed with gurus and babas on social media and TV and closely followed six of the most famous and rich of the lot. I noticed that they were all associated with politicians, who were devotees of the gurus, though their devotion stemmed from their desire for power. The gurus had huge followings and millions would vote for the one they championed. Even in small towns there were babas who supported the local candidate. In return, they enjoyed political patronage, and rich followers helped them live luxurious lives. Besides, they got loads of free publicity when politicians and celebrities followed them; then common people flocked to them as well in the belief that there must be something good there. Thus, the gurus themselves became celebrities. They could not prove logically that God is omnipresent, but they themselves were everywhere!

I figured that most Indians are followers of one guru or another, or of spiritual healers or astrologers, and happily offer them anything from a few rupees to millions in cash and kind. Even if only half the population – 650 million people – were followers, this meant that every eleventh person on earth is a devotee of a guru.

Every sixth person on the planet is an Indian. Less than 4 per cent of them pay taxes and most of them pay just a few hundred or a few thousand rupees. The rest manage to prove that they are not in the tax bracket. Basically, Indians do not wish to pay taxes for the development of their own country, but most devotees of gurus happily pay gurus and religious shrines in the hope that their place in heaven will be reserved or they will have a good life in the next birth. More than twenty times the money paid in taxes goes into the hands of religious trusts and gurus.

I was shocked when I learnt these facts. I went to my favourite God, Lord Google, to look for answers. I made a list of the twenty richest and most famous gurus and the twenty richest shrines in India. The wealth of these put together constituted a major chunk of India's GDP. I searched for details of their expenses. There was no clear picture, but a new fact came up that really surprised me – there were piles of gold, diamonds and other precious stones in the locked underground vaults of many central Indian and south Indian temples. The government had tried to uncover this wealth, but the trustees of the temples would not allow it to touch the treasure. There were all kinds of stories of how unlocking this wealth would invite the curse of the Gods on the local populace. The government even appealed to the Supreme Court to intervene, but the matter still rests there.

'What kind of Gods are these?' I wondered. 'Why is God so greedy for material possessions when His children live all round Him in abject poverty?'

Then I reminded myself that I was an atheist, and as far as I was concerned, God did not exist.

'It is the godmen running their business in the name of God.'

'So are all gurus conmen and thugs?'

'No,' I reasoned. 'Many of them follow the faith they preach. Only a few are cheats. But why do most of them do nothing to help the needy?'

I was convinced that this habit of never questioning anything has made Indians 'dumb'. It is just confined to religion – Indians do not question anything that is deemed to be ancient knowledge.

If an astrologer were to be asked, would two children born at the same time in the same place, one the son of a rickshaw puller and the other the son of a businessman, lead the same kind of life, would he be able to answer this? Common sense tells us that the life of the two children would be different because their upbringing would be different. In exceptional cases, a rich man could become very poor or a poor man very rich. But in general, that is never the case.

My life had been full of many ups and downs, but I had negotiated it with help from family and friends and by the use of my own common sense. I never felt the need of advice from godmen or astrologers. Once a friend visited an astrologer and later told me that the astrologer's daughter had lost her husband in a car accident.

'Did Panditji foresee the accident?' I asked.

The friend shook his head sadly. If the astrologer could not foresee his own daughter's future, how was he going to predict anyone else's?

I was convinced that using one's mind to question everything was the key to finding the real thing. Without questioning, one just gets sucked into the trap laid by these thugs. I wish there were more saints like Mother Teresa or Bhagat Puran Singh and fewer charlatans who call themselves gurus. In the present day, that seems to be mere wishful thinking.

A famous and popular guru was arrested in Gujarat for sexually exploiting two girls who lived in his commune. The two had lived there with many other girls and with the consent of their parents to serve Guruji, so that they would gain spiritual learning and lead fuller and happier lives. But Guruji's blessings came to them in the form of lust. They were forced to sleep with him. They were told that they would go to heaven, their next lives would be happier because when they pleased him, they pleased God.

One girl chose to use her mind and resisted his advances. He tried to rape her, but she fled from his ashram in the middle of the night and went home and told her parents what had happened. Her father wanted to keep the matter quiet, but her mother was furious. She went with her to the police station and filed an attempt to rape complaint against the guru. The police officers were reluctant to record her complaint and warned the mother and daughter of dire consequences if they defamed the guru. The threat did not deter the two and they went to Ahmedabad, where another girl from the ashram joined them. They went to the press and reported the goings-on in the ashram. Two media channels picked up the news and splashed it across the nation. Newspapers followed up on the story and the police was forced to record the statements of the girls. The hue and cry that ensued encouraged many other girls to come forward and register similar complaints. They told the police that goons of the ashram had threatened them; some had been advised by parents to say nothing and many had never before told anyone about their sexual exploitation.

The guru was arrested, though his forty-year-old son, who was also accused of molestation, managed to run away and was arrested three weeks later. I expected the 5 million followers of the guru to be shocked and shamed, but to my complete surprise, they came out in full support of the guru and accused the girls of making up stories against the guru and his son. A few came forward as witnesses and some left the guru in disgust. The guru's henchmen killed two of the witnesses and threatened to kill the girls and their families, but the police protected them and the guru and his son are in prison awaiting trial.

Media reports estimate the guru's wealth to be above 12 thousand crores, accumulated over fifteen years. The guru was an illiterate *tanga* driver who discovered an easy way to fool a lot of people. He disappeared from his hometown and later surfaced as a godman in a remote village in Gujarat. Stories were spread of miracles that he performed and word of mouth did the rest.

Another guru, who claimed to have 40 million followers, had three criminal cases against him in the CBI court. He was accused of murdering his driver, castrating many men living in his commune, so that they could have no sexual relations with the girls there, and of raping a minor. This guru was from a small village in Rajasthan. He did not complete his schooling but became a devotee of an ailing local guru. The ailing guru appointed him successor and eight years later he became the guru of millions of lower-caste people who found their identity through him. Guruji encouraged them to stop believing in the caste system and treat everyone as equal. To the lower castes, discriminated against since centuries, this gave them dignity and a sense of power. The guru even assigned them a special surname, which became the identity of his followers.

Two eyewitnesses testified in court in the murder case and the CBI summoned the guru for the final hearing. Guruji left for court from his dera in a cavalcade of 300 luxury vehicles. Thousands of his followers lined the roads and he stopped at three places to address them. The followers firmly believed that their guru was above the law. Almost 90,000 supporters gathered outside the CBI court and raised slogans, convinced that their guru would be exonerated. But the overwhelming evidence confirmed his guilt, and he was sentenced to life imprisonment in the murder case. The hearing in the two other cases was fast-tracked. Guruji's followers went berserk and attacked the police and then everything that was in their way. The police had to fire at the mob and forty people died. Thousands were injured, hundreds arrested and property worth billions was damaged. The CBI judge was given special security. The government learnt its lesson and the other two cases are being heard in-camera.

The media uncovered many unsavoury details of the guru's vast empire – 300 deras in five states and real estate worth Rs 16,000 crore. Cash, jewellery, cars, gadgets, foreign currency, arms and ammunition were found in the headquarters, where 150 girls formed a private army to cater to his needs. The guru had made his own movies in which he played the lead, performing all sorts of death-defying stunts and miracles.

Not one politician came forward to condemn the man even after he was sentenced. The vote bank of his followers was just too large.

The conviction by the courts and public exposure of the fraudulent gurus made me feel bold enough to speak out against godmen in public, hoping to be heard out. No such thing happened.

GODMEN AND CRIME

Sandeep Gupta threw a party to celebrate his twenty-fifth wedding anniversary. My family and me, his friend for thirty years now, were invited. At the party, I met Rajat Mehra, an old acquaintance who I had not seen for a while. Rajat's son was there too, and during a conversation, he told me that he would be taking up science in college. I knew that Rajat was religious and superstitious, so I asked the boy how he would reconcile the teachings of modern gurus and superstitious beliefs with scientific theories. Rajat's family were ardent followers of a guru whose institution had branches all over Europe and other rich nations. The boy said that he had questions about the logic in the teachings of the guru and he doubted that he would be able to follow the guru blindly after studying science.

Rajat, who had been listening to this conversation, interrupted to tell me that his son would never doubt or betray his guru and that scientists also believed in God. I tried to pacify him by saying that it was just a general conversation about science and religious beliefs and such discussions opened up the mind. Rajat was not convinced, but he took the opportunity to invite me to a seminar a week later where his guru would be addressing a large gathering at a five-star hotel in Amritsar. The main speaker was from Nairobi and pupils from other European branches would also be there. Rajat said he would send me VIP passes.

I told him that I was not a believer and he should offer the passes to Sandeep and his wife instead. Rajat was offended. He thought this was an insult to his guru and told me that people were desperate to hear Guruji and only the blessed got tickets. People were willing to pay a lot of money for them. I gave in, but insisted that Sandeep Gupta also be given passes, so that we could come together. Rajat agreed and delivered the passes the very next day. He was convinced that once I heard his guru, I would turn a believer, though Jasmina joked that it was more likely that the guru would start doubting his own teaching after a conversation with me!

A few days before the seminar, the Punjab and Haryana court issued non-bailable warrants against a small guru with about 3 million followers in Haryana. His followers all lived within 30 to 40 kilometres of his dera. Before the police could get there to arrest him, 70,000–80,000 followers surrounded the dera and dared the police to arrest the guru. Women formed the first line of defence. The media was present in full force and the police did not want to take a wrong step. The guru had been taunting the government from within the dera, but outside, his followers were prepared with sticks and stones to attack the police and also threatened to kill themselves if the police did not go away.

There was tension all through the first day. On the second day, paramilitary forces were deployed in large numbers. It was the month of June and the temperature was 45 degrees Celsius in the afternoon, making it difficult to stand under the scorching sun, but the followers stood their ground. They got food, water, portable fans and sheets from the dera. The government, on the other hand, had a hard time feeding all the policemen on duty, providing them with toilets and tents. The area had been cordoned off by cutting the supply lines from the villages to the dera, but there was enough stock inside to withstand the siege. The Supreme Court directed the central government to assist the state government if necessary. Messengers were sent into the dera to negotiate with the guru. Instead the guru warned the judge that God would paralyse him as a punishment for issuing the arrest warrants! He then invited the media inside and told them that he was willing to surrender, but his followers would not allow it. If he were to be arrested, his followers would block the roads and immolate themselves. Thousands would die. He suggested that he should be allowed to stay on in his dera and the government could consider it house arrest.

Once the media entered the dera, images of the luxuries within flashed across screens all over India. There was an indoor heated swimming pool, a gym, a personal theatre, indoor and outdoor play areas, lavish bathrooms fitted with jacuzzis, smart TVs and music systems, Italian marble floors and more amenities than any five-star hotel. This was where Babaji, the spiritual head of thousands of poor people from the lower castes, wanted to live under house arrest.

Of course, the government rejected his suggestion and offered to airlift him by helicopter. Many politicians had visited this dera and there was a helipad inside. However, no politician or political party came forward to ask the guru to surrender. The police had arrived there on a Thursday, and finally on Saturday night, they rushed into the compound when most of the tired followers were fast asleep. Hundreds were arrested and many injured; three people died. The guru was finally arrested and taken to jail in a police van.

Jasmina and I watched all this live action on TV with our morning tea. The media, which had ignored the guru so far, now delved into his background. I wondered why they did not do so before these gurus' smooth tongues helped them amass such large followings.

NO ANSWERS TO MY QUESTIONS

I was reluctant to go to Rajat Mehra's guru's seminar, but Sandeep persuaded me, saying the ladies would enjoy it and the organization was very different and had enlightened many souls in Europe and America. Nearly one-third of the following was of white people and, Sandeep argued, if they could follow this guru, why couldn't Indians listen to what he has to say?

At 5 p.m., we reached the venue. The office bearers of the organization were all dressed in white kurtas and pyjamas, with badges indicating their position. It was women who primarily ran the institution; they wore only white saris and never married. They were known to be the most learned spiritual scholars in India. I had found out that though the organization had branches in many nations, it was located in the well-to-do areas everywhere.

'Where there is money, there is a saint,' I said to myself.

The hall was full of the influential people of Amritsar, with the commissioner of police, the district collector and a member of Parliament all seated in the front rows. The show started with a prayer and then two local, well-known ladies interviewed the eighty-year-old founding member of the organization. Later, the main speaker, Mr Idris from Nairobi, came to the dais. He was a rich, seventy-year-old Muslim businessman. He went on to advocate the ideology and support the noble cause of enlightening the minds of the audience through three theories: the theory of karma, Kalyug and Satyug, and God's master plan.

I was dismayed when I heard what I believed was totally irrelevant in my experience.

Mr Idris began by saying that he was talking of Vedic spirituality though he was a Muslim who should not speak of any other religion. But he believed that it was the good deeds of his past life that had given him the opportunity to serve this noble cause in this life. Simply put, he said that good deeds ensure a better life next time, while bad deeds mean a hard life in a hard place. I raised my hand to ask a question, but a volunteer said I could not disturb the speaker mid-session.

Then came his discourse on Kalyug, and he told the gathering that time was divided into four yugas. It began with the golden period of Satyug, but now we were in the darkest phase of Kalyug. I raised my hand, but once again a volunteer asked me to sit down. Mr Idris also noticed me this time, but he continued with his final point, which was that God had already preordained our lives. Every little thing was predestined; even the people who were sitting in the hall listening to him were destined to be there. This was too much for me.

Before anybody could stop me, I got up and said, 'Sir, I have a question.'

There was silence in the hall and the speaker looked slightly irritated. Rajat ran up and asked me to sit down. But I pointed at the stage and told him that I disagreed with everything the speaker had said. Rajat asked me to come out of the hall. I realized that everyone was staring at me, some in anger and others with curiosity. I walked out behind Rajat and told him that I had questions to which I needed answers. If these people claimed to enlighten minds, then they should answer my queries. I was really angry and agitated.

When we heard applause from the hall, signifying the end of the talk, Rajat led me backstage. Mr Idris came there a few minutes later. About twenty girls dressed in white lined the passage. Rajat introduced me and said that I had some questions. Mr Idris shook my hand and nodded his head.

'How does the theory of karma work? Isn't there a first time for everything?'

'Yes,' replied Mr Idris.

'That means our first birth was not governed by karma, and God put us wherever He pleased? Some in poor houses and others in rich, some in happy situations and others in difficult ones.'

Mr Idris agreed.

'So that first time, the environment we grew up in defined our mindsets and dictated our deeds. So, if that first birth was not by our choice, then how could God punish us for our bad deeds in our next life?'

Mr Idris was silent.

'Any other question?' he asked.

'Yes, sir. But after you answer the first one.'

'You go and see Sister Narayani. She will guide you.'

'Sir, you preach theory. This is your ninety-ninth event. You also preach on TV. You must have preached to millions of people. I am also among those millions, please answer my question yourself.'

'Ok, I will answer. What is your next question?'

The twenty women had now surrounded us and Mr Idris seemed anxious.

'You say that the Kalyug is the darkest period in human history. But according to me, this is a golden period. The world's estimated population is around 770 million. In 2002, 1,000 Muslims were killed in Gujarat. In 1984, 4,000 Sikhs were massacred in Delhi and other parts of India. In 1947, 1 million people were killed and 5 million displaced due to the Partition of India. In the Second

World War, the Nazis killed 5 million Jews. At that time, the world population was 230 million. Hitler, the killer of these people, was a hero in his country. Germany now gives refuge to millions of war-affected Muslims from Syria and Afghanistan.'

'What is your question?' said Mr Idris impatiently.

'Two more minutes, please. If you go further back in history, kings brutally killed enemies and even innocent citizens. Millions of people were killed in wars when the population of the world was one-fifth of today. In fact, the further back we go, the more barbaric we find people to be. The plight of women has been horrific. Our history is full of violence and brutality.'

'Yes, yes, what is your question? I have to go now.'

'You say this is Kalyug and the past was Satyug. But isn't it the opposite? The population has multiplied many times, but no leader can now kill any person and become a national hero. Leaders today have to step down if they are caught in corruption scandals or murders. Women's liberation has made a difference to the lot of women in our society. You can't even slap a child as before. So, I think this is Satyug and the past was Kalyug. What do you think?'

'Very valid question. But it's a long question based on the long history of mankind and needs time to explain. I suggest you go to one of our centres and talk to someone there. You will get all the answers. I really don't have time now. I must be back on stage for the closing ceremony.'

Rajat immediately agreed.

But I said, 'So you have no answers to my questions? Then you should stop preaching ridiculous theories to people who ask no questions.'

Mr Idris gave me his calling card and asked me to write to him.

I said, 'Sir, you claim to enlighten people and alleviate their misery. But aren't you meddling in God's master plan where everything is predestined?'

'Rajat, let's go,' said Mr Idris and they walked off.

The women looked at them and then at me, some in anger, some in appreciation and others in bewilderment.

I walked into the hall where Jasmina, Sandeep and his wife were watching the closing ceremony. Jasmina looked anxiously at me. A lady on stage was explaining how telepathy worked. But I had had enough. I asked Jasmina to come out. Sandeep and his wife also followed us. They wanted to know where I had been. I told them that I was seeking answers to my questions, but Mr Idris was unable to provide them and it had caused some bitterness between Rajat and me. Sandeep told me that there was no need to question people. I should listen quietly and then follow or not follow what was said, as I wished.

'We should concentrate on the snacks and tea,' he smiled.

'It is my problem that I cannot sit and listen like a dummy,' I retorted, irritated. 'That is why I did not want to come here in the first place. I agreed only because you were with me and Rajat had said they would address queries from the audience.'

'You should have stayed at home and watched the Discovery or Nat Geo channels,' said Jasmina angrily.

'Yes, that would have been better for me.'

A WRITER IN MY HOME

When I was changing that night, I found Mr Idris's calling card in my pocket. I handed it to Jasmina and told her that he had asked me to write my questions to him. Jasmina said that it was better for me to write privately to preachers instead of making a public spectacle.

'They preach in public, don't they?' I said. 'Then they should answer questions in public, too.'

But the next morning I got up early, opened the bedside table drawer to get my glasses and saw the calling card. I immediately wrote an email on my phone repeating the three questions and requested an early reply. I felt strangely calm and happy after writing it. Jasmina noted the look of satisfaction on my face and remarked that some people found release of their tensions in writing and this made them happy. I recalled that my great grandfather and his grandfather always wrote a daily diary and Jasmina said that Aashna did the same, though she refused to show anyone what she wrote. Jasmina had tried reading

Aashna's diary once, while cleaning her writing desk, but Aashna had walked in and snatched it from her, claiming it was private.

Jasmina was delighted to know that Aashna was carrying forward a family legacy. She told me that Aashna also wrote poems and articles for her school magazine. She was shy and had to be persuaded by her teachers to reveal her talent. I was thrilled. I had found such solace and joy in writing that I decided I would always write whatever was in my heart.

At dinner I asked Aashna what she liked to write, but Aashna was annoyed. Jasmina quickly stepped in to say, 'I told Papa that you love to write. Papa has also started writing and finds it very relaxing.'

Aashna turned to me with a surprised smile and asked, 'What have you written?'

'An email,' I replied, and we all laughed.

'You should write whenever your heart is heavy; it eases the pain,' Aashna said. But when I asked to see her poems, she refused.

'They are not for public reading.'

'We are not the public; we are family,' protested Angad.

But Aashna said she would show them when she wrote something that wasn't private. I probed a little more and discovered that she wanted to be a writer and do a screenplay writing course. Immediately, I whipped out my phone and googled the best writing courses in India and shared the results with her.

'Papa, you are just too impatient,' said Aashna. 'I still have to complete class twelve. Then I will take a break year and travel the world. After that I will look at college.'

'You are too young to roam the world alone,' I said to her. 'Wait for another three or four years, grow up a little more and get street smart, then you can travel on your own.'

Aashna was all ready with arguments, but Jasmina and Angad both agreed with me, so she gave in.

'Besides, a three-month break after the twelfth board exams is enough time to relax. After that you should join college. The three-year writing courses all start in June and July next year, so you must prepare to live away from home from the coming summer,' I told her.

I was so excited about Aashna's writing aspiration that I began investigating the four institutes I had shortlisted and from them selected the two best – Film and Television Institute of India (FTII) and Whistling Woods. My own desire to write was strong and I thought my daughter could help me with the English language and vocabulary. I had never had the opportunity of a stable school and college life, and I felt I was illiterate. But now I started writing every day.

A month later, I had an appointment for counselling for Aashna at Whistling Woods in Mumbai. The option of FTII had to be shunned as it was for postgraduates.

I love Mumbai. It is the city of Bollywood movies, which had fuelled my fantasies when I was young. Films had also introduced me to the divide between the rich and poor in Indian society. In old Hindi movies, the hero is always a noble and mostly poor man in love with a girl from the upper-middle or rich class and the story generally revolves around how their love breaks down the class barriers. Modern Hindi movies are full of rich people living rich lives, completely disconnected from the reality of the common man.

I was already dreaming that my daughter would be a successful screenplay writer and her stories would be made into hugely successful movies. Her movies would be based on the lives of the poor and the middle class. Mahatma Gandhi, a true Indian, had given up wearing anything but a dhoti when he saw that most Indians were so poor that they could barely clothe themselves. He brought India to the centre stage of the world by identifying with the majority of its citizens – the poor. I was sure that Bollywood could do the same. I was sure Aashna could hold up a mirror to Indian society because she was a sensitive person.

MINDLESS BELIEVERS

Kulwant, my driver, asked me for a loan of Rs 20,000. I was taken aback because he had taken an advance of Rs 15,000 just a couple of months ago and had not yet repaid it. I demanded to know why he needed so much money. Kulwant hesitated, but I refused to give him any more money until he answered, so he told me that his wife was in hospital since three days and the bill had crossed Rs 25,000 this time.

'This time?' I asked, surprised.

'This is the second time in two years that my wife has had a miscarriage,' said Kulwant. 'The last time, too, my son died in the womb.'

'Son? How do you know it was a son?'

'Our babaji told me that I had been blessed with a son both the times, but some ghost or witch is causing them to die. It does not want me to have a son to carry my name forward. I only have two daughters,' Kulwant said, sadly.

I was furious, but knew that at such a time I could neither preach to him that daughters and sons were equal nor be angry with him.

'Take me to the hospital,' I said. 'I will pay the bills there.'

I checked the bill and was appalled to see that medicines and even bottles of glucose were charged far more than their actual cost. Even the doctors' fees and surgery charges were high for a mid-level hospital. Though Kulwant's wife was in a room shared with three other patients, she had been charged the rent of the whole room. I protested strongly and the bill was reduced to Rs 21,500. Kulwant was very grateful to me.

'I do not want this money from you,' I told him, 'but only on the condition that you will not make your wife pregnant again just because you want a son.'

Kulwant nodded his head.

'Ji, sahib,' he said.

I knew he did not mean a word of it.

Rajat and his wife visited us one Sunday. I apologized for the unpleasant scene I had created at the seminar. Rajat was still upset.

'You should have waited for the event to end and spoken to other members of the organization,' he said. 'Why did you accost the speaker?'

I reminded him that he had given me passes to the event and took me to Mr Idris saying that it was meant for people like me and my queries would be addressed. I added that if he could answer those questions, I would be happy to apologize to Mr Idris.

'We are ordinary people and do not understand the spiritual aspects of the gurus,' he said, angrily. 'We do not feel the need to question them.'

'If common people cannot understand the deeper meaning of spirituality, then why do gurus preach? Why do they waste their own and other people's precious time?'

Rajat did not know what to say. He said that he had come there to tell me that I had not done the right thing at the seminar. Because of my behaviour, he had been pulled up by the managing committee and removed from the core group for a year.

To ease the tension between us, I changed the subject and offered to go for a movie and dinner in the evening. Rajat, after some reluctance, agreed, and the rest of the time was spent in near normal conversation.

THE JOY OF WRITING

Jasmina, Angad, Aashna and I went to Mumbai for Aashna's counselling at Whistling Woods. Aashna and I went into the counsellor's cabin, while Jasmina and Angad waited outside. Suparna, the counsellor, was a young thirty-year-old woman, who looked twenty and talked like a teenager. She was very friendly. She asked me about my family and told me about hers, which put us both at ease. Then she asked Aashna to narrate one of her stories. Aashna began hesitantly. I interrupted mid-way to say that I did not find any hook point in the story and it did not revolve around the main protagonist. Suparna listened in silence. At the end of the story, I pointed out that Aashna had unintentionally revealed the mystery of the suspense thriller.

Suparna asked me if I was a writer too.

When I said no, she said, 'Well, you should be one, because you have instinctively pinpointed where the story went off track.'

She suggested that my daughter and I could be a team since Aashna had very expressive language and I had the knowledge to create content for cinema. I was puzzled and wondered what I should write.

'Your heart will tell you that,' said Suparna.

At dinner that evening, Jasmina and Angad smiled knowingly at me and Jasmina said, 'So now we have two writers in the family!'

'Buy one, get one free!' quipped Angad.

They had both heard the entire conversation through the cabin's window.

Three days later, we were back to our daily routine in Amritsar. I was sitting in my office going through the YouTube during my lunch break, when a video of Javed Akhtar sahib abruptly popped up on the channel titled "Acha nai lagta" with his picture on it. Finding it attractive, I opened it without any specific thought. This was his poem where he points out that we do not like to endorse ideas which might have merit if we do not like them. It poked my inner conscience, and somehow, I connected to it strongly. I was moved as well as motivated to write about topics which are not well accepted socially. In the beginning, I picked up a pen but could not write a word. I had not even written my diary after the first day. But the writing bug had bitten me. After twenty minutes, I set aside the pen and paper and picked up the newspapers and went into the washroom. The lead story that day was about the daughter of an IAS officer who was stalked by the son of a powerful politician. The girl was on a scooter and the boy in an SUV. She stopped her scooty and called the police. The incident was recorded on CCTV cameras. The media picked up the story and it received wide coverage. No arrest had been made so far. A politician's son harassing a girl was nothing unusual, but the girl confronting him and being supported by her father was news.

I started writing a story on the memo pad in my mobile. I wrote for two hours, ignoring all calls on my phone. I called the story 'Pehchaan', meaning identity, and it was about the misuse of powers by influential people and the struggle of a common man to get out of the trap. At noon, I sent all the memo notes to Jasmina to take printouts. Jasmina was amazed that I had written the whole story in one go.

I switched on my work phone and found loads of messages and missed calls. The factory and warehouse staff were awaiting my instructions. I gave detailed instructions each morning because I could not bear mismanagement or negligence, and when travelling, I often handed over written notes. Gagan usually took over both administrative and marketing work in my absence.

I went over the story again at night. I had forgotten about it in the day, but when I read it again I was very pleased. It was a crime thriller with a message, I felt, and Jasmina agreed.

The next morning I sat with my pen and paper again, but no ideas popped up and the paper remained a pristine blank. As usual, I picked up the newspapers and headed for the washroom. I was bored with my daily routine. I wanted to do something different. The Sunday paper carried a story about a nine-year-old ragpicker girl who was killed by stray dogs. That triggered something and I picked up my phone and started writing a story, 'I Wish to Be a Dog', about the sorry plight of ragpicker children. I finished it in fifteen minutes. Then I googled ragpickers and learnt that India has two million ragpickers. Many of them are bitten or killed by stray dogs in the dumps where they work.

Jasmina was very moved when she read the story and encouraged me to write more stories with such socially relevant content. But I could not write to order; stories just came to me when they came.

At 5.30 a.m. the next day, I woke up with a story in my head that demanded to be written down immediately. When Jasmina got up at 8 a.m., I was still writing and sushed her when she started talking. She was offended, but asked me if I wanted tea, which annoyed me even more, and I glared angrily at her. She left the room in a huff.

At 9 a.m., the story 'DNA', based on the caste system, was complete. I emailed it to Jasmina and then went to look for her. She was busy scrolling through her Facebook and refused to look up. I sat in front of her, put her feet in my lap and started pressing them. She usually relented when I did this, because in India, a wife touches her husband's feet in respect, never the other way round.

As usual, she smiled slowly and moved her feet away. She printed out the story and brought it to me to read. But I wanted her to read it first. I had written it in one urgent flow and there could be many errors. I went off to work and at 4 p.m. Jasmina's WhatsApp message arrived with a smiley face. She really liked the story. She had corrected the few mistakes that she found.

In the next five weeks, I wrote ten short stories, three long stories and some childish, immature poetry. I mailed everything to Jasmina, except the poems, which I thought were too silly to be shared. I wanted other opinions on my writing, so I took my children on a long drive with some wine and snacks and narrated two short stories and one long one. They liked them very much and my confidence rose.

Mr Jatin Shah organized plays in Amritsar and I narrated two of my stories to him. He liked the stories too, and he advised me to learn script writing. The stories were detailed, he felt, but more like plots than screenplays. He recommended a professional writer who could give me better advice. I met the gentleman and narrated two other stories to him. This writer found my stories very interesting. When I told him that my English was very poor, he told me to write in Hindi or Punjabi.

'Language is just a medium to communicate with others,' he said.

I said, 'But I prefer to write in English because I want my stories to reach as wide an audience as possible.'

'The greatest difficulty is finding a good publisher or a someone in the film industry who will at least look at your work.'

I decided right away that I would get some established writers in Bollywood to assess my writing. If it was any good, I would continue to write, otherwise, I would give it up. However, writing gave me such solace that I thought it would be nice to write irrespective of anyone's opinion of it.

Jasmina had an aunt in Mumbai whose husband was a close friend of Mr Umesh Mehra, a successful erstwhile producer in Bollywood. Though he no longer produced movies, he was still closely connected with the film world.

Jasmina asked her aunt to introduce me to Mr Mehra. As luck would have it, Nancy *bua* told Jasmina that a whole group of her friends, including Mr Mehra, were going to be in Amritsar on a pleasure trip a week later and she would certainly arrange for me to meet him.

I met Mr Umesh Mehra at a coffee shop in the hotel where they were putting up. He heard two stories and then declared that I was an *ulti* writer – a rare breed of writers who vomit out a story in one go. He said one of my stories was old wine in a new bottle, but the other could easily be a hundred-episodes serial. He suggested that I get my stories registered with the Screen Writers' Association (SWA), otherwise, when I narrated my stories to film and TV serial makers, the concepts could be stolen.

I decided to go to Mumbai a week later and register with the SWA. I was very excited, but wondered how I could quickly learn to write scripts. I searched YouTube and found a Mr Rathore who guided aspiring writers with a book and a CD. I immediately ordered the book for Rs 5,000. The slim book could be read in two hours and the CD ran for an hour.

After going through the book and the CD with me, Jasmina was doubtful if I would have the time to write a script. I realized that I was not a real writer – I could not write a single line if someone told me to. My stories came from my own subconscious and emotions. I did not create them; they were created in my mind when something I heard or read triggered the process. To become a professional screenplay writer, I would have to take a full-fledged course, and I could not spare any time from work. But I knew that it was important to register with the SWA in Mumbai.

Aashna had decided to join Whistling Woods. She had to appear for the entrance examination in Mumbai two months later, but I, impatient as I was, could not wait that long. I wanted to find out if there were agents who would take my stories to film directors and producers. I called Mr Rathore who invited me to Mumbai.

I wrote another plot for a full-length feature film a day before I left for Mumbai. It was a comedy called 'Five Desi Americans' and could also be adapted as a TV serial.

Jasmina called her cousin, Harjas, in Mumbai and asked him to find a writer who could read and assess my stories for a fee. Harjas was a businessman with no idea about the film world, but his friend, Alia, was a screenplay writer and worked for TV channels. He told Jasmina to contact her. Alia spoke to Jasmina and asked for a synopsis of my story. Jasmina sent it to her and reminded her again two days later to read it.

Alia called me just as I was entering Mr Rathore's office building in Mumbai. She said she had read the story and it was interesting, but it needed to be developed into the proper format. I thanked her and asked how long it would take for the story to be converted into a script. She said that it would take six months to a year, with someone working full-time on it. I told her that I had written the story in ninety minutes! She was impressed. But when she heard that I was going to meet Mr Rathore, she warned me that in Mumbai, my stories and concepts could be stolen in a jiffy and I should be very careful.

Mr Rathore was a friendly person. He asked me to narrate a story, but with Alia's warning ringing in my head, I narrated my story but changed it so much that it was quite directionless in the end. Mr Rathore was disappointed and told me that I did not have the ability to be a writer and he was unable to help me.

My heart sank.

'To tell you the truth, I twisted the story because I was warned that my plots and concepts could be stolen,' I said.

Mr Rathore laughed and asked me to narrate a story that no one would steal. I started telling him the story of my own life, beginning with the anti-Sikh riots of 1984. The events of my life came alive as I narrated them and I had to stop and sip some water to prevent my tears from spilling over. Those traumas still had the power to unsettle me completely.

Mr Rathore was in tears too by the time I finished and I was on the verge of breaking down completely. I just wanted to leave, but Mr Rathore offered me a cup of tea. He called his assistant, a young man called Srivinay, Sri for short, and told him that my story was different and engrossing.

I narrated the story again, this time with a bit of fiction where religion and the judiciary were involved. When the story ended, Sri and Mr Rathore looked at each other in disbelief. Mr Rathore said it was the best story he had ever heard. Sri said that it was a story for a novel that could later be made into a movie. I was amazed. I had just discovered the story in my own life.

I asked Mr Rathore if there were ghost-writers who could write scripts. But he said I should forget everything else except 'Once There Was Me'.

I went to the SWA office, filled forms and submitted my papers, and waited to deposit the membership fees. I looked at the pictures of writers on the walls, many of who were dead, but whose words are still alive in the minds and hearts of people. I imagined that after forty or fifty years, my picture would also hang on these walls. The cashier called me and I deposited the money and bought a Bollywood directory. I headed for the airport and on the way highlighted names of people I most admired, like Mr Rajkumar Hirani and Mr Javed Akhtar. I called Jasmina and told her that there was a new story that would take me months to write.

The next morning, I started writing 'Once There Was Me'. It was tough. I had to revisit the dark corners of my past, but I could also relive the joyful moments. I weaved some fiction into the story, events from other's lives that were rarely talked about. I was immersed in writing my story, when one morning, out of the blue, demonetization jolted the country. Small factories and businesses were badly hit. Some of my clients shut down their businesses and many others were on the verge of collapse. Small-scale industries that supplied commercial quality, low-cost products to rural areas, which were not covered by big brands, could not survive. This had a terrible effect on my business. Almost 20 per cent of it was lost. I needed to work harder and put in more time to revive it. But all I wanted to do was write my book. I had no desire to spare extra time for the business. My expectations and needs were never too high, and I knew that I could survive with less money.

GOD'S MONEY FOR GOD'S CHILDREN

My stories had churned up another great desire in me – I wanted to do something for the underprivileged. The more I wrote about the plight of the unfortunate, poor people in my stories, the more empathy I felt for them. But did not know how a common man like me could do anything to alleviate the suffering of even 1 per cent of the underprivileged. Through my stories, I wanted to change the way people thought, so that they would be inspired to do whatever they could for the poor. That could take a long time.

Then one day, it suddenly struck me, 'Why can we not use God's money for the welfare of God's children?'

All this money that was donated so abundantly to temples and to godmen should somehow be brought into rightful use for people who needed it most. But first, I would need to have an idea of how much money there was with temples and godmen. No one would reveal this information willingly. Some trusts did have information publicly available, but it was hard to tell how correct and complete it was. However,

I collected whatever information was available. I stopped writing for a while and surfed the Internet and found data from some shrines and a few gurus' ashrams. I jotted down rough estimates, thoroughly searched Wikipedia, and perused websites and articles. Then I chose twenty gurus and twenty shrines for this purpose.

Armed with this list and information, I went to Mr Rakesh Kothari, an activist, and requested him to prepare a Right to Information (RTI) application against the shortlisted gurus. Unfortunately, Mr Kothari's own guru's name happened to be on the list. He was very annoyed. He told me that it was important to highlight the teachings of these gurus, not their incomes. All of them were not charlatans; some of them were very good people.

I tried to tell him that I was not against any guru; I only wanted to know their worth and the kind of wealth they had. Mr Kothari was unconvinced and told me that he could not file any application anyway, because only government departments come under the purview of the RTI Act. Besides, he believed that this wealth belonged to God and not to humans. I tried to argue that God had no need for material possessions, that the poor were also His children and needed His help, but Mr Kothari remained unmoved.

After this meeting, I was convinced that every other person was the follower of some guru. There are around 4,200 religions in the world, each further divided into different sects. In fact, some religions have more than thirty sects and others, hundreds of sects. On an average, it meant that there are at least 80,000 different ideologies flowing in and out of human minds. New Age gurus have now come up with their own theories and concepts, further dividing the already divided.

I decided that I needed to file a Public Interest Litigation (PIL) in the Supreme Court. I would bring the huge wealth of the temples and ashrams to the notice of the Honourable Supreme Court and highlight the plight of more than half of India's population living in sub-human conditions.

People offered money to God to better their lives, so why could this money not become blessings for His children? It should be taken over by the government and used to build skill development centres, hospitals, schools, orphanages, old age homes, cottage industries in villages, small factories to be used as training centres. There was so much to do. Though the government did something for the upliftment of the poor, the problem was so large that it could make only a small difference. Besides, corruption in government swallowed up a large part of the resources meant for the poor. Perhaps the fear of God's wrath would prevent misuse of God's money by corrupt officials. The government had been trying hard to bring back black money stashed in Swiss and other banks abroad. Why not concentrate on the money stashed at home in temples and ashrams? Everyone from every religion would benefit by this, so there could be no objection to it at all.

I collected a huge amount of data and information, but I was afraid that my PIL would be rejected. I planned to say in the PIL that the shrines and gurus could keep more than a year's income in reserve for any emergency or unforeseen expenditure.

The plan was to first seek information of the monthly income and the monthly expenditure of these places from the Internet. In most cases, the monthly income far surpassed the expenditure and grew rapidly. Someone who will not give Rs 500 to his sick worker will happily donate Rs 5,000 to a guru or a shrine. I also decided that in my PIL, if approved for hearing, I would request the court that there should be a limit on what can be spent on construction of new temples, mosques, churches, etc. Instead, the money should be used to restore and maintain old historical and religious places. It agitated me to see how much money godmen charged to say prayers for their followers. If God heard and answered the prayers, there would be no poor and hungry people on earth.

Jasmina noticed that some of my google searches were about a Sikh guru and a Sikh shrine. We both knew how religious Sikhs are. Jasmina was afraid that including them in the PIL would invite their wrath and harm to our family. But I disagreed.

I said, 'There is langar in every gurudwara, big or small. Sikhs are kind and generous, and always willing to help. They will be happy if my PIL is accepted.' Jasmina had her misgivings, but she knew I was adamant. So she simply prayed for my safety.

My research showed that nine gurus and babas had been arrested in the past year, and the media was now very alert and vocal about them. It gave me great confidence. I knew that it was just the tip of the iceberg, and sooner or later, thousands more would be exposed. I wrote down all the points I wanted highlighted in the PIL:

1. Gurus should be registered like any service provider and should pay taxes including service tax, since they sell God, who should be free for the public, at high prices;
2. Income tax raids and searches should be done on their premises;
3. There should be mandatory questionnaires for them to fill in which they have to disclose their past lives;
4. Their deras and ashrams should be registered just like other small, medium or large enterprises and should be taxed accordingly;
5. They should explain and live their spiritual teaching, which most of them don't;
6. Advertisements by them should be banned, including hoardings and flyers, since they cost money that rightfully belongs to the public. Besides, advertising increases their following, which increases superstitions and illogical beliefs;
7. Treasures in the vaults of shrines should be made public and used for the welfare of the poor;
8. There should be government supervision in deras and shrines to check malpractices and CCTV cameras should be installed where donation boxes are opened and offerings counted and listed;

9. Honest government officials should be deployed to ensure that these rules are complied with and they should be shuffled around different shrines and deras so that they do not have time to get hand in glove with the institutions;
10. Political parties should be barred from using religion as a political plank;
11. Science and Logic, which encourages students to think, should be compulsory in government and private schools so that children learn to use their minds and question what they are told.
12. All religious shrines, deras, gurus and babas should come under the purview of the RTI act since they also claim to work for the people.

I hoped that my PIL would be accepted. If it was rejected, I had no idea how I would pursue the case. The media was certainly more alert and more willing to expose them, but those who needed a guru simply switched from one to another. Every day new gurus seemed to be popping up on TV, and sometimes they accused each other of wrongdoing!

THE BIRTH OF AJAB PRODUCTIONS

A famous north Indian Hindu saints' organization published a list of all fake gurus and babas, and the list was carried in newspapers and broadcasted on TV. The organization also promised to update the list regularly. But the only gurus on the list were those that had already been exposed. I was amazed at what these gurus could get away with, without being challenged by their followers. The famous guru with a sweet smile said that India would become Syria if a Hindu temple was not built on a disputed piece of land. This case was still being heard in the Supreme Court at that time, but this did not prevent him from making this grandiose and absurd statement.

'How,' I wondered, 'can I get my message across if the PIL is not accepted?'

The only way was to use the media. I could produce short films and serials or documentaries on social issues. But the film industry was based in Bombay. Besides, I had little time to spare from my business, which needed more attention now.

'But where there is a will, there is way,' I told myself. 'Life is short and unpredictable and one should follow one's heart.'

I knew that Jasmina would help in every way she could. As for the geographical constraint, India is full of creative people and not all of them can go to Mumbai. Why not produce in Amritsar what is being produced in Mumbai?

This was a very exciting idea. Naturally, it occurred to me in the very early hours of the morning and, of course, I had to wake up Jasmina and tell her about it. At 6.30 a.m., I shook her awake.

'I will sleep in another room from now,' she said angrily.

'Not after you hear my plan.'

'I don't want to hear anything. Why must you ruin my sleep and your life?'

'We will go back to sleep, but only after you hear me out.'

Jasmina reluctantly sat up. She called the maid on the intercom and asked for tea. I immediately started telling her about my plan to start a film and dubbing studio in Amritsar. It would be fully equipped, just like the studios in Mumbai.

Jasmina stared at me in total disbelief. The maid walked in with the tea.

'Your Bobby bhaiyya is going to be a hero, a writer, a producer, a director, a lyricist and everything else,' Jasmina announced to her.

The maid was flummoxed and simply smiled and left.

'And what is the name of your production house?' asked Jasmina, jeeringly.

'Ajab Production,' I said promptly.

'*Ajab*...means strange...Why Ajab?' she asked.

'Strange, yes, but in a good way, a positive way,' I said.

'But why "Ajab"?'

'A for Aashna, J for Jasmina, A for Angad and B for Bobby. Ajab is me and you and our children,' I said with a smile.

She was awestruck with my creativity. 'Go for it,' said Jasmina. 'You are unstoppable.'

FINALLY, A LAWYER FOR MY PIL

I continued to look for information on the godmen's wealth on the Net. Most shrines are managed by trusts and their estimated wealth is easily available. There was also data on the estimated wealth of different gurus and their ashrams and deras, which, though not factual, did give an idea of their worth. It ranged from Rs 2,500 crore to almost Rs 18,000 crore, including the value of their real estate.

I needed a good Supreme Court lawyer in Delhi who handled PIL cases. I shortlisted four and emailed each of them, clearly explaining that I wanted to file a PIL against the top twenty shrines and twenty godmen, asking them to disclose their annual financial statements and their landholdings, buildings, cash, jewellery, vehicles, etc., so that their wealth could be evaluated and used by the government for the welfare of the poor. According to the data available, the combined wealth of these twenty shrines and twenty godmen came out to be approximately Rs 23 lakh crore. I proposed a scheme in my PIL in which a sum of twelve months of expenditure could be kept aside by them as their security and the rest be taken away. Each month they could keep their expenditure to themselves and handover the rest of the offerings to the government to be used. I found the mobile numbers of two lawyers and called them in the evening. One of them said he did not deal with PILs. The other heard what I had to say and then said that he worked only for corporates. When I pointed out that his profile said that he handled cases for NGOs and for the poor, he explained that these were cases that came to him through his corporate clients for their corporate social responsibility.

The next day, I called my architect, Robin Joshi. Robin is a young man who had renovated my office and remodelled our warehouse. I explained to him that I wanted to build an indoor studio and office building for a production house, both fully equipped like studios in Mumbai. Robin was amazed. Amritsar is famous for its Golden Temple and its wonderful food, but there has never been a film studio in the entire region. Robin said he had no idea or knowledge about studios. He could only get the construction done if the layout plan was given to him. I smiled and told him that I had no idea about the various formats and styles of writing scripts or novels, but I wrote stories in all genres without any training. I also had no idea what a studio looked like – in fact, I had never been inside a film studio in my life – but I hoped to successfully write scripts and produce movies through my own studio, because my heart was in it.

Robin realized that I would not take no for an answer. He decided to find people who knew about such things and bring a layout plan for me. The studio would be built on a 1,300 square yards plot that I had bought for investment a year ago, just a kilometre away from my house and office.

Two lawyers, whom I had not called, replied to my emails. One asked me to attach all the details for the PIL and said that he would charge Rs 5 lakh per hearing. I deleted his mail. The other lawyer, Mr Krishnan Iyer had written only two words, 'Call me' and his mobile number.

Mr Krishnan Iyer was a sixty-three-year-old Tamilian Brahmin. Brahmins are upper castes and have the authority to preach religion. They are in top positions in almost every Hindu shrine. I doubted that he would accept the case. If he read the content of my PIL application, he would most likely be angry with me. Maybe that is why he had asked me to call, so that he could give me a piece of his mind or preach to me.

So I first sent him a WhatsApp message asking if I could call now. His WhatsApp profile picture scared me – it showed a man in a long white kurta and lungi, with a big red tilak on his forehead. He wore a chain with a large locket on which was a picture of a Hindu deity. Before I could change my mind, Mr Iyer messaged, 'Yes'. I took a deep breath and called him. A mature voice and positive tone greeted me.

'Yes, Bobby, tell me,' he said.

'Sir, you must have gone through my email; I have written my heart out. I want to help people with their own money that they have donated to God, hoping for good luck in their lives, but they don't know that good times are in their own hands and can come to them with their own money, which they and their ancestors have donated to God in small instalments over a long time,' I said all in one breath.

I expected the phone to be disconnected or some angry response.

'Why not?' said Mr Iyer. 'We will try to make these rich shrines and deras contribute to this noble cause. I think the PIL should be accepted with all the data that you have already provided. I will also try to get more information and we will legally establish the points and convince the judge to accept the PIL for hearing.'

I could hardly believe my ears.

'When I saw your WhatsApp picture, Sir, I was sure that you would refuse to take the case, because you seem to be a very religious man, Sir,' I said.

Mr Iyer laughed. 'You are absolutely right,' he said. 'I am very religious, which is why I say my own prayers and donate nothing to temples. I prefer to give money to orphanages and other charities.'

I could hardly believe that such people existed in India. I asked him what his fees would be and was again surprised.

'I will not charge anything,' Mr Iyer replied. 'This is a social cause and I do not charge fees for such cases. It is my duty towards society and the poor. I will send you the form for the power of attorney. Sign it and send it back to me with your ID proofs. Also send me any other information regarding this matter that you may have with you.'

'Sir, you have opened my eyes,' I said. 'I always thought that religious people were not rational, but now I realize that I was wrong.'

THE RUMOUR

It took me some time to digest this new perception of Indians, and I decided that the tag line for me as a writer and a producer would be 'Changing Perceptions', since human beings learnt new things all the time and their perceptions changed continuously.

That weekend, Jasmina, the children and I met my cousin Tarun and his family for lunch at a restaurant. We were meeting after a long time. Tarun told me that he had met Rajat at a wedding a few days ago and he was bad mouthing me.

'Have you had a fight with him?' he asked.

I was surprised. I had been in touch with Rajat and my impression was that things had been sorted out between us. That was obviously not true, at least for Rajat. I demanded to know what Rajat had said about me, and after some hesitation, Tarun told me that the conversation had started with a discussion about business, how everyone had suffered because of demonetization. Rajat said that the only one who had not suffered was I because I was in the kind of business where demand increased when times were bad.

He said that I was dealing in drugs and that is why I was so rich and had bought such a big house and two Mercedes cars in such a short span of time.

I gulped down the wine in my glass, stared at Tarun and asked, 'And what did you say?'

'I do not respond to such people. I ended that conversation and left.'

I felt deeply hurt. Why did Tarun not object, why did he not stand up for me? But Tarun said that he had no desire to argue with the likes of Rajat. It was better to avoid such people. I said nothing.

At home, I told Jasmina what Tarun had said and she was worried. If Rajat had said this to someone so close to me, he would have certainly said it, and worse, to others, too. I had to find out. I invited Sandeep Gupta and all my other friends, except Rajat, for dinner. Nine of us met at the club. Once we had all settled down and enjoyed some harmless conversation, I asked Vishal when he had last met Rajat. Vishal said that it was a long time ago. I asked if he had said anything about me, but Vishal said he had said nothing specific.

'Did he say I am a drug dealer?' I asked.

Vishal was shocked. He looked at the others and then said, 'Yes.'

Rohit, another friend, said that they had all heard this nonsense from Rajat and from others Rajat had been talking to. I looked at both the Sandeep Guptas. They would not meet my eyes.

'Do you believe him?' I asked.

They all said at the same time, 'Are you crazy?'

'Have you gone mad?'

'Why will we believe that bastard?'

'Thank you so much for believing in me,' I said. 'But did any of you object to him saying such things?'

None of them had.

'People actually enjoy it when someone talks ill of another. We may not agree with a person like Rajat, but we all enjoy the moment, so we are all guilty,' said Sandeep.

I reminded them that we are all friends and the only thing that binds us together is trust.

'If we cannot trust each other, we cannot remain friends. You all listened to Rajat in silence, so somewhere in your hearts, you believed him.'

There was complete silence.

I changed the topic and it was never discussed again. But that night, I realized that it is only the family that is truly on one's side. I was shocked that Rajat's faith in his guru was so strong that he would stoop to defame an old friend. I had worked tirelessly for thirty long years to reach where I was today. For all that to be dismissed and to be labelled as a drug dealer had hurt me very deeply.

'Forget small people like Rajat and move on with your life,' said my inner voice.

Jasmina also encouraged me by saying, 'Elephants never change their paths just because dogs are barking in their way.'

But I felt like an ant, not an elephant. Then I told myself that an ant could get into the trunk of the elephant and bite it, the elephant would run towards the lake for water, but the lake would be dry! I was going to be the stubborn ant that would bring down an elephant with my stories and with the PIL.

INTO THE LITERARY WORLD

The next morning, I sent off all the required documents to Mr Iyer. I hoped for the best, but if the PIL got rejected, I would tell people about the underprivileged through my movies and serials and stories. If the regular channels did not accept my serials and movies, I would start my own YouTube channel to take my cause forward.

It was around this time that I read about the Jaipur Literary Festival. It is a huge event in which authors, publishers and other speakers from all over the world come together to discuss books and the business of books. Three hundred thousand people were expected to attend the event this year. I decided to go there too and learn about the world of books. I took Aashna and Jasmina along, because Aashna wanted to be a writer and Jasmina was already helping me with my writing. Angad also accompanied us, and since 26th January was a holiday, I turned it into a family vacation. Jasmina obtained the delegate passes that gave us access to all the areas where speakers, publishers and authors held meetings and round table discussions as well as the cafeteria where they spent their free time. I wanted to immerse myself in the world of these intellectuals so that I could listen and watch, and most importantly learn.

The thought of attending the festival and the filing of the PIL so excited me that I found it hard to concentrate on work. Government policies towards China had changed and I needed to devote more time to my business. All three products that I imported from China faced anti-dumping cases. The Indian corporates who had filed the cases were most likely to win. If I didn't find an alternative, my business would be finished. It would take a lot of time to find new suppliers in new countries, and time was something that I did not have. I decided to focus on my passion and ignore my dying business. For the first time, I chose what to do with my life. Till now, life had handed out situations and circumstances and I had dealt with to the best of my abilities.

We reached Jaipur late at night a day before the festival began. I had shortlisted the events I wished to attend. The first was a conversation between two authors and a publisher. Mrs Preeti Gill, editor and literary agent, was the moderator. The session lasted for an hour and I was very impressed.

I then attended a session where a famous author answered the audience's questions. He said that he was from a business family and his father was very upset when he started writing because he took two years to complete his book and neglected his business during that time. Once the book was complete, he could not find a publisher. He chased more than ten publishers for five years, but each one rejected his manuscript.

It is very hard for a first-time author to find a reputed publisher in India. Only one in ten manuscripts are accepted and of the thirty books that are published every month, twenty-nine are by established authors. The famous author gave all these details and also said that he had to self-publish his first book. It was successful and a well-known publisher then published his second book.

I was now very worried about my two manuscripts – a collection of forty-one short stories called 'Stories of Us' and my semi-autobiography, 'Once There Was Me'.

That evening I closely observed the writers and speakers at dinner. They all seemed to glow with contentment. Most of the women did not wear any make-up and were simply dressed. The men mostly wore traditional Indian clothes and looked dignified. I found them charming and believed that it was the ability to observe the world around them and portray it in words that gave them that glow. I asked Jasmina if she found this gathering very different from our usual social circle, and she too agreed. They were more confident and graceful, and there was no show of wealth as in the business community, especially in north India.

On the last day, I attended Preeti Gill's conversation with a European author. This was her third event that I attended and I was enormously impressed with her. I had read about her in a newspaper and knew that she was from Delhi, but her in-laws' ancestral home is in Amritsar. After the session, Jasmina and I walked up to her. Preeti Gill was sixty years old, tall and graceful, with short hair and dressed in a salwar kurta. I told her that we were from Amritsar and had attended the Jaipur Literary Festival for the first time. Jasmina said that I was an aspiring writer and wanted to show her my work. I would greatly appreciate her critical comments on my writings.

Much to our surprise, Preeti told us that we could meet her in Amritsar the following month. She and her husband, Kamaljeet Gill, had set up a cultural hub called Majha house, in her father-in-law's bungalow there. Preeti assured us that she would guide me.

A CASE AGAINST GODMEN

When I returned from Jaipur, I collected more data from the Internet for the PIL. I learnt that most godmen spent fortunes on security and did not move out of their deras without guards armed. The principal disciples, who formed the first ring of staff members, also made a lot of money. They were the first point of contact between rich businessmen and politicians and the godman, and they made full use of these opportunities to line their own pockets. Godmen spent a lot of money on advertisements and the construction of new premises. They travelled first class when they went abroad to preach simplicity and contentment. The happiness that they claimed to spread among people was actually confined just to them and came from making utter fools of so many people.

I also discovered that the primary followers of these godmen were women, mostly housewives. They spent their free time listening to them and then encouraged their families to follow, with tales of miracles and spiritual powers. 'This is one more reason why the education of women is so important,' I thought.

Further research uncovered the fact that there are two kinds of godmen – one kind preach about the goodness of God and the other profess ways to deal with the Devil and his evil force. Both took money from their followers to perform rituals to alleviate pain and tension and improve their lives. With urbanization, black magic was denounced and slowly went out of favour. In the rural areas, it is still prevalent. 'It is only money that makes this work,' I thought. When there is no money given to these godmen, whether good or evil, their business dies down. Most of them never work to uplift the downtrodden, but they make a lot of money in the name of faith.

I prepared to drive to Delhi the next day for the presentation of the PIL in court. I asked my driver, Kulwant, to come early. Mummy believed I was going against the messengers of God and was angry with me. A day before I was to leave, she went to the Golden Temple. Kulwant, who was as religious as her, drove her there. She told Kulwant that she had to pray for me because she was worried about me and then poured out her fears about the PIL that would prove that godmen had untold wealth and that many of them were fake. Kulwant was horrified to know that he would be driving me to Delhi for this sinful purpose.

The next morning, when I came to check if the car was ready, Kulwant said that he could not drive me to Delhi because his guruji had told him in a dream that he should not be a part of this journey.

'You will just be driving the car, so you won't have to face God's curse,' I said with a smile.

I guessed that my mother had been talking to him.

Jasmina also told Kulwant that he would have to drive me, since she trusted no one else to drive on the highway, not even me. Kulwant said nothing but looked unhappy.

It was a beautiful morning and my mind was full of fresh ideas. I watched the people on the road, the milkmen, hawkers and farmers heading for the markets. At 8 a.m., we passed the industrial area on the Ludhiana highway. A lot of factories were located there and migrant workers on their way to work clogged the bypass on the outskirts of the city. I thought of how hard life was for all these people who woke up at the crack of dawn and headed for work. The rich could afford the luxury of sleeping till late.

At 10 a.m., we stopped for breakfast. I bought breakfast for Kulwant as well and carried the tray towards him. Kulwant came forward to take it and thanked me.

Then he hesitantly asked, 'Why are you doing this? Why are you dragging God to court?'

I explained to him that it was not God that I was taking to court, but the false godmen, so that they would be accountable to their followers, from whom they accumulated so much wealth.

Kulwant said, 'Godmen are like God and taking them to court is akin to taking God to court.'

I was shocked, but told Kulwant that all that the courts would ask for were their financial records and not question their teachings or preachings.

But Kulwant was not convinced. 'It is a sin to ask such question,' he said.

'Asking questions is never a sin,' I retorted and ended the conversation.

At Mr Iyer's office, I signed a few papers and then waited for the court proceedings to start. Mr Iyer was in his usual simple attire with a red tika on his forehead, red and orange religious threads round his wrist, the picture of a Hindu deity on the locket around his neck. I would never have approached him if I had seen him first. But this deeply religious man was all set to challenge godmen and shrines from all over India. He told me that he was very happy to be a part of a PIL that he himself would have filed had he thought about it first. In thirty-two years of practice, he had never come across such a PIL. I was very relieved to hear that someone other than Jasmina appreciated what I was trying to do.

'Will it be accepted for hearing?' I asked.

'Yes, yes,' said Mr Iyer. He explained that there was a bench of three judges who all were quite rational. 'One of the judges had already heard a case against a religious shrine which has been asked to open its treasure house to government scrutiny.'

I pulled out the previous day's newspaper, which had reported that the Archaeological Survey of India had been allowed by the Odisha government to open the treasure chest full of ornaments in the Jagannath Temple after thirty-four years. The ornaments were expected to be of a huge market value. Mr Iyer immediately attached the newspaper report to the file he would present in court.

Finally, we stood before the judge, who scrutinized our file. Mr Iyer told me the rough estimate of the income and expenditure of the twenty shrines and twenty deras in the country.

'This is just a sample survey, my Lord,' he said. 'It is just letting the court and the government know what kind of enormous wealth they possess, which should be used for the welfare of the poor people of this country.'

'The source of this information is not authentic and the figures seem fictional,' said the judge.

'The financial numbers of many shrines have been published by their trusts, my Lord, and are available to the public. But many don't publish their financial details. Most godmen talk about the spiritual balance sheet and hide their financial balance sheet under it,' Mr Iyer replied. 'There are many more sitting on huge unaccounted piles of cash, real estate, foreign bank accounts and vehicles,' he added.

He narrated all the important points from my file.

The judge looked at me and asked, 'Gentleman, are you going to stand by your PIL to the end? I have seen and heard many who withdraw such cases halfway.'

'It has taken me years to come to this point, Sir,' I said. 'There is no question of backing out. But I am afraid for the safety of my family and request the court not to make its proceedings public if the PIL is accepted.'

Mr Iyer intervened to say that it was not the court that invited the media to become a party to the case, but the parties who wanted the media involved so that their case was highlighted. Such cases caught media attention through word of mouth or through the routine court reports in the newspapers.

I asked him to try and keep the case as quiet as possible so that no one would know that the PIL had been filed by me. Mr Iyer did not reply.

Finally, the judge said, 'Well, I believe your client has taken this courageous step for a social cause. I expect him to remain very careful while speaking in court. This is a very sensitive matter. We need to confine it within judicial language.'

Mr Iyer smiled. 'My client won't have to speak, my Lord. I will be his mouthpiece in court and even before the media, if required.'

The PIL was accepted and the judge issued orders to the twenty shrines and twenty godmen to appear before court with details of the past three years' income and expenditure, income tax returns and a list of their moveable and immoveable assets.

I was bursting with happiness. I wanted to touch Mr Iyer's feet, but Mr Iyer hugged me with joy and asked me to wait in his office. When I switched on my phone, it was full of messages from Jasmina, Mummy and even from my brother, and an almost equal number of missed calls. I was nearly in tears and could not talk, so I messaged Jasmina and Gagan, 'PIL accepted. Hearing after twenty-five days.' I told Jasmina and Mummy not to worry about me; it was time for the godmen to worry about themselves.

At 4 p.m., Mr Iyer gave me the documents and a copy of the PIL with the court's acceptance of it. He advised me to be careful and not talk about the PIL so that no one learnt of it before the case hearing date. I had Rs 2 lakh with me in a plain white envelope. I tried to give it to Mr Iyer, who gently smiled and told me that he had a lot of money and didn't require any more. He thanked me for the many ideas that the PIL contained of schemes for the welfare of the poor.

I headed for the car park where Kulwant waited for me. Seeing my happy face, Kulwant looked grim.

'What happened, sir?' he asked.

'*Ho gaya* – it has happened,' I said.

Kulwant got into the driver's seat without a word. I was surprised. He usually opened the door for me. However, I got into the back seat without a word and was soon engrossed in answering emails and messages. At 9 p.m., we stopped for dinner. I asked Kulwant what he would like for dinner, but he was still miffed and said he would buy his own food.

'As you wish,' I said coldly.

Kulwant relented and said I could get him whatever I wished. I smiled and bought dinner for both of us. We ate at the same restaurant, at separate tables, as usual.

When we were back on the road, Kulwant asked me what I would do if I lost the case against God.

'Against godmen, Kulwant, not God,' I corrected him. 'I won't stop if I lose the case. I will write stories and make movies and serials and documentaries about these godmen. I will also talk about poor people and how they should get their basic right to live a dignified life.'

This made Kulwant happy and he wanted to know what kind of films I would make.

'They will be stories about ragpickers, manual scavengers, prostitutes, homeless people, old people, the handicapped and transgenders...'

Kulwant's phone had been ringing often since the start of the journey, and he had disconnected the calls. It was unusual. I knew that Kulwant always answered the phone when it rang, without even checking who was calling. But that day he kept checking the number and disconnecting. I found it strange but said nothing.

At home, I found Jasmina and the kids in a celebratory mood, but Mummy was very angry. She was waiting up for me and asked me to take back the case. I tried to explain my stand to her but she would not accept it.

'You will lose the case,' she told me.

'No problem. I will still not let these godmen sleep peacefully,' I laughed.

'Oh, do whatever you want,' she said and added, 'God Bless you,' and hugged me.

Jasmina warned the children not to talk about the case since people did not see it the same way that we did.

The next morning, I repeated everything that had happened to Gagan. Gagan was a very religious person, but like Mr Iyer, he was against the hoarding of unaccounted wealth when so many were in need of help.

'DO NOT DEFAME GOD...'

A few days later, Preeti and Kamaljeet Gill came over. They were preparing for the inaugural event of Majha House. They spent two hours with Jasmina and me, and enlisted Jasmina's help in the organization of the event. I was impressed with their enthusiasm and determination to get this project going. Jasmina had a dual interest in the event – she would enjoy helping Preeti and it would further my writing career.

Fifteen days later, Mr Iyer emailed to say that the court's summons had been dispatched to all forty parties mentioned in the PIL. Many shrines had responded positively and appointed lawyers to appear before the court, but only two of the deras had responded so far.

Mr Iyer believed that at least four or five corrupt godmen would join hands against my PIL and would also try to involve the media and politicians to stop the hearing or even threaten me. Mr Iyer had received information through professional detectives and other sources. I offered him money, since he had to spend on detectives and informers, but Mr Iyer refused again.

The Majha House event succeeded beyond expectations. Well-known authors, speakers, publishers and performers came from all over India. This was just the beginning, and I was delighted that I would be able to attend such events in Amritsar itself.

The first hearing of the case came up and I had to go to Delhi. I was surprised that there had been no leak to the media about the case when the summons had already been served and must have made many people very angry. But Mr Iyer said that many godmen were getting together to fight me jointly.

Three days before I left for Delhi, Kulwant knocked urgently on my door. He normally never came up to my room and generally went about his work in the garage and the lower floor. He told me that two unknown men had come to his door early in the morning and asked him to tell me to withdraw the PIL or else I would be in trouble. They left as soon as they delivered this message.

Now I was really worried. I could not ask for police protection because that would make the case public knowledge. I pretended to be unperturbed and told Kulwant not to talk about this to anyone. Kulwant wanted to know if I would still pursue the case, and I said I definitely would and I was not afraid of anyone. If I were harmed, the court would not spare the assailants.

I pretended to be very brave, but I was scared. I loved my family and I loved myself. I had no desire to be killed.

Then I remembered the line from the *shabad* of Guru Gobind Singh, 'Subh karman te kabhun na daro' (don't fear when you are on the right path). I told myself, 'You are a Sikh and Sikhs are fearless. They do not abandon the battleground.'

But I remembered that I could not be a Sikh if I was an atheist and it dawned upon me that I could never disassociate myself from my community. Despite being an atheist, I was trying to do what the Sikh religion truly taught.

The next morning, I walked into the kitchen for a glass of water and overheard the maid talking about Kulwant and his wife.

'Do you know that Kulwant's wife has had another miscarriage? Kulwant said that his guruji told him that he and his wife would never have a male child because he works for Bobby sahib who is an atheist. His salary comes from an atheist and that money runs his kitchen. It is a curse that passes into the food and kills the foetus in the womb.'

'How is that possible?' asked the other maid. 'We all receive money from Bobby sahib too, but nothing happens to us or our sons?'

'I don't know. But Kulwant is planning to leave this job next month.'

I was aghast to hear that Kulwant, who was more like a family member than a mere employee, held me responsible for the miscarriages his wife suffered and would actually quit his job. I immediately wanted to talk it out with him and explain to him that miscarriages have medical reasons, not such irrational ones.

Aashna was planning to go visit her friend in Hyderabad via Delhi, and when she heard that I was going to Delhi, she insisted on going with me. Her plan was to go to Delhi and fly from there to Hyderabad. I agreed.

The next two days were very busy with clients who had come from the US. I had to go to Delhi for the hearing and Jasmina tried to book me on a flight, but it was full. There was no option but to drive through the night. Aashna too didn't mind that. Kulwant, reluctant as usual to drive me for the hearing, seemed even more taken aback at Aashna's plan. He kept saying that she would have to be awake all night and it would be a strain. None of us thought much of his agitation. He was very fond of the children and always concerned about their comfort.

Aashna was already in the car when Kulwant picked me up from the hotel where I had taken my business guests for dinner. I decided to talk to Kulwant about his superstition on the way.

In the car, after some desultory conversation with Aashna, I first answered all my emails and messages. I sent the daily instructions to my office and warehouse staff, since I would have to switch off the phone in the court the next morning.

Later during the journey, when we were about to reach Ambala, Aashna was feeling very tired and dizzy. At this point Kulwant suggested that she be dropped at Chandigarh from where she could take a direct flight the next morning and reach Hyderabad comfortably. Both Aashna and I agreed.

We detoured to Chandigarh and dropped Aashna there. I thought Kulwant looked relieved, and for a moment, something niggled at the back of my mind. But then I thought I was being fanciful and brushed it away.

Traffic moved fast in the night and we were only 160 kilometres away from Delhi when my phone rang. It was a private number. I assumed that it was a call from the USA or Canada.

A heavy voice said in Punjabi, 'Bobby Sachdeva, turn your car around and go back to Amritsar. Otherwise, face the consequences of trying to defame God.'

'If I defame God in court, God will punish me Himself,' I answered.

The caller laughed. 'I am God in this territory and I have the authority to punish you.'

'I am doing this to protect people from inhuman beings like you. You are not God, you are a dog.'

The caller abused me loudly in Punjabi. Even Kulwant could hear him. He kept looking at me in the rear-view mirror.

The phone call disturbed me. So I started talking to Kulwant, asking him if he really believed that his kitchen was run on the money of a sinner and that a cursed salary from an atheist employer paid for the food he ate.

Before Kulwant could answer, his phone rang. He looked at the number, answered the phone and said, 'Ji achcha, Paaji – Yes Brother,' and disconnected.

'Who called at this time?' I asked curiously.

'My brother-in-law. He works the night shift at the factory. He called to say that he will go to my house in the morning to deliver some clothes sent by my wife's parents.'

I wondered what was so urgent that he would call at this time of the night. But before I could ask any more questions, Kulwant said that he thought the brakes of the car were not working properly. He wanted to stop and check them. I could not see any warning light indicating any fault on the dashboard, but Kulwant insisted that something was wrong, so I told him to stop under a streetlight and check everything thoroughly. The toll plaza was only 500 metres away. I was feeling strangely restless and I asked him to play my favourite song on the CD player, a Pakistan Coke Studio rendition of '*Hum kyun chalein us raah par jis raah par sab hi chalein, kyun na chune woh raasta jis par nahin koi gaya...'* (Why should I walk the well-trodden path, why not choose a road less taken).

The music filled my ears. I noticed that road-widening work had started on that stretch of the highway and the oncoming traffic had been diverted. Traffic from both sides was plying on the same side of the road. I was a little sleepy and closed my eyes. Over the music, I could hear the sound of trucks coming down the road.

It took a few seconds for the roar of a truck coming too fast, too close to register. My eyes flew open, but the bonnet was open and there were blazing lights right upon the car.

The car flew up in the air and landed upside down on the road, totally crushed.

Kulwant had disappeared.

***

Hum kyun chalein us raah par
Jis raah par sab hi chalein,
Kyun na chune woh raasta
Jis par nahin koi gaya...

Bobby was gone.

What remained was his intense desire to help the poor, downtrodden people of his country, to make those who sell religion to them as a panacea for all ills accountable and to inspire everyone to do the same in whatever measure they can.

I WILL FIGHT THE GOOD FIGHT

Aashna sat in Mr Iyer's office with a fat sheaf of papers in her hand. She felt uncertain and nervous, but forced herself to be calm and focussed. It seemed unreal that her father was gone. Just three days ago. She could hardly believe that he would not call her, ask her about the stories she was writing or tease her any more. But despite the tragedy, her mother had been adamant that the case should be carried forward to its logical end. Aashna and her brother had agreed. This was the least they could do. So here she was, in Mr Iyer's office, trying to understand what exactly she had to do, what the intricacies of the case were, telling herself again and again that this was the least she could do for her father. She looked with unseeing eyes at the shelves full of files and papers, the dusty books, the people at the adjoining table discussing some case loudly. For a moment, panic gripped her and she wanted to get up and run away from that strange and unfamiliar place. 'I cannot do this,' she thought. 'I have no clue what to do here. Surely Papa would not expect me to be here....' Then she remembered how important this was for him. No, she could not run away. She would do this. She could do this.

Mr Iyer turned to look at the young girl, sitting upright on the steel chair, fear and determination flickering across her face, and his eyes filled with compassion and admiration. He would do the best he could for this brave young girl. He put a gentle hand on her head, reassuring her that he would help her every step of the way.

They spread the papers on the table and he began explaining to her what had been done and what remained for her to do...

EPILOGUE

I, Bobby Sachdeva, am still very much alive to live my dreams.

I will continue writing short stories and books and Ajab Productions is a reality that will soon bring movies and documentaries to screens, both big and small.

This book is part autobiographical, part fiction, because some identities had to be protected, and where religion and the judiciary were involved, some fiction was necessary. Names have been changed in some instances.

The aim of this book is to kickstart the process of helping the poor and needy and implement practical solutions for the problem.

I hope that you too will raise your voice for those who are too weak to raise their own.

Bobby Sachdeva